DO YOU DO EXTRAS?

NIKKI ASHTON

Do You Do Extras?
Published by Bubble Books Ltd

Do You Do Extras
First published July 2018

Cover design – JC Clarke from The Graphics Shed

Formatting by—JC Clarke from The Graphics Shed

Edited by – Brooke Bowen Herbert

This book is dedicated to my grandad, Bill Barlow, who I've been thinking and talking about a lot recently. He was a quiet man, but when he spoke you listened.

When I was a teenager, he told me it didn't matter if I didn't succeed, as long as I tried.

Well, I tried Grandad and I hope I made you proud

CONTENTS

Please be aware that some of the spellings in this book are American English, due to the nationality of some of the characters

CHAPTER ONE

Phoebe

Do you ever get to the point where you've held your wind in for so long your stomach feels like it harbours Mount Vesuvius? Yep, me too. At this very moment the inside farts are rife. As the Pope walks past me, a huge one bubbles and churns, and I'm sure he heard it. The Pontiff continues walking, however, still munching on a tuna roll.

It isn't the real pope, of course. He's an extra for the latest film I'm shooting. I say I'm shooting it, but not in the sense that it's my film and I'm the director, or even the lead. I'm actually '*Third girl in Vatican Square*'. I'm the one with the map in my hand, waving it at two other girls who are both looking around faking confusion. Yep, I'm an extra in films, TV shows, even advertisements. You need someone to look suitably nonchalant in the background, then I'm your girl.

I'm Phoebe Drinkwater, age twenty-six and I live with my sister Beth and her two adorable twin boys, Callum and Mackenzie. It works for us; she needed help with the mortgage after her deadbeat husband, Steven, left her with twin boys of a year old. All because his nubile, twenty-one year old assistant 'sucked dick magnificently'. I kid you not, that was one of the lines from the 'Dear Beth' note that he left on the bedside table. Beth, nor the boys, have seen him since that miserable, rainy Wednesday over five years ago. Personally, I think she's better off without him. He was a big head who thought every woman wanted him and every man wanted to be him. Let me tell you, he wasn't all that. He may have been okay looking, but his breath smelled like rancid meat – which is probably why Miss Cock Sucker, the assistant, chose to blow his cock rather than kiss his mouth. Anyway, I digress. Beth needed help with the mortgage and I can't get a mortgage because, as I said, I'm an extra. Extras don't have long-term contracts. We never know when we're going to work next and the pay is shit, but we do it because we feel like we're actors, only without the fame and fortune, which suits me just fine. Anyway, my beautiful sister cleared out her sewing room, squeezed a double bed and chest of drawers in there, and welcomed me with open arms. I was also grateful because after flat-sharing with two gay guys, Andy and Dermot, I didn't want to go back to my childhood home when the boys decided to move to Andy's homeland of Australia. I have a somewhat fractured relationship with my parents - basically they hate me because *'I'm such a disappointment'* and will never be as wonderful as my younger sister, Melania. Melania is a blonde haired blue-eyed, perfect size ten; with a loving husband, who is a brain surgeon, and two perfect children who behave impeccably. She's also a successful doctor with her own practice, but is sought out by hospitals all over the world to help them diagnose bizarre and unknown diseases. Perfect isn't she? Yep, and she also doesn't exist. She's a figment of my parents' imagination and musings when they're letting me know exactly how disappointing I am. Being compared to a figment of their imagination doesn't exactly bring family harmony, so seeing them as little as often works for all of us, me especially.

"We should have gone ahead and had Melania," my mother said to my dad one day when I'd been thrown off a film set in Finland for belching loudly during a death scene. I have no idea what the fuss was about. They were able to reshoot it and the light just about held up – I didn't know they only had around five hours of daylight that time of year. And okay, it was the last day of the massively over budget movie and time was tight, but I defy anyone not to belch after eating herrings on toast for lunch. "She would have been such a beautiful daughter," Mum continued while Dad shook his head and rolled his eyes at me. "I know, Deborah," he replied, sighing heavily. "She'd be working in third world countries by now, saving lives and making us proud."

So, that was why I didn't want to go home to 37 Grosvenor Drive, Rickeby. As for Beth, well she never hesitated offering when I cried out in pain after she asked me if I was going to go home. She immediately said, "Phoebes, you're coming to live with me and the boys. We'll work out your rent later, but you can help me with the boys when you're not working, which means I can do some overtime. It'll be great."

I tried to argue that she wouldn't want me around, cramping her style – surely there must be a man in her life, I asked? I knew there wasn't. We told each other most things, and I knew the only sexual experience Beth had had in the years since Steven disappeared was when she accidently brushed her hand against her boss's cock when she'd squeezed past him behind the counter of the bank that she worked in. Apparently Gerald, her boss, almost chocked on his own spittle and Beth almost peed herself from laughing with her friend and colleague, Angela, in the break room. Gerald, her fifty-eight year old, very married and very rotund boss, went home with a migraine and didn't return until the following week.

Beth, the boys, and me had a lovely time living together. We were the Fantastic Four, according to Mack, and we fought crime in the dead of night. That boy had a vivid imagination. Callum, on the other hand, had told his friend's mum that he had two mothers, and that Beth and I were in a lesbian relationship. The mere thought had me puking in my mouth on many occasions. I'm not homophobic, please don't think that, it's the thought of being a lesbian with my sister – wrong on so many fronts. She's very beautiful, with her dark auburn hair and brown eyes, but she's my sister and to be honest, I'm a cock girl through and through.

As the last scene had been shot – the lead man running through the streets of Rome with a seven foot tall man-mountain chasing him, we were all in the dressing trailer removing our costumes. Thankfully, the only things left to do were close ups on the lead actors for the final scene of the film, so it was my last day. That meant no standing around for continuity photographs, no hanging around to be fitted with another outfit, and no more shitty on-set food that totally disagreed with my bowels on a regular basis – hence the wind and subsequent inside farts.

"Where you go next?" Policeman number six asked me, pulling off his jacket.

"Back home," I replied with a sigh. "I've got a job on the new Addison Yates movie. It's being shot locally to where I live."

Addison Yates was an action series that was now on its fourth movie and for some reason it was being shot in Manchester at the studios with some location shots in the city. Usually they were big, Hollywood blockbuster type of movies with huge money spinning effects and amazing car chases. I wasn't sure how it was going to look without the gorgeous sunshine and California backdrop, but I didn't care too much. It meant I got to work on a big budget movie and go home at night to see Beth and the boys. The fact it was big budget also meant I was paid better, which meant Beth could stick to her usual three days of working for a while. Plus I had two lines of dialogue, which meant I got a speaking part stipend – thank goodness I had a great agent, Barbara, who insisted on it. I would also be working in scenes with the leading man – Grantley James. I was playing a 'studious looking tech girl who worked for Addison's security company'. Grantley had played Addison Yates in the last movie, taking over from the previous lead, Ryan Rushton. Ryan had become a little too fond of the nose candy and when his septum practically dropped off during an interview with Ellen DeGeneres, the studio decided enough was enough and replaced him with Grantley. What had caused uproar was soon forgotten when Grantley brought a whole lot more sex appeal to the character of Addison. Ryan was hot, but Grantley was better looking and also ripped to perfection – he was another level, with his sexy stubble and taper fade haircut that was always styled to perfection. He also had a penchant for chunky rings and leather bracelets, giving him more of an edge than the immaculately put together Ryan. Rumour had it Ryan's six-pack was spray painted on, but there was nothing fake about Grantley. Even the three-inch scar on his left forearm was real. The studio explained that away with Addison having a scuba diving accident on his vacation after his last job, i.e. the last film – no one knew the reason why Grantley had a scar in real-life, but I doubted it was from scuba diving.

All in all, I was looking forward to shooting the movie. The director, Alexi Rodrigo, was known for encouraging the whole cast to mix together and become a family. Extras weren't hidden away, they were encouraged to mingle with the lead roles, so it was definitely going to be a different experience for me.

"I 'ope you enjoy," the policeman said about my next job, in his sexy Italian accent. "You wanna fuck tonight?"

He lifted his chin as he asked his question. His dark eyes hooded and sultry.

I looked him up and down, hands on my hips.

"Yeah, okay. Let me get changed and I'll meet you by the food trailer."

"Si," he replied. "We can have dinner first."

As he left the trailer, I shook my head and continued to undress. Who said romance was dead – not the Italians, that was for sure.

CHAPTER TWO

Grantley

"Is this fucking rain ever gonna stop?" I asked Barney, my security guy.

We were in the hotel and all I could see through the damn floor to ceiling window was rain, rain, and more fucking rain.

"Any chance that fucker will break its banks?"

Barney chuckled his usual deep boom. "That fucker is the River Irwell, I believe." He shook his head and smiled while he continued to tinkle the keys of the baby grand piano that was in my room.

"Whatever," I grumbled. "The point is, if this weather keeps up are we likely to be flooded?"

"I checked the forecast, and the rain is due to stop around eight-thirty."

"That fucking exact, hey? Well great, just another three hours of this shit."

I heaved a sigh, missing the LA sunshine and pushed away from the window, making my way to the kitchen of my suite.

"You want coffee?" I asked.

"Nope, I'm good."

Barney had been with me for almost three years, and as well as my security he was pretty much my only friend, seeing as most of my old friends had gotten sick of my miserable ass a long time ago. Sure, when I'd hit the big time a few crawled back out of the woodwork, but I'm smart enough to know when I'm being used – hence it usually being just me and the big guy.

I'd employed him after I'd seen him deal with a real stupid dude who tried to get into the LA club where Barney was doing security. The prick, having already been thrown out, thought he could rush Barney and get back in – needless to say the guy ended up out cold, on his back, on the sidewalk. I'd just got a part in a movie and knew it was gonna be big, which meant in turn so would I. Call me a big-headed prick if you want to, but I know how fucking good an actor I am. With fame comes Paparazzo, horny housewives who literally want a piece of you, and idiot douchebags who want to gain their own bit of fame by being the guy to put you on your ass – hence why I employed the 250 pounds of black muscle.

"I'm not sure I'll be able to take this place, if the weather is like this all the time," I called back to Barney, scratching at the stubble on my chin.

"Maybe if you quit moaning like some pansy-ass-pussy, you'd stop worrying about it."

"You do know I fucking pay you to take care of me, not insult me, don't you?"

"Yep."

That was followed by another deep laugh and a new tune on the piano. I smiled as I heard Beyonce's, 'Crazy in Love' being played. Who'd have thought an ex-brawler like Barney could tickle the ivories to a pretty good standard.

"You called your mom?" I asked.

"Yep, you called yours?"

I paused putting the stupid little pod into the coffee machine. I mean come on, what the fuck is wrong with grounds, hot water, and a jug?

"Did you?" Barney's deep voice growled.

"No, and I'm not going to."

As I reached for a mug, the piano playing stopped and I knew Barney was on his way into the kitchen. We had the same argument at least three times a week – why hadn't I called my loving mother? That would be because she's a drunk bitch who couldn't give two shits about me. She never had and never would. As long as I deposited money into her account every month she didn't give a damn whether she ever saw me again.

"Grantley," Barney said from behind me.

"Listen Barney, we've been over this. I give her money and that's about the sum total of my devotion to that woman. You have no-"

"I have no idea what it was like growing up with her as my mother." Barney placed a huge hand on my shoulder. "I know Grant, you've told me many times, but take it from someone who knows, don't leave it until it's too fucking late."

I shrugged my shoulder from under his hand and turned away. I never let anyone see the hurt that I knew was in my eyes when talking about my mother. Barney had no idea what I'd gone through as a kid. All he knew was that he was at odds with his dad when the guy dropped dead of a heart attack and he would never forgive himself and thought I should take heed from his mistakes. Me, well I was a cold-hearted fucker who didn't care whether I never spoke to my mom again. I only gave her money to stop her selling stories about me for cash. I could hand on heart say, if she died tomorrow there would not be one microscopic bit of guilt on my part. Fuck it, I might even throw a party with fairground rides and fire-eaters.

"I'm not discussing this with you, Barney. We'll agree to disagree."

Barney sighed and reached around me to snag an apple from the display of fruit that the hotel replaced every damn day – another total waste of money. A few grapes, a couple of bananas, and some berries in the refrigerator would be perfectly acceptable. That's what you got for being a Hollywood movie star, I guess.

"Okay, but just think about it."

"I have, not gonna do it again and I've decided she can go fuck herself. Okay?"

I looked at him with wide eyes and arched brows and waited, finally he nodded and turned to leave the kitchen.

After a few minutes, I followed him and found him standing by the couch, scrolling through his cell.

"You mind if I go out for a while?" he asked, without looking up at me. "Mr. Rodrigo said he'll send someone around, if you'd feel safer. In fact, my friend, I think he told Marcia you were never to be left alone."

"For fuck's sake," I muttered. "I'm not a fucking baby, or more to the point, that dick- Ryan Rushton."

Alexi Rodrigo was the producer/director and franchise holder of the Addison Yates movies and after what happened to my predecessor – he lost half his fucking nose through snorting too much blow -was paranoid about anything happening to me, so he was a little over protective. Marcia Silva was my agent and was one of the best in the business – mainly because she didn't take shit from anyone- directors, producers, and certainly not her clients.

"I'd love to know what Marcia said about that," I muttered, imagining her telling Alexi to go fuck himself at trying to tell her what to do with her client.

"Yep, I'm thinking the same," Barney replied with a deep chuckle. "I think he's pretty glad she's stuck in Tahoe trying to get Jen out of that movie."

Jennifer Barbuda was a stablemate of mine and her previous agent had signed her up for some shit, soft-porn movie without telling her. When it became apparent that Jen was going to have to do some pretty salacious scenes, without a body double, Marcia took the first flight out there to, in her words, 'sort the fucking ass wipe's clusterfuck out and rescue Jen'.

"I think I'll be safe in the suite and I'm definitely not going out in this rain. I'll do a final read-through for the scenes we're going to be shooting tomorrow. Where you going anyway? Unless you don't want to tell me of course."

I grinned at Barney as his head lifted. I hated arguing with him, so I felt relieved when he flashed his teeth at me in a wide smile.

"Lady I know lives nearby."

"How the fuck does a man from the Bronx know a woman who lives in Manchester, England?"

"She worked in New York for a while, a couple of years back. Used to come to the club most Friday nights and we got...shall we say, friendly."

I rolled my eyes and flopped down onto the couch, grabbing my script with my spare hand. Lifting my coffee mug to my lips, I looked over at Barney, who was punching out a text.

"You coming back tonight?"

He looked up at me, his thumbs still flashing across the screen of his cell. "Yep, not sure what time, but I'll be back in time to wake you, don't worry."

I nodded and let out a long exhale. I rarely slept well through the night, usually dropping into a real deep sleep just before dawn. It then became a huge struggle to wake. One time, Barney had to douse me with a vase full of water I was in such a deep sleep. In the past, I'd missed my studio car a couple of times and one time slept through my shoot time. That had nearly cost me the job and ultimately it would have been my reputation in the john, so since then Barney was always around to wake me.

"You sure you'll be okay?" Barney asked as he came out of his bedroom, dressed to impress and smelling of *my* fucking cologne.

"I will if you stop stealing my stuff." I complained, taking off my black-rimmed glasses. "Don't I pay you enough to buy your own cologne?"

"Sure do, but I'm thinking my lady might like me smelling of the great Grantley James."

"She'll have no fucking clue what I smell like." I shook my head and pointed at him. "Is that my fucking sweater, too?"

Barney shrugged. "Maybe."

"Well I can't fucking wear that again, can I?" I protested. "You're as wide as a fucking tank, it'll be stretched now."

"Gee, sorry boss."

The fucker winked at me and opened the door. "Call me if you need anything."

"Just go you thieving bastard." I waved a hand at him, dismissively. "And have a great time."

"I will."

When the door clicked behind him, I picked up my glasses and went back to my script. A script that I could recite backwards if I needed to. I was ready for the next day, in fact, I'd been ready for months. The script was engraved deep into my brain, my body was sculpted to perfection after hour upon hour in the gym, my mind was clear and I was hungry to start. So why the fuck did I feel as though something scary was about to happen?

CHAPTER THREE

Phoebe

The rain had finally let up, but the tiny piece of the sun peeking through the clouds still wasn't enough to provide any warmth.

I finished off my take-away coffee and threw the corrugated, cardboard cup into the bin before turning the corner for the studio security gate. I flashed my pass at the guard and smiled at him as he nodded me through.

You'd think I would have been excited about starting a new film, especially one with Grantley James as the lead, but I couldn't summon up any enthusiasm. I didn't know why, but I wasn't getting the usual flight of butterflies in my stomach that the first day of shooting brought. *And* I had lines - that in itself was worth a little hop, skip, and a jump. I picked up my pace and did a little jump in the air, but nothing. My legs felt leaden and I knew there wasn't a skip in them.

"Hey Phoebe."

The shout that came from behind, startled me. I looked over my shoulder to see Declan, a guy who I'd been on quite a few things with, including two movies and three episodes of Coronation Street. Appearing on Britain's longest running soap gave you kudos in the world of extras, believe me.

"Hi, Declan. What are you shooting?"

Declan gave me a supercilious grin and a little head wobble. "Only the latest Addison Yates movie. What about you? You playing dead body number three again in that daytime hospital drama?"

God, what a dick he was. Just because he'd had a lead role in a thriller once, about ninety years ago, he thought he was better than everyone else. You'd think he'd won an Oscar for his performance, but in reality, had never won a lead role since – or any role for that matter.

"Oh, well," I said with an air of nonchalance, "we'll be working together then."

Declan stopped in his tracks. "What? You're on it as well?"

"Yep. In fact, I have some lines. How cool is that?" I asked, twinkling my eyes at him. "I'm going in as an extra, but coming off it as an actor."

Declan's lip curled – result, he was pissed off.

"*You got lines,*" he said in astonishment. "How on earth did you manage that?" He puffed out his chest underneath his bright blue *Puffa* jacket that was unzipped and showing off a *Ted Baker* shirt that was stretched to its limits.

"Barbara, my agent, put my name forward, I did a quick test and they said yes. The director said if there'd been a bigger part available it would have been mine."

He didn't of course. I hadn't even met him. I dealt with one of the casting team who had half-watched and half-listened to me at the same time as texting on his phone. Declan didn't need to know that though. It wouldn't hurt to bruise his ego a little.

"I wonder why Raymond didn't put my name forward," Declan mused, swiping the back of his hand at the beads of sweat that were forming on his massive forehead.

"You okay, Dec? You're looking a little bit..." I waved my hand up and down in front of his face, "hot and bothered."

He made a strangulated groaning noise from the back of his

throat and pushed my hand away, before striding towards the main building.

"Stupid little arsehole," I muttered, as I watched him stomp away.

Declan pulled open the door with force and, without glancing back, he walked inside letting it slam shut. I sighed and shook my head. He was always so jealous. He hated it if someone got even a single word of dialogue, he hated it if someone was in shot longer than he was, and he hated it if someone managed to get a proper acting job where they appeared on screen for longer than a minute at a time and got dialogue of more than a couple of lines. In truth, he hated everyone except the leads and as far as they were concerned, he hadn't got the nickname Brown Tongue for nothing, the big arse licker.

As soon as I walked inside the building, I noticed the massive difference in temperature. While it hadn't been arctic conditions outside, the rain had caused a cold, damp air to linger. I unravelled my scarf and unzipped my coat as I walked over to the PA at the registration desk; a large woman with long hair and thick glasses, who had red painted lips in a wide smile.

"Morning," she sing-songed. "What's your name, hun?"

"Phoebe Drinkwater." I showed her my pass and my driving license.

After studying them, she looked down the list, her forefinger snaking down the page of names until she finally stopped halfway down. She stabbed at the paper and then with a flourish, struck a tick next to my name.

"Lovely." She smiled up at me. "Do you have your booking sheet?"

I handed it over and the woman signed it and then stamped it with the studio stamp.

"There you go." She handed it back to me with my voucher. "Go to dressing room three and then onto the holding area once you're ready. You'll be called from there."

"That's great, thank you." I replied, returning her smile with one of my own.

"You know where you're going?"

I nodded. "Yes, I do thanks. I've worked here before."

"Enjoy, but a word of warning," she whispered, quickly scanning the corridor. "Our leading man is a little testy today."

"Okay, thanks for the heads up." I replied with a giggle.

"My advice," the woman said, "admire him from afar."

"I'll try and avoid him."

I'd heard that Grantley James could be a little difficult at times, but I was always one to give people a chance. I never listened to gossip, preferring to find things out for myself. Wondering whether this was one time I should listen to gossip, seeing as it had come from the PA, I started towards the dressing rooms. All filming for the next few days was going to be on the interior set, so only a few extras would be around. This meant we were using the studio dressing rooms, rather than a trailer which was the usual. Knowing where I was going, I began walking down the corridor. I had only gone a few steps when my phone buzzed in my pocket.

Pulling it out, I looked down at the screen to see a text from Beth.

Beth: Good luck for today, sis x

It was accompanied with a cute photograph of the boys, heads together and each giving me a thumbs up.

I started to type out a reply when I went smack into a long, hard body.

"What the..."

"Oh God, I'm so sorry."

"Could you watch where you're going instead of looking at your damn cell?"

I hadn't really registered who was standing in front of me, not until I realised I was listening to an American accent. Very slowly I lifted my head, and inch by inch, took in the specimen of perfection that stood before me.

"You're Grantley James," I gasped as my gaze landed on his face.

His pale green eyes stared at me through his dark brown hair that was sexily dishevelled.

"Yeah I am," he snapped. "And you're damn clumsy." He reached down and rubbed his knee. "Fuck."

"Sorry did I hurt your knee?"

I dropped my head to look at his injured joint and as I did, Grantley lifted his, and his skull cracked against my forehead with such force I felt my teeth rattle.

"Ah shit," I cried. "That hurt."

Grantley took a step backwards and glared at me as he rubbed his head.

"Are you determined to kill me?"

"It was your head that hit mine." I felt for a bump on my head, worried that I wouldn't be able to film if I had a big purple egg on display.

"You weren't watching where you were going," he growled. "That's the exact reason why fucking cell phones should be banned."

He pointed at the mobile phone still in my hand.

"So you don't have one?" I narrowed my eyes at Grantley, waiting for him to respond.

"Nope, I don't."

He ran a hand over the scruff on his chin and looked at me with defiance in his eyes. If I hadn't been around actors for the last five years, I'd have probably believed him – he hadn't won a Critics' Choice award for Best Young Actor on his first film for nothing. Yes, he was good, but I still saw it; the tell-tale look to the side. It was quick, I'll give him that, but I saw it.

"Liar!"

Grantley straightened and put his hands to his hips and the slight thrust he gave, drew my attention. I glanced down to see he was wearing grey sweat pants and I registered a number of things.

1. He was definitely commando. I could see the outline of his dick against the grey-marl fabric.
2. It was a fair size dick, because 'It' rested at least eight inches down his leg. (I'd had a job in a menswear shop for a year after college, so knew these things.)
3. His pants were hanging so low, I wondered if he was a *wankster*.
4. If he wasn't a *wankster,* was he actually someone's bitch?

Grantley's growl brought me back to the matter in hand –the fact that I had an angry, Hollywood movie star standing in front of me – with no undies on.

"Did you call me a liar?" he asked, leaning forward from the waist, into my space.

"Yes," I replied, surreptitiously breathing in his delicious smell. "You said you don't have a mobile and I think you do."

"If I say I don't have a *cell,* then I don't have a *cell.*"

"And I call bullshit."

Grantley glared at me with his nostrils flaring. "What's your name?"

"Why?" I dropped my bag and scarf to the floor and folded my arms over my chest.

"I want to know. I'm guessing your working on my movie in some capacity, and I want you off it."

My eyes widened as I gasped. "You can't fire me just because I called you a liar."

"Can't I?" He cocked a brow and smirked.

"No, you can't. You'd have to give me a verbal and then a written warning first, otherwise I'd call my union and get this film brought to a halt quicker than you can say 'liar, liar, knickers on fire'." I gave him a sarcastic smile, knowing I had him.

"You wouldn't dare."

"Wouldn't I?"

We stared at each other, both waiting for the other to break, but no way was I losing – I played this game with Callum and Mack all the time. I was the reigning champion.

Grantley's chest heaved in time with mine as we continued watching each other and then the silence was broken.

His bloody mobile rang, chiming out the chorus of 'Hangin' Tough' by New Kids on the Block. Totally forgetting the reason for our argument- I squealed, clapped my hands, and did a little hip wiggle – I bloody adored 80's music.

"Oh God," I cried. "I love this song."

"Fucking Barney," Grantley hissed, and reached into the back pocket of his sweat pants for his mobile.

"Yes, yes, yes," I shrieked realising what was happening. "I knew it, you do have a mobile."

Grantley curled his lip at me and stabbed at the screen.

"What do you want and when the fuck did you change my ring tone?"

I heard a deep chuckle on the other end of the line, and then whoever it was started talking. I watched as Grantley listened and stared back at me.

"Just a minute," he snapped down the phone and then looked at me. "You can go now, but I'll be watching you."

I rolled my eyes, picked up my bag, and walked away. I had only got a few steps when I heard a roar behind me. I quickly turned to see Grantley sprawled on the floor, but to his credit he still had hold of his mobile.

"You okay?" I asked, rushing over to him.

He lifted his head and exhaled deeply before speaking back into the phone.

"I fucking tripped over a scarf that some idiot had left on the floor."

With a quiet gasp, I looked down to see my scarf tangled around Grantley's feet. I must have dropped it, but I wasn't telling him that.

"Oh dear," I said, holding back a giggle. "You should watch where you're going instead of looking at your damn *cell.*"

I didn't hang around because the words that came out of Grantley James' mouth were just rude if you ask me.

CHAPTER FOUR

Grantley

"Please tell me she's not."

"Not what?" Penny the make-up girl asked, as she touched up my nose.

"Her." I gave a quick nod to the side. "She's not playing the nerdy assistant?"

Penny glanced to her left before sighing and continuing to dab at me with a sponge.

"Don't tell me, you've upset her too."

Penny was my regular make-up girl on the Addison Yates' films, so she was well aware that my reputation of being a miserable dick was justified. She was also someone else that I saw as a friend.

You see, I didn't just have Barney as a friend, I had Penny too; go me.

Penny and I were drinking buddies from time to time, but as I wasn't a big drinker, more often than not I ended up being Lone Wolf while she flirted her way around the bar. Usually resulting in me grabbing a cab back to whichever hotel we were staying in, while Penny disappeared with her latest hook-up.

"I haven't upset her." I snapped. "*She* almost crushed *my* skull in and broke both *my* legs."

Penny rolled her eyes. "I'm guessin' you're over exaggeratin' as usual, honey," she drawled in her rich Texan accent. "She's such an itty bitty little thing. Can't see how the hell she can have hurt you as bad as you say."

"Well she did." I pouted as Penny blotted my cheeks and forehead to remove the shine.

"She's real pretty." Penny grinned and winked at me.

"Keep your hands off. If I get her thrown off this damn set, I don't want to have to socialize with her because you've hooked up with her."

Tall, tatted, and gorgeous, Penny liked girls and girls, both gay and straight, seemed to like her - a great deal. In fact, I'd known many straight girls who jumped in the sack with Penny – she had an innate sexual chemistry that oozed from her. I should know. I hit on her on our first night out together, on my first Addison Yates film. She soon put me straight – so to speak.

"I'm jokin' honey. She's a knife, no doubt about it."

Penny liked to use a cutlery analogy for women's sexual orientation. Straight women were knives, bi-sexual ones were forks, and gay ones were spoons – you get the idea.

"She's still pretty hot though. Don't you think?" She grinned at me.

"Haven't noticed," I replied.

"And I call bullshit."

"What the fuck is it with people calling me a liar today?" I moved away, shrugging away Penny's hand. "Are we done?"

"So you *do* think she's hot?" She tapped the end of my nose with one of her brushes. "*And* she drives you crazy. Boy this is going to be fun."

Penny walked away giggling like a fucking girl.

"You ready, Grantley?" the Third Assistant Director called. "We're going to shoot the office scene first."

"Be right with you."

The Third AD nodded and went back over to Alexi Rodrigo,

who looked to be making changes to the shooting order with the First AD. I glanced over at my new nemesis, who was having photographs taken for continuity. I couldn't believe I was going to have to act in a scene with her. At least she only had three lines before Addison dismissed her from the office. Even I could be professional for three lines of dialogue.

A few minutes later, myself, the extra girl, and Don Paisley, a seventies icon movie star who played Addison's boss, were all on our marks, ready to go.

"And action!"

"You sure this information is correct, Arthur?" I pointed at the papers in my hands that were supposed to be the business and bank files of a drug and people trafficking ring, running under the guise of a British Software company.

"Imelda is the best hacker in the business." Don, playing Arthur my boss, turned to the ass pain playing Imelda.

She was dressed in a black pant suit with a white blouse underneath. It was pretty tight and I had to be honest, she had some pretty sexy curves. The black, bobbed wig and scarlet lipstick were hot too, it was just a pity she was so annoying.

"I thought the guy who created their software was a genius? Doesn't he go by the name of Red Wizard, or something?"

I delivered my line to Don, half turning my back on 'Imelda'. She then pushed my shoulder and stared me straight in the eye to reply.

"I can assure you Mr. Yates, I know what I'm doing. Andrew Green, or Red Wizard, whatever you want to call him, may well be a genius, but he's no match for me – I can promise you that."

"I'm sure you can, Imelda." With a deep, sultry whisper, I delivered what was supposed to be a flirty line, perfectly. So perfectly in fact, I saw *Imelda* squirm a little. I couldn't help but smirk at her – I'd turned her on. So much so, she missed her next line.

"Cut!" Alexi shouted. "Sweetness, is there a problem? You have three lines, please don't tell me you've forgotten them."

"Take a breath, Phoebe." Don said, being his usual kindly, gentlemanly self.

So, her name was Phoebe. It sounded a little like some sort of tropical plant, but it was kind of cute and suited her. Fuck, what the hell was my brain doing – thinking she was cute just because I could see what a fine ass and tits she has. Okay, I was officially shallower than a kid's pool in the park, but a man can't help being a man.

Phoebe took the breath that Don suggested, nodded, and stood back on her mark.

"Okay quiet everyone," Alexi shouted. "Let's go again."

This time she delivered her lines perfectly. A little stilted maybe, but you could hardly get into the psyche of the character in three lines. Shit, I was defending her as well as calling her cute. That get-up she had on must have had some magical sex scent sprayed all over it.

"You're happy then?" Don/Arthur asked.

"Yeah, I'm happy." I turned to Imelda/Phoebe and gave her a chin lift. "You can go now, Imelda."

Imelda nodded, turned, and walked out of shot. I couldn't help but look at her ass and almost choked.

"What the fuck," I gasped.

Pinned to the back of her jacket, was a piece of paper with, "Grantley is full of Bull sh*t" on the back.

"Cut! What the hell, Grantley?" Alexi ran a hand through his unruly curls. "What's wrong?"

"Sorry, but she kinda put me off." I pointed in the direction of where Phoebe had disappeared between a camera and a boom operator. "Did you not see it?"

"Not see what?"

"On her back."

I paced forward, ready to go and search for the little minx, but was stopped by Alexi's booming voice.

"Take it from your line again. Phoebe, get back on your mark."

Phoebe appeared and walked toward us with a grin on her face.

"Turn around," I blasted at her.

"Grantley, man," Alexi said from his chair to our right, "we need to get this scene down. I have another thirty fucking indoor scenes to do today."

"I think I'm shining." Don said, raising his hand.

"But her back," I blustered.

Phoebe made a show of turning around and looking over her shoulder.

"Is there something wrong with my jacket?" she asked in all innocence.

"Can I get make-up, please?" Don called like a diva.

"Don't give me that shit," I hissed, leaning in closer to her. "What did you do with the sign *Phoebe*?"

She shrugged as she chewed on her top lip.

"I should damn well get you thrown off this fucking set."

"Okay, guys. We all ready?" Don asked, returning from having his make-up touched up.

We ran the scene again and this time it went without a hitch. Phoebe left and as she stood out of shot, I was desperate to grab hold of her and find out what the fuck she'd been playing at.

Once we finished a couple more scenes, we broke for lunch and I went on the warpath looking for her. I found her queueing at the buffet table. Without thinking, or caring what anyone thought, I grabbed Phoebe by the elbow and pulled her out of the line.

"Hey," she cried. "I was almost at the front of the queue."

"Tough shit."

I stormed to the back of the dining hall, dragging her with me.

"I should fucking fire your ass," I growled as we stopped near the exit door. "I'm the lead on this damn movie and you do not mess with me."

"Oh, it was a joke," Phoebe huffed, "but if you have no sense of humour, that's not my fault."

"I have a sense of humor, sweetheart, but not when I'm working. If you can't be professional then you should *not* be on this set."

I stared at her, giving her my most vicious snarl. Props to the girl, she stood tall and her gaze never wavered.

"I'm sorry, okay," she finally snapped. "I thought it might make you laugh after what happened earlier."

"Yeah, well it didn't." I thrust my hands into my suit pants' pockets and leaned the top half of my body forward. "And you pull another fucking stunt like that and I swear to God, you'll be off this fucking movie and I'll make sure you never get any work ever again."

"That's a bit harsh." she replied with a gasp. "It's not like I murdered your mother or anything."

I snorted, knowing that if she had, I'd probably be getting her a starring role, not threatening to get her kicked off set.

"That should show you just how seriously I take my work."

Phoebe rolled her eyes and huffed. "Fine. I'll be on my best behaviour for the rest of the shoot."

"Just be grateful I'm in a good mood."

Her eyes widened and she snorted out a laugh.

"Sorry," she said, when I gave her a warning look. "I'll behave I promise. It was quite funny though, don't you think?"

"No, I fucking don't. I'm a serious actor and you're making me look like a dick."

Phoebe chewed on her lip and considered me. "Hmm, I think, to be honest, not wishing to sound rude, but you're doing that yourself. I mean, come on it was a joke – everyone plays jokes on the first day of shooting."

"Not on my movies they don't. Do I make myself clear?"

She saluted me and nodded. "Yes, sir." She stamped a foot. "I'll make sure I behave sir."

My jaw tightened and I knew my dentist was going to give me shit about grinding my teeth.

"Just make sure you do."

I pushed away from her and stormed across the dining hall, no longer in the mood for lunch. I couldn't believe how much she'd pissed me off.

I had a good sense of humor.

I could take a joke.

I could laugh at most things, but I couldn't get the vision of her fucking ass out of my head.

CHAPTER FIVE

Phoebe

Grantley James did not take my little joke well – at all. In fact, I'd say it was an epic fail of gargantuan proportions.

Penny, the make-up girl, thought it was hilarious when I showed her and explained why I was doing it. She said he'd 'love it'. Yeah well, he didn't.

But what did I care?

Actually, an awful lot if he followed through and got me thrown off set.

I needed to help Beth with the mortgage because, yet again, Steven had failed to transfer the child support he was supposed to pay. To be honest, Beth was lucky if she ever got any, but after five months of no money at all, and payments before that being sporadic to say the least, she'd finally consulted a family solicitor. Two days after the solicitor's letter was sent, Beth received a paltry three hundred pounds into her account, but nothing since.

I'd tried to tell her to take the stupid arse to court, but she always said she didn't have the time or energy. She'd only consulted a solicitor because he was a friend of Angela's husband. I went with her and had to admit, the solicitor was pretty hot and hoped maybe I could do a little match-making for my gorgeous sister, but Mr. Devine was well and truly married.

Anyway, I digress – again. I needed the money and could not afford to be sacked because Grantley James had zero sense of humour and walked around as though he had a banana up his arse. He was a miserable git and well and truly played the part of spoiled film star perfectly.

"Hey hunni."

I turned to see Penny walking towards me with a worried look on her face.

"I am so sorry. I honestly thought he'd laugh it off."

"It's fine," I sighed. "I just have to behave or he's going to get me thrown off the film."

Penny shook her head. "I know he can be difficult, but he can take a joke, usually. I'm real sorry, I truly am."

"Honestly, Penny please don't worry. You're not the one who frog-marched me from the canteen in front of everyone."

"He didn't?" Penny's nostrils flared and as she inhaled a deep breath, the snake tattooed across the swell of her breasts rippled as though it was real.

"Wow." I gasped.

"You looking at my titties or my tatties?" Penny asked with a huge grin.

"What?"

I looked up, my mouth gaping.

"You looking at my tits or my tattoos, hunni?"

She pointed at the snake with one finger and her left boob with the other.

"Oh God, your tattoos, every time. Not that you don't have nice boobs, you do, but..." I trailed off, swirling my finger in the vicinity of Penny's boobs.

"Relax, I know it's not my tits that interest you. Thanks for the compliment about the tats though. My brother does them when I'm back in Dallas."

"Do they hurt?" I asked, leaning forward to peer at the tattoo of an apple on her neck – the apple the snake was obviously heading for. For something so simple, it was amazingly life-like and looked almost 3D.

"Kind of like an angry kitty constantly scratching you. You got any?"

"No, I don't have any pets."

She burst out laughing. "No tattoos, hunni, not cats."

I shook my head. "Oh right. Nooo, too scared."

"Well maybe if you're ever in Dallas, I'll hook you up with Benny, my brother. Or even his ex-boss, Dex. He has a studio, Heaven & Ink, around here somewhere. I could find the address for you."

I shook my head. "No thanks, but one thing. Your brother is called Benny?" I asked, sputtering out a laugh.

Penny rolled her eyes. "Yeah. Our parents never thought of the consequences of our names being shortened. Anyway," she said glancing at the huge watch on her wrist, "I gotta go and touch up Harriet - again."

I grimaced thinking about Harriet Hinckley- the middle-aged, ex-musical theatre actress who was playing one of the 'bad guys' in the film. She tended to sweat profusely and I knew make-up generally had to touch up her make-up for almost every shot.

"Poor Harriet," I replied. "I wonder if she's menopausal."

Penny laughed and shook her head. "I have no idea, but whatever it is, I've had to designate a set of brushes and sponges just for her – no one wants to be touched up with a damp brush."

I shuddered at the thought. "Okay. You'd better go."

"But listen, don't worry about Grant. He really is a good guy, he just forgets he's allowed to be a normal human being at times."

"Hmm, most times."

"He really is okay. He'll warm to you, you'll see."

Penny gave my shoulder a squeeze and walked away, leaving me wondering whether torturing Grantley with a match under his feet qualified as him warming to me.

CHAPTER SIX

Grantley

"Cut!" Alexi called. "Get that in the can please. Okay everyone let's take a break for lunch. We'll do the street chase scene in one hour. We've got around two hours before rain is forecast people, so don't be late to the outside lot."

As Alexi strode away, I stood and waited for Penny to come over and stick some tissue into the collar of my shirt, so as not to get make-up on it during lunch, seeing as I would be in the same outfit for my street chase scene. I always felt like a complete tool walking around with it floating around my neck, but it was kind of necessary.

"Hey honey," Penny said as she approached me. "Nice work there."

I shrugged. "It won't win me an Oscar, but thanks. So, how's your day going so far?"

"Meh, you know, okay I guess."

"How so?" I asked, craning my neck to allow Penny access to my collar.

"I got blown off by a really cool girl last night. I thought we were on the same page, but turns out we weren't."

"Ooh Penny Wade crashed and burned, totally unacceptable."

"Yep sure is." Penny laughed and stood back. "All done, now you can go get lunch."

"So, this girl, would I like her? Is it worth me giving her a call?"

Penny folded her arms across her chest and shook her head. "You really are one big ego, aren't you?"

"Hey, I'm just a realist. The ladies like me."

"Well this one wouldn't. She's most definitely a spoon, but seemingly, I'm not big enough or butch enough for her."

"Ah okay. Well, her loss." I leaned forward and kissed Penny's forehead. "One day your princess will come."

"I'll sure have some fun while I'm waiting though. Okay, I'm gonna grab some chow. You coming?"

I nodded and waved for her to go ahead and followed behind. As we reached the dining room, I heard cursing behind us. Turning around to see who had such a foul mouth, I saw the pain in my ass; Phoebe. She was looking down at her cell and stabbing her finger at the screen, while strutting toward us.

"Hey, shouldn't you watch where you're going?" I called. "Last time you were so engrossed in your phone, you nearly killed me."

Phoebe's head shot up. "What?"

"I take it you mean pardon?"

"Oh shit," Penny groaned. "I'm too hungry to stand here and watch you peacocking. I'll see you in there."

"What?" I asked, turning around to see her disappearing through the door.

"I take it you mean pardon?"

I turned back to Phoebe to see her watching me with a shit eating grin.

"You really are a pain in my ass, aren't you?" I questioned.

"I have no idea what you mean. Anyway, you were the one listening to my private conversation."

Frowning, I shook my head. "You weren't even talking to anyone. You were cursing to yourself. Sounding like a New York dockhand, I might add."

"Oh, I'm sorry if I upset your sensitive nature. I'll be sure to keep my mouth shut in the future."

Then she damn well clicked her tongue at me and rolled her eyes.

"Did you just roll your eyes at me?" I accused, thrusting my hands to my hips.

"No," she lied, "you're seeing things. Maybe you need glasses."

"I already have them for reading. I know what I saw."

Phoebe grinned. "Wow, do you? I would never have imagined you in spectacles. Did you find it difficult to find a pair to suit you?"

"No. Why?" I asked incredulously, wondering whether she was always so random.

"It's just...no, I shouldn't really say."

I gave a long exhale. "You may as well say it now, otherwise I'll forever be damn well wondering until my dying day."

"Now you're just being sarcastic."

"No, no way. I'm truly interested," I said – sarcastically. "Just spit it out."

"Okay, you asked." She shook her hair back and lifted her chin. "I expect it would be difficult to find spectacles that suit you because you've got quite a fat head."

My mouth dropped open as I stared at her.

"Sorry," she muttered, looking down at the floor, "but you do."

"I do not have a fat head. I'll have you know I was voted second in Men's Health's Sexiest Man of The Year poll."

"Really?" She asked with what sounded like genuine interest. "Who won?"

"Ryan Gosling," I replied petulantly.

Shit, I still felt the sting.

"Ah." Phoebe nodded knowingly. "That explains it."

"What does?"

"That he came first."

"Are you trying to say you find Ryan Gosling more attractive than me?" I thrust a hand to my chest. "Because if you are, that hurts."

"He has his qualities," she replied earnestly. "I can see what women see in him. I just find his lips to be a little too thin."

"Ah, is that so?"

I couldn't help but smirk. It was often commented how full and pouty my lips were.

"Hmm." Distractedly, Phoebe looked back down at her phone. "Stupid idiot."

"Who is?"

Her head shot up. "So you are eavesdropping?"

"You're here in front of me," I cried incredulously, sweeping a hand in front of me. "I can't help but hear."

"If you must know, it's the delivery man who is supposed to be delivering my trampoline. He's left it at the wrong house and won't go back for it. Well he wouldn't, but after I threatened to call his manager he's relented."

Suddenly images of Phoebe bouncing up and down on a trampoline filled my head – specifically her tits bouncing up and down.

"The address is quite clear," she continued. "It's not my fault he doesn't understand the difference between Grove and Road. Although, I've always said having a Cedar Grove and a Cedar Road was utter madness. I even called the council about it, you know."

Yep, she was definitely high.

"So, you use a trampoline?"

Okay, so I changed the subject back to the trampoline, but the images just wouldn't go away.

"Oh yeah," she scoffed. "It's good fun and keeps me fit – helps to improve my pelvic floor tremendously."

Fuck there was that eye roll again. What the hell had I said wrong this time?

"Obviously, I'm annoying as well as have a fat head. Anything else wrong with me? Because you know, you may as well tell me, now that you've started."

The little shit actually thought about it for a second and then shook her head. "Nope, not that I can think of off the top of my head.

Although," she said with a laugh, "if it was you, you'd say 'off the top of my fat head'."

"Once again, I do *not* have a fat head. It's a perfectly normal size." I shook my perfectly sized head in disbelief. "I could have you thrown off set for talking to me like this you know."

"What, for telling you the truth? Seriously, you've surrounded yourself with too many arse lickers if you can't take a little criticism."

"You said I've got a fat head. That's just damn fucking rude."

"Well Ryan Gosling did beat you, so..." she trailed off, giving a shrug.

"What are you trying to say?"

Phoebe sighed. "That he has a normal size head."

"You've got to be shitting me. His head is the same size as mine." I put my hands up to feel the shape and size of my head.

"You'd think that," Phoebe said, tilting her head to study me. "But when you look at it close up, it is fairly large. Not overly so, but enough to lose you a few votes."

"Seriously, you think that's it?"

"Hmm, I do. Anyway, I'd better get some lunch. See you around Grantley."

With that she walked away, giving me a little wave over her shoulder.

"Fuck." I muttered. "I have a bigger head than Gosling."

CHAPTER SEVEN

Phoebe

When I finally got home, dragging my weary body through the door after standing on the train and then sitting next to a rather badly odorous man on the bus, I was disappointed, to say the least, that I couldn't smell food cooking. Beth always had dinner ready for me.

"Oi, you lazy bugger," I cried, making my way into the lounge. "Where's my dinner?"

I threw my bag down next to the sofa and looked at my sister with wide, expectant eyes. As soon as I saw her face, I knew something was wrong.

"What is it?" I asked, plonking myself next to her and grabbing hold of her hand. "Beth?"

She looked up at me with tears in her eyes and took a deep breath. "I've found a lump."

"What? Where? Have you called the doctor?"

I must have squeezed her hand too tightly because she winced a little.

"Sorry," I apologised. "Have you?"

Beth nodded. "Yes. I went a few days ago, but I've had a letter from the hospital. They want me to go in tomorrow for a mammogram. Dr. Phillips rushed it through. That's bad right?"

"No," I shook my head. "Not necessarily."

"I'm so scared, Phoebes."

Beth's bottom lip trembled as she looked up at me.

"I'll be with you, so don't be scared. What time is the appointment?"

Beth shook her head. "No, you can't. You need to work. You can't afford to be away from the set."

"I can and I damn well will," I protested. "They'll have to sack me if they won't let me take the time."

"I thought you were doing the reverse shots on your dialogue piece tomorrow?"

She looked so lost and worried, I dragged her against my chest and hugged her tightly.

"Fuck it and fuck stupid Addison Yates."

Beth pulled away. "No, you need to go. Honestly, I'll be fine. I won't hear anything tomorrow and my appointment is early, so I'm sure it'll be a quick in and out and I'll be back at work before the first brew is due."

"Are you sure?" I felt extreme guilt wrap itself around my throat at the thought of letting her go alone. "I'm sure I can get Mr. Roderigo to reschedule it."

"Nope. Not a chance. If you could drop the boys off at Wendy's though, that would be a big help."

Wendy was the boys' child-minder in the school holidays when both Beth and I worked.

"Consider it done. No problem at all." I said dragging her to my chest, for my own comfort as much as hers.

The next morning, the boys were not in the mood for doing anything that I asked. Beth had gone off to the hospital for her eight-thirty appointment and I needed to be on set by ten-thirty, which meant the boys needed to cooperate.

"Please, Mack," I pleaded on the edge of hysteria, "leave the box where it is."

"But it needs to go into the bin," my eco/society conscious nephew complained. "People shouldn't leave rubbish."

He was right. I knew he was but at that precise moment I didn't give a shit who had dropped their take-away carton onto the pavement without a care. I was going to be late for my call if I didn't get to the station within the next hour.

"You're stinky," Callum shouted at his twin, while kicking at a piece of dried up dog shit.

"Am not. You are."

"Boys, please," I cried, closing my eyes and hoping when I opened them I'd miraculously be on a train heading into Manchester. "Neither of you are stinky. Mack, leave the box and Callum stop kicking the dog shi- poo."

They both looked at me murderously as if I'd just informed them that that the Easter Bunny was a ridiculously insane marketing ploy made up by chocolate companies to help increase their profits.

"Please, move it."

"Why are you taking us to Wendy's anyway?" Mack asked, running his hands along some garden railings.

"Your mum explained this. It's because she had to go into work early this morning." I repeated the lie that Beth and I had agreed to tell the boys.

"Oh no."

I rolled my eyes and prayed for patience as I watched Callum drop to his knees to tie his shoelace – something which he couldn't actually do, but always insisted he could.

"Callum, please we're two minutes away from Wendy's. You can leave that for now."

The concentration on his face was evident as a tiny tongue poked out of the side of his mouth. If I let him carry on we would be there for at least ten minutes before he gave up and had a frustrated strop.

"Auntie Peepee," Mack insisted. "We can't go to Wendy's today."

"Mack, will you stop it. You're going to Wendy's and that's final. Callum, please just leave the shoelace."

Callum stood up with a sigh and crossed his little arms over his chest. "Mack's right. We can't go to Wendy's."

"Why not?" I cried, almost stamping my foot like the six-year-olds standing in front of me might do.

"Because she's in Terror reef."

"Where?" I glanced across the road to where I could see Wendy's house. The porch door that was usually open, wide and welcoming, was firmly closed.

"Terror reef," Callum repeated.

"See I told you," Mack added. "We can't go today because she's in Terror reef."

"Where the hell is Terror reef?" I muttered, anxiously glancing at the house once more.

"It's on holiday," Mack said in a voice that indicated I was the most stupid adult ever to darken his doorstep. "You go on a plane to it."

"It takes ages to get there," Callum offered.

I looked at them both wracking my brains and suddenly realised what they meant.

"You mean Tenerife?"

"That's what we said," Callum sighed.

"You mean she's not there." I pointed at the house.

Mack shook his head. "That's what I've been telling you for the last hour."

I pulled my head back and furrowed my brow. "Excuse me, I think you'll find it was about five minutes tops."

"Well, it seemed like an hour," he grumbled.

"Auntie Peepee, please can I tie my shoelace now?"

"No." I gave Callum a cursory glance before turning back to Mack. "So, you're telling me Wendy, her husband, and kids have gone on holiday?"

"Yep. They went yesterday."

"So how do you know this, but your mum doesn't?"

"Mummy does. She properly forgot."

"Probably forgot," I corrected.

It wasn't surprising that she had forgotten - going to the hospital was probably the only thing on her mind. I pulled my mobile out to call her, but when I thought about what she was in the middle of dealing with, changed my mind.

"Okay boys, let's turn around. You're coming to work with me today."

"Do we have to?" Callum groaned.

"It'll be fun," I said, grabbing hold of both boys' hands and walking back the way we'd came. "You'll be able to see all the cameras and the actors."

"Will we see Addison Yates?" Mack asked excitedly, ever the little boy enthralled by action.

"Yes, dickhead will be there," I muttered under my breath.

"Who's Dick Head?" Callum asked. "Is he an actor too?"

Shit those kids had bionic hearing, unless it was when Beth was shouting for them to get to sleep.

"Oh, it's no one."

"Is that Addison's real name?" Mack asked. "Dick?"

"Well, no not really."

"So why did you call him that?"

"I didn't."

"You did," Mack replied. "You said, yes Dick Head will be there."

I looked down at the two earnest faces looking up at me and conceded defeat.

"Yes, that's his secret name, but only certain people are allowed to call him that. It's short for Richard."

"Will we be able to call him Dick?" Callum asked. "Or do we have to call him Richard?"

"Should we call him Addison?"

"Or do we call him Mr. Head?"

"God no," I snapped, quickly crossing the road to the bus stop. "You can call him Addison or Mr. James."

"Why Mr. James?"

Please let me close my eyes and start the day again. And what sort of school do they go to that they've never heard the phrase dickhead before?

"That's another one of his names. He only lets his friends call him Dick, so maybe just call him Mr. James or Addison."

I felt Mack shrug. "Okay, but I think I'll call him Addison."

"He might let us call him Dick," Callum added, stumbling over his untied shoelace.

"Can I tell my friends that I met Addison Yates?" Mack asked. "When we get back to school after the holidays."

Having reached the bus stop, I let go of the boys' hands and stooped down to Callum's shoe.

"I don't see why not."

"We'll have to get evidence," Callum added, placing his tiny little hand on the top of my head to steady himself, while I tied his lace. "Auntie Peepee will need to take a photograph."

"Woah that would be cool."

Mack high-fived his brother and giggled.

"Just think Cal, me and you on a photograph with Dick Head, everyone will be dead jealous."

"Yeah, us and Dick. How cool is that?"

I groaned inwardly and knew without doubt today was going to be challenging to say the very least.

CHAPTER EIGHT

Grantley

I was waiting on set for my call, when I heard hissing and whispering behind me. Turning slowing in my chair, I noticed it was *her* and she had two little people with her. Two little people that looked identical to each other.

Twins!

Twins freaked me out – Village of the Damned and all that shit, and didn't they talk to each other in some strange language or via telepathy? Plus, what the fuck were they doing on set? I knew Alexi encouraged a friendly, family atmosphere, but bring your kids to work day was pushing it too far.

"Good of you to turn up," I said as Phoebe caught me looking at her.

"I'm not late," she snapped. "Our call for the reverse shots isn't for another ten minutes."

I chose to ignore the fact that she was correct. "Who are they?" I nodded at the matching pair of evil, suddenly wondering whether she was married with a brood of kids.

"My nephews. My sister had an appointment and her child minder has gone to Tenerife and Beth forgot, so I took the boys there this morning and ended up bringing them here because I didn't want to worry my sister, so I was going to leave them in the dressing room but Pauline, who is an extra in the dinner party scene, said it might be dangerous to leave them alone whereas on set someone could keep an eye on them, so I checked with Alexi and he said it was okay as long as they didn't make a noise, so I've warned them that they have to be quiet and -."

"Okay, okay," I cried, cutting her off. "Take a breath, otherwise we'll need to get a doctor on set."

She took a deep breath and looked down at the boys and lifting their hands one at a time said, "This is Callum and this Mackenzie – well, we all call him Mack."

"Hey." I gave them a short wave, noticing both were staring at me open-mouthed.

"You're Addison Yates," the one called Mack said, his tone laced with awe.

"Yep, I sure am."

Looking at them both, I could see they were slightly different. Mack had darker hair than Callum and where Callum had dimples in his cheeks, Mack's was in his chin. Maybe they weren't so freaky after all.

"You jumped out of a plane without a parachute," Callum added.

"I did," I replied seeing no point in telling them it wasn't actually me, but Bruce, our stuntman.

"Woah. You're really cool, Dick."

Phoebe squealed. "Callum!"

Callum looked up at her and frowned. "But he is."

"Aaah you're in trouble," Mack said with mischievous grin. "Auntie Peepee said we weren't to call him Dick. We are supposed to ask or call him Mr. James."

"She said that it was okay, didn't you Auntie Peepee?"

I looked up at Phoebe who was breathing rapidly and shaking her head, evidently having been ratted out by the little terrors. *And* Auntie Peepee? That was fucking hilarious.

"Auntie Peepee said my name was *Dick*, did she?"

I narrowed my eyes on Phoebe who was now a deep shade of red.

"Yep. She said you only let your friends call you Dick, but you might let us call you Addison or Mr. James. What *can* we call you?" Mack asked, giving a little shrug.

"I think Dick will be fine." I kept my eyes on Phoebe as I answered the boy, loving the discomfort she was obviously feeling.

"I'm sorry," she spluttered. "They misunderstood or misheard or something. I said they were to call you Mr. James. Didn't I boys, didn't I say you were to call him Mr. James, *because that's his name?*"

She ground out the last few words, staring hard at the boys and silently begging them to save her ass.

They both nodded and Phoebe let out a breath.

"But you did say Dick Head was his secret name."

And good old Mack threw her right back under the bus.

"*MACK!*"

"Well," I said. "Only a few people call me that, but I think your Auntie Peepee calls me that all the time. Isn't that right, Peepee? Usually Dick 'Fat' Head, I believe."

"I'm so sorry," she said in a strangulated voice, as though she was choking. "I didn't say...I mean...I...your head isn't really that fat, I was joking."

"Ah, you're both here," Alexi gushed, appearing at the side of my chair. "Let's get these reverse shots done and then you can go and get changed for the dinner party scene, Phoebe."

Alexi didn't tend to like to use the same extras in multiple scenes, but he did have a trusted few that were, and it looked like Phoebe was one of those bad pennies that would keep turning up.

Phoebe looked down at the boys and then back up at Alexi and nodded. "Okay." She then stooped down to eye level of both boys, and gently pulled them in front of her. "Now, remember you have to be extra quiet as soon as Mr. Rodrigo says 'action', okay?"

Both of them nodded and gave her a grin. I had to admit they were pretty cute.

"You boys want to watch through a camera?" Alexi asked.

They looked at Phoebe, who nodded, and then turned back to Alexi and gave him their own grin.

"Be good," Phoebe warned, checked her wig and walked off to her mark.

"See you later boys."

I pushed up out of my chair to follow their aunt.

"Bye, Dick," they chorused.

After doing the reverse shots of the office scene, I was dressed in a tux and moved on to the dinner party scene. In the scene, Addison is in some fancy ass restaurant eating with friends when the bad guys storm in and take his 'love interest' hostage during the melee, so as I talked with Alexi about the way he wanted the scene to go, I watched the extras get into place in my periphery. They were milling around, taking their spots, and getting last minute direction from Monique, the Second AD. It was then I spotted her, smack bang in the middle of them, wearing a tiny fucking sequinned dress – Auntie fucking Peepee, with the longest, toned legs I'd ever seen.

"Fuck me," I growled under my breath.

"Something wrong?" Alexi asked, looking over his shoulder.

"No, nothing. Just remembered something I've forgotten to do."

I tore my eyes away from Phoebe and gave Alexi a quick smile.

"Okay, let's do this," Alexi said and slapped me on the shoulder.

As he walked away I noticed the boys sitting on chairs, both wearing a huge pair of headphones each and watching everything that was going on. Mack spotted me first and gave me a thumbs up before nudging Callum and pointing toward me. Callum waved and I gave them a quick wave back, wondering why they made me smile so fucking big. I'd never spent much time with kids – didn't have any friends who had them, had no siblings and so had no nieces or nephews, yet I instantly liked these two boys and wanted them to like me. I wondered whether my getting tight with them would mean Auntie

Peepee would consider wrapping those amazing legs around my neck.

Woah – where the hell did that thought come from?

Concerned at the shit my brain was coming up with, I glanced over at Phoebe again. She was bending over talking to some guy with a beard, who was sitting at one of the dining table set ups. While Phoebe talked to him, the damn douche canoe's eyes were firmly on her cleavage which, it had to be said, was as fucking spectacular as her legs.

Did that make me a douche canoe as well, for noticing her tits?

I suppose it did, but at least I was doing it on the sly. The bearded guy may as well have held a placard up that said, 'I'm looking at Phoebe's tits, bring me a towel for the drool'.

What a prick.

I seriously considered storming over and covering her with my jacket, when Alexi shouted for everyone to take their places. I was back to being Addison Yates and Phoebe's tits and legs would have to wait.

The dinner party scene took hours to shoot. There was a lot of action in there, with hand to hand combat and some explosive special effects, so Alexi wanted it done perfectly. We'd choreographed the fight scenes weeks before, so they all went well, but when a table cloth was set on fire, it had got a little out of hand, pushing things back a while. While the set was redressed to a suitable starting point, I talked to Bruce, who was not only our stuntman but also our Stunt/Fight co-ordinator. I was checking he was happy it all looked realistic enough, yet the whole time, I had one eye on Phoebe.

Even though her nephews were watching her, she never lost concentration or let her eyes stray to them. She kept to her marks and did her job. Credit to the boys, they were quieter than I ever thought was possible from kids. There wasn't one peep from them and when I looked over, they were watching with rapt attention at what was going on. The only time I heard a noise from them, was their screams of delight at lunch when they saw all the mini burgers and hot dogs that catering had provided. I'd eaten with Alexi and Francesca, who was playing my love interest, as Alexi wanted to discuss some of the location scenes in a couple of days' time. The whole time though, I'd kept one eye on douche canoe, Phoebe, and the boys, wondering what they were talking and laughing about.

After lunch, we were straight back to it until finally, Alexi was happy. Even though it was only around four, we were all tired and smelling of smoke, and as the following day was going to be on location, he called an early end to the day's filming. The extras were all herded off set and while I had my hidden Lavalier mic removed, which we use alongside the boom to pick up dialogue, my eyes were drawn to Phoebe, wanting to get one last look of her legs in the that dress.

Douche canoe had disappeared, thank fuck, but Phoebe was listening to the boys while they talked animatedly to her, both flinging their arms around and throwing their bodies from side to side. I had a feeling they'd enjoyed the fight scenes and would be re-enacting them for a few hours at least.

"There you go Mr. James," Bailey, the assistant sound guy said, taking a step away from me with the mic in his hand. "You're free to go."

"Thanks, Bailey. See you tomorrow." I gave him a quick head nod and stalked away, hoping to see Phoebe before she left.

Why?

I had no fucking clue.

CHAPTER NINE

Phoebe

I couldn't believe how well behaved the boys had been while I'd been on set, but I also couldn't believe that Mr. Rodrigo had allowed them to watch. I'd heard from a friend of mine, who'd done a film with him in Australia, that he was laid back and extremely approachable, but never expected him to agree to have two six-year-old tearaways on set.

"Dick was amaaaazing when he was fighting," Mack cried excitedly, as we walked towards the bus stop. "Did you see him hit that man with the big scar?"

"Yeah, and when that other man went to punch him, and he picked up the table and put it in front of him and the man got his fist stuck in it."

"Awesome."

Callum and Mack were buzzing and so happy, I just hoped that Beth's day had gone just as well as theirs. I don't know what all of us would do if it turned out to be bad news. She was the glue that kept us together, the one who chivvied me along when I thought about quitting and getting a proper job, the one who the boys adored. We'd all be devastated if anything happened to her, but I wasn't sure the boys would *ever* get over it. She was their only parent, because Steven sending a few quid every now and again certainly didn't constitute parenting.

My heart thudded rapidly at the thought of the boys having to go to Steven. Not a chance would I let that happen. I'd fight tooth and nail to keep them. Not that he'd want them anyway. Two small boys did not fit in with the lifestyle of holidays, expensive cars, and designer clothes- that he was evidently leading with Miss Cock Sucker – according to his numerous social media accounts, which Beth and I stalked when we were pissed on cheap white wine.

As Mack karate chopped Callum, I pushed the dark thoughts from my head and plonked myself down on the bench seat under the bus shelter.

"Boys," I called, "stop Kung-Fu-fighting and come and sit down. The bus will be here soon."

"What's Kung-Fu-fighting?" Callum asked, his cheeks rosy red from the exertion of battling with his brother.

"What you were just doing."

"No we weren't," Mack said breathlessly. "We were doing unarmed combat. I'm Addison Yates and Callum is the big, ugly, bad guy."

"Why am I him? You've been Addison for ages. It's my turn to be Addison now."

"It's my game," Mack protested. "You should have thought of it if you wanted to be Addison."

I took a deep breath and counted to five – they might well have killed each other by the time I got to ten.

"Okay boys, enough of that game now, but next time you play it, Callum is Addison. Okay?"

Both looked at me with a frown. Their little brows pinched and cupid bow lips pouting. They were so damn cute, I dragged them both into a hug.

"I love you two," I sighed, inhaling in their scent of fresh air and baby shampoo that Beth still used on them.

The boys squirmed a little and while Mack pulled away, Callum, the one who always loved a cuddle, gave me a little squeeze before following his brother.

"When will the bus be here?" Callum asked, pushing himself up on to the bench next to me.

"Not long, ten minutes," I lied.

We'd missed a bus by five minutes and there wouldn't be another for a half hour. The boys, however, did not need to know that.

"I'm hungry," Mack groaned, leaning his head against the grubby Perspex of the shelter.

"I'm thirsty." Callum decided to join in.

"Well, I don't have any food or drink on me, so you'll just have to wait until we get to the railway station."

"Can we have a burger?" Callum cried excitedly.

"No. You had burgers at lunch. In any case, your mum might have made something by the time we get back."

"Can't you text and ask her?" Callum asked. "She might say we can have burgers."

I shook my head. I didn't want to text Beth again. I'd sent one earlier telling her I'd pick the boys up from Wendy's on my way home – I didn't want to remind her that Wendy was away and she'd forgotten, it would only make her feel bad, and I didn't want her to. I was putting off another text because I was scared that this time I'd get more back than an 'Okay, thanks' as I had earlier. What if she gave me bad news? I knew she probably wouldn't have any results yet, but it still worried me. What if they had noticed something and taken her in straight away – yes, logically I knew she'd have called me if that was the case, but fear still tapped at my breast bone.

"You're not having another burger. I'll get you a cereal bar and some juice."

Callum and Mack pulled identical faces – tongues out and eyes crossed.

"G-r-oss," Mack complained.

"Tough, that's my final offer."

I heaved a sigh and pulled my phone out of my bag, contemplating again on whether to call Beth or not. Before I decided, I flicked through a couple of emails and a text message from my service provider offering me more data. Okay, I was putting it off, but what was wrong with that.

"Auntie Peepee," Callum hissed, pulling on my sleeve. "Look."

"What?" I asked, looking up.

Stopped at the side of the road was a huge, black, four by four. It had blacked out windows and black alloyed wheels – it was big and sexy and looked extremely expensive. As I admired it, the back window slowly whirred down, to reveal the handsome, tanned face of Grantley James.

"Woah," Mack cried, running towards the car. "It's Dick. Hey, Dick."

I cringed as Grantley stuck his head further through the window and looked directly at me.

"Boys," he said, addressing Mack and Callum, finally taking his eyes off me. "Did you enjoy yourselves today?"

"It was so cool," Callum cried, excitedly. "When you punched that big man, it was amazing."

"I liked the fire too," Mack added, jumping up and down on the spot. "It went, whoosh."

Mack threw his arms up into the air, demonstrating the licking of flames. I glanced at Grantley and noticed a warm smile spread across his face, as he listened intently to the boys.

"Well it sure sounds like you enjoyed it a lot."

"Oh we did, Dick. Didn't we Mack?"

Mack nodded enthusiastically and stepped forward next to Callum and, standing on tiptoe, tried to peer through the blacked out windows.

"Mack," I warned. "Don't be rude."

"It's fine." Grantley laughed. "What are you doing here, anyway?"

He looked directly at me again and gave me a small chin lift.

"We're waiting for the bus to the railway station," I replied, glancing over my shoulder at the bus shelter.

"You have to get a bus and a train to get here?"

"Yep. But it's no biggie, lots of people have much worse journeys to work."

"But you did that journey with the boys too?"

I nodded. "Yep. They didn't mind though did you boys?"

The boys ignored me, now too interested in the good looking black guy in the driver's seat, who had opened the passenger door and was letting Mack and Callum have a look inside.

"I think they're more interested in your car." I rolled my eyes. "I'm sorry, they're not normally so easily distracted. Usually I can bring them to heel with a whistle and get them to beg with a click of my fingers."

Grantley's lips twitched and then he let out a quiet laugh. "They're well behaved kids, their parents must be proud of them."

I glanced at the twin trouble. "Beth, my sister, their mum is, but their father is absent and has been since they were a year old. They're all down to Beth."

"Their mom has brought them up alone all that time?" Grantley looked at them anxiously with his brow furrowed.

"Pretty much. I moved in about four years ago, and help out where I can, but it was just Beth before that. She's pretty amazing to be honest."

A lump formed in my throat, as I thought about Beth and what she might be about to face. No one deserved cancer, but Beth had worked so hard to provide a good home for the boys, it seemed even more unjust.

"What, their dad just up and left?" Grantley asked. His nostrils flared a little as he clenched his jaw. "And he's never been back since?"

I shook my head, a little taken aback at his evident anger over the boys' and Beth's situation.

"We do okay though," I replied, feeling the need to explain and to calm Grantley's ire.

His head suddenly disappeared and the man talking to the boys, leaned between the two front seats. After a few seconds, the rear passenger door opened.

"Come on," he beckoned with the tilt of his head. "Get in, we'll give you a lift home."

"It's really not necessary."

"Woah cool," Callum shouted. "Can I sit in the front?"

"No, I want to sit in the front."

"I asked first."

"Please Callum," Mack whined.

Callum, the first born by twenty minutes, shook his head and rooted himself in the car doorway, arms firmly planted across his chest confirming his stature as the eldest.

"Boys, I didn't even say we were going in Mr. James' car. The bus will be here soon."

"We're giving you a lift and that's final." Grantley growled and then turned to pick up, what looked like scripts, which were spread across the back seat.

"Really, it's not necessary," I sighed.

"I said *we're taking you all home.*"

Grantley stepped out of the car with a pile of papers under his arm and moved to the open passenger door where the boys were having a stand-off. Callum wasn't budging from his spot, but Mack was determined, trying to pull him away by his arm.

"Okay guys," Grantley said breezily. "To save any arguments, I'm gonna ride shot-gun and you both can sit in the back with your aunt."

"But-."

"No arguments, Cal," Grantley replied, shocking me that he knew which twin was which. "In any case, I think you'll be pleased when you see the DVD player in the back. There's already a Marvel film loaded up and ready to press play on."

Callum almost bowled Mack over as he ran and flung himself up the high step-up into the car, sprawling across the back seat.

"Callum," I admonished, glancing warily at Grantley. "I'm so sorry. I'll pay if he's scratched the leather or anything else."

Grantley gave me a small smile. It was tiny in fact, a simple twitch of his lips at the sides, but pure amusement glittered in his pale green eyes.

"What's so funny?"

"You really think I care about some scratched leather in a rented car?"

"You will if you have to pay for it." I pointed at the seat, which now Callum and also Mack were sitting on and bouncing up and down. "*Boys, stop it.*"

"They're fine," Grantley said softly, ushering me to the door. "Now get in and we'll get you home."

"Honestly-."

"Please just get in the damn car," he sighed.

"But it's probably miles out of your way. It will take you almost an hour to get there."

"Barney doesn't mind, do you?"

Grantley leaned down to peer inside the car, flashing a grin at the driver, Barney.

"Nope, call it my good deed for the day." His voice was deep and rich and images of him serenading someone with a sexy love song while he gyrated around them sprung into my mind.

I really did watch too many music videos.

I sighed deeply and looked down the road, wishing for the bus to suddenly appear. Although how I'd get the boys out of that damn car if it did, I had no idea. I was about to succumb when I spotted Declan running towards us.

"It hasn't gone yet, has it?" he huffed, pulling his bag higher onto his shoulder.

"Not yet," I replied as a red-faced, puffing Declan ran up beside me.

With his chest heaving, Declan looked between myself and Grantley, his mouth dropping another inch with each little bit of realisation that I was talking to a Hollywood star, and my nephews were sitting in the back seat of said star's car.

"Oh," he said before snapping his mouth shut.

"Hi," Grantley said, giving Declan a tight smile.

"Mr. James," Declan simpered. "It's a pleasure to meet you. I'm Declan Johnson. I'm an extra on the film alongside Phoebe."

Declan held out his hand to Grantley, who took it and shook it firmly.

"As in prick."

I gasped and snapped my eyes up to Grantley's that were surveying Declan's face intently.

"I'm s-sorry," Declan stammered.

"Johnson," Grantley said with an even tone. "It's what we Americans call a prick, a dick. We call it a Johnson."

Declan visibly sagged at the realisation that Grantley wasn't, in fact, insulting him. Although, the way Grantley was perusing him I wasn't so sure.

"Do you need glasses?" Grantley snapped, closing the gap between him and Declan.

"I-I don't think so," Declan stammered, looking a little perplexed. "Why?"

"I just thought you might," Grantley replied, flicking some dandruff off Declan's shoulder. "Seeing as you kind of look at Phoebe's chest more than her face."

"*Grantley.*" I gasped. "That's not..."

I was going to deny that was the case, but it was actually true. Declan's eyes rarely moved higher than my knockers if there was any part of them on show. Actually, come to think of it, he pretty much stared at them the *whole* time. I'd played one of several nuns once and he was one of several priests and he still managed to give them a good once over – more than once.

"I can assure you, I would never objectify Phoebe like that," Declan protested.

Grantley slapped a big hand on Declan's shoulder and gave him a tight smile. "Good to hear it. Now, if you'll excuse me, I need to get Phoebe and both the boys home."

I was pretty sure the look of astonishment on my face matched that of Declan.

"Seriously, Grantley, I can get the bus and train."

"No arguments. The boys have already started to watch a film, so get in." Grantley shouldered Declan out of the way, to give me room.

"Hey, Grant," Barney called from the depths of the car. "We should get going man, you've got that thing tonight."

"Okay, Barney." Grantley turned to Declan. "Great to meet you, Johnson. Now, Phoebe get in."

Knowing I had very little choice and giving Grantley a look that I hoped, but doubted, evoked fear in him, I got into the car and sat next to the boys.

Grantley got in and as soon as his door was closed, Barney moved away from the curb and sped away. I looked over my shoulder to see Declan watching us, shock written all over his face.

"You okay back there?" Barney asked, giving us a quick glance in the rear-view mirror.

The boys, engrossed in the film, where I spotted Scarlett Johansson running alongside the Incredible Hulk amongst other people, failed to answer.

"We're great, thank you." I answered for us all.

"No problemo. Now, you wanna give me the deets of your address and I'll get you guys home."

I gave my post code to Barney, who keyed them into the in-car *Sat Nav* and sat back into the soft cream leather.

"You okay if I work?" Grantley asked from the front seat.

"God yes, that's fine," I gushed. "Please don't let us stop you. It's really very good of you to do this. It really wasn't necessary."

"Please," he sighed. "Stop thanking me and sit back and enjoy the journey home without hundreds of other people stepping on your toes, or pushing into your back – or even that bearded prick we just left, looking where he shouldn't."

I glanced at the boys, both were enthralled, so they hadn't heard Grantley call Declan a prick. Not that he wasn't, he truly was, but the boys didn't need to hear that sort of thing.

"How did you know he's always looking where he shouldn't?" I asked, interested to know.

"I saw him today," he replied, reaching into his pocket. "He was looking at your cleavage during the dinner party scene."

Ugh, he really is a dirty, creepy bastard.

"Nothing new there I'm afraid," I replied.

"Seriously?" he asked over his shoulder.

"Yep. He does it all the time."

Grantley turned to look at me and was now wearing a pair of black-rimmed glasses. Those, paired with the rings and thin leather bracelet he must have put on after filming, well, he looked – shit, how to describe what he looked like.

Hot.

Sexy.

Gorgeous.

And did I say hot?

And yep, they suited him because newsflash, he didn't really have a fat head.

"Yeah," he said, rousing me from my thoughts. "He most definitely has the right name."

He then turned back to his scripts and left me wondering whether I'd wet my knickers when we went over a speed bump a few seconds earlier, or I was one more woman not immune to Grantley James' charm and horny as hell spectacles.

CHAPTER TEN

Grantley

I tried to concentrate on my script as we drove along, but the animated chatter in the back seat kept distracting me. It wasn't pissing me off or anything, but those kids were funny and I found myself smiling more than once at what they were saying.

"No way," Mack exclaimed. "Dick could smash The Hulk on the head with a piece of wood."

"But he couldn't," Callum retorted. "I'm not being mean about Dick, but the Hulk is *The Hulk,* he can kill anyone, he's like a giant or something."

"But Dick is the best at punching."

"Yes, I know, but the Hulk has got these massive hands, as big as your head, and all he'd have to do is crush Dick's skull."

I heard Phoebe sigh. "Please boys, stop calling him Dick." She said quietly, but not quietly enough that I didn't hear and feel amused by it.

"But that's his name," Callum protested.

"His secret name," Mack added. "Only his friends call him Dick, and he said we could."

"Well I'd rather you didn't. Now, watch the rest of the film."

I looked over my shoulder and caught her staring at me with an anxious look on her face. When she realised I was looking, she jumped slightly in her seat.

"Sorry, are they disturbing you?" she asked, thumbing toward the boys.

"No not all. I was just checking you're all okay back there."

Phoebe nodded and flickered a weak smile. I should probably have told her I didn't mind the fact that she'd obviously called me Dickhead to the twins, because weirdly I didn't, but I didn't want her to know I'd been listening in on their conversation. Plus, it was kind of funny to watch her squirm – call it payback for calling me a dickhead.

"Okay, here we are," Barney pronounced pulling into a tree-lined street. "What number was it again?"

"Oh sorry, 121," Phoebe said, leaning forward in her seat to speak to Barney. "Just up there on the right, behind that white car will be great."

Barney nodded and slowly drove forward.

"Thank you so much for this. It really was very kind of you."

"Not a problem." I waved her away and turned to look back through the windshield.

It was a nice road. The houses were two-story, neat and tidy, and each one looked pretty much like all the others. All the lawns at the front were hidden behind fences or hedges, and each had a driveway running up the side.

"Your sister lived here long?" I asked.

"About nine years. She lived here...before."

I took it that 'before' meant *before* the boys' fuck-up of a father abandoned them – for another woman, no doubt. In my experience, men who left their wife and kids only ever left for someone else – it was never because they'd decided married life wasn't for them and they'd be a better parent living alone; no, never for that reason. That's what my own shit of a dad had done – left us for someone else when I was just five years old. I suppose I was lucky he'd stuck around that long, but when a younger, less drunk model showed him some attention, he didn't waste any more time. Don't get me wrong, I don't blame him for leaving. Sue-Ann Miller, my darling mom, was a Grade-A pain in the ass, whose idea of getting the vitamins she needed, was taking OJ with her vodka. What I *did* blame him for, was leaving me with her. Dad and I were tight. He took me fishing and let me help him fix his bike, read me stories at bedtime, he even had my name tattooed on his arm, yet he still rode away while I sobbed on our front lawn begging him to come back. He never tried to contact me, not even when I became a movie star – which I guess is props to him.

He was still living and breathing. I knew because I hired a PI to track him down. I didn't want to contact him, but I suppose I wanted to tie up my loose ends before I signed on as Addison Yates. I wanted to know whether he was likely to come at me for cash, or even have some story printed in the newspaper about being my long-lost father. Apparently, he didn't need me or my money. He worked as a mechanic at a bike shop and was married to some woman ten years younger than him, who cut hair and did mani- pedis for a living – she wasn't even the one he'd left me behind for. They lived in a quiet cul-de-sac in Dayton, Ohio, had no kids, and rode with a mom and pop motorcycle club on the weekends. He lived the simple life of any normal, fifty-eight year old man and appeared to have never looked back – not the day he rode his bike from our house, or ever since.

As soon as Barney pulled up alongside the curb, the boys had their door open, ready to bolt.

"Hey, boys," Phoebe said. "What do you say to Barney and Mr. James for the lift home?"

"Thank you," they chorused, high-fiving Barney's raised hand.

"Yes, thank you both. It was really very kind of you." Phoebe flashed us both a smile and bent to pick up her bag from the floor board.

"You have to come in and see Mummy," Mack chimed, leaning between the two seats.

"Mack," Phoebe warned, glancing at me. "Mr. James and Barney have things to do. They probably need to get back."

"Yeah," Callum gasped. "Come and have tea with us."

"I don't drink tea, buddy." I shrugged.

"No, not tea you drink, silly. Tea that you eat. Tea, tea."

"He means dinner," Phoebe explained, although I already knew; I was just messing with the kid.

"Maybe we could come in for a few minutes."

I had no idea what made me suggest it, the words just fell from my mouth without any thought from my brain. Yet, I didn't hate the idea. I *wanted* to go in and meet their mom.

"I-I don't know," Phoebe stuttered, looking between me and Barney. "Beth has, well she's been-"

At that moment, a slim, pretty woman, about Phoebe's height but with dark auburn hair, approached the car, bending to peer around the open door and into the car.

"Mack, Callum, what's ...what are you doing in that car?" she asked with a hint of trepidation.

"Beth, it's fine," Phoebe called, stooping down so her sister could see her. "I'm here. We got a lift back from the studio."

Beth appeared in the rear passenger doorway and opened it wider. "Wow," she exclaimed looking inside. "This is nice."

She then turned to look at me and as soon as she recognized me, her mouth dropped open into a huge o shape.

"Hi," I said, giving her a quick wave. "Grantley James, you must be Beth."

She nodded, her eyes widened and her mouth still gaping.

"Isn't it cool Mummy?" Mack said. "We've watched a film and Dick said he's going to come inside for a few minutes."

Beth looked at Phoebe and then back at me.

"Only if that's okay with you," I replied, giving the shocked woman a winning smile.

She nodded again.

"Dick was awesome today Mummy. He punched this big ugly man." To demonstrate, Callum started to throw punches into mid-air.

"Dick?" she asked Phoebe, furrowing her brow.

Phoebe didn't answer, but shook her head.

"That'll be me," I said, flashing a grin at Phoebe. "It's a name the boys gave me for some reason."

"Oh, okay." Beth looked at Barney, me, and then Phoebe. "*Would* you like to come in?"

"If that's okay with you," I replied, already unfastening my belt. "We have time, right Barney?"

Barney nodded. "Yes sir. We can spare some time."

"I thought you had a thing," Phoebe said, her brow furrowed.

"I do, but a few minutes won't hurt. So, lead the way Beth."

The boys scrambled out of the car, pushing Beth to one side, who stared after them, evidently totally dumfounded about the Hollywood Star visiting her home.

CHAPTER ELEVEN

Phoebe

"I'm so sorry, Beth," I hissed, as we both stood in the kitchen.

Beth was making a pot of coffee, while I put some pizza and garlic bread into the oven. I glanced up at her, anxiously waiting for a sign of any kind of how her appointment at the hospital had gone. We hadn't had a chance to talk since Grantley James had strolled into the house, looking every inch the Hollywood star that he was. Mrs. Herbert from next door almost fainted into her open wheelie bin when she spotted him.

"God, don't apologise. Do you know how many cool points this will give me with all the young ones at work? Grantley-flipping-James in my house." Beth fanned herself and grinned. "Do you think he'd do a selfie with me for proof? Those little shits at work will never believe me otherwise."

I chewed on my lip and watched my sister carefully. She certainly didn't look devastated, but was she just putting on a show because Grantley and Barney were here.

"Beth, how did it go today?" I asked, brushing her hair from her face. "I didn't dare call you in case it was bad news."

Beth gave me one of her beautiful smiles and grabbed my hand.

"They don't tell you anything on the day, sis."

"Really?" My heart sank, knowing that we would have days, if not weeks, of tormented waiting.

"Listen, I know I was a total mess last night, but once I calmed down I remembered that Dr. Phillips said she thought it might be a cyst and the mammogram was a precaution. So, that's what I'm going with."

I watched Beth as she went back to the coffee making. If she could look on the positive side, then so could I.

"Anyway," Beth said, suddenly turning to me. "How come Grantley James gave you a lift all the way back from Manchester, and why were the boys with you?"

"Well," I started with a quiet laugh. "You forgot that Wendy was in Tenerife, so I had to take the boys to the studio with me."

Beth gasped and slapped a hand against her mouth. "Oh my God, I did. I'm so sorry. Shit, did you get into trouble?"

I shook my head and leaned closer to speak quietly into her ear. "No, the director is really lovely, and Grantley appears to have become best buddies with the boys. I'm so shocked Beth, he's been nothing but a dickhead since we started filming, but with the boys today, he was brilliant."

Beth started to giggle. "You called him dickhead in front of the boys didn't you? Which is why they keep calling him Dick."

"Yep," I groaned. "But that's the other thing, he appears to have taken it really well."

"He seems perfectly lovely to me." She sighed, and gazed at me with dreamy eyes.

"To look at maybe, but up until today, he was a misery without a sense of humour."

"Who's that you're talking about?"

The sexy, almost throaty voice of Grantley James echoed around Beth's kitchen and if I could have squeezed myself into the washing machine to hide, I would have.

"Oh, my neighbour next door but one," Beth said without

pausing – shit she was good. "He's a miserable old sod, but he told the boys a joke this morning."

Grantley looked at me, folding his arms over his chest. It was a very nice chest, it had to be said. Solid, but not too buff or big, but stretching his black t-shirt quite nicely. Anyway, he was looking at me so intently I wondered if he was reading my mind. When he parted his jean clad legs, almost posing, his eyes still on me, I was positive he was.

"Yes, Mr. Douglas," I said, with a wide smile. "He's normally rude but today he took us by surprise. I was just telling Beth about it."

"Okay." He nodded and turned to Beth. "So Beth, I hope you don't mind, but Mack and Callum persuaded us to stay for *tea*."

I couldn't stop the 'no' that rushed from my mouth in a gust of air. Grantley looked at me and smirked.

"No?"

"You...well you have that thing, Barney said." I pointed towards the wall that I assumed Barney was on the other side of.

"Barney is making my apologies as we speak."

"But, we're having pizza and garlic bread."

"Barney and I love pizza."

Grantley's smirk was almost indistinguishable, but I saw it. I saw the twinkle in his eye and the twitch of his lips.

"We only have one. Beth, that was the only one in the freezer."

"No worries," Grantley said, with a hint of laughter. "I'm guessing there's a pizza take out place around here." He turned to Beth again. "If you don't mind us staying, I'd like to buy us all pizza for dinner. It would actually be my pleasure."

As I watched Grantley smile at Beth, my heart missed a beat. He was looking at her so reverently, with a gentle smile touching his lips. Oh my God, he fancied my sister.

"You don't need to do that," Beth said brightly, evidently not seeing what I saw. "I'm sure I can find another pizza at the bottom of the freezer somewhere."

"No," Grantley said, shaking his head. "I insist. When you see how much Barney and I eat, you'll be glad I offered."

"Well, if you insist."

Beth opened up the junk drawer and moving aside a tube of glue and two screwdrivers, she found the menu for the local take-out place. She passed it to Grantley.

"They've got most things, but it's no Pizza Hut."

Grantley looked down at the menu for a few seconds and then back up to Beth, flashing her one of his best Hollywood smiles.

"Looks good to me. I'll go and check what the boys want."

"I've already got a pepperoni pizza in the oven," I said, hearing a definite flatness to my tone.

That was exactly how I felt – flat and dejected. How could I be so mean, just because Grantley liked my sister? She was beautiful, so why shouldn't he like her? What would it mean though? What if they fell in love and she moved to Hollywood to be with him? What if I stopped being an idiot and thinking ahead of myself?

"Okay, great." Grantley nodded, flashed another smile and left the kitchen.

"Ooh isn't he lovely," Beth gushed and turned back to finally finish the coffee.

"So come on," Grantley laughed, running his finger around the rim of a wine glass. "Why Peepee?"

The boys had long since gone to bed, and the four of us adults were still sitting around the dining table, drinking wine and picking at cold pizza. The boys hadn't wanted to go to bed. There'd been a lot of cajoling and arguing, but eventually, after Grantley had promised to come to tea again, another time, they'd succumbed, and according to Beth, fallen asleep almost the instant she'd pulled the duvets over them.

My sister, who was a little squiffy after four glasses of wine, let out a loud burst of laughter at Grantley's question. I tilted my head and gave her a warning stare.

"I'm sensing there's a story here," Barney chuckled, in his deep baritone as he lifted his glass of *Diet Coke* to his lips.

"There isn't, I promise." I rolled my eyes and reached for the jug of water, feeling the need to dilute the wine, seeing as the following day was going to be a long one for me. I had to be on set for nine, but would be called sporadically throughout the day until late into the evening.

"Bullshit," Grantley said, narrowing his eyes on me and repeating what I'd said to him on our first meeting.

"There's no story," I protested, kicking what I thought was Beth's shin under the table.

Grantley jumped. "Ow," he cried, frowning and pouting all at the same time. "You just kicked me."

"I did not."

"Yes you did, you thought I was Beth." He pointed at me and narrowed his eyes. "You were kicking her to keep her mouth shut. Admit it."

"No."

"Yet again I call bullshit, now spill it, *Peepee*."

Beth snorted and almost spat her wine over the table. Grantley leaned forward and passed her a paper napkin from the lid of the pizza box – I'd tried to put plates out, but Grantley insisted that pizza tasted much better out of the box.

"You may as well tell us, Phoebe," he stated, sitting back serenely in his chair. "If you don't I'll ask Mack and Callum."

I blew out a breath and looked up at the ceiling. He was right, if I didn't tell him the twins would, and they'd just embellish the story to make it sound worse. Not that it could sound any worse than reality.

"Oh just tell him, Phoebes," Beth cried. "It's funny."

"It's embarrassing," I griped.

"Come on," Barney urged. "Spill it hon'."

"Alright." I tsked, took a gulp of water and cleared my throat.

"The boys were only small, around three, and Beth and I had taken them to the zoo." I looked at Grantley who was grinning and closed my eyes briefly. "Do I have to do this?"

"Yes!" The three of them chorused.

"Okay." I reached for my wine and took a long slug. "Anyway, I was desperate for the loo, so we went to the public toilets and the line for ladies was huge. Apparently the men's were out of order, so they were having to use the ladies' and there was an attendant letting men in when they'd finished letting women in and so on, so it was taking an age."

"She's right," Beth giggled. "The queue was huge."

"And what happened?" Grantley asked, leaning forward and resting his elbows on the table.

"Like I said, I was desperate. I asked if I could push to the front, but everyone in that queue, bar none, were absolute tossers and said no. How mean is that?"

"Yep, real mean," Barney grumbled.

"Whatever, keep going." Grantley moved his hand in a rolling motion urging me to continue.

"Okay," I sighed. "Well it was a gorgeous day, really warm and the boys were having the best time ever. We loved it too, didn't we Beth. In fact," I said, giving an earnest nod. "Did you know that to let a male giraffe know she's available for mating, a female giraffe urinates in his mouth?"

Beth howled with laughter while Barney groaned and muttered something about knowing a few women like that himself – ugh.

"Stop stalling, Phoebe," Grantley warned, cutting into what I thought was an extremely interesting conversation about the mating rituals of giraffes.

I rolled my eyes. "I had to go or was going to wet myself, so decided the only thing to do was to go in one of the bushes near the monkey enclosure."

"No way," Barney laughed. "You didn't?"

"Ssh," Grantley said, waving a hand at Barney. "I need to hear this from Phoebe."

"Okay, okay," I continued. "So I decided to go in the bushes, but I was wearing an all in one thing, it was shorts and a top in one."

"A playsuit," Beth giggled.

"Yeah a playsuit," I grimaced. "Stupid thing. Anyway, to be able to pee I had to take it totally off. So, I did and I had the best pee of my life. You know that real sense of pleasure you get when you finally get to empty your bladder, it's the best feeling ever. You get a little shiver of delight, don't you?"

I smiled at them all and took another swig of my water.

"And." Grantley pressed. "That is *not* the whole story, I damn well know it."

"Oh no, there's definitely more." Beth giggled and poked me in the arm. "Carry on."

"I hate you," I hissed. "Like I said, I had the best pee ever, and was just finishing off when I heard laughing and shouting and then there was this really high pitched screaming."

"That big woman with the fat kid," Beth reminded me.

"Why were they screaming and shouting?" Barney asked.

"Because," I said with a huge swallow. "Because I wasn't aware that behind me was a wall made up of mirrors and I wasn't totally hidden by the bushes. Everyone could see my bare arse, with my knickers and playsuit around my ankles while I peed in the bushes. Let me tell you, once I realised, after some kid shouted 'look at her bum', I have never peed so fast, there was some force behind it. I actually got my feet a little wet in the process. As for loo roll, well I had one tiny little tissue that I'd already use to wipe ice cream from Mack's mouth."

"So that's why the guys call you Peepee?" Grantley asked, looking at me intently.

The look of supreme smugness on his face told me that he knew there was more to it, but my lips were well and truly sealed. That was all he was getting.

"Noooo," Beth cried. "It gets better."

What the hell happened to family loyalty?

Grantley's eyes widened and his gaze shot back to me, the smug look even smugger now that he knew he'd been right all along.

Some people are simply too confident for their own good.

"So it's something much better than you taking a piss in some bushes and showing your ass?"

"Much better." Beth snorted before taking a sip of wine.

"Okay, lay it on us."

I rolled my eyes.

"It really isn't that funny or interesting. That's it, that's why the boys call me Peepee, because I had a wee in some bushes at the zoo."

"Oh Phoebe, you liar," Beth cried. "You know it's so much more and so much funnier than that."

I glared at Beth, but she was having far too much fun to care.

"You may as well tell them."

"Yep, you may as well," Grant chimed in. "If you don't, Beth will."

"Yeah," Beth added. "And I might embellish it a little too much, so it's in your own interest really."

She was right, if I didn't spill then she would, and she'd make it sound *so* much worse than it was.

"Okay, okay," I grumbled. "I was so shocked by the scream I started peeing again. It was like some involuntary fear reflex, but I wasn't taking care in what I was doing and peed all over my playsuit. So when I pulled it up, encouraged by a couple members of the zoo staff, who had responded to the stupid woman's pathetic screaming fit, it was wet down the front, right in the crotch area."

I banged my head on the table, reliving the shame of dozens of adults and kids firstly seeing my bare arse and then the humiliating sight of my wet crotch.

"When she came out from behind the bushes," Beth said around a belly laugh. "The boys pointed at her and shouted 'Mummy, auntie's had a peepee. Auntie peepee'."

"They shouted it right up until we got home and I was able to change out of my clothes, even though it had dried off by then. The next day, they wouldn't call me anything else and it stuck. People just assume it's because they couldn't say Phoebe when they were smaller, and," I said, glaring accusingly at Beth, "that's the version I usually stick to."

"But really it's because you wet yourself," Beth added *helpfully*.

Grantley and Barney were laughing loudly, both with shining eyes – Barney was even clutching his sides.

"It's not that funny," I groaned. "It really isn't."

"Oh shit, it is." Grantley slapped a hand against the table. "Not only did everyone see your ass, but you pissed yourself, too. That's damn hilarious."

"Yes," I replied through gritted teeth. "Although if we're being factually correct, I didn't actually wet myself in the sense that I didn't get my knickers down quick enough. It was only because I was shocked and missed my aim."

I let out a long breath, hopeful they'd laugh for a few more minutes and then forget about it. But, trust my sister to make matters horrendous.

"That's not the best bit," Beth said, nudging me a little forcefully and almost pushing me off my chair. "Tell them the rest."

"What, there's more?" Grantley asked, his eyebrows shooting up.

"We got thrown out of the zoo." I gave Beth a glare, silently warning her I'd get her back someday.

"Shit, you were escorted from a kid's zoo. Did they handcuff you?"

"No Barney, they didn't handcuff me, but the security guard wanted to call the police and have me done for indecent exposure. Luckily, his friend thought I was cute, so I gave him my number, flirted my way out of there and then blocked his number once I got home."

I looked around the table and huffed at the three imbeciles laughing uproariously at my nightmare.

"Tell...tell...tell them the other bit," Beth said in between gasps.

"No!" I snapped, glaring even harder at her.

Sometimes a tiny piece of evil showed through my sister's charming personality, and this was one of those occasions.

"Shit, there's more," Grantley cried. "What else? Ah fuck, this is priceless."

"No, it's not. It's a hideous nightmare I desperately tried to forget, and almost had until my beloved sister decided it would be a great after dinner story."

"You tell us, Beth," Barney insisted, wheezing out another laugh.

Beth looked at me and burst out laughing.

"I hate you more now than I did two minutes ago, and I'll hate you even more tomorrow," I growled at my sister. "You may as well tell them."

"While Phoebe was peeing, with her bum on show," Beth said, looking between Grantley and Barney. "The chimpanzees were watching."

"And?"

"And," she continued. "They obviously liked what they saw because two of them were wanking off and pointing at her."

Grantley gasped and looked at me with his mouth agape. "No way, please tell me you didn't cause the chimps to throw one out."

With shame and mortification, I slowly nodded my head.

"Yes," I replied, quietly. "My name is Phoebe Jane Drinkwater and I made a chimpanzee masturbate and I am deeply ashamed."

Grantley, Beth, and Barney roared with laughter, all doubling over and clutching their sides, each other, and the table to stop themselves from falling off their seats.

"Hey," Grantley finally said amidst huge roars of laughter. "Did they ask if you do extras?"

"Haha, very funny."

"Oh shit," Beth squealed. "Now I'm going to pee myself. Do you do extras, that's so funny; you know because you're an extra."

"Yes, Beth, I get it," I bitched through gritted teeth.

"One thing's for sure," Grantley said.

"And what would that be?" I sighed, knowing it was going to be some crappy joke.

"At least you can say you've had monkey sex."

As everyone rolled around, I sat back in my chair and watched them. I wanted to be mad, but I hadn't seen Beth this happy or laughing so much since – well since, I'd peed in the bushes at the zoo and the chimps had wanked off because they fancied my peachy little arse. I also realised how Grantley looked even more beautiful with a smile on his face.

At that moment, I felt happy and content and was really glad that two little boys had melted Grantley James' hard exterior, because ultimately it had caused my gorgeous sister to forget her worries and laugh like a drain.

CHAPTER TWELVE

Grantley

It was almost eleven-thirty when Barney and I left Beth's house, and we'd had a great evening. Yeah, it had mostly been at Phoebe's expense over the whole Peepee affair, but props to her-she'd taken it like a man.

"Shit," I muttered as Barney drove us through the quiet streets, back toward Manchester. "I've got a voicemail from Marcia."

Barney grimaced as I put my cell to my ear.

"She's probably heard you bailed on dinner."

"Probably."

I was supposed to have gone to dinner with a British director who thought I'd be 'just perfect' for his upcoming World War 2 comedy. I mean come on, firstly, how the fuck do you joke about a damn war, and secondly, me-do comedy – nope, not a chance. I barely cracked a smile on a daily basis, never mind a fucking joke. Although, it had to be said, I'd laughed and smiled plenty around Beth's dinner table.

I hit the button to listen to my messages and heard the ladylike words of my agent.

"Grantley, you little fucker," she snapped, in her thirty smokes a day growl. "I set that fucking dinner up for you and you get Barnabus to tell the guy you're ill with the fucking craps. What the fuck is going on? You no more have the craps than I have an intact hymen. Ring me as soon as you get this, you lying little cunt."

And that, ladies & gentleman, was my mild-mannered agent. People often asked why I put up with her, the answer – she loves me and treated me more like a son than my own mother ever had. Yes, she was foul-mouthed and pissed with me most of the time, but she cared.

"Ooh, she's mad," Barney said, having heard every word.

"Yep, but isn't she always." I pressed the delete button and turned off my phone. "She knows I don't want to do the movie, so I have no idea why she set the meeting up in the first place."

"Her own commission, I'm guessing."

"Yeah well, she's going to have to rethink that one. I've told her if I'm going to do anything in between this and the next Addison Yates movie, it has to be something with depth."

I was planning for my future and Marcia knew that, but God loved a trier, and she tried more than most to get her own way. While I enjoyed playing Addison and it payed damn well and had given me a level of fame that most actors dreamed about, it was pretty easy to do. I didn't have to put much characterization into Mr. Yates – he was basically me with a gun and fast cars. I'd signed on for four movies in total, so besides the one we were currently filming, I had two more to go. After that I was saying adios to Mr. Yates, so I needed to make sure people in the industry knew I was actually a good actor, not just someone who looked great fighting bad guys while wearing a dress suit.

"Was tonight worth it?" Barney asked. "Pissing Marcia off and maybe losing out on a role, I mean."

I shot my gaze to him. "Yep. Most definitely. Don't tell me you didn't have fun."

"Oh yeah," he chuckled. "I sure did, but I'm not the one who was supposed to be meeting an important director."

"He's not important," I snapped. "Not to me anyway. He's important to Marcia."

Barney glanced at me, momentarily taking his eyes off the road. "So, you got a thing for her then?"

"Who, Marcia?"

I *knew what he meant - fucker*.

"Yes, fucking sixty-year-old Marcia, who eats more than I do, has the manners of a caveman, and has bigger balls than both of our nut-sacks put together. Fucking Phoebe, and you know it."

I inhaled deeply and felt my heart miss a couple of beats. It had fucking snuck up on me, so damn stealthily even I'd been surprised. Yeah, I'd thought she was hot and pretty, but I also thought she was fucking annoying as hell. It wasn't until I'd seen the prick with the beard ogling her that I'd realised I felt something in my gut. Not jealousy because, and it may make me sound like a douchebag, that guy was no threat to me if I wanted Phoebe. No, what I felt was something akin to how I'd felt as a kid, when Bobby Turner from down the street rode my skateboard – a skateboard I'd bought with all my tips I'd saved from the job I had delivering newspapers. Now, when I tell you folks only tip the newsboy at Christmas or Thanksgiving that shows how long I'd damn well saved for. So, when Bobby did a perfect Railside on my coveted board, I felt sick with the need to claim her back – she was *my* board, not his, and he had no rights putting his fucking dirty, grubby Chuck on her, never mind get her to do a trick that I still hadn't quite mastered. *That's* how I felt when Declan, the prick, ogled Phoebe's tits.

"You gonna answer me?" Barney asked with more than a hint of damn laughter in his voice. "Do you have a thing for Phoebe? Or maybe it's her sister, you were kind of looking at Beth as though she'd just saved the planet."

"Fuck off," I snapped. "I think she's a great mom, is all. It couldn't have been easy bringing up twins alone, but those kids are amazing and that's all down to her. My fucking mother barely managed to drag me up, so I have the uttermost respect for Beth, and that's it."

"Ah, so that's what the fuzzy little smile was all about?"

I let out a laugh. "I don't have a fucking fuzzy little smile. I barely smile, period."

"You do around those two sisters. A fuzzy little one for Beth and a 'shit I really wanna kiss you' one for Phoebe."

He wasn't wrong there. I think I really did want to kiss her – fuck it, I *knew* I did.

"She's a cool girl, I'll give you that."

I looked out at the side window, watching the scenery as we joined the freeway – or whatever they called them in the UK.

"Just admit it man," Barney chuckled. "You've got a boner for the girl."

I swung my head around. "Hey, watch your damn mouth."

"I'm sorry, but that kind of proves what I'm saying." Barney grinned at me and slapped the steering wheel. "Well, I'll be."

"Ah shut up and drive." I growled but couldn't help the smile that was spread across my face.

The next morning, it took me forever to get out of bed. I hardly drank, so the three glasses of wine I'd had at Beth's had left me feeling a little heavy headed. Plus, as usual, I'd slept like shit. I didn't drink because I'd seen first-hand what a destructive thing alcohol was. I also didn't drink because above everything, I was a professional who wanted to get to the top of his career – I'd seen too many actors waste their potential and talent by drinking or doing drugs. I'd worked too fucking hard to throw it all away on a bottle of Jack.

I'd known from an early age that I wanted to act. I'd never dreamed I'd be a movie star, but I hoped that I could make a decent living from it. I think my love for acting first started after my dad left. Life was so shit, I'd play act in my room, pretending that I lived a different life. I was Grantley Miller - the doctor, or Grantley Miller- the cop, or spy – anyone but Grantley Miller- the thin, short, neglected kid of Sue-Ann Miller and abandoned son of Trent Miller. I started to read aloud to myself, using different voices for the characters and eventually borrowed copies of plays from the library and performed them to no one but myself and the various bears and toys dotted around my room.

Then, when I was sixteen and I'd grown tall and filled out, I finally plucked up the courage to join the drama club at school. I'd always shied away from it before, choosing to play baseball instead. Don't judge me, I was a teenager desperate to get laid and a high school sport was a more reliable means to an end. I only really joined drama club because Stacie Kimble did. She was blonde haired, blue-eyed, and had the best tits in school and every guy wanted her. The next play being performed by the club was to be a modern version of Romeo & Juliet and I figured Stacie would be a shoe in for Juliet. This meant that if I joined I'd get to be Romeo and maybe get to kiss her. I admit I was an over confident prick who didn't rate any of those already in the club, but it turned out I was right to be so. We got the leads and I got my onstage kiss with Stacie, which led to me fucking her backstage at the last night party – that was also the night I got my first blowjob. In hindsight, it wasn't a great BJ, but when you're sixteen just the sight of a girl's lips around your dick is enough to cause an explosion at the yogurt factory.

Aside from the sexual experience, joining the drama club was the best thing I ever did. My teacher saw something in me. He saw my talent and pushed me to go for an audition for the part of Sebastian in a stage version of Cruel Intentions. If I got it, it'd be a huge step for me – it was being performed in a proper theatre, the Paramount in Cedar Rapids, sixteen miles or so South East of Shellsburg where I lived. Mr. James coached and helped me and I would be forever grateful, because I got the part. Yep, I used his name when I registered with SAG; why not, he believed in me, unlike my shit of a father whose name I unfortunately inherited. I got that first break when I was just eighteen and after the run finished, I packed my bags and moved to LA. Within a year, I'd managed to get Marcia to take me on as a client and after a couple of years of bit parts in theatre, some TV ads, and a minor role in a daytime soap for a three-week stint, she got me a supporting role in a movie. According to the critics, I outshone the lead actor in the fast cars and loose women movie about a guy trying to escape a Mexican drug cartel – I played the part of student doing some travelling who got caught up in the drama. After that, I got the lead in a buddy movie about a guy trying to decide whether he should propose to his girl or not. The role was nothing like Addison Yates, but the studio must have seen something, because I was the second person they called to take over from Ryan. Okay, so it smarts a little that I was only second, but I figured Jake Gyllenhaal probably deserved the call first. Thank fuck he didn't think it was for him, because at twenty-six I was living the dream and would do whatever I could to keep it that way.

"You okay?" Barney asked, shoving a mug of coffee at me.

"Yep, just know it's going to be a long fucking day."

"You've got some time before we need to leave." Barney looked at his watch. "Your call isn't for another hour and thirty."

"I'll drink this and then take a shower."

Barney nodded and left me to drink my coffee, eat my toast, and read through the day's script. I was just about coming around, when my cell shrilled out with the ring tone of a nuclear war siren – *my fucking mother*.

I looked at the screen for a few seconds, wondering how many times she'd call back if I dropped the call, but before I could decide what to do, Barney's huge hand appeared, picked it up, and answered it.

"Sue-Ann," he said, looking at me with a huge-ass grin. "Yep, he's here."

"You fucker," I muttered and snatched my cell from him. "Sue-Ann, what do you want?"

"I'm your damn mother, Grantley, so why do you insist on calling me by my name?"

"Because you'd kind of need to deserve to be called mom, *Sue-Ann,* and in no sense of the word are you deserving of that moniker."

She sighed on the other end. "I did everything I could to be a good mother to you. You have no idea how hard it was bringing you up alone."

"I have an idea, seeing as I kind of brought myself up." I drummed my fingers on the table, my impatience almost bubbling over. "What do you want, as if I have to ask?"

"I don't always want money, Grantley," she replied sulkily.

"Oh okay, you just called to see how I was? Or, to wish me good luck with the movie? Or did you call to tell me you're moving to Africa to work as a humanitarian envoy?"

"There's no need to be so sarcastic or rude, I'm still your mother."

"Un-fucking-fortunately," I hissed under my breath. "So, I'll ask again, what do you want? No actually, Sue-Ann, I'll rephrase that, how *much* do you want?"

"Nothing, I don't want any money. So, what do you have to say about that Mr. Smartypants?"

"Well, I'm shocked to say the least," I said, and I was, but I was also wondering when the other shoe would drop. "If not money, what?"

Bang - my size twelve, Italian leather, tan colored brogue fell to the fucking floor.

"I want to come visit. In fact, I've already bought my ticket."

CHAPTER THIRTEEN

Phoebe

"You like him, don't you?" Beth asked as she turned into the railway station car park.

She was taking the boys out for the day, so she had given me a lift. It had meant Mack and Callum getting up early, for a non-school day, but they were still buzzing from meeting Grantley and being on set, so it wasn't too difficult a task.

"Who?" I reached down for my bag, wondering which of the numerous pockets I'd put my rail pass into.

"You know who. Grantley," she whispered, glancing at Callum and Mack in the back seat through the rear-view mirror. "I can tell by the looks you were giving him."

"I was not."

And I really wasn't, not to my knowledge anyway. I didn't think I looked at him any differently than I did Barney.

"Anyway, it's you he has a thing for." I grinned at her.

"Hah," Beth spat out a laugh. "That's ridiculous and you know it, you're just trying to deflect."

"No I'm not."

"Yes you are, just like you did last night over the zoo incident."

I couldn't help but smile. "Yes, and I haven't forgiven you for that either."

"Ah, don't be a spoilsport, it was funny." Manoeuvring into a parking space, Beth called over her shoulder. "Okay boys, grab your coats and backpacks."

"Where are we going?" Mack asked.

"You'll see when we get there, it's a surprise."

"Where are you going?" I asked, opening the passenger door after she pulled to a stop.

Beth shrugged. "No idea, depends which train comes in first, but probably Liverpool."

"Well, I'll be late tonight, so don't bother with any dinner for me."

"Okay," Beth nodded. "We probably won't be back until early evening anyway, so we'll eat out."

Once outside the car, I bent to kiss the boys.

"Have a great day you two."

Callum kicked a stone. "I wish we could go and watch the film again and see Dick."

I grimaced inwardly at him calling Grantley, Dick, but hey it was done now.

"Ooh you meanie," Beth cried, clutching a hand to her heart. "I can't believe you don't want to spend the day with me, your amazing mum."

Callum looked horrified that he'd upset her. "No, I do, but I wanted to see Dick and it's so exciting watching the film being made."

"There's loads of fighting," Mack added, grabbing Beth's hand and shaking it excitedly.

"Not today, buddy," I said with a sigh. "It's a really boring day today. Lots of scenes with just talking, no action at all."

Mack nodded. "Okay."

"Will you say hello to Dick for us?" Callum asked. "And don't forget the picture."

"I won't," I said ruffling his hair. "It's safe in my bag."

The boys had drawn a picture for Grantley as a thank you for the lift home and for staying for dinner. Neither of my nephews were budding artists, so I imagined it wasn't going to be particularly good. I didn't know because they'd put it in an envelope marked 'Dick Private', which made the school girl inside me giggle.

By the time I reached the studio, I just had time to go over to catering and grab a coffee, before I needed to get to the holding area. There were a few crowd scenes being shot, and we were all being bussed out to the location.

After grabbing a coffee and stuffing down a chocolate croissant, I was making my way out of the canteen, when Grantley came striding in, his phone glued to his ear. He looked at me so I gave a wave, but he didn't respond and stormed straight past me, up to the counter.

"I need you here, Marcia."

His voice was loud and hard, causing everyone to turn and look at him. As he reached the counter, he banged his hand down and demanded 'coffee, black'. Claire, one of the catering girls, used to prima donna actors didn't bat an eyelash and poured Grantley his coffee, popped on the lid and passed it to him. How they did that I had no idea. I hated rudeness and Grantley had just been plain rude. I watched as, resting his phone between his neck and chin, he snatched up a packet of sugar, ripped it open, pulled off the lid and poured the sugar into the coffee, before throwing the empty packet on the counter top and slamming the lid to the cup back on. There was a bloody waste bin only a couple of feet away from him. This wasn't the same man who had insisted on cleaning up wine glasses and pizza boxes before leaving Beth's house the night before.

As I was about to turn and leave, Grantley started walking my way. His eyes turned towards me and as they did he growled into the phone.

"Get here Marcia, no excuses."

He stabbed at the screen on his phone and stood in front of me.

"Hi," I said, looking up at his tall frame.

Grantley's eye twitched a couple of times before he finally spoke. "Morning. How are you?"

"Fine. You?"

There seemed to be a tension between us and I wasn't sure why. He'd left on perfectly good terms the night before. Maybe that was it, he was regretting giving me, a lowly extra, a lift and then staying to have dinner with me and my family. Well if that was it, he could shove his attitude where the sun didn't shine, i.e.-up his bum.

"Not really," he sighed, taking a sip of his coffee and wincing. "Fuck, this coffee is shit. Why the hell don't they get some decent stuff? I swear it's that instant stuff you Brits insist on drinking."

"Maybe if you spoke to Claire, the girl behind the counter," I pointed to Claire who was busy pouring a cup of tea for someone, "and told her your preference to fresh coffee, she would make sure that's what you got. Otherwise, it's likely you're going to get the instant stuff that we Brits insist on drinking."

Grantley tilted his head and shoving a hand into his jean pocket, studied me.

"What?" I asked.

"I'm just wondering why you always feel the need to repeat things back to me when you're giving me crap."

"Take it as a compliment," I said, turning to walk away. "You're obviously so eloquent I can't think of anything better to hit back at you with, except your own words."

Grantley let out a laugh and shook his head, looking up at the ceiling. "You brighten my fucking day, Peepee, you really do."

I wasn't sure what to say to that, so decided to say nothing and walk away.

"Hey," Grantley called. "Where are you going?"

"The holding area."

I didn't turn but kept walking, only for Grantley to fall into step beside me.

"I'll be nicer to catering," he said, bending slightly to speak into my ear. "I promise."

I glanced at him and frowned when I saw a grin on his face. A strand of hair fell into his eyes and my hand twitched at my side, wanting to brush it away so I could see his eyes that were unusually full of humour. They didn't show it often, usually they were dark with surliness or anger – he really should try it more often, they were beautiful when he did.

Clearing my throat, I turned away. "Well make sure you do."

"Promise."

I didn't need to look at Grantley to know he was laughing at me.

"So what's crawled up your backside and bitten your nadgers, to get you in such a bad mood?"

Coffee spurted out in front of us as Grantley spluttered out a laugh.

"What the fuck are my nadgers?"

I stopped in my tracks and looked up at him with cocked brows.

"Your nuts, your bollocks, what else would they be?"

Grantley shrugged. "I had no idea. Sorry, it's not a word I picked up from watching EastEnders on the BBC World Service channel."

"You don't watch that, you liar."

"What the BBC World Service or EastEnders?"

"Either."

"I watch both, or I did. I had a really small part as a British college kid in an episode of Breaking Bad."

My eyes widened. "No way, I bloody love Breaking Bad. I don't remember any British college kid."

"There wasn't; I was cut from the scene. I went into Walter's classroom to give another kid a message and for some crazy reason they wanted me to be British. Because I'm a true professional, I wanted to deliver my three lines with the correct accent, so I watched the BBC and particularly, EastEnders, for three weeks solid."

I burst out laughing. "And they still cut you?"

Grantley nodded with a sigh. "Yep, I ended up on the cutting room floor."

He actually looked hurt as he pouted around the lid of his corrugated take-out cup.

"Sorry," I replied.

"Ah it's fine, but the point is I've never heard the word nadgers."

"Well, now you have. So, you still haven't answered me. What's got you so moody? Are you regretting taking me and the boys home and staying for dinner?"

I had very little filter when something was concerning me. I liked open and honest, even if it was with the leading actor in the Hollywood movie that I was on as a mere extra. Grantley must have been a little taken aback too, because he pulled up and straightened his shoulders.

"Why the hell would you think that?"

I shrugged. "I don't know. You were fine when you left and then just strutted past me like I was invisible."

He rubbed a hand over his stubble and closed his eyes.

"I can assure you it's not you, your nephews, or your sister that has me so antsy."

At the mention of Beth, I pulled in a sharp breath and felt a little stab in my breast bone. God, what a bitch I was. If he liked Beth, which I was pretty sure he did, I should be happy for her. She deserved some fun and someone to care about her.

"Beth really enjoyed your company last night," I said, looking down at my shoes and making a mental note to polish them when I got home.

"Well I enjoyed it too, honestly."

"You could take her on a date," I blurted out. "I'd look after the boys."

Grantley's eyes doubled in size as he leaned his upper body closer to me.

"What? I-I like Beth, but-"

"Honestly it's fine. I know you're not here for long, but you could just be company for each other."

He looked around the room and everyone who was watching our interaction all turned away, or carried on their conversations.

"Seriously Phoebe," he hissed. "I don't have a thing for Beth. Not like that."

"Well like what then?" I slammed a hand to my waist. "Because if you think she'll agree to be some sort of 'location fuck buddy', she won't."

"God no," he gasped. "I think she's an amazing woman and mother, bringing the boys up alone, but I don't have any romantic feelings for her."

It was my turn to go bog-eyed as an elongated 'oh' escaped my mouth.

"Yeah, oh."

Grantley's lips pinched together as he studied me. Shit, now was the time he threw me off the set.

"I'm so sorry. I know I said I'd behave, but I was just trying to help. I thought that you-."

"Phoebe," he snapped, "just stop will you."

"But if you throw me off set, what happens if we have to do some reshoots. Alexi will be really mad, he'll have to get another extra in to say my lines."

"Phoebe, seriously, I hate to break it to you but Penny could deliver those lines."

"I thought I played the part extremely well," I said indignantly.

Grantley gave a weary laugh and pinched the bridge of his nose.

"You were brilliant, but-."

"Oh, now you're being sarcastic."

"No, I'm not." He sighed and I could sense his patience was wearing a little thin.

"Sorry, I should shut up."

"Yep, maybe you should."

Grantley flicked out his tongue and licked his bottom lip and I couldn't take my eyes of it, as it moved from one corner of his mouth to the other.

"Listen, I think Beth is an amazing mother and I have the utmost respect for the job she's done. I know it's public record that I have a fractious relationship with my own mother, so my admiration of your sister comes from the knowledge I have personally on how shitty a fucking mom can be. And that is why I'm so pissed this morning."

"Because Beth is a good mum?"

"No, because mine isn't, but is insisting on coming here to visit me."

"Maybe she's trying to make amends," I offered. He was right, it was public knowledge about the frostiness between him and his mum. One paper even reported that he'd tried to run her over with his car once –although it was the same newspaper that said Angelina Jolie was actually Brad Pitt and vice versa; they simply liked dressing up as each other to fox the press.

"Nope." Grantley shook his head and started to walk again. "Sue-Ann Miller doesn't apologize for any reason. Sue-Ann Miller does what she can to help herself. She's coming here for a reason, but I can assure you, it won't be to see her only son."

"So what are you going to do?" I pushed open the double doors out of the canteen area, leading us into the very corridor that I first bumped into Grantley.

"That's what the call was about," he explained. "I was telling Marcia, my agent, to get herself over here and sort it out."

"You told her," I said, tilting my head. "Not asked?"

Grantley huffed out a laugh. "No, Phoebe. When you meet Marcia you'll realize you don't ask her to do anything. She'd much prefer you to tell her, because then she can tell you to fuck off, fly in, and save the day when you're least expecting it and love her forever because of it. Plus, it means you owe her."

I nodded slowly and the main thing I took from it was when he said 'when you meet Marcia' and wondered if that meant we were friends.

Grantley looked at the large but elegant watch on his wrist and groaned. "I've got to go, I've got to record some dialogue with Don before we go on location. The sound was muffled."

"Okay. Well, have a good day."

Grantley paused as though he was going to say something else, but nodded and started to walk away. As he reached a door to another corridor, I remembered something.

"Oh Grantley," I called. "I have something for you."

"For me?"

Grantley turned and made his way back to me. I jogged to meet him halfway, while rummaging in my bag.

"Ah, here it is." I pulled out the boys' picture and handed it to him.

Ripping open the envelope, Grantley took the picture, drawn on stiff, light green paper, and looked down at it. As his brow furrowed, I began to worry he hated it and if he did then I seriously couldn't like him any longer. I knew the boys weren't that good at art, but they were my little munchkins and no one dissed their efforts. Just as I was about to snatch the paper from him and storm away, he let out a huge laugh.

"Oh my God, that's fucking brilliant."

"It is?"

"Yeah it is. I wasn't sure who it was supposed to be at first, but then I saw this."

He turned the picture to me and there at the top of the page in capital letters, were the words DICK HEAD, with an arrow pointing to a man with neat stubble, aka Grantley James, Hollywood Movie star.

CHAPTER FOURTEEN

Grantley

I was in my trailer and I finally felt warm. It was our second day on location and we were filming at an old warehouse out in the boonies and it was fucking cold enough to freeze off my nuts. Production and the set designers had done a great job, making the warehouse look like some sort of fortified drug factory, but you'd have thought they'd have put some damn heating in because the industrial hot air blowers just weren't cutting it.

Wrapping my hands around a mug of coffee, I looked down at the shooting schedule on the table in front of me and sighed. Our next location, in two days, was a moat house just south of Manchester. It was only the lead actors and some secondary actors going there, and I was fucking pissed because we were going to be staying there for three days.

You'd think I'd have been grateful for three days away – Sue-Ann was arriving the day we left, so our mother/son reunion would be delayed, thank fuck, but I couldn't help but think that it was three days away from the set. Three days away from Phoebe and three days that Declan, the prick, would be around her, staring at her fucking rack.

Yeah, it kind of worried me that I felt that way if I was being honest. I guess it was because apart from Barney and Penny, she was the only person I spoke to at any length. I chatted with the rest of the cast, but I'd never been one to get too involved with my fellow actors. I'd never had an off-screen relationship with a co-star during filming. I didn't party with the gang on down days. I pretty much kept to myself and I liked it that way. I couldn't think of anything more torturous than having to put effort into trying to be nice to people after a long, exhausting day. Plus, actors are a delicate bunch, especially if our egos aren't stroked regularly, so me being a miserable fucker to the woman I'm supposed to have a sex scene with the next day, wouldn't bode well. I did not want to be the victim of a booby-trapped modesty pouch just because I didn't romance the leading lady enough the night before.

Which led me back to Phoebe. She took me for who I was. She didn't give a shit that I was the lead actor or a movie star. She called me out. She gave me shit. She made me fucking smile and there weren't many people who could say they'd managed that and I was going to damn well miss her.

The last couple of days on location, we'd started eating lunch together. It wasn't such a huge thing because Alexi encouraged that the whole cast mix in, but I always made sure I got a seat next to her; usually at the end of one of the long tables where we all ate. She talked a lot about the boys and Beth, a little about her parents, who sounded as fucked up as mine, and she told me funny stories of her time as an extra. I listened intently to every word that came out of her mouth and found her totally captivating. The fact that she was damn nice to look at was becoming an added bonus rather than the main factor of why I wanted to be around her.

Three days at the moat house meant I'd have to interact with other people, something I was not looking forward to. I knew that Francesca, who played my love interest, would use her time wisely to try and entice me into her bed. I could see it in her eyes – the idea that bedding the famous Grantley James would get her the publicity that she craved. Well, it would not be happening.

I drank the rest of my coffee, took my glasses off and put them on the table, then got up to take the mug to the sink. The trailer I had was pretty cool; with a big ass white leather couch, a stainless-steel kitchen, and a huge TV. At one end there was even a day bed with more fucking pillows on it than they probably stocked at Bed, Bath & Beyond. It was ridiculously plush considering I probably spent a sum total of two hours a day in it. No doubt that would change when we did some night shoots once we got back from the moat house. Night shoots could be ridiculously long – you didn't rely on the light, so directors tended to keep going for hours.

I wasn't due back on set for another hour, so after washing my mug, I flicked on the TV and scrolled through the channels. The UK channels didn't have much to interest me, but I found one that was showing reruns of *Malcolm in the Middle,* an old favorite of mine – I always dreamed of having a family like Malcolm's. No matter how dysfunctional they were, they were definitely better than mine. I was just settling down to watch the Halloween episode - where Lois gets arrested for kidnapping when she picks up the wrong kid- when I heard a loud knock at the door.

I considered ignoring it, but the second hard knock was followed by an 'Oow, shit that hurt', in a voice that I recognized as Phoebe's. I quickly pushed up from the couch and rushed to the door and opened it.

"Hey," I said, not able to stop the huge ass grin from seeing her dressed in a pair of white coveralls and blue hair net on her head. "Get inside you must be frozen."

I ushered her in and quickly closed the door, shutting out the cold air.

"It's not that cold," she remarked, looking me up and down, no doubt taking in the thick sweater, fingerless gloves, and wool scarf wrapped around my neck.

"It fucking is."

"You Americans are such wimps." Phoebe's giggle danced around the space, and suddenly I felt a whole lot warmer.

"Just us SoCal dudes," I mocked, finishing with a surfer drawl.

"Aren't you from Iowa, according to Wikipedia? Don't they have cold winters there?"

She paused and leaning over the couch, regarded the shelf above it and tilting her head, looked at the few books that were stacked on it.

"I haven't lived in Iowa for almost nine years," I replied, watching as she picked up my worn copy of *The Grapes of Wrath*.

"I prefer Neville Shute's *A Town like Alice*, from that period," she said, flicking through the pages. "I always found Steinbeck to be a little miserable, if I'm honest." Phoebe put the book back and turned to me with a huge grin. "So, I suppose I shouldn't be surprised that you like him."

She sucked on her bottom lip to stop the smile, but her eyes were glistening and I damn well liked it.

"I'm not miserable, and I'll have you know neither is Steinbeck. Have you ever read it?" I nodded toward the book.

"No, I read *Of Mice and Men*, which was enough to put me off him."

"Well maybe you should. It's a fantastic example of people striving to remain dignified during times of hardship."

"Are you saying I'm undignified?" Phoebe asked narrowing her eyes, but with a little smirk on her lips.

"Couldn't be further from the truth," I replied, smiling right back at her. "I just think you might enjoy it if you gave it a go."

"Maybe I will, if I ever find myself stranded on a desert island with just Steinbeck's back catalogue for company."

"You're a damn philistine." I laughed and shook my head. "I got a similar response from Sue-Ann when I suggested she read it. Her, I get it – she has the attention span of a Kardashian in Target - but you, I expected better."

Phoebe's mouth gaped. "You're not dissing the Kardashians are you? How dare you?"

"Please don't tell me you buy into all that crap. My estimation of you has dropped even further – not only do you hate Steinbeck, but you like the fucking evil enemy that is trying to take over the world."

Phoebe grinned and flopped down onto the couch. "I don't really. I've never watched the show. The only opinion I have is that arse is ridiculous – sorry, I'm not sure even which one it belongs to. In fact," she said crinkling her brow, "maybe the arse should have its own show."

"Hey, come on now, Kanye is probably far too busy."

Phoebe burst out laughing, rocking back in her seat and lifting her legs in the air. As she did, the legs of her coveralls lifted to reveal a pair of slim ankles, which weirdly I found damn sexy. Who knew ankles could be a turn on?

"Why the hell are you dressed like that, anyway?" I asked, joining her on the couch.

"I'm in the factory scene. I'm one of the people packing the drugs."

"Oh okay." I nodded and looked down her body. "Do people who work in factories wear that shit?"

Phoebe shrugged. "No idea, maybe if they're packing cocaine into toy dolls they do."

"Actually I'm not sure they would. People who work in factories packing drugs would probably be doing it in their underwear."

"Really?" she asked, screwing up her cute little nose.

"Yeah. No place to stash the drugs in case they think it might be a good idea to take a sample."

"Well I'm glad we're not being too realistic. There's no way I'd want to sit next to Declan in my bra and knickers."

"But you wouldn't mind being on film in your underwear?" I asked, grinning at thoughts of her in a skimpy bra and panties.

"What can I say, I'm a martyr to my art," she replied, nonchalantly looking at her nails.

I laughed and poked her leg with my foot.

"Anyway," I said, leaning my head back on the couch and turning to look at her. "What did you come over for?"

A little blush pinked her cheeks, as she averted her gaze from me. "Was bored, so I thought I'd pop over and check on you."

"How can you be bored? Aren't you supposed to be packing drugs into baby dolls?"

"There was an incident."

Phoebe started to mess with one of the buttons on her coveralls, unfastening and then refastening it.

"What sort of incident?" I asked tentatively.

"It wasn't my fault really."

"What wasn't?"

Shit, what the hell had she done? If it was something major, Alexi might throw her off the set. Funny, seeing as I'd been the one to threaten it a couple of times, yet now I was desperate for her to stay.

"I punched Declan," she finally replied on a sigh.

I shifted on the couch, pushing myself up straighter. "Why the fuck did you feel the need to punch that prick?" I asked, feeling my teeth start to clench. "What did he do?"

"He got a little close to me when we were packing the cocaine. He kept moving his stool closer to mine, until his knee was touching mine. So I asked him to move."

"And he didn't," I stated.

Phoebe shook her head slowly. "I moved and then he moved, and I just got a little mad."

"So you punched him?"

My emotions were mixed – I fucking loved that she'd kicked the little prick's ass, but I fucking hated that she'd felt that she needed to. I knew that little fucker was...well, a fucker.

"Kind of. I pulled my arm back to push him away, but my stool kind of propelled forward and the flat of my hand hit him smack on the nose."

I felt like high-fiving her, but knew I should retain some semblance of professionalism.

"Okay, so did you break his nose?"

"No, but it did bleed all over his costume. In fact," she said, looking a little perplexed, "he bled an awful lot."

"So they had to stop filming?"

Phoebe nodded and sighed. "Yep. He screamed, too. Anyone would think I'd stabbed him with the noise he was making. He ruined the dialogue, you know."

"Are you in trouble?" I put my hands on the couch, readying myself to get up and go fight her corner.

"God no," she exclaimed. "Rosie who was next to me, told Alexi that I'd head butted Declan by accident." She giggled. "Apparently she caught Declan looking at her boobs the other day, so she was pretty pleased with what happened."

I let out a long breath, thankful that she wasn't in trouble, but when I looked at her face I could see that behind the smile there was worry.

"Hey, what's wrong? Alexi didn't say anything did he?"

"No, honestly. He was lovely about it, even though we're going to have to break for a while so they can clean Declan and the cocaine up."

"Clean the cocaine?"

"Hmm, when he bled, it also spurted over some of the cocaine and the conveyor belt. It needs to be cleaned and disinfected for health and safety reasons."

"Who said that?" I asked, wondering how bad a mood Alexi would be in after being delayed over some ridiculous, bureaucratic ruling made by some inflexible, little idiot.

"Oh I did," she replied with a beautiful smile. "I'm the Health and Safety rep."

CHAPTER FIFTEEN

Phoebe

Once we started filming again, the day went pretty quickly. I was in a couple more scenes in the 'drug factory', one of which Grantley was in.

He was posing as the leader of a drug cartel looking to get in on the action, but really, he was Addison Yates and he was not only looking at ways to bring the drug lords down, but also find Madelaine - played by Francesca Woodfield- the girl kidnapped in the restaurant scene. It was amazing watching him do his thing up close and personal. He really was a great actor, making Addison and the plot seem believable even though it was actually quite farcical – I mean, how many Security Agents would have hand to hand combat with a guy one day and the next, look him in the eye and not be recognised just because he was wearing glasses and a bleached blond wig. Even so, when Grantley delivered his lines you could hear a pin drop on set, everyone was so enthralled by his performance.

Alexi had called cut on my final scene for the day and I was just heading out with the rest of the extras when a hand landed on my shoulder. I turned to see Declan. His nose looked sore and he looked extremely pissed off. He also looked extremely stupid, with two huge wads of tissue hanging out of his nostrils. Lucky for Declan we didn't call an ambulance, because they would have stuck tampons up his nose. Shame, we really should have called them.

"What the hell did you think you were doing, hitting me like that?" he asked, his swollen nostrils flaring around the tissue.

"You know why," I replied. "And I didn't actually do it on purpose."

"Like hell you didn't. You've turned into quite the Prima Donna, you know that. Since you got your lines and are all pally-pally with Grantley, you strut around as though you own the place."

I tried to take a step back. It was instinctual to want to get away from him, but also his breath absolutely reeked of the chorizo and garlic chicken we'd had for lunch, and not in a good way. It was more like gone off chorizo and garlic chicken.

"That's not true and you know it." I pulled away with a little more force, causing Declan's hand to drop from my shoulder. "Leave me alone Declan."

"No!" he snapped. "You punched me."

"I didn't do it on purpose, I was trying to push you away."

"Everyone is saying it," he scoffed, curling his lip, "that you think you're something special."

Deep down I knew he was lying, but something still punched at my stomach. I knew everyone always felt envious of the extra who got lines, but I'd tried not to make a big thing of it. It was only three lines after all. I didn't even want to be a leading actress, the thought of having to learn all that dialogue and pull out all those emotions every day, just didn't excite me. I was quite happy with the odd line and being in the background. I could understand Declan being pissed off about it, he knew I didn't want to be anything but an extra, whereas he was desperate for the limelight – no wonder he was jealous and maybe a few more were too, but no way did I think I was someone special.

"If anyone thinks that," I sighed, "then tell them to come and talk to me about it. Now please, can I go? I don't want to miss the bus back to the studio."

"Your boyfriend not giving you a lift?"

"No. That was purely coincidental that Grantley drove past and saw me waiting with the boys. He did that more for the boys than me."

I had no idea why I was justifying it to Declan, it wasn't anything to do with him. Him or anyone else.

"Everyone thinks you got the lines because you're shagging him."

"Well I'm not," I spat back at him. "Even if I was, Grantley couldn't or wouldn't, get me some dialogue just because we were sleeping together."

"Everyone is calling you a whore, pretty much."

The pain couldn't have been worse if *he'd* punched *me* in the nose.

"No," I gasped.

Declan smirked at me and nodded his head, very slowly. "Oh yes."

"You're a liar. Nothing is going on between us, not like that anyway."

"So what's it like, Phoebe? Do tell me. Did you get the lines before you shagged Grantley or after?"

My throat tickled as tears welled in my eyes. How could he say things like that? How could everyone else think that? I would never do anything like that.

"You hateful man," I said around an emotional gasp.

"You whore."

He verbally punched me again and this time it was too much. I turned and ran, pushing past people making their way to the dressing rooms, as I let the tears fall. Ricocheting off Claude, a huge, grey-haired man, I slammed into a wall, winding myself.

"You okay?" Claude asked, stooping down to look at me. "Phoebe, what's wrong?"

He bent to look at me closely, resting a much more comforting hand than Declan's on my shoulder.

"I'm not a whore," I sobbed.

"What?"

He looked down the corridor where I'd come from and then back to me. People passing us gave curious glances, some of them whispering to each other as they went by.

"I'm not. I didn't do what he said."

As I pulled the hideous blue hairnet from my head, the tears were flowing rapidly and my chest was heaving as I thought about Declan's words.

"I don't know what it is you're talking about sweetheart," Claude said, running a hand through his mass of curly hair. "I-."

"Hey, what's going on?"

Suddenly Claude was pulled away from me and Penny was standing in front of me, pushing my hair from my wet cheeks.

"What's wrong, hun?"

"I don't know," Claude replied. "She banged into me and she was just like that."

Penny rolled her eyes. "I was asking Phoebe. Since when do I call you hun? I don't even know your name."

Claude snorted out a girlish laugh for a man so large. "Ooh sorry. I thought you were talking to me."

"Nope. Listen, you go. I'll take care of her."

Penny turned back to me, pushing a slim, tattooed arm around me and hugging me against her.

"Come on," she whispered in my ear. "I'll take you to Grantley."

"No," I cried. "People will say-."

"Fuck what people say. Have you not left yet, big guy?" she said without even looking at Claude.

"Thank you, Claude," I whimpered, giving him a small smile.

"No problem. Glad I could help."

Penny tsked and started to walk me down the corridor amongst the throng of extras making their way to the dressing rooms to change out of their costumes. When we got to the end, everyone turned left, but Penny steered me right towards the exit of the warehouse. We passed a few technicians and some of the other main actors, but no one gave us a second glance. Finally, Penny pulled me to a stop outside Grantley's trailer. She banged on the door.

"Grantley, open up. Phoebe needs you."

Within seconds, Grantley's door was swung open and he was standing in the doorway. He was already out of his Addison Yates' clothes and wearing a pair of faded jeans and a grey t-shirt.

"What the fuck's wrong?" he asked, stumbling down the metal steps and pulling me against his chest. "Hey, Phoebe, what happened?"

"I figured you'd look after her."

With my face against Grantley's chest, I couldn't see Penny, but I could tell she was smiling. Her voice was full of warmth and tenderness.

"How...?" Grantley said.

"I have eyes, hunni. I'm gonna go. I still have my gear to pack up. You gonna be okay?" she said into my ear.

I turned my face to look at Penny, giving her a smile.

"Thank you, Penny."

"My pleasure, sugar." She ran a hand down my hair and with a punch to Grantley's bicep, turned and left.

"Come on, let's get you inside. It's fucking freezing out here."

"No it's not," I said around a small laugh.

"It fucking is."

"You're going to have to tell me some time," Grantley cajoled, placing a mug of coffee into my hands.

"I actually don't." I sighed and took a sip of the muddy liquid. "Ugh that's disgusting."

"No it's not, that's proper coffee. Now tell me what got you so upset."

"Seriously, Grantley, I'm fine. Penny shouldn't have brought me here. I'll drink this and then leave you to it. I'm sure you've got plenty of things you need to be doing."

He planted himself on the sofa next to me and leaned forward, resting his forearms on his knees. "Penny did the right thing. We're friends."

I turned my head sharply and raised my brows. "We are?"

"You know we fucking are." He narrowed his gaze on me. "I admit you were a pain in my ass at first, but I'd say we are most definitely friends. Now damn well tell me what got you so upset."

This was how it had been for the last twenty minutes, him pushing me to tell him why I'd been crying and me saying I was fine. I didn't want to tell him, because I knew what would happen – Declan would get thrown off the film and then I'd be the biggest bitch alive.

"I really am okay, I swear. Just something stupid upset me."

Grantley's eyes darkened as he took hold of my chin with one hand and with the other, took my mug and placed it on the coffee table.

"I want to know, Phoebe," he said softly. "Penny must have thought it was serious to bring you to me."

"I'm so sorry about that. You don't need me here, crying on your shoulder."

And boy, what a shoulder it was. I don't think I'd ever felt as safe as when he had his arms wrapped around me. Unfortunately, I think I got snot on his t-shirt, but he hadn't seemed to notice when I surreptitiously wiped it away. I hadn't wanted to leave his embrace and forgo his clean citrusy smell and warm, hard chest.

"Tell me." His gaze was steely and commanding and made my heart thunder.

"I was being silly."

"Maybe, maybe not, but I won't know unless you tell me," Grantley said in a tone so soft and tender, I wondered whether he was actually hypnotising me.

"Promise you won't do anything, because if you do it'll only make things worse."

Grantley sat back against the soft leather of the sofa, eyeing me warily.

"So it's something bad enough I'm likely to go nuclear on someone's ass?"

I winced, knowing he was right.

"Swear to me, Grantley. Please."

He watched me for a few seconds and then nodded.

"Okay."

I took a deep breath and told him all about mine and Declan's 'friendly' conversation.

"The fucking asshole," he cried, pushing up from the sofa. "I'll have him thrown of this damn movie quicker than he can say 'I'm named after a fucking prick, because I am one'."

"You promised," I said, pulling on his hand. "If you do anything, it'll just prove it right to those who think it."

"I don't give a fuck what they think," he stormed, pulling away from me and starting to pace up and down the trailer. "I'll get every-fucking-one of them that said it, or even thought it, thrown off too."

"I don't want that," I protested.

"Well I do. They can't say that."

"They actually can. We live in the free world."

"Not on this fucking movie we don't. This is my movie and if I want the fuckers gone, they're fucking gone."

He turned quickly, snatching his phone up from the coffee table. "I'm going to call Alexi."

"No!" I cried, making a grab for the phone. "Please don't, Grantley. Please."

Lifting it to his ear, he paused and stared at me. "Why don't you want me to get the ass hat kicked off?" he asked. "Surely you don't want to be around him after he upset you."

"Because it would make what he said seem true. It really would look like I only got the lines because you and I are...well you know."

Heat flooded my veins, as I considered what Declan had said. I couldn't lie, a little picture flashed through my brain. A picture of Grantley supremely naked and doing naughty things to me.

As if he read my mind, Grantley's lips curled into a small smile – the first I'd seen since Penny had deposited me at his door.

"I don't really care what they say. You know that right?"

I nodded.

"We're friends, even if you don't think it, and I'd do the same for any of my friends. But," he said on a sigh, "I won't do anything about it, because you don't want me to. Although why you don't, I have no fucking clue."

"I just don't want things to be even more difficult. Not that I thought they were, until Declan said what he did."

"Yeah well, that all sounds like a crock of shit to me." Grantley puffed out his cheeks and looked at me intently. "I'm pretty sure he's making it up and no one else has said that about you. That only makes me want to dick punch him even more."

"Well I think he's probably been punched enough for one day."

Grantley tsked. "Nah, I'm sure he can manage one more. Anyway, I won't say anything, but if he does anything else, all bets are off. Okay?"

I grinned and nodded. "Thank you. I do appreciate you wanting to get rid of him for me, but I'll be fine."

"You sure?"

"Honestly."

Grantley took a step towards me and lifted his hand to my face. His fingertips whispered against my sticky cheek and the lightness of his touch took my breath away. Standing as still as a statue, I raised my eyes to look at him. His strong jaw was taught and beneath the light spray of whiskers I could see a nerve twitching. Eyes the colour of winter grass looked down at me as I held my breath. When Grantley's breathing quickened, I knew he was going to kiss me. Slowly, his hand moved around to the back of my head as he narrowed the gap between us. The air grew stifling and all I wanted to do was feel his lips on mine.

"I have no idea what's happening here," he whispered, inching closer. "But I know I *have* to kiss you."

We were nose to nose and I couldn't believe I was going to get to kiss him.

"Well do-."

"Grantley, open up this fucking door now. I'm freezing my fucking titties off out here."

Grantley's hand fell from my hair and he took a step away from me, letting his head drop back with his eyes closed.

"I cannot believe this," he groaned. "Fucking Marcia."

CHAPTER SIXTEEN

Phoebe

As Grantley strode to the door, I quickly ran a hand over my hair and straightened my ugly white overalls. I knew I hadn't *been* kissed, but that near kiss had been pretty hot – God, imagine what an actual kiss would be like.

"What the hell are you doing here?" Grantley asked, a cold breeze rushing around me as the door was opened.

"You fucking asked me to be here, you asshole."

I turned and watched as Marcia stomped through the door. She was wearing an extremely tight white skirt with a fitted black and white stripe jacket on her tiny frame, and carrying my dream handbag; a black Mulberry, Bayswater. Her bleached blonde hair was bigger than she was and as she tottered forward on a pair of towering, black stiletto shoes, which were probably as expensive as her handbag, she slapped Grantley around the back of the head.

"What the...what's that for?" he asked, rubbing at the spot she'd slapped.

"For making me come to this godforsaken hell hole," she screeched. "You just wouldn't take no for an answer, would you?"

"I told you why," Grantley protested. "Sue-Ann is coming and you're the only who can put her in her place."

"I know I have the honor of that ability, but it doesn't mean I always have to be the fucking one to do it."

"But you do it so well," Grantley said with a grin.

I watched their interaction, silently waiting on the side-lines and wondering whether I should simply slink away. Before I had a chance to decide, Marcia turned her head towards me – I say she turned her head but more like her face turned to me, and her hair looked as though it stayed where it was. It was so solid with hairspray, I wondered if she ever dared go near a naked flame.

"And who the hell are you?"

"I...I-."

"Marcia, this is my friend, Phoebe," Grantley said on a sigh.

My gaze shot towards him, and while he wasn't smiling, there were little creases at the corners of his twinkling eyes.

"Why the fuck are you dressed like that?" she cried, waving a finger up and down at me. "Do you clean the drains around here, or are you some sort of fucking sexual freak and I'm going to be reading about this experience in People Magazine in a month?"

"Marcia!" Grantley snapped. "Stop it. Phoebe is an extra on the movie. She's just finished filming a scene."

"You're letting a damn extra spike your pole? Grantley, what the fuck have I told you about messing with the help? You. Don't. Fucking. Do. It."

My eyes widened as she pushed past me and strode up towards the other end of the trailer where there was a small bed, piled with cushions. Bending, she pulled off the cushions and then the white cotton duvet.

"I'll make sure this lot is burned," she growled. "We don't want her scraping your damn spunk off here and claiming some little bastard as yours – that's assuming you've used protection and she hasn't saved the damn condom in her purse."

"Marcia!" Grantley bellowed. "That's e-fucking-nough. Don't you dare talk about Phoebe like that. We are not having sex. We haven't even kissed."

Thanks to you, Marcia, and I just know it was going to be amazing.

"Doesn't mean she isn't going to try." Marcia winked at Grantley. "She wouldn't be the first little whore to try it."

"Marc-."

"Hey," I cried. "I am not a whore. How the hell dare you?"

"Ah jeez, Grantley," she cried. "This one has fucking balls."

"We *are* just friends. What Grantley says is true, but even if we were more than that, you should not be calling me a whore. You don't even know me. You stroll in here, being rude to Grantley the moment you walk through the door, and call me horrible names without even saying kiss my arse."

"Oh my God, you are a fucking sex freak," she groaned, horrified. "You want me to kiss your ass?"

"No," I snapped. "It's a turn of phrase. The point I'm making is, you haven't even spoken to me and have already made your mind up that I'm out to pull a fast one on Grantley."

"A fast one – what like pull a gun on him?"

She was playing with me, she knew exactly what I was saying.

"I mean it, Marcia. Leave Phoebe the fuck alone." Grantley pointed a finger at Marcia as she kicked at one of the pillows on the floor. "She's my friend. She makes me laugh and I enjoy her company. She has no fucking hidden agenda. She's so fucking good and kind she wouldn't have a damn clue where to start."

Marcia grinned at him and ran a hand over her candy floss hair. "Well fuck me, I do believe you like the little ballsy one."

"I just said that," Grantley bellowed, throwing his arms into the air. "She's my friend."

"Whatever, lover boy."

Marcia waved him away and moved over to the kitchen area and ran a finger along the counter top.

"At least it's clean. Now, when does Teen Mom get in?"

Grantley rolled his eyes. "I've told you before she wasn't a teen mom, no matter what Sue-Ann tells you. She was not twelve-years-old when she had me. You've only got to look at her for Christ's sake. Does she look thirty-eight to you?"

"Like hell she does," Marcia laughed.

"Exactly. She was twenty-three and had been married to my dad for two years. The only time life became hard for her was when he left, and that was only because it meant she didn't have a built in babysitter while she went out and got fucked up on vodka and weed with her friends."

Grantley's face was contorted with anger and pain as he raged at Marcia. I knew he didn't rate his mum, but the look on his face made me think it was so very much more than her making bad choices.

"Oh my god, she's going to be fifty." Marcia roared with laughter. "I am so going to enjoy that day."

Grantley shook his head, impatience seeping through his every pore. He turned to me. "I'm sorry, Phoebes."

The smile he gave me and the fact that he called me 'Phoebes' made my heart stutter. It was silly, only a few people called me that, those who'd known me a long time, who were comfortable with me. Grantley felt comfortable with me and it made me happy.

"I'm fine." I nodded and grinned at him.

"You sure? You know, after what happened." He took a step towards me, holding out a hand.

I looked down at it and then back up to his face. His eyes were soft and pleading. I reached out and linked the tips of my fingers with his.

"Honestly, I'm good. Declan is an idiot and I know he was just trying to upset me."

There was a crackling silence between us as we stared at each other, both of us watching the other carefully.

"Okay, okay," Marcia squawked. "As much as I'm enjoying watching the crappy Hallmark love story unfold, I didn't come here for that. You said you wanted my help, so here I am to save the day. Yet again."

Grantley closed his eyes, and his mouth started to move. He was silently counting to ten.

I pulled on his hand. "I'm going to go."

Grantley's eyes flashed open. "I'll give you a lift home."

"No, no, no, lover boy." Marcia stepped between us, pushing a flat palm against Grantley's chest. "You and I need to discuss the Sue-Ann situation and also the reason you fucking bailed on the meeting I set up for you. Little Miss Snogie here can move that little ass of hers back home on her own."

"Snogie?"

"Frozen." Marcia and I answered in unison.

"Whatever," Grantley said. "But if I want to take Phoebe home I will."

"Honestly Grantley, it really is okay."

He looked down at his watch and then back at me.

"Sorry Phoebes, but I think you've missed the bus back to the studio."

His tone was self-satisfied and he had a matching smile. It was funny, I'd seen him smile more in the last couple of days than I had the whole last week on set, or in any photograph in the media.

"Listen, lover boy," Marcia said. "Take her home or don't take her home, but I let my car service go, so you're gonna have to take me to my hotel first."

"Where are you staying?" Grantley asked impatiently.

"Not the damn Lowry, that's for sure. I do not want you knowing what I get up to off the clock."

"Marcia, you know and I both know I have no interest in what, or who, you do *off the clock*."

Marcia shrugged. "You're just jealous that I can still pull the guys and yet you have trouble with the broads – present company excluded."

She smiled at me and then turned back to Grantley.

"I need to shit and shower, so move it."

Marcia rolled her hand, encouraging Grantley to hurry.

"Marcia! I do not want to know about your bathroom habits." Grantley pinched the bridge of his nose and sighed. "Okay. I'll take you first."

"Honestly Grantley, just drop me at the railway station. It's fine."

Grantley shook his head. "Nope. Go get changed, and I'll get Barney to bring the car to the front. We'll take Marcia back to her hotel and then you and I will have some dinner in my suite."

I immediately looked down at the ground, wondering whether anyone else had heard my heart drop to the floor.

Dinner in his suite.

"Grantley-."

"I insist," he said, turning to pick up his coat from the back of the chair. "It's the least I can do after my uncouth agent called you a whore. And," He looked pointedly at Marcia, "it's all on her."

"Fuck you," Marcia cried, and gave Grantley the bird.

CHAPTER SEVENTEEN

Grantley

I couldn't believe fucking Marcia, She insisted that Phoebe ride shotgun while she and I sat in the back. According to her, she wanted to talk business. Yeah, right. It had taken all of five minutes for her to drop her head back and start sounding like a rusty saw, snoring her head off. Not that anything was going to happen in the car between me and Phoebe, but Marcia was the fucking biggest cock-blocker around.

"You'd best wake her," Barney called over his shoulder. "We're two minutes away from her hotel."

"Can I do it when we pull up?" I asked, glancing at her open mouth. "It'll give me a couple more minutes of peace."

Phoebe giggled and turned to look between the two seats.

"She looks quite sweet like that. Just a sweet, little old lady."

"I fucking heard that, you little cu-."

"*Marcia,*" I snapped, cutting her off. "Don't."

"Do you know how fucking insulting that is?" she growled at Phoebe, sitting up straighter. "You ask any fucker in showbiz, I am not damn sweet."

"Hey now," Barney said, looking at her in the rear-view mirror. "You're one of the sweetest women I know."

"That's because all the women you know are sleazy, two-bit whores. Just pull up in front."

With a deep laugh, Barney saluted her and signaled to pull up in front of the old, Victorian looking hotel.

"Here you are ma'am," he replied with a smirk.

"Thank you Barnabus and when you take him and her back to the hotel, make sure he's got condoms." Marcia poked me in the shoulder.

"I told you, we're just-."

"Yeah, yeah, I know," she drawled. "Just friends. But while you're being just friends, make sure you wrap it before you tap it."

As Barney pulled to a stop, Marcia swung her door open and stepped out.

"I'll speak to you tomorrow and talk about what we'll do about your mother. But, do not call me before midday – damn jet lag."

"Okay," I sighed. "But Sue-Ann gets in the day after tomorrow, so we need to be sure we have a plan."

"I said that, didn't I?" Marcia rolled her eyes and turned to Phoebe, who was watching us carefully. "And you, don't you dare try and pull that fast one of yours on my boy here. You do anything to jeopardize his career and I'll rip those perfect titties of yours right off."

Phoebe's hand flew to her chest. "I wouldn't."

"Marcia," I said, wearily. "Just get out."

"See you fuckers tomorrow. Barney," she barked, "take my damn luggage inside."

And then she was gone.

CHAPTER EIGHTEEN

Grantley

Walking into my suite, I sensed that Phoebe was dragging her feet and was feeling a little uneasy. I knew it was because we were alone, since after seeing us up to the suite, Barney had gone off to see his lady-friend.

"You want a drink?" I asked her while shaking off my coat.

"A cup of tea would be lovely," she replied. "I'll make it."

"What, you don't trust my tea-making skills?"

"Well," she said with a smile. "You are American."

"What are you trying to say about my people?" I laughed, realizing with a certain amount of shock that she'd made me laugh, yet again.

"That you're rubbish at making tea."

Phoebe took off her own coat and went to hang it over the back of one of the dining chairs.

"Hey, let me put that in my closet," I offered, reaching for her long, blue coat.

Phoebe's cheeks blushed as she handed it to me and she looked so cute, I just wanted to kiss her. Shit, I'd wanted to kiss her since Marcia turned up.

"Thank you."

"No problem."

I gave her a quick wink and walked into my room, hanging our coats next to each other in my closet. Listening to Phoebe opening cupboards and clattering cups in the kitchen, I went into the bathroom and reached for my mouthwash. I didn't want to jump the gun, but if I did get to kiss her, I didn't want my breath smelling like shit.

After taking a quick swig and then spitting, I reached for my cologne and dabbed a little on to my neck. It was my favorite one and was not the one that I advertised – that one smelled like horse nuts-well, at least to me it did. Fresh breath and sexy smell, hopefully meant I was fully prepared if I got lucky enough to kiss Phoebe.

Taking a deep breath, I left the bedroom. I didn't feel nervous per say, but there was excitement buzzing around in my gut. Phoebe was a pretty girl; with her fair skin and caramel hair with matching eyes, but more than that, she was funny and interesting. She wasn't a yes girl just because I was the movie star. She was honest and real, and in my business, you rarely met anyone like that.

"Hey," I said, as I walked into the kitchen area. "Did you find everything you need?"

Phoebe swung around and gave me a dazzling smile. "This coffee machine is amazing," she replied with an enthusiastic sing-song to her voice. "I need to get Beth one of these for her birthday."

She turned back around and continued watching the mug being filled. The excitement on her face warming my heart.

"I prefer a jug myself."

As I moved to stand beside her, Phoebe looked up at me with a twinkle in her eyes.

"No way, this is much more fun."

"If you say so." I chuckled and gave her shoulder a squeeze.

I didn't miss the little shiver her body gave and it excited me. I wanted her to want me. I wanted her to care about me. I wanted her to enjoy being with me. I wanted her, period.

When the machine finished, Phoebe passed me the mug and then turned back to stir the cup of tea that she'd already made.

"Sorry," she said, without facing me. "You do take it black, don't you?"

"Black is perfect." I replied, watching her carefully.

Her arms were slim and elegant, and her hands tiny with long fingers. With her long hair pulled over one shoulder, I could see her smooth neck and the jut of her chin as she looked around with a teabag on the end of a teaspoon.

"Where's the bin?" she asked, turning to look at me.

I reached around her and opened up a cupboard door.

"Et voila." Inside were two trash bins, one grey and one green.

"Oh how cool is that too." She slapped the teabag into the grey bin. "We've just got a boring pedal bin at home. I tell you, Beth really needs to see this place."

"You could come over one weekend, with Beth and the boys. If you like."

What the hell was happening to me? The Grantley James from two weeks ago would never have invited her over, never mind a couple of kids and their single mom. But the Grantley James from two weeks ago hadn't met Phoebe Drinkwater.

"Oh I don't know about that," she replied, with a tinkling laugh. "I'm not sure you'd like the noise the boys would make with that piano."

"Well, maybe we could all do something," I heard myself saying. "I hear there's a couple of great museums in the city."

She looked at me and nodded. "That sounds good. So, Barney has a girlfriend close by?"

And that was the subject changed.

"Oh my goodness," Phoebe sighed, rubbing her stomach. "That was amazing."

"You've still got your caramel ice-cream cheesecake to eat."

"My what?"

She screwed up her little nose and furrowed her brow.

"Caramel ice-cream cheesecake."

"You mean ca-ra-mel," she giggled.

"That's what I said, caramel."

"No, you said carmel. You left the second 'a' out."

"No I said it correctly. You're the one who said it wrong."

I leaned back in my chair, watching her closely. God damn she was pretty.

"You Americans say everything weird," she muttered, taking a sip of her wine.

"I think you'll find you're the ones who can't pronounce words properly."

"Okay, look at the way you say route."

"Route." I corrected her.

"It's not spelt r.o.w.t. There's an oo in the middle."

"You know you're wrong." A smile flickered at my lips at the horrified look on her face.

"No, I'm not. It is called the *English* language or have you forgotten that?"

"Nope, but doesn't mean you say it right."

"Yes we do. Seriously Grantley, I have no idea how you can think leverage should be pronounced levaridge. Ridiculous."

She really did look pissed and I wanted to laugh. She had her hands thrown in the air and her voice had a real tone of despair.

"Tomayto, tomahto," I replied with a grin. "Who cares?"

Phoebe's eyes narrowed on me as she smiled. "You're so annoying."

"Yep, I know. Now, do you want your carmel ice-cream cheesecake?"

"No thank you," she said haughtily. "But I will have my caramel ice-cream cheesecake."

I shook my head and rolled my eyes.

"Whatever."

With a chuckle, I got up and went into the kitchen to retrieve our desserts from the refrigerator. When I opened it up, I noticed another bottle of wine in there and decided that a couple more glasses each wouldn't hurt. I had to be up fairly early for the drive to the location shoot, but I could sleep in the car if necessary. Managing both desserts in one hand, I picked up the wine with the other.

"Here you go," I placed the plates on the table. "It looks pretty good."

"Wow, look at you," Phoebe said, sitting back in her chair and pointing at me. "Were you a waiter in a past life?"

"Actually, yeah. I waited tables for a summer when I first got to LA."

"Really? Was it a nice restaurant?"

I laughed out loud and shook my head. "God no. It was a crummy backstreet diner, but they made the best pancakes around and it was close to Fox studios, so producers and directors were always coming in."

"So you gave them your best customer service?" Phoebe asked with a smile.

"But of course." I tilted my head and winked at her.

"And did it work?"

I burst out laughing. "Like hell it did. Every damn waiter, barman, and store clerk in LA is an actor looking for a break, so they were pretty adapt at ignoring me. I did meet Marcia there though. After she relocated from New York."

"It was definitely worth it then."

"I guess so. She got me where I am today. I owe her a lot."

I sighed, thinking back to how many free breakfasts I had to give Marcia before she'd even agree to talk to me. She'd been a hard nut to crack, but she'd been behind me all the way since then.

"What made you want to be an actor?" Phoebe asked, pushing her cheesecake around her plate with a dessert fork. "I have to admit, I Googled you and it said you were a promising baseball star at High School, but gave it up when you were sixteen."

I cringed inwardly, wondering what else she'd read about me. It wasn't a secret Sue-Ann had raised me alone and that we didn't get along, but me and Marcia had worked hard to be sure no one knew how bad my life had been with her. Yeah, it may have made a great story, but I didn't want every interview I did to be about me overcoming adversity to make it big. I just wanted to be asked about my acting.

"I always liked the idea of acting," I finally said. "I just thought I'd get more girls by playing baseball."

Phoebe rolled her eyes. "Why does that not surprise me?"

"What does that mean?" I asked, nudging her leg with my foot.

"Well, you're a bit of ladies' man aren't you?"

She forked a small amount of cheesecake and popped it into her mouth. Her lips closed around it and she momentarily closed her eyes, obviously savoring the taste.

"Good?" I asked.

"Hmm." She nodded and grinned around the fork. "Delicious. Anyway, stop avoiding my question."

"Didn't realize it was a question," I retorted, knowing that's exactly what it was. "I thought you were making a statement."

"Well whatever, you are a ladies man. At least I think you are."

"And I think your accusations are unfounded, Miss Drinkwater. Do you ever see me in the media with lots of different women?"

She thought about it, twirling her fork around in the air. "Hmm, now you mention it, no not really."

I tipped my glass to her. "There you go. I've had two serious girlfriends in the last five years. Before that, I admit I was a serial dater, but there wasn't always sex involved."

Phoebe's cheeks pinked and she quickly looked back down at her dessert. Shit, was she a fucking virgin? Or was she just one of those uptight Brits?

"You want to change the subject?" I asked around a laugh.

Phoebe's head shot up. "No. You can talk about your dating history if you want to."

I leaned across the table and whispered. "Just not the sex part."

"I said you can if you want to." Phoebe began to tuck into her cheesecake again, feigning nonchalance, but her still pink cheeks said otherwise.

"Nope," I replied. "I don't want to."

It was true, I didn't want to. I didn't want to talk to her about the many girls I'd slept with, because being in LA was like being a kid let loose in FAO Schwarz with unlimited credit. I didn't regret it, but all kids grew out of wanting toys eventually. I wasn't ashamed. What young guy wouldn't spread the love if it was handed to him on a plate? I just didn't talk about anything that wasn't important to me, and call me a douchebag, but those girls weren't important to me – just as I wasn't to them either.

"Okay, so how serious were your girlfriends? I didn't see anything on Google about them."

"Wow, you really did do some research didn't you?"

"God, I'm sorry." Phoebe blushed again. "Please don't think I'm stalking you or anything like that."

She looked at me anxiously, sucking on her bottom lip, and I had a real yearning to set it free with my thumb - mainly so I could suck on it myself. Giving myself a little inward shake, I moved my eyes away from her lips and attempted to concentrate on the conversation.

"I'm not mad, Phoebe," I said softly. "I'm in the public eye, my story is out there for anyone to see. You just won't find much about me before I moved to LA, being a high school baseball star aside."

"I guess people are only interested in your acting career."

I shrugged. "Maybe. Or maybe, I just buried it."

Phoebe's mouth dropped open as she stared at me. It was written all over her face that she was wondering what had happened in my life that I'd felt the need to keep it hidden. But, when she picked up her wine glass and took a sip, it was evident that she'd decided not to ask. Maybe it was the fear of hearing my story, because there was worry etched on her pretty features. Worry that I didn't want her to feel.

"It was nothing horrific, Phoebe," I said softly. "I just don't want people knowing that my mother was probably one of the worst moms on record."

"Please tell me she didn't hit you or..." Her barely audible voice trailed off, but I heard the words she didn't say.

"No," I replied with a sigh. "She didn't hit me or anything else. What she did do was neglect me. I pretty much brought myself up after my dad left."

Phoebe's eyes glistened as she leaned forward to listen to me and I could feel the sympathy emanating from her.

"I've never told anyone but Marcia and Barney about this," I said, pushing away my wine glass.

"You don't have to tell me either. Honestly Grantley, it's your business and I should never have brought it up."

I watched her carefully. Seeing the apprehension on her face and the compassion in her eyes, I knew I wanted her to hear it. She was my friend and friends shared their deepest secrets. Yeah, it didn't escape me that I had never told my two serious girlfriends anything at all about my childhood, and I'd lived with one of them. Living with Serena had been really short-lived, just a couple of months, even though we tried real hard to make it work. Yet, I never divulged any of what I was going to tell Phoebe.

"When my dad left, I'd like to say it was what made Sue-Ann fall apart, but it wasn't. She was an out of control drunk way before that. I think my dad covered for her being a shit mom while he was around. He was the one who took an interest in me, and in hindsight, I realize he was the one who kept Sue-Ann together and cajoled her into behaving like a mom. Once he left though, there was no one to cover for her and it was pretty clear she was not meant for motherhood."

"And yet your dad still left you with her?" Phoebe took in a deep breath. "Oh my God, that's awful. He's as bad as her."

I nodded and gave her a tight smile. "Yeah, you're right, he's just as fucking bad."

"Yet you still call him dad, but she's Sue-Ann."

I'd never thought about that before, but she was right. I had no idea why I did that.

"I don't know, maybe because he was a great dad before he left – the best in fact – that still gives him the right to be called dad. Who knows?" I shrugged. "I guess most of my memories are of her and the miserable life we had together."

"I know I have a bad relationship with my parents," Phoebe replied. "But they did at least care for me and kept me safe."

"Well Sue-Ann was all kinds of shit." I laughed emptily. "She would leave me for days at a time, alone in the house without much food, while she went off and got stoned or drunk with whatever guy she was lusting after at the time. I always knew when she was going to do a disappearing act, because she'd give me ten dollars before I went to school. She'd always say 'just in case you need anything, baby boy' and then that night I'd get home and she'd be gone."

"Oh my God," Phoebe gasped. "Did no one help you? Did your neighbours not see what was going on?"

"I was pretty good at hiding it. For as much as I hated her and the life we led, I knew it would be a lot worse if I was put in the system. I learned to do laundry and how to make that ten dollars last. I ate a lot of ramen noodles and bought a hell of a lot of bruised fruit. No one, not even my teachers realized what was going on. I even kept up my school work, doing my homework after I'd washed and dried my clothes and cleaned up the house. Anything not to bring attention to the situation."

"How old were you when your dad left?" Phoebe pushed away her half-eaten dessert and clutched a hand to her chest.

"I was almost six."

"The same age as the boys," she whispered. Her head shot up as she looked at me with understanding. "That's why you took to them."

I smiled and nodded. "That and they're pretty cool kids."

"I can't imagine Callum and Mack having any clue how to look after themselves."

"I can't imagine them ever having to. If Beth weren't around, they'd have you."

Phoebe's head dropped and she took in a long breath. Twisting her napkin in her hands she nodded.

"They'll always have me," she replied.

She sniffed and swiped at her cheek; she was crying. The thought of the boys being in my position had really got to her.

"It won't happen," I said, reaching over to touch her cheek. "Beth is a fantastic mother and would never do that."

She lifted her gaze and gave me a small nod.

"You're right, she wouldn't. I just can't believe your mother put you through that, Grantley." She sniffed again. "I can't stop thinking about how scared you must have been."

"The first couple of times." I shrugged. "But after that I got used to it. She didn't do it all the time, but she went missing at least a couple of times a year. And to be honest, when she was at home she was pretty absent. I was more like the parent than she was. At first I made sure she ate, and actually got out of bed each day – I think I thought that she was heartbroken about my dad. But after a few months I realized the way she was and knew that was why he left in the first place. When I was about eight or nine, I started to look forward to her going. My life was easier for those peaceful few days that she was gone."

"She never remarried?" Phoebe asked.

"God no, she was getting too much child support from my dad. I'll give him that, he paid for me right up until the day I turned eighteen. Plus, I think most of the men she went after realized pretty quick what a loser she was. She was never one of those women that went for deadbeat men who I'd feel threatened by. Oh no, she always went for the guys with good jobs and money. The couple that she actually brought home were pretty cool guys – one was a dentist. Brian Turnblatt was his name. A balding guy with more than a few extra inches on his waistline. He was nice, always scruffed my hair and asked me how I was doing. She was actually normal while she was with him. She cooked and cleaned and even made sure I showered."

"So what happened?"

"She stole from him." I raised my eyebrows and shrugged one shoulder. "It was inevitable. She had a good thing going and fucked it up. She took money from his wallet and the keys to his practice and gave them to a drug dealer ex-boyfriend who she owed money to. He got in and stole a load of prescription pain meds. Sue-Ann had no idea that the practice had a silent alarm that went straight through to the cops. Of course her ex snitched on her, but Brian being the good guy that he was decided not to press charges. We just never saw him again."

I reached for my glass, which was still half full, but after looking at it, I pushed it away again. We hadn't even opened the second bottle, what with things getting so serious so quickly.

"I'm sorry, Phoebe," I finally said. "I wanted us to have a nice dinner, not talk about my shitty childhood."

She looked up at me and smiled. "I'm just sorry you had a shitty childhood."

"Don't be. I survived and I never got hurt. Well, not really."

"What does that mean, not really?"

I stuck out my left arm and pointed at the scar on it. It was raised and jagged, a silver line against my tanned skin.

"She did that when she was drunk and high one night."

Phoebe gasped. "No."

"Yeah. She didn't mean to, but she still never said sorry."

"What happened?"

"It happened when I was around eleven. She was dancing around the room with a bottle of vodka in her hand and she tripped and caught it on the side of the coffee table. The bottle smashed and so she was lurching around holding onto the neck of it, and I was worried she was going to cut herself. I didn't care about her too much, but I didn't want her cutting her own throat by accident and me having to go into foster care. I made a grab for her arm but she struggled and the jagged glass ripped my skin. It was pretty deep and wouldn't stop bleeding."

"Oh my God, what did you do?"

"I bandaged it up and put the broken bottle into my school bag. The next morning when I got to school, I dropped the bottle in the school yard, stuffed the bloody bandage into the bottom of my bag and then made a big show of falling over. I knew the school would take me to the ER and no one would ask as many questions as if I'd gone in with my drunk mom the night before. They stitched me up and I was fine."

"And no one guessed?" Phoebe asked incredulously.

"Nope. Although my teacher, Miss Kingston, couldn't understand how from falling over I'd managed to get the bottle into the top of my arm, or for that matter, how the bottle got there. I remember our janitor getting into real shit with the Principal for that. Miss Kingston asked a lot of questions, but I stuck to my story." I grinned at her. "Even then I was a fucking good actor."

Phoebe smiled. "You evidently were."

We fell silent again and I decided that we'd had enough talk of Sue-Ann Miller and her amazing mothering skills.

"So," I said with a grin. "Now it's your turn. Tell me all about your sex life."

Phoebe groaned, screwed up her napkin and threw it at me before starting to laugh.

"You are so rude."

"Yep, I know," I sighed. "But you still think I'm amazing."

She didn't answer, she just looked down at the table and I knew that I'd never before wanted anyone to think I was amazing as much as I did at that moment.

CHAPTER NINETEEN

Phoebe

It was almost ten and I knew I should get going. My last train home was at eleven-thirty, but I didn't want to travel on that one. It was usually full of drunken people scarfing down stinking burgers and trying to engage me in their inebriated conversations that made little or no sense. I wasn't averse to that when I was drunk myself, but when I was sober it wasn't much fun.

"Grantley," I called through to the kitchen area. "Is it okay if I call reception to get me a taxi?"

Grantley appeared around the corner, sucking something off the end of this thumb and looking extremely gorgeous.

"A taxi?"

"Yes, I need to get up to the railway station. I'd like to catch the ten-thirty train."

He glanced down at his watch. "I'll get Barney to come back. I don't want you getting on a train at this time of night."

"God, no," I cried, shaking my head and walking towards the desk where the phone was. "Don't do that, he's out enjoying himself. Honestly, I'll be fine."

"Shit," he muttered. "I'm sorry, I never thought about you getting home. I'd drive you, but I've had too much to drink and of course, Barney has the car."

"Don't be silly, I'll be fine on the train."

Grantley shook his head. "No. You're not doing that."

"Well how else do I get home?"

Grantley's eyes glittered with a hundred possibilities and there wasn't one of them that I wanted to say no to – come on, I remembered that anaconda he hid in his sweat pants on the first day of filming. Unfortunately though, I had to say no.

"Grantley-." I started.

"Nope, it's not happening. I know what you can do -."

It was my turn to interrupt him. "No, I'm not staying. You don't have a spare bedroom and I wouldn't feel comfortable with you sleeping on the couch."

I was sure I would regret not staying with the possibility of petting his snake, but I'd undoubtedly regret staying even more. While I chastised my own stupid decisions, Grantley cleared his throat. When I looked up at him, he gave me a smirk as he crossed his arms over his chest.

"I was going to suggest that I pay for a taxi to bring you all the way home."

I closed my eyes and groaned. What a stupid, bloody idiot. I wanted to crawl up into a tiny ball and disappear. Or maybe invent a time-machine so I could erase my stupid ramblings. As neither were going happen, I opened my eyes, only to see Grantley now had a full on grin. The smug bastard.

"I just...shit...I."

"I know what you thought, Phoebe. You thought I was some sort of douche, who would persuade you to stay the night on our first date..."

Grantley's voice trailed off, and now it was his turn to colour up as he scrubbed a hand over his face and laughed.

"You never said that this was a date." I fluttered my eyelashes and lay a hand over my heart. "Well, Mr. James, aren't you just the romantic one."

Grantley rolled his eyes, but was still smiling.

"I was making a point about the sort of person you think I am. You know, a *ladies' man*."

"Now who's using my words back at me?"

Grantley laughed and came to stand in front of me. "Whatever, but I'm neither a douche nor a ladies' man, so I would never suggest you stay over." His gaze roamed lazily down my body and then back up again. "Unless of course you want to."

Of course I wanted to. My nipples and vagina were most definitely up for a sleepover.

"No, you idiot." I slapped at his arm and turned back to the phone. "A taxi to the station is fine, thank you."

"Nope. A taxi all the way home otherwise you get the couch, and I have to warn you, I walk around naked in the mornings."

Shit, I'd get to see his mammoth weapon. Then again, sweat pants could be very deceiving.

He watched me as I contemplated his offer.

"Okay, fine," I sighed out. "But you do know it's going to cost you a fortune."

"It'll be worth it to be sure you get home safe."

Then without warning, he leaned forward and kissed my cheek while stroking a hand down my hair. His touch and his kiss were both gentle, but took my breath away and made my heart thump wildly. Grantley pulled away slowly and as he did, he gave my nose a little rub with his own. Our lips were now inches apart and I held my breath; he was going to kiss me. This time however, there would be no interruptions and I knew he would blow not only my socks off, but my knickers too, because I had no willpower whatsoever.

As Grantley's lips hovered over mine, I looked up at his eyes and then back to his mouth. His top lip was a little fuller than his bottom one, but both looked enticing and I was desperate to capture them with my own. Grantley swallowed and threaded the fingers of one hand into my hair, while the other rested against my neck, the metal of his rings cooling my heated skin.

"So pretty," he whispered. "So *damn* pretty."

I lifted onto my tiptoes and let out a small breath, opening my lips for him – inviting him in. Grantley's hand moved from my hair to the small of my back, and pulled me against him. The minute our bodies slammed together we became a tangle of arms, pulling at each other, as our tongues played and our lips explored. Our breathing got heavy amidst the moans of enjoyment and satisfaction. My body was thrumming in time with the waves of electricity rushing through my veins. I'd never been kissed like this before. I'd never felt such dizzy heights of pleasure, simply through having a man's lips on mine.

He was amazing, and from what I could feel, those sweat pants had not been deceiving at all.

Grantley hooked his hands under my thighs and lifted me from my feet. Turning around, he walked us back to the dining table and put me down on it, using his tall, sculpted body to force my legs apart and position himself between them. I edged forward, needing to feel some sort of friction, and groaned when the buckle of his belt rubbed in just the right place.

"Grantley."

"Oh fuck."

Evidently we'd said enough because we stopped talking and continued kissing, with Grantley's hand snaking up my side and under my shirt. The trail of his fingers caused my skin to pebble and a shiver of delight to ripple through me. Grantley's mouth left mine and started to land warm kisses down my neck, sending me onto a higher plane of need. Moving my hands from around his neck, I put them behind me, leaning back to give him better access to my heated skin.

Arching my back, my chest heaved as Grantley moved his hand up and dragged his thumb along the side of my boob. His kisses along my neck became more heated as they continued all the way down, over the swell of my breast, to the last closed button of my shirt.

"I'm so fucking hard right now," Grantley groaned as his hand twisted in my hair. "You've done this to me, Phoebe."

As I moved closer to the edge of the table, Grantley pushed forward and I felt exactly how hard he was. He was steel-hard and long, and the idea that I'd made him that way made me more sensitive and needy. The seam of my jeans and the friction his movement was causing, gave me a tiny amount of relief – but it was nowhere near enough. I was throbbing and wet and knew I would never experience a kiss like this, ever again. Even if I spent a lifetime kissing Grantley James, this one would top them all.

"Grantley, I...Oh God," I moaned, my legs widening to accommodate more of his body.

Grantley grabbed my bum in both of his hands and pulling me forwards, slammed me against him and I cried out, consumed with a craving for more. Then his lips were back on mine and he picked me up and carried me away from the table. I flexed my hips, desperate to detonate the pressure inside me, anxious for him to quell the throb between my legs.

"I need to cum," I cried, not thinking about either my embarrassment, or how close my mouth was to Grantley's eardrum.

"Shit," he grumbled, sticking a finger into his ear.

"Oh God, I'm so sorry," I gasped, my hips still writhing of their own accord, obviously knowing what I needed.

"It's fine." Grantley's mouth went back to my neck, nipping and kissing along it and his hands went back to caressing me.

"I hope I didn't deafen you." I pulled at Grantley's hair, pushing my body closer to his to try and gain a little more friction.

"You didn't," Grantley said against my skin. "But thanks for the heads up."

"Really?" I asked breathlessly. "Because the slightest of touches would be all I needed."

Grantley chuckled and took a nibble of my bottom lip.

"Pretty girl, what are you doing to me?" he groaned.

Grantley's arms wrapped tighter around me as he groaned into my mouth and thrust his hips.

"Oh shit, I'm sorry."

Barney's deep voice rumbled behind us and just like that my need and desire curled itself up and puff, it was gone.

"Fucking hell, Barney." Grantley's forehead fell to my shoulder. "Shit."

I squirmed in his arms, urging him to put me down.

"I can't," he groaned. "I might poke Barney's fucking eye out with my boner."

I couldn't help but laugh and buried my face in his neck. He smelled so delicious, I nearly asked Barney to ride around the block for a while.

"Hey guys, I'm real sorry."

I couldn't see him, but I knew he had to be smiling.

"Can you give us a minute?" Grantley asked, carrying me back over to the table, while I clung to him like a baby monkey.

"Yeah sure, I'll go make some coffee or something."

I risked a glance over my shoulder to see the back of Barney with his shoulders shaking with laughter.

"I'm so fucking sorry," Grantley whispered, closing his eyes and shaking his head. "I wasn't expecting him back. He stayed out all night last time he went to see her."

I took a deep breath and smiled. "It's okay. I suppose he did a good thing by coming back."

"He did?" Grantley asked incredulously. "How the hell do you work that out?"

"I…we…well we shouldn't have let it go any further. I'm not a prude or anything, but I'm also not the sort of girl who jumps into bed with someone, just because they're the best kisser on the planet."

"Just this planet?"

Grantley grinned at me and my stomach did another little flip.

"Maybe this and Pluto," I replied, tilting my head as though thinking about it carefully.

"Shit, Pluto is really small," Grantley gasped. "In any case, Pluto isn't classed as a planet any longer, so that doesn't really count."

"It isn't?" I asked with a smile. "Well, I'm a little stuck now as to which other planet that you may be classed as best kisser on."

Grantley looked at me with amusement, brushing some hair from my face.

"Okay. What about Earth and Jupiter? Jupiter is pretty big you know and I think that kiss was more than worthy of Earth and Jupiter's votes."

I thought about *that kiss* and grinned. He was probably right.

Grantley dropped a kiss to the end of my nose and then pulled back to look at me. "You're right, I shouldn't have kissed you like that, I'm sorry."

"No, don't be sorry. It was a great kiss." I cupped Grantley's face with my hand and sighed. "It was just a little too hot and heavy, especially as we weren't even on a date."

Grantley grinned and slowly pulled away, leaving me sitting on the edge of the table. I watched him, swinging my legs, as he ran a hand through his hair and looked towards the kitchen area and then back to me.

"I'll ask Barney to take you home," he said with a hint of disappointment – which I happened to like.

"No, I'll get the train."

I looked at my watch. I'd probably missed the ten-thirty, but could definitely catch the eleven o'clock one.

"No damn way," Barney's voice thundered from the kitchen area. "I'll take you."

I turned around to see Barney reappear. He was still grinning and when I glanced at Grantley, I saw him give his friend the middle finger.

"Barney," I replied with exasperation. "It'll be gone midnight before you get back, and that's if we leave now."

"Not a problem."

"Why are you back anyway?" Grantley asked, moving towards Barney. "She give you the brush off?"

"No, she's going away on business in the morning, so needs to get a good night's sleep."

"Whatever." Grantley punched at Barney's stomach as he walked past, but Barney didn't even flinch. He just flashed a pure white smile.

"Okay Phoebe, you want to get your stuff together?"

"Are you sure?" I asked, jumping down from the table. "I really can get the train."

"Don't make me throw you over my shoulder, sweetheart."

I gave him a big smile and nodded. "Okay, thank you."

I picked up my bag and remembered that my coat was in Grantley's wardrobe. I turned to ask him for it, but he wasn't there and I didn't want to go into his room without asking.

"Erm, my coat is-."

"Here," Grantley replied, handing my wool coat to me.

I took it from him and noticed he had a black hoody on.

"Where are you going?" I asked.

"I'm coming with you." He winked at me and stuffed his wallet into the back pocket of his jeans.

"Ah shit," Barney groaned. "Please don't tell me you're gonna be making out in my back seat."

Grantley twinkled a smile at him. "Maybe."

Warmth spread through me as Grantley's fingers linked with mine, and I hoped that Barney took the long way home.

CHAPTER TWENTY

Grantley

"You gonna tell me about last night?" Barney asked, as he drove us to the Mill House.

I wasn't sure I was going to tell him, because I didn't know how I felt about what had happened. I liked Phoebe; she was great, she was sexy, she made me laugh, and she was going to be here when I left in four weeks' time. Yes, I could stay for a while after we wrapped up filming; I had a couple of months break coming up, but what after that? The fact that I was even thinking about it scared the shit out of me. We'd kissed just once, admittedly it had been the hottest kiss I'd had in a long, long time, but here I was wondering how we could do the long distance thing. When I'd moved in with Serena I hadn't given it this much thought. Because all I'd done, all fucking night, was think about Phoebe and that kiss. I'd jerked off thinking about it, I'd gone for a run on the treadmill in my room at four-thirty in the morning thinking about it and I'd showered, oh and jerked off again, thinking about it.

"What the hell are all these plastic bears about?" I asked, pointing to the third one I'd seen, on the side of the road.

"I heard it's a local tradition thing," Barney replied. "It's known as bear town and don't change the subject."

"I wasn't."

I fucking was.

"She's a good kid, Grant, don't do this if you're not on the same page as her about it."

"What's that supposed to mean?" I turned in my seat to look at the big man.

From his profile I could see he wasn't joking around. He always got a fast pulse in his jaw when he was being serious and that fucker was throbbing to a pretty wild dance beat.

"It means, she doesn't seem the type to want some sort of fuck buddy. I'm guessing she's an all in type of girl."

"And how do you know that's not what I want too?"

Barney glanced at me with one eyebrow cocked.

"I'm not some fucking man whoring douchebag, you know that about me."

"Yes I do," he replied in his deep, rumbling tone. "But I also know you don't do commitment. Fuck, you lasted two months living with Serena and you loved her." His gaze shot back to me again. "Or are you telling me that you're actually in love with Phoebe?"

"No," I spluttered, "of course I'm not."

She'd be pretty easy to fall in love with though.

"I just want you to think about what you're doing, that's all. Make sure she knows what you're wanting before she falls in too deep."

"Yes, Dad," I muttered.

"I'm fucking ten years older than you, so it's not physically possible. Doesn't mean I won't beat your ass though if you carry on giving me shit."

I laughed, but deep down I knew he was right. I did need to have that conversation with Phoebe, but I didn't want to. What if she wanted everything that I didn't, we wouldn't be able to carry on and I hated that idea.

It was almost eight in the evening by the time we finished filming for the day, and all I wanted to do was shower and sleep. I didn't even have the energy to eat, but Alexi had insisted we all sit down together for dinner. I didn't even have Barney for my socially inadequate self to talk to. He'd gone back to Manchester to drive Marcia around and help her with my mother when she finally arrived. Apparently she'd decided to have a stop-over in Paris, so was arriving a couple of days later than originally planned. I'd said no at first, but when Marcia threatened to get back on a plane to LA without waiting for Sue-Ann to arrive if I didn't loan her Barney, I had to change my mind.

Stepping out of the shower, I wrapped a towel around my waist and rubbed another through my hair, before wiping the steam off the mirror over the sink. Leaning forward I peered at my reflection. I looked as tired as I felt. There were grey circles under my eyes and my skin was pale. These damn films took it out of me, with the long hours and all the action scenes I had to film – hence why we only shot one every year and a half. I needed that time for my body to repair. I winced as I rotated my arm. I'd fucked up my shoulder when I was filming a scene where I was thrown against a basement floor. Henrik Dietler, playing the main drug lord, had been a little too enthusiastic in that scene.

With a sigh, I reached for my electric razor, needing to make sure my scruff kept to its usual two-day length. It was surprising how many film critics picked up on shit like that. Turning it on, I started to carefully tidy up, being sure not to go too short. I was pretty much done when I heard my cell ping with a text message. My heart lurched. Only a couple of people had my number, so I just hoped to God it wasn't Marcia or Barney letting me know my mother had already landed and was causing trouble. Finishing off my shave, I moved into the bedroom and found my cell on the mahogany night stand. It was a number I didn't recognize, but when I read the text, I couldn't stop the huge ass grin.

Unknown: Hey it's me, Phoebe. Barney let me have

your number. Just wanted to say hi and hope it's going OK.

I quickly saved her number and started to type out a text then thought better of it and called her instead. As her number rang, I began slowly pacing the room, still smiling. That was what Phoebe did to me – she made me smile.

"Hello."

Phoebe's voice was a little tentative and I wondered if she thought I was mad at her for texting me.

"Hey, pretty girl."

I was right. She gave what sounded like a relieved sigh on the other end.

"Was it okay? Barney giving me your number?"

"God yeah. It was nice getting a text from you," I replied, as I dropped down onto the edge of the huge, four-poster bed. "In fact it was great after a long, tiring day."

"I wasn't sure whether you'd be finished, which was why I sent a text. I didn't expect you to call me back. I just wanted to say hi."

I caught my reflection in the mirror over the dresser and noticed I had a pansy-ass look on my face. Shit, she really was making me a pussy.

"Well hi."

"Hi." It was a soft whisper and I really wanted to see her face and kiss her.

"What're you doing while we're here? You working on anything else?"

"I'm working on Coronation Street tomorrow for two days."

I had no idea what that was, but she sounded excited.

"That's good right?" I asked with a laugh.

"Yes," she cried. "Oh my God, it's fantastic. You really need to Google it. It's our equivalent of The Bold & the Beautiful, but without the bold or beautiful people."

"Not my thing, but I get the picture, so I'm excited for you."

"Hmm... the only problem is, Declan is on it too. We're playing a couple having a meal in the bistro. Which means I've not only got to sit for hours forking cold food around a plate and drinking lukewarm, watered down apple juice out a wine glass, but I have to do it opposite him."

My mood suddenly soured at the thought of her sitting with that prick while he stared at her fucking tits.

"Grantley, did you just growl then?"

Fuck, I think I might have.

"Can't you ask to do something else?" I asked, trying to keep the bitterness from my tone.

I had no damn right to ask her, we only kissed. We weren't even dating.

"It's a really small cast of extras," she replied. "There isn't much else I could ask to do."

"Well if he gives you shit, tell me."

I wanted to add: 'and if he looks at your tits tell me, because I'll punch him in the face', but thought it best not to.

Phoebe sighed. "I'll be fine. He just caught me unawares last time. I'll be ready for him."

"You shouldn't have to be ready for him, the fucking douche. I should've had him thrown off the shoot at the time."

"No, you shouldn't have," she protested. "It would have made things much worse."

I rolled my eyes and decided that was enough talk of Declan, he wasn't worth the oxygen.

"What you doing tonight, pretty girl?"

"Just chilling with Beth and the boys." There was a smile in her voice as she spoke of her family and it made me smile right along with her. "We've been watching *The Secret Life of Pets*, it's hilarious."

I chuckled. "Yeah, I watched it on the flight over here. You're right, it's pretty funny."

"You watched it?" she asked incredulously. "Aren't you a little old?"

"Hey, I'm a kid at heart. Plus, I'd pretty much seen everything else, even been to the premier of two of those showing."

"Ooh listen to you, Mr. Showbiz."

"I try," I replied with a laugh. "Well, say hi to all of them for me."

A warm feeling spread through me as pictures of Phoebe, Beth, and the boys sitting around watching movies flitted through my mind.

"I will. Anyway, I'd better let you go."

I reached for my watch on the night stand and looked at the time – I was going to be late for dinner, but I couldn't give a fuck. I much preferred the idea of talking to Phoebe a little longer, for a couple more hours, if I could.

"It's fine," I replied. "You'll be back on set on Thursday, right?"

"Oh yes, this is just a couple of days' work."

"That's good, it wouldn't be the same without you to talk to at lunch."

Phoebe laughed on the other end. "You really do need to learn to socialise more, Grantley."

"Nope, I'm good."

We continued talking and as Phoebe told me about one of the soap actors falling over and spoiling a scene, there was a knock at my door. I ignored it the first time, but when it happened again but a little louder, I thought I should answer it.

"Hey Phoebes, someone's at my door, just hang on a second."

"Okay."

I padded over to the door and swung it open, to find Francesca on the other side.

"Hey Grantley," she said in her sickly-sweet voice. "Aren't you a sight for sore eyes."

I looked down at myself and realized I was still only dressed in a towel.

"Hey Frannie, sorry, I'm running a little late."

"That's okay, I can come inside and wait." She licked her top lip, and didn't hide the fact that she was ogling my body. "Maybe catch a little more of that body, although there's not much of it I haven't already seen."

"Give me five and I'll be right down."

Francesca nodded. "Okay, I'll save you a place right next to me."

I flashed an empty smile and watched as she sashayed away. Closing the door, I put my phone back to my ear.

"Hey Phoebes, I'm going to have to go."

"Okay. Take care and have a good night," she replied in a quiet, flat tone. "And I hope the next two days go well. Night, Grantley."

"Night Phoe-."

That was it, the line went dead. With a frown, I dropped my cell onto the bed and went to my closet for a pair of jeans and a light sweater, cursing Francesca the whole time for spoiling my night.

CHAPTER TWENTY-ONE

Phoebe

I barely slept the night before, thinking of Grantley and Francesca. I'd heard their conversation at the door and it was evident that she'd had sex with him, if her comments about already seeing him naked were anything to go by. I knew they hadn't done their sex scene yet, so that wasn't how she'd gained knowledge of it. No, they must have had sex before and now they were on location staying in the same house, probably in rooms next door – or maybe even in the same room. And he'd called her Frannie. I'd only ever heard her called Francesca, but Grantley had a pet name for her, just like he called me Phoebes.

God, I hated feeling like this – sick with jealousy and all knotted up inside. It wasn't me. I didn't allow men to get to my heart and make me vulnerable. I'd seen the pain Beth had gone through and didn't want that for myself. No, men just weren't allowed in; until Grantley. He'd wormed his way in there. God, I was such an amateur at being a cold-hearted bitch. I was a very poor three out of ten at keeping my heart locked up, or was it simply I'd never met anyone who I'd wanted to get to my heart before – until Grantley.

All in all, it had been a shitty night, followed by an even shittier morning. Declan was being as hateful as he'd been a few days earlier.

He'd been throwing barbed comments out at me all morning and when there was a break in filming, he felt it necessary to share his disdain of me with Jack and Peter- two other extras who were supposed to be two businessmen having lunch on the next table. Then to top it all, Declan continued his pecking at my head over our lunch break.

"Don't you just hate people who use who they're sleeping with to get better parts?" he asked Jack.

"It didn't work for me, Declan," Jack replied with a laugh.

"Who was that then?" Peter asked, weirdly taking a sip of the cold tea that was supposed to be a pint of beer.

"Why have you brought that with you?" I asked, pointing at the murky liquid. "You do know the lunch truck has refreshments."

Peter nodded. "Yeah, but I like this. Anyway Jack, tell us who you sold your body to for a part you didn't get."

"The game show host," Jack declared. "He promised me a part in a new sitcom he was writing."

"Oh no," I groaned. "Who got it instead?"

"Would you believe, Whoopi Goldberg?"

Peter and I exchanged glances, words unspoken as we looked back at the freckled faced, ginger haired Jack.

"I know right," Jack said, with a knowing nod of his head. "Thankfully, it never made it to TV. According to the reviews from the rushes, Goldberg just didn't cut it as a gay, English man."

"Excuse me," Declan said, holding up a palm. "But you don't quite understand what I'm saying."

"Yes we do," Peter said. "Never shag a bloke for a part unless you get it in writing first."

I burst out laughing at the exact moment I began to chew on a piece of chicken. As I laughed, I took in air that caught in the back of my throat at the exact same time as my piece of chicken, and it caused me to have a coughing fit.

"Shit, take a drink of water," Jack said, passing a glass to me. "Don't die on us, love. Are you okay?"

"Yep," I croaked, before taking a swig from the glass.

"It's that bloody chicken, it's far too chewy," Peter complained, shoving his food around his plate and peering down to inspect it.

"That's why I had the beef," Jack added, patting me on the back. "Better?"

I nodded, took another sip of water, and croaked out a 'yes'.

"Are you sure that's beef?" Peter asked. "It's a bit grey to be beef."

"Yes, it's beef. At least it said it was beef on the chalkboard."

"You're still not getting my point," Declan complained.

I sighed heavily, deciding I'd had enough of his bitching. "Listen, Declan," I said looking up at him.

"What?"

Every word that I wanted to say slipped from my mind. I was blank, because hanging in Declan's wiry black beard was my piece of chicken. I shot a look at Peter, who seeing my widened eyes guessed something was wrong. He turned to Declan and as soon as his eyes landed on him, a huge smile enveloped his face.

"Declan-." I started, before feeling a sharp kick to my shin as Peter cleared his throat, and gave a short shake of his head.

"Phoebe, what is it?" Declan was irritated.

I shook my head, declining to answer.

"I'll tell you something," Peter said with a grin. "This chicken is so chewy I'm sure it could bounce right off the plate."

Declan huffed and pushed his plate to one side. "You people are so..."

"So what?" Jack asked, looking up from his beef. "Oh shit, right." He'd spotted the piece of errant chicken and started to laugh.

Declan scraped his chair back and stood up, looking down on the three of us, while chicken still dangled from his beard.

"I'm going to the green room for ten minutes meditation. I feel my stress levels rising."

"You do that," Jack called after his disappearing back. "And maybe have a little snack while you're there. You know, keep your energy levels up."

"Yeah," Peter added. "I highly recommend the chewy chicken."

I couldn't stop laughing as Declan gave a disdainful look over his shoulder and disappeared.

"You two are terrible. You should have let me tell him."

"No way," Peter replied. "He's a tosser, he deserves it."

"Yeah, he does," Jack added. "Now, tell us who you slept with that's got his undies in a twist."

The rest of the day went by without another word from Declan. I wasn't sure whether Jack or Peter had warned him to be quiet, but he didn't speak a single utterance to any of us. Even when the director asked us to be more animated and actually look like we were having a conversation, all Declan said to me was 'blah, blah, blah'. He threw a few dirty looks my way, and Peter and Jack's way too, but no words - plus his beard was clean too, so it was a huge relief all around. I'd explained everything to Peter and Jack and swore on the spirit of Sir Alan Rickman that I hadn't actually slept with Grantley. I admit, I left out the part about the kiss in his hotel suite, but that was more an omission of the facts than a lie, so Sir Alan could rest in peace.

So after what had been a crap day, finally, I was home and walking into the hallway with a huge sigh of relief.

"Hi," I cried. "I'm home."

"In the kitchen," Beth cried. "Opening wine. The boys have gone to their friend, Toby's house for a sleepover."

I entered the kitchen, shrugged off my coat, dumped it on a chair with my bag and grabbed a glass from Beth's hand.

"Oh God, thank you," I said, closing my eyes as I sipped the cool, crisp wine. "I've had to sit opposite Declan and pretend I like his company all bloody day."

"Ooh," Beth groaned. "Nasty."

"I know. He's been a total dick. Dropping hints about me sleeping with Grantley, just so I could get three sodding lines."

"Shit. Have you slept with him?" Beth's mouth dropped open as she plonked down onto a chair.

"No. You know I haven't."

"I know no such thing," she protested. "I know he brought you home at almost midnight the other night, after spending the evening in his suite."

"Yes, and I told you that we kissed. So, you know I'd tell you if I'd had sex with him."

"Would you?"

"Yes!" I cried and then belched. "Oops sorry, I've been drinking warm apple juice all day. And again, yes, of course I'd tell you."

"If you do have sex, you will be careful, won't you?"

I slapped at Beth's arm, shocked at her suggestion. I'd always been super careful when having sex. I loved kids, but didn't want one with someone I wasn't going to spend the rest of my life with and I certainly didn't want any nasty diseases, thank you very much.

"I always use condoms, as well as being on the pill."

Beth rolled her eyes. "I didn't mean take physical care of yourself, although that's a given. I meant I want you to take care of yourself mentally. I don't want you to end up with a broken heart."

My mind warped back to the conversation I'd heard between Grantley and Francesca and how I'd felt all day because of it.

"I think it's too late to take mental care of myself," I sighed.

Beth reached out a hand and rubbed my forearm. "You've really fallen for him, after one kiss?"

"Yeah, but it was one hell of a kiss."

"Well he is Addison Yates, I wouldn't expect anything less."

She giggled and drank more of her wine before we fell into silence, me contemplating the stem of my wine glass and Beth looking through the kitchen window, to the darkening sky.

After a few minutes, I glanced at my sister, to see her pretty face was masked with worry and I hated that she was feeling that way. Whether it was the boys, herself, or even me that had put that look there, I didn't care. I was supposed to be making sure she didn't have any stress while we waited for her results.

"Beth," I whispered. "Please don't worry. Everything is going to be okay. I know it is."

She looked at me with tear filled eyes and let out a long breath. "What if it isn't Phoebes? What if I have cancer and they can't cure it? What happens to my babies?"

"Firstly, you're not going to have it and secondly nothing will happen to them."

"If I die, you do not let Steven get them. Promise me." She wagged a finger at me as the tears now started to trickle down her cheeks. "You have to fight to keep them, and please don't let Mum and Dad have them because, ugh, that would be worse."

"You don't even have to ask that," I replied, feeling a huge rock of pain in my chest. "I will always take care of them. He'd never get them, neither would Mum and Dad. Even if I had to leave the country and give us all false identities."

She giggled through her tears and caught hold of my hand. "You really would do that, wouldn't you?"

I nodded and shrugged my shoulders as though it was a given.

"But what if you're not here?" she asked. "What if you and Grantley fall in love and he takes you to live in Hollywood? What happens then?"

"Do you actually think I'd go if you were ill? And that's not likely to happen, anyway."

"What?" she asked. "You falling in love with him, or him taking you to live in Hollywood?" Her smile was soft and gentle and I had to wonder, as I had a thousand, million times, how Steven could have left her.

"Both," I replied.

"Really, you don't think it's likely that you'll fall in love with him?"

I wanted to say I wouldn't, that it would never happen, but for some reason my tongue was suddenly too big for my mouth and I couldn't form the words. What the hell was happening to me? Why couldn't I just say 'no, I will not fall in love with Grantley James'?

"Because you know you probably will."

"Shit," I groaned. "Did I say that out loud?"

"Yep, you did."

"Oh fuck."

"Yeah," Beth said with a grin. "Oh fuck."

"I can't, Beth," I protested. "You're not to let me. I'll be right in the shit if I do. He lives in America and I'm pretty sure he's had, or is having sex with Francesca Woodfield."

"But he kissed you."

"I know." I chewed on my lip, hoping drawing some blood might stop me thinking about the sickie feeling in my stomach.

"So is he definitely sleeping with her now?" Beth's eyes were now wild with anger, as she gulped back the rest of her wine and reached for the bottle. "He kissed you and is shagging someone else?"

"I don't know for certain, it's just what I overheard."

I recanted the telephone conversation I'd had with Grantley and what I'd heard when I was holding on the line. I told her and then kind of wished I hadn't, because it made me feel even more jealous, if that was possible.

When I finished, Beth looked at me, perplexed.

"That doesn't prove anything. She might have meant she'd seen him with no top on, or didn't he do one of those Men's Health, take care of your bollocks, ad campaigns?"

My memory flicked through everything I'd read about Grantley, but I didn't recall a naked photo-shoot of him cupping his balls, or anything like that.

"I don't think so."

"Well there may be an explanation for what she said. Don't jump the gun until you've asked him."

I almost spat out my wine. "Ask him? You have got to be joking? No way, that makes me sound even more stalkerish than Kathy Bates in Misery. Nope, I'll just keep my distance."

"But he might not be sleeping with *her*, which then means *you'll* miss out on sleeping with him and I'm sure you don't want to risk that. I mean," she said with a deep breath, "what if he's really, really good."

I thought back, to seeing the outline of his dick in his sweat pants and how big and hard he felt in his jeans when he kissed me. Shit, she was right. What if I gave the possibility of *that* up, just because he wasn't a virgin and may have entered Francesca's tower with his magic sword.

"Hang on a minute," I cried. "How did we get from talking about the boys' future, to my possible future sex life in a matter of sentences?"

Beth shrugged. "Dunno, we're just good I guess. Anyway, whether you like it or not, you fancy him like mad. You could possibly end up falling in love with him, so you have no alternative but to ask him what's going on with not only you two, but him and Francesca as well."

"I really don't think he thinks of me that way."

Just then a text beeped on my mobile. I glanced down and saw it was from Grantley. Snatching up my phone, I swiped the screen to read it.

Grantley: Hi pretty girl. Just wanted to check in and say I'm looking forward to seeing you on Thursday – G x

I couldn't help but smile, even if he was having sex with Francesca, he still made me want to grin and sing Donny Osmond songs – hey don't judge me, my mum loved him and played his stuff non-stop when we were kids. They were my formative years and she ruined me musically, what can I say.

"Is that him?"

Beth evidently hadn't missed the soppy look on my face either.

"Yes." I turned the phone to show her the text.

She grabbed it off me and shoved it closer to her face. Then before I had chance to realise what she was doing, she shot up from her chair rushed into the downstairs loo and locked the door.

"Beth!" I roared. "What are you doing? Please don't tell me you're texting him back."

Silence.

"Beth, I mean it. If you're doing what I think you're doing, I'll kill you."

The lock clicked open and Beth came out of the loo with a big grin on her face.

"You can thank me by telling me how good he is in bed, when the time comes."

She dropped the phone into my hand and sauntered back into the kitchen.

"What have you done?" I groaned, bringing the screen to life. "Oh for fuck's sake, Beth."

Phoebe: Hi. I'm fine. Thank you handsome, but tell me, are you shagging Francesca Woodfield?

"BETH!"

CHAPTER TWENTY-TWO

Grantley

"What the fuck?" I stared down at my cell, reading the text that Phoebe had sent to me.

Was I sleeping with Francesca? Where the hell had she got that idea from? Why the hell did it concern her?

Okay, scratch that last one, I guess when you've almost got someone off with a kiss it kind of is their concern if you're sleeping with someone else, but why she'd ask me that, I had no fucking clue. I dialed Phoebe's number – this wasn't something we could discuss by text. It rang a couple of times and then went to voicemail.

"You've reached Phoebe's phone, sorry I can't answer, but leave your number and I'll call you back... maybe." She ended the message with a giggle, which for some reason wound me even tighter.

"Phoebe, I think we need to talk."

I hung up and looked down at my phone. Maybe I should have said more than that, it might sound like I had something I needed to tell her – like 'yes I have slept with Francesca, but I need to tell you personally.'

I dialed her number again, but this time it went straight to voicemail – she'd damn well dropped my call. Okay, a text it was then.

Grantley: Phoebe answer your phone.

I waited a couple of minutes and tried again, but once more it went straight to voicemail.

Grantley: I mean it Phoebe. Answer your fucking phone this time. I want to talk to you, not fucking text.

I dialed her number and waited, fully expecting her to answer, but once again the little minx dropped it. I was slowly losing patience and wondering whether one damn kiss was worth all the hassle. But I guess the fact that I was desperate to get ahold of her and put her ridiculous notion to bed, kind of told me it was.

Grantley: I'm seriously pissed now, Phoebe. I'm going to call one more time and if you don't answer your god damn phone, I will not be responsible for my actions when we get back on set.

I dialed her number again and waited, my fingers drumming on the arm of the chair I was sitting in. Finally, I heard her breathing on the other end of the line.

"What the hell makes you think I'm sleeping with Francesca?" I went straight in there, no need for the formalities.

"I-I. It wasn't me," she replied tentatively.

I sighed. "What wasn't you? What the fuck are you talking about?"

"I didn't send the text. It was Beth."

"And why the hell did Beth send the text?"

It was almost silent on the other end, apart from her soft exhales, which were fucking turning me on. I was imagining her lips slightly parted and her chest rising and falling slowly while she blinked those damn long lashes of hers. Fuck, I was fucked beyond fuckdom if just the sound of her thinking got me hard.

An image of Phoebe about to touch herself was pushed from my head as she spoke.

"It was my fault. I told her that I thought you were sleeping with Francesca." Her words were rushed and while I couldn't see her face, I knew it would be red with embarrassment.

"Why would you think that, pretty girl?"

I let out a breath, wishing that we didn't have one more day shooting at the Mill House. I didn't know what this girl had done to me, but she made me feel all kinds of soppy shit.

"I heard her when we spoke on the phone the other night. It sounded like she knows what you look like naked and you called her Frannie."

I furrowed my brow, wondering what the hell she was talking about.

"That's her name."

"Her name is Francesca, but you called her Frannie, like you...oh shit, I'm being ridiculous. Honestly Grantley, ignore me. I'm being stupid and what you do really is no business of mine. It was one kiss and I have no right to question you."

"Okay," I replied. "Firstly, I've always called her Frannie, so I'm not sure why that's upset you, but we'll come back to that-."

"Really Grantley, I'm being silly. Please, can we just forget about it?"

"No, we can't forget about it," I snapped before softening my tone. "It was obviously important for you to ask, or to at least mention it to Beth. So let me clarify, I'm not and never have slept with Francesca, *and* it was almost two kisses, but if you've forgotten that then I'm obviously losing my fucking touch."

Phoebe giggled on the other end, causing me to let out a sigh of relief.

Told you, totally fucking fucked from here to fuckdom come.

"I am sorry," she whispered. "I shouldn't have said anything."

"No, you should have asked me." I pushed up from the chair and walked over to the lounge window, watching Alexi shooting a scene with Francesca and Henrik over by the mill pool. This was a real beautiful place, but I just wanted to be back at the studio. "What you heard," I continued, "was Francesca flirting with me, because I kind of forgot I was only wearing a towel when I answered the door."

"How do you forget that?" Phoebe asked incredulously.

I grinned. "Because I was talking to you. You've kind of messed with my head a little."

"Ooh." She sounded surprised.

"Yeah, I'm a little shocked too." I paused, waiting for Phoebe to respond, but when she didn't I continued. "So, is there anything else you want to ask me?"

"Yes, actually there is," Phoebe replied.

"Okay, go on."

I held my breath, wondering what she was going to ask. I had nothing to hide from her but if she was going to ask me what my feelings were toward her, well, I wasn't sure how I was going to answer.

"You say you forgot you had a towel on, but couldn't you feel how cold your nadgers were when you opened the door?"

Fuck, this girl slayed me.

CHAPTER TWENTY-THREE

PHOEBE

I don't think I had ever been so excited to go to work. The sun was shining, my train was on time, it wasn't packed with sweaty commuters, and Grantley was going to be back on set.

The first few scenes that were being shot didn't include any extras, so we had to hang around in the holding area. It was boring as hell, but at least I managed to read some more of my book, which also kept me away from Declan. I saw him holding court over at the card table, talking in a loud voice about his two days 'on the street', but no one was really very interested in what he had to say. We'd all been on a soap opera a time or two, he was no one special. At least his mum would enjoy seeing him on screen in a few weeks' time - apparently she invited her sister around to watch every one of Declan's appearances.

"Hey, you okay?" Trish, one of the other extras asked, sliding into the armchair next to me.

"Oh hi, Trish." I closed my *Kindle* and smiled at her, even though I was getting to a good bit and really wanted to finish the chapter. "I'm fine thanks. How about you?"

"Fine, a little bored. I forgot to bring my book with me." She nodded down at my *Kindle*. "Yours any good?"

"Yes, really good. So," I said looking around the room, "it's a little busy in here today."

"Yeah, apparently after we've done our evacuation of the factory scene, Alexi wants to reshoot the casino scene, so they've all had to come back in."

I nodded in understanding. A lot of directors used the same group of extras for every scene, but because this film had quite a few crowd scenes, Alexi didn't want the same people to be shown on screen all the time – he liked to think using different extras for different scenes gave the film realism. Says the director of a film where the leading man flies in through a church window on a para glider.

"I heard about Declan, by the way," Trish said, leaning closer to me. "What he said to you."

I drew in a breath and rubbed at my forehead, concern washing over me. Was Trish also going to tell me that I was a whore?

"He's a twat," she said. "We all think so. No one really thinks you got the three lines because you slept with Grantley James."

"They don't?" I asked, looking up at her expectantly.

"No, do they heck. Even if you did, good for you. Who wouldn't want to ride that pony? I'd have been happy with one word if it meant I got the chance to see whether he lived up to his reputation."

"Reputation?"

"You know," she replied, thrusting up her hips manically. "Mister Lova-Lova."

I couldn't help but laugh. "Well I have no idea, we really are just friends."

"Well if I was just friends with that sexy hunk of a man, I'd be doing everything in my power to make sure he realised exactly how good a friend I could be." Trish winked at me and pushed up from her chair. "Right, I'm off for a pee. See you later. Oh, looks like you're being called."

I looked over to where she was nodding and saw Joey, one of the runners coming towards me

"See you later, Phoebe." Trish waved at Joey and walked away.

"Hi Joey," I said, smiling up at him. "You need me on set for something?"

Joey bent down and spoke closely to my ear. "Grantley has asked if you can go to his trailer. He's in between shooting outside shots."

I watched Joey carefully, wondering whether he thought the same as Declan about me, seeing as I'd been summoned to Grantley James' trailer. His face was unreadable though, probably because he had to do this sort of thing a million times a day on film sets.

"Okay, thanks."

He gave me a shy smile and walked away. Yep, he definitely thought I'd been called for a booty call.

When I got to his trailer, the door was flung open and there at the top of the stairs was the beautiful sight of Grantley James dressed in a slim black suit, with a white open-necked shirt and, swoon upon swoon, he was wearing his glasses.

"Hi," I said, giving him a huge smile.

"Hey, pretty girl."

The smile he returned was beautiful, but also a little sad. There was no light in his eyes and his face barely moved a muscle.

Standing to one side, Grantley gave me room to get through the door. As soon as it was shut behind us, I was turned by the shoulders and pulled into his arms. Soft, welcoming lips landed on mine as his hands moved up to thread through my hair.

It was a quick, intense kiss. Nowhere near as suggestive as the one in his suite, but it was pretty good nonetheless.

"Wow," I said, leaning my head back to look at him with starry eyes. "That was an amazing welcome."

"I missed you."

Grantley dropped his forehead to mine and pursed his lips to kiss the tip of my nose. He didn't move, but took in a long, slow breath.

"Hey, what's wrong?" I asked, running a palm down his cheek.

Grantley didn't say anything but wrapped his arms around my shoulders. My heart thumped wildly as my own arms snaked under his jacket to hug him back. There was little to no space between us, and we were breathing in unison. The room was silent and everything about the moment seemed so much more than it possibly could be. We barely knew each other, he was a Hollywood Star and I was a nobody, we'd had one amazing kiss but standing there holding each other, it felt as though we were two lovers taking comfort from the one person in the world that we knew we could rely on. I wasn't stupid enough to think it was anything more than Grantley needing a hug for some reason, but I didn't care because he needed a hug from me.

"Sue-Ann arrived," he said quietly against my shoulder.

As he said her name, I noticed how his body stiffened. I didn't blame him, she was a crap mother from what he'd told me, and she made mine seem as protective as Sarah Connor in Terminator.

"It's been bad then?"

Grantley nodded. "Yep, she's a fucking nightmare."

He started to pull away from me and I really wanted to cling on for dear life and keep him there, but that would have been weird. So, when his arms dropped to his sides, I let my own fall too and took a step back.

"Has she done anything particular, or is she just being your mother?"

Grantley let out a humourless laugh. "No, if she was being my mother she'd have Skyped me and asked if I was eating properly, blown me a kiss, and told me she loved me. No, instead she turns up at my hotel at almost midnight, having missed her earlier flight and not telling us, leaving Barney hanging around the airport for almost two hours wondering whether she'd been picked up by Customs and was having a full anal cavity search."

"Oh dear." I had no idea what else to say. "So how did she get to the hotel?"

"A fucking taxi that I had to get out of bed and go down and pay for because she had no cash on her. But that wasn't the best part," Grantley said, his nostrils flaring. "She comes up to my suite, insists I throw Barney out of his bed, so she could have it and then proceeds to rip the lining of her case and produce two huge fucking bags of coke."

"Oh shit," I gasped. "You're not joking are you?"

Grantley shook his head. "Nope, I'm fucking not. That was the reason for the stopover in Paris. Apparently, she owed a dealer a favor and that was it. Sue-Ann became the mule for probably five-grand worth of cocaine. Small fries I guess, but enough to get her thrown in jail and get me sacked from the franchise."

"Oh shit."

"Yeah shit, but do you know what she fucking said when I screamed at her?"

I shook my head.

"If you gave me enough money, I wouldn't have to do this for a living. Then she called me an ungrateful brat."

Grantley looked totally broken. His shoulders were sloped and his usual ramrod straight back was hunched over.

"I'm so sorry," I whispered, reaching for his hand.

"I fucking hate her, Phoebe. She's a fucking leech on both me and society and I swear I actually wouldn't care if she got caught and had to wear orange for the next twenty years. And let me tell you, I for one would not be visiting her."

"What are you going to do?"

He breathed deeply and pulling his hand from mine, ran it through his hair.

"I made her call the dealer and tell him to meet her first thing this morning – Barney followed her and watched her hand over the back-pack. Other than that, I have no idea. I'm hoping Marcia manages to get out of her what she's doing here, because all she keeps saying to me is 'can't a mother visit her child', which is a fucking joke. She has a reason for being here and as soon as I found out what it is, she's on the next plane home."

"Can't you just give her some money? Didn't you say she said you don't give her enough?"

"I asked her how much she wanted, but she said she didn't want any."

"You just have to hope Marcia cracks her then." I chewed on my lip, having no idea what advice or help that I could give to him. "I wish I could help, but I don't know her to have any idea what her plan is."

Grantley looked up at me and winced. "Well actually, that's a favor I was going to ask you."

"W-what?" I stammered, recognising unease in his eyes. "What can I do?"

"Have dinner with us tonight," he rushed out, grabbing my hand and pulling on it pleadingly. "She's insisting that we eat together in the hotel restaurant and she got hold of my phone and saw our texts so is also insisting that you come."

"How did she get your phone?"

"She took it from my room while I was sleeping."

My mouth gaped open.

"Yeah," Grantley said with an eye roll. "She's a fucking joy. She's done it before, looking through my contacts for people that she thinks she can fucking get favors from when I'm not around to hand out the ready cash. Unfortunately, she thinks it would be 'the best thing ever to meet your English chick'."

"She actually called me that?" I winced.

"Yeah, and I'm so damn sorry. If you don't come to dinner, she'll come to the set and I cannot risk that Phoebes. She'll ruin my fucking career."

I put my hands to my waist and paced away from him, thinking about Grantley's request. Would one dinner hurt?

"She does know that we're just friends doesn't she?"

Grantley sighed and shook his head. "Phoebe, you know and I know we're not just fucking friends. I can't contemplate what the hell we are at the moment, not with having to deal with Sue-Ann, but 'just friends' doesn't fucking cut it."

With anger seeping from him, Grantley pulled off his glasses and rubbed his eyes.

"If you don't want to do it, fine," he snapped. "But please don't start with this shit now."

"Hey," I cried. "I have no idea what we are, so don't you dare shout at me. If I started calling you my boyfriend you'd damn well freak out, so stop being a knob. You tell me what we are Grantley, so I know what to say to your damn mother at dinner."

Grantley threw his hands in the air. "I have no idea, either. I just know I missed you and needed to hug you and tell you about my fuck up of a mother. That's all I can give you right now, Phoebe."

"I haven't asked for anything." I threw my arm out at him. "You're the one who said we aren't just friends. I'm simply trying to understand what possible reason she could have for wanting me there."

"I have no clue." He shrugged. "Probably just to make me look like a dick, knowing her. It's like it's her life's plan to make my life shit, so if she can put you off me she will."

"Well isn't she a piece of work?" I shook my head and blew out my cheeks. "I'll come to dinner, *because* you're my friend, but if she starts on me Grantley, I won't be responsible for what I say to her."

"Thank you," he gasped and once more pulled me into a hug. "Don't forget what a waste of space she is."

"I won't," I groaned. "Now let me go, before you suffocate me."

Grantley let me go and grabbed my hand, bringing it to his mouth.

"Thanks for being a good friend, Phoebes. I can't tell you how much I appreciate it."

I gave him a small smile and hoped that I didn't regret it.

CHAPTER TWENTY-FOUR

Grantley

I couldn't believe I'd persuaded Phoebe to have dinner with us. In fact I couldn't believe I'd wanted to persuade her. Introducing her to Sue-Ann was a fucking crazy idea, especially if I wanted us to see more of each other.

My mother wasn't known for welcoming my dates or girlfriends into the family fold – not that I'd introduced her to that many. Who wanted a woman they liked to know that they came from stock so shit you had seriously considered having a vasectomy to nullify the bloodline? After careful consideration, I hadn't gone through with it, but that was mostly because I was a pussy. Thinking about having someone touch my dick and nuts for something other than pleasure, made said nuts shrivel up in fear.

Barney was taking Phoebe home to change, and then bringing her back for dinner, leaving me alone in my suite with Sue-Ann, because fucking Marcia had insisted she meet us at dinner. I was damn mad as shit about that idea. I'd asked her to come over to the UK to help me get rid of Sue-Ann, not leave me alone with her. Marcia though, told me to 'shut the fuck up' and let her handle it her way. Trouble was, I didn't see her handling it at all.

I was just finishing getting dressed, tucking my dress shirt into my pants, when Sue-Ann started shouting and banging on my door.

"Grantley, where the hell is the vodka?"

I rolled my eyes and sauntered over to the door, slowly pulling it open.

"What?"

"I asked you, where is the vodka?"

I looked her up and down and shook my head slowly. "Not a chance are you wearing that to dinner."

The microscopic skirt in a fucking hideous green lace fabric, just barely covered her ass, with her spindly, bruised legs hanging out the bottom like the legs of a fucking baby bird hanging out of a nest. The top half of her outfit wasn't much better. I had no idea what you called it but it looked like a scarf that she'd wrapped around her chest and then wound and tied it around her neck. The fact that gravity was playing a big part in things, meant it looked less than desirable.

"What the hell's wrong with it?" she cried, looking down at her body.

"Well if you have to ask, you're more of a drunk than I thought. You look like a hooker trying to score a john to get money for drugs. Oh, I'm sorry," I cried. "That's exactly what you are."

"Don't you speak to me like that. I'm still your mother."

"Yeah, I know, so you keep saying. But, I mean it. You're not eating dinner with me dressed like that. At least put on a bra and a blouse."

"This is my newest outfit," she complained. "There's nothing wrong with it."

"Yes there is. Change it and no I don't have vodka."

With that I slammed the door in her face. I could not look at her one more minute.

Where the fuck were Barney and Phoebe and why the hell had I agreed to Marcia meeting us at dinner?

There was another knock on the door and a screeching of my name on the other side, but I ignored it and finished up getting dressed. Finally, once I was ready, I picked up my cell and shot Marcia a text.

Grantley: I don't care what your plan is, just make sure it works!

I got nothing in return, because I knew she'd be ignoring me. That was how Marcia dealt with me most of the time – ignore me until she had what I wanted. She just better make sure I got what I wanted this time.

Finally, after a half hour of hiding in my bedroom like a damn sulky teenager, I heard the door to the suite open and Barney's deep voice speaking. I snagged my wallet off the dresser and rushed from my room, just in time to see Sue-Ann standing with her arms crossed, surveying Phoebe.

"Pretty girl," I said in a low voice as I approached her.

Phoebe swung around to face me and crossed her eyes and stuck out her tongue – a move I was guessing she got from the boys. I grinned at her and felt relief seep through me that Sue-Ann hadn't managed to put her off in the two minutes they'd been alone, because let me tell you, she's that fucking bad she could do it easily.

"You look hot," Phoebe said winking, before smiling wide and calming me down.

"And so do you."

I took hold of her hand and tugged her to me so that I could kiss her rose pink lips. She smelled damn good too, not her usual flowery perfume, but a little muskier.

"You ready for this?" I murmured against her ear, sneaking a glance at my mother, who was now at least wearing a shirt, albeit a little tight.

"As I'll ever be."

I moved in front of her, to see Sue-Ann watching us carefully, her beady eyes narrowed on us.

"Sue-Ann, this is Phoebe."

"Yeah, I kinda gathered that honey," Sue-Ann drawled. "You're not what I expected."

"Oh, okay." Phoebe gave a nervous giggle and held her hand out to Sue-Ann. "It's great to meet you anyway."

Sue-Ann looked disdainfully at Phoebe's offered hand and then slowly back up to her face. After a few seconds she curled her lip and lifted her chin to me.

"Are we going for dinner or what?"

"Not unless you show some manners." I moved to Phoebe's side and picked up her hand that was now at her side. "You take Phoebe's hand and shake it with the goodwill in which it was offered."

Sue-Ann looked as though she was thinking of something to say – her tell was the way her cheek twitched – but evidently nothing came. She took Phoebe's hand and gave it a limp shake.

"Pleasure to meet you, I'm sure." Sue-Ann's voice was simpering as she flashed a tight smile at Phoebe.

I. Will. Fucking. Kill. Her if she ruins this for me.

"Let's go and get this over and done with."

I took Phoebe's hand back in mine and gave it a reassuring squeeze. Whether it was to reassure her or me, I had no fucking clue.

"Are you coming with us, Barney?" Phoebe asked as we moved toward the door.

I gave my friend the wide-eyed look that said 'please come with'. He quirked his lips up at one side and studied me for a few seconds before nodding.

"Sure. Should be a fun night."

I groaned under my breath. Marcia and Sue-Ann at each other's throats was bad enough, but if either of them upset Phoebe, I wasn't sure I'd hold it together. She'd come tonight to support me, as a *friend* and I would not tolerate her being made to feel uncomfortable because of the shit-fest going down at the dinner table.

When we reached the hotel restaurant, after an uncomfortably silent elevator ride, I was relieved to see it was fairly empty but for a couple of business dinners and an elderly couple. I'd chosen the hotel restaurant rather than somewhere more public, because with Sue-Ann in tow, I couldn't risk getting photographed by the press. It didn't bother me normally, it was part of being famous, but I *did not* want the mother from fucking hell being snapped alongside me.

When the Maître De led us to our table, Marcia was already sitting there. She looked less than amused to be there, if her pinched mouth and drumming fingers was anything to go by.

"Hey Marcia," I said, bending down to kiss her cheek. "You been waiting long?"

"No, I'm trying to limit the time I have to be here," she snapped, turning her head towards Sue-Ann, who was pushing herself up against the Maître de who had shown us to our table. "I've been making calls, but came up with nothing."

"Shit," I muttered. "Okay, let's keep on it."

I held a chair out for Phoebe, putting her in between Barney and me, which meant Marcia and Sue-Ann were sitting next to each other, unfortunately. That could go one of two ways; they'd play nice and get along for my sake, or Marcia would stab my mother with a salad fork – my money was on the latter, with a steak knife to the eye for good measure.

"Are you okay?" Phoebe asked, as we sat down. "You look as though you're going to burst out of your clothes and go green at any moment."

I reached under the table and snagged her hand again, as I leaned closer to speak quietly without my mother hearing. "Marcia's been trying to find out what Sue-Ann wants, why she's here, but she's come up with nothing."

"She may just want to visit you." Phoebe sounded hopeful.

"Nope. No way. She's got an ulterior motive and it scares the shit out of me that I have no damn idea what it is."

"You're sure it's not just money?"

I nodded and reached for the water jug. "Yes, I told you, I asked her to name her price and she didn't want it. So no, it's not money."

"It might be part of her plan, because she wants a *huge* amount of money. An amount that she knows you'll say no to."

"Maybe. I guess she knows she'll only get so much from me," I sighed. "But whatever it is she wants, she's not getting it from me. She had her chance."

As I looked over, I heard Sue-Ann asking for a bottle of vodka to be brought to the table. Thank God I asked for a table with as much privacy as possible, because I knew without doubt that the night was going to go to shit.

CHAPTER TWENTY-FIVE

Phoebe

We had only just finished our starters and to say Sue-Ann was pissed was an understatement. She'd downed half the bottle of vodka she'd insisted on having brought to the table, interspersing each shot with a swig of wine. She'd barely touched her scallops, pushing the plate away after just one mouthful. And, of course she was getting louder with each passing minute.

"So Phoebe," she slurred, draping her arm over the back of her chair. "How many of your leading actors have you slept with?"

I shifted in my seat and inhaled a long, patient breath.

"Keep your voice down," Grantley hissed, looking over at a table of business men who kept looking over.

It may well have been him that they'd recognised, but I wouldn't be shocked if it wasn't the drunken, pitiful figure of his mother that had drawn their attention.

"Jus askin a quesion," Sue-Ann said almost incoherently. "Well?"

"None," I replied, through gritted teeth.

"Sue-Ann." Grantley snarled her name out in warning. "Keep your dirty mouth shut."

"Oh chill out, I'm only asking your girlfrien a quesion any mother would ask. I mean," she said, pointing at me, her eyelids drooping. "You don't wan her givin you somein nasy, do you?"

It was getting more and more difficult to understand her, and Grantley was definitely about to lose his temper, big style.

"Hey," Grantley hissed, leaning over the table and pointing a long finger at her. "Shut your damn drunken mouth and give me that bottle. *Now.*"

Su-Ann clutched the bottle to her like she was cradling a child, which was bloody ironic, considering the sort of mother she was.

"I haven't finished yet," she pouted.

"Oh yes you fucking have." Marcia reached across and grabbed it from Sue-Ann's arms. "You're a damn embarrassment. All it takes is for someone to snap a picture of you and it'll be all over the press."

"Thas wha happens when you a movie star." Sue-Ann reached for Grantley's hand. "Baby boy, you know I jus lookin out for you, right?"

"Don't call me that," Grantley snapped, his body stiffening. "I'm neither a baby nor a boy."

"You're my baby boy," she simpered with a childlike giggle.

"Sue-Ann," Barney said softly. "Why don't you go to the bathroom and freshen up a little. By the time you get back your chicken parmigiana will be here."

"I don't *need* to freshen up, *Barnabus.*"

Her head lolled as she sneered at poor Barney, who was merely trying to play the peace maker.

"Go to the damn john, Sue-Ann."

"Wha you gonna do if I don't, *Marcia*?"

Marcia gave her the sweetest of smiles and grabbed Sue-Ann's hand and evidently squeezed it a little too hard, because Sue-Ann let out a little yelp.

A couple more heads turned our way and I could see Grantley was becoming more uncomfortable. His eyes looked around the restaurant, searching out anyone with a camera.

"It's okay," I whispered, putting a hand on his. "No one can see us that well."

We were positioned in a corner behind a couple of huge plants. Yes, they'd hear us, but no one would know it was Grantley, unless they'd seen us walk in.

"If you don't go and fucking sort yourself out, I'll damn well march you in there myself and flush your head down the fucking toilet. Understand?"

Sue-Ann grabbed at Marcia's hand, pulling it free of her own. "Fuck you."

As she pushed up from the table and wobbled towards the bathroom, I heard Grantley exhale and saw him place an unsteady hand onto the table.

"I need her to leave. I want her on an airplane back home as soon as fucking possible."

"Just fucking tell her to go," Marcia said, looking in the direction that Sue-Ann had gone. "Give her a fucking check and a plane ticket and say sayonara bitch."

"It's not that easy, you know that."

"He gave her a check," Barney added. "He told her to name her price, but she didn't want it."

I looked from one to the other, feeling totally out of my depth as to how I could help. There was nothing that I could offer, except be there for Grantley.

I placed my hand over his and leaned into him. "She'll slip up soon enough and once she does, you'll know how to deal with her. I think you're right, her saying she doesn't want money is a load of old codswallop."

"What?" Grantley gave a short laugh. "Cods what?"

I rolled my eyes. "Codswallop. A load of rubbish."

Grantley kissed the end of my nose and sighed. "Thank fuck for you being here."

"I haven't done anything, except annoy her."

"Nah, it's not you, pretty girl. She's just naturally mean."

"She's not mean, Grantley," Marcia said, reaching for the wine. "She's just a fucking drunk, cock-sucking bitch."

"Who unfortunately is my fucking mom."

Grantley dropped his head to my shoulder and groaned. "Can we just go and leave her in the bathroom?"

"Nope," I said, kissing the top of his head. "We can't. Just think of it as your payment for entry into heaven."

"Well if that's what's required, I'll take hell."

"She's on her way back," Barney said.

I watched him as he watched Sue-Ann stumble her way back. His face was full of concern and I wondered why he never seemed to lose it with her in the same way that Grantley and Marcia did. I didn't think it was anything sexual, she was much older than him for a start, but Barney most definitely gave Sue-Ann a little more leeway than anyone else.

"Okay?" Barney asked her.

"Wha ever." She waved a hand at him and reached for her wine glass.

Barney cleared his throat and pushed it away with a finger. "No more, Sue-Ann," he said softly.

She looked at him for a few seconds and then snapped her head to Grantley, who was watching silently, his body tense.

"Where's that damn chicken?" Sue-Ann finally asked and picked up a glass of water to take a long swig.

The rest of the meal went without incident, if you could ignore Sue-Ann falling asleep with her head lolled forward. Grantley managed to keep up a cool demeanour throughout, talking about the film and a future project that Marcia thought would be good for him.

Finally, we were all finished; coffee cups drained and my nerves were on high alert. I assumed that Barney would be taking me home, but nothing had been mentioned. Barney hadn't had any wine over dinner, so he could drive me if necessary, but I didn't want to assume. Plus, I really wasn't ready to go. We were having a day off from filming the next day, so it would be okay to have a few more drinks and maybe go dancing.

God, who was I kidding? I didn't want to go dancing, I wanted to be kissed for a few hours by Grantley. Although dancing would be great too.

"We'd better get you home," Barney announced. "Just let me get Sue-Ann up to the suite."

Grantley inhaled sharply and moved around in his seat. "I... erm.was wondering whether you wanted to stay tonight?" he asked, his voice unusually unsure.

"Grantley," Marcia warned. "What the hell have I told you about fucking the staff?"

As Grantley's hand banged down on the table, I jumped in surprise.

"Marcia, do not start on me. After this fucking sideshow of a dinner, I don't need or want your advice. If Phoebe wants to stay, I'll take the other couch by Barney."

"Shit man," Barney growled. "It'll be like damn summer camp. You wanna get some torches and we'll tell ghost stories?"

Grantley chuckled and flipped Barney his middle finger. He turned to me and licked his lips.

"It's up to you. I just thought we could have a few more drinks." He paused and glanced over at Sue-Ann. "I'm not ready to let you go home just yet. But I swear there's no pressure. I'm happy to sleep on the couch."

I looked at his dark eyes, which were full of sadness and knew I wasn't ready to go home either. However, I wasn't sure I was ready to share his bed just yet. I wasn't a prude or a virgin, but I wasn't stupid either. I wasn't a girl who got all dreamy about a man just because they'd smiled at me. I said it before, my heart was cold – before Grantley. My problem was, Grantley had the power to ruin me. He had the power to melt the ice around my heart and leave me broken beyond repair. I knew that my feelings were already more than they should be at this stage. We were barely at the second date stage if this was a normal relationship, in a normal life, but everything about this relationship seemed heightened because it was Grantley and because we were conducting it around the filming of a movie.

So, for now I would be that stupid girl, because I didn't care. I felt alive and I wanted this.

Leaning closer to Grantley, I whispered. "You don't need to take the couch, but I'm not ready for that next step. So, if you don't think you can manage that, well you'll be going to summer camp with Barney."

Grantley's eyes raked over my face as his hand came up to cup my cheek.

"I can manage whatever you want," he whispered. "But I will want to hold you."

"You will?"

He nodded. "Yeah, what can I say, I'm a clinger."

I tilted my head and perused him. "Okay, but your hands stay above the waist."

He looked at my knockers and grinned, giving a little chuckle.

"I'm definitely on board with that."

I smacked his arm. "Behave. You know what I mean."

He smiled slowly and then dropped a soft kiss to my lips.

"Yeah, I do," he replied as he pulled away. "And I'm totally on board with that too."

"Good."

"When you two have stopped acting like high school sweethearts, you think we can go?" Marcia asked impatiently. "I need to be up early in the morning, I've got a five am call."

"Yeah," Grantley breathed out, looking at Sue-Ann. "Let's go. You okay to get her upstairs, buddy?"

Barney gave him a two-fingered salute and pushed up from his seat. Moving over to Sue-Ann, he shook her shoulder, gently rousing her.

"I'll get a taxi from the lobby," Marcia said as she rummaged through her bag. "I'll call you tomorrow."

"Not too early. I have a day off remember."

"How could I forget."

As Barney lifted Sue-Ann to her feet, Marcia gave a wave over her shoulder and weaved her way out of the restaurant. It was strange, no one had really taken much notice of Grantley throughout the evening, but the wiry, skinny, elderly woman drew everyone's gaze.

"Night guys," Barney said, putting an arm around a drowsy Sue-Ann. "Try not to wake me when you get up to the room."

"Hah, whatever," Grantley scoffed. "You know you'll be engrossed in *Suits* for the next few hours."

Barney let out a deep chuckle and with a wave of his hand, slowly moved away with Sue-Ann.

"So," Grantley said. "You want to go to a club?"

"Really? Won't you be recognised?"

Grantley shrugged. "Maybe, but the concierge told me there's a club not far from here that is full of local TV celebrities. If I've learned anything from this business, it's that celebrities will go out of their way to ignore another celebrity."

I thought about it for a nanosecond and nodded my head. "Let's go."

"I hope you have your dancing shoes on, pretty girl, because we're not stopping until we drop."

"One thing I need to ask," I said.

"Yeah."

"What am I going to wear in bed?"

Grantley moaned quietly and closed his eyes for a couple of seconds. When his eyes landed on mine, his were full of desire.

"I'd say me," he said with a smirk. "But I'm guessing that's a poor joke, so I'll say I have plenty of t-shirts that you can wear."

I nodded but deep down was thinking, yeah I'd be up for wearing Grantley James, and maybe I should just sod the consequences. After all, wasn't that why I'd packed a spare pair of knickers in my handbag?

CHAPTER TWENTY-SIX

Grantley

The music was loud, the drinks flowing, and Phoebe was dancing like no one was watching her. She wasn't the best dancer, but the joy it gave her was evident as she bounced around, singing along to every song. I'd tried to keep up with her but after almost two hours, I needed a break, so I was watching her from our private booth.

God love Marcia, I'd texted her that we were going to the club, and despite the hour and that she'd left the restaurant in a less than stellar mood, she'd called on ahead for us. We were guided to our table by a hostess in a tight black skirt and crisp white blouse, who then advised me that our bill had been paid for by my agent.

You see, the woman did love me after all.

As the song changed, Phoebe whooped with excitement and came running to me.

"Grantley come and dance. It's a remix of Freedom by Wham."

"I have no idea what you're talking about." I reached up and pushed sticky hair from her sweaty face.

"Wham! George Michael?"

"Oh yeah, I know who he is."

"This is Wham, so come on. Dance."

She grabbed hold of my hand and dragged me up onto the dancefloor, holding my hands as she jumped around like Tigger. Her elation was infectious and I found myself singing along to the chorus, which I had to say weren't George's best lyrics. As Freedom finally flowed into some dance tune, I pulled Phoebe against me and kissed her hard. I kissed her as though I'd never get to kiss her again. I kissed her with a need I'd never felt before. But as my hands moved to her ass, I felt a tap on my shoulder.

If this was someone recognizing me and wanting a damn selfie with me, I would not be happy. I ignored the tapping for a little while, but it was insistent. Groaning, I pulled my lips from Phoebe's and looked over my shoulder. A tall guy with a shaved head, wearing a collared shirt and vest, was looking at me with raised brows.

"Yeah?" I asked, tucking Phoebe under my arm.

"No petting on the dancefloor," he shouted loudly into my ear, making it buzz. "If you want to do that go get a room."

"You're kidding right?"

He shook his head and silently thumbed in the direction of the exit.

"Okay, okay. No petting on the dancefloor."

"Thank you," he said. "Enjoy the rest of your night."

As he strutted away, Phoebe started to giggle.

"I've never been told off in a nightclub before."

"Certainly not for *petting*." I shook my head and taking Phoebe by the hand, dragged her back to our booth. "Maybe it's time for a break anyway."

We flopped down onto the leather seat, with Phoebe snuggling up to my side. I kissed the side of her dance sweaty head and took a drink from my beer bottle.

"You had a good time?" I asked her.

Phoebe grinned, lifting her own bottle of beer. "The best. Thank you."

"Don't thank me, thank Marcia. She's paying."

"You see, I told you she was sweet."

"Well I'm not so sure about that."

I dropped a kiss to her lips that tasted of beer and sat back in the booth. Stretching my arm around the back, I drew circles on Phoebe's shoulder with my thumb. Her black and white stripe dress was sleeveless and showed off her tanned, toned arms, as well as those spectacular legs of hers, and I couldn't understand why she hadn't been snapped up before now.

"When was your last relationship?" I asked.

Phoebe looked at me quizzically. "Why do you ask?"

"No reason, just interested."

"You sure?" She half turned in her seat, and put her bottle down on the table. "It's a bit out of the blue, you asking."

I shrugged. "I guess I'm curious why you don't already have a guy."

"I suppose it's because I'm not the relationship sort of girl."

"I don't for one minute think you're a one night stand sort of girl either." I thought about what she'd said, about not being ready for the next step, even if she slept in my bed.

"I'm not. I suppose you could say I'm the cautious sort of girl. After what happened to Beth, I don't want to find myself in the same position."

I ran my fingers through her hair and studied her pretty face wondering how this thing between us had happened. I'd thought she was a pain in the ass at first, but within days she had me bewitched, yet she hadn't even tried to.

"Not all men are like your sister's douche of an ex, you know."

"I know," she sighed. "But she was devastated, Grantley. She was absolutely heart-broken and if it hadn't been for the boys, I dread to think what she would have done."

Phoebe's eyes filled with tears and the very real fear of what Beth might have done was evident in the way she pulled in a shuddering breath.

"I'll try not to hurt you," I whispered, leaning in to kiss the corner of her mouth.

"The fact you said that actually makes me feel a little hopeful."

She gave me a small smile and then looked out toward the dancefloor. "You didn't say you wouldn't hurt me, but you'd try not to."

"Because I will – try not to, I mean."

She turned back to me, her eyes soft and warm. "Which is more damn honest than saying you *won't*."

Phoebe's warm lips landed on mine, and stayed there for a few seconds before she slowly pulled away.

"I need the loo," she announced.

"Okay. Nice to know."

We both laughed as Phoebe pushed back along the seat to the edge of the booth.

"Won't be long."

As she walked away, I watched her carefully. There was no strut or hair flicking to attract attention, she was just Phoebe. She had no hidden agenda, as far as I could see, and she was the most open person I'd ever known. I'd known her for a few weeks and yet I felt like I could trust her implicitly and I knew that I didn't want to let her go – definitely not in a month's time, and maybe not ever.

CHAPTER TWENTY-SEVEN

Phoebe

I woke up with a large hand splayed across my stomach, something hard pressing into the crack of my bum, and Grantley James snoring softly in my ear, and it was the best feeling ever.

We'd had an amazing time in the club, dancing until the soles of my feet burned and laughing until my sides ached. Grantley had been right, no one gave us a second glance – well they did, but didn't approach us, or take sneaky photographs on their phones, thinking we wouldn't notice the flash going off. We were left alone to have a great time, apart from the bouncer who scolded us for kissing on the dance-floor. I'd thought he was going to make us leave, but thankfully he didn't, because that would have just been a sour end to a great couple of hours. I couldn't say we'd had a great evening up to that point, because dinner had been pretty awful. Although, it was much easier once Sue-Ann was asleep. The club made up for everything though.

Once we got back to the hotel, it was almost three in the morning and we were both exhausted. Barney was sleeping soundly on his back, with one of his huge arms lying over his face. He'd left a small side light on, so Grantley turned it off as we tiptoed towards the bedroom. The sound of snoring was coming from Sue-Ann's room. It was a deep, alcohol induced, throaty snore, so it was unlikely even a brass band marching through the suite would wake her.

"Both the kids are fast asleep, that's good," Grantley joked, as we entered his room.

After turning on a bedside lamp, Grantley found me a t-shirt to wear and told me he'd got housekeeping to leave a few things I might need in the bathroom. When I went in I was surprised to see face wipes, a toothbrush, deodorant, some hair-ties and a pale blue gift bag.

I peeked inside to see three tissue paper wrapped parcels. I pulled them out and unwrapped each one. There was a pair of jeans, in my size, a gorgeous black lace top, in my size, and a couple of pairs of knickers, also in my size. My heart jumped as I looked at everything on the counter. How had Grantley managed to get them all for me and how the hell did he know my size? But even if he'd got the wrong sizes, I'd have been impressed at the sheer effort that he'd made.

Once I'd removed my make-up, cleaned my teeth, slipped on his t-shirt, and pulled my hair back into a ponytail, I went back into the bedroom. I almost gasped when I was met with a half-naked Grantley. He was wearing only his black boxer briefs and had his back to me, standing by the dresser as he unbuckled his watch. His back was broad and toned, and every muscle moved with languorous fluidity. He was a beautiful sight and I wondered whether sleeping in the same bed as him was foolish. I'd asked him to keep his hands above my waist, but I wasn't sure I'd be able to do the same.

"Hey," I said, softly. "I found the gifts."

Grantley turned around and gifted me again, this time with a gorgeous smile. "I knew you'd need stuff for tomorrow. Is it all okay?"

I nodded. "Perfect, but you really didn't have to."

"I didn't want you to feel awkward in the morning," he replied, taking a step towards me. "We know that nothing is going to happen, but you walking out of here in the dress you wore tonight may give others the wrong impression."

I almost ran and climbed him like a baby chimpanzee. His thoughtfulness amazing me.

"Thank you, that's really kind of you," I said, trying to keep the breathiness out of my voice.

He grinned and looked down at my legs, which were bare up to the top half of my thighs. "To be honest, I wish I'd just let you wear that shirt and forget about the jeans. It looks pretty hot on you."

I giggled and pulled at the hem. "I'm not sure I would dare walk out in public with this on."

"Well that's good, because I wouldn't have wanted to share that view with anyone."

"So which side?" I asked, nodding at the bed.

Grantley shrugged. "I tend to starfish, so you'd best pick."

Nervously, I edged to the right hand side of the bed and drew back the duvet. "You sure?"

"About you sleeping in my bed, or about you sleeping on that side?"

I licked my dry lips and took a deep breath. Suddenly, with the buzz of the alcohol wearing off, I wondered whether this was a good idea. We definitely weren't going to have sex, but this – sleeping next to each other, in very little clothing – seemed just as intimate. Lots of people had sex, but often that didn't include sleeping in each other's arms afterwards. We were going to do this because it was what we wanted. Grantley could just as easily sleep on the sofa, but I didn't want him to and he didn't want to either, despite me telling him I wasn't ready for the next step. That had to mean something, didn't it? Or maybe he was playing me, thinking he'd change my mind once we were in bed. I had no idea, but I wasn't going to think about that.

"Phoebe," Grantley whispered. "I can just as easily grab the other couch, I'd be cool with that."

"No," I said, straightening my back. "I'd like you to stay, as long as you know there will only be sleeping."

"No kissing?" he asked, a smile on his upturned lips.

"Maybe *some* kissing."

Grantley laughed and then nodded to the bed. "Get in pretty girl."

His voice was soft and gentle and I instinctively knew he wasn't playing me. I might get burned by this man one day, but for now he wanted us.

At first, Grantley kept his distance from me, and all I could feel was his breath on my neck. My body was full of tension as I tried not to stray onto his side of the bed and touch him. As he moved slightly, the mattress moved and because I was so close to the edge, I almost toppled out.

"Ooh, shit."

"You okay?" Grantley asked.

"I nearly fell out of bed."

I inched back a little more, stopping as soon as I sensed Grantley's body was close. Holding onto the edge of the mattress, I snuggled down, only to have an arm wrap around my body and drag me backwards.

"I won't bite, Phoebes," Grantley chuckled as he pulled me against his chest. "I told you, I'm a clinger."

With one arm wrapped around me, he placed his other on the pillow above my head.

"Better?" he asked, placing a kiss on the back of my head.

God, yes. It felt amazing to be in his hold.

"Much," I replied, on a yawn.

"Good, now sleep well, pretty girl."

"Night, Grantley."

He gave me a squeeze and another kiss, this time on my neck, and I felt my body relax into sleep. The next thing I knew I was waking up with Grantley's hand and boner, reminding me that we were in bed together. He'd been the perfect gent all night, his hand had stayed on my waist, never straying lower or higher, so I couldn't complain about the python being woken up.

I turned slowly, so as not to wake him and looked at his handsome face. He looked peaceful and stress free and I was glad that sleep took him away from his insidious mother in the next room. We'd obviously slept well, because I'd woken in pretty much the same position that I'd fallen asleep in.

Grantley made a little sigh and blew air through his lips and then started his quiet snores once more. Craning my neck, I could just about see the digital clock on Grantley's side of the bed – blimey, Grantley's side; that made us sound like a real couple – as I processed that thought, I noticed that it was almost nine-thirty. I couldn't remember the last time I'd slept that late. Even if I wasn't working, the boys and their noise usually woke me pretty early.

Stealthily, I lifted Grantley's arm and slipped from under him and out of the bed. As my feet touched the thick, plush carpet, I held my breath, hoping that he continued to sleep. It wasn't that I wanted to sneak away, he simply looked peaceful and must have needed it as he was still sleeping so soundly.

Slowly opening the bedroom door, I heard voices in the suite and wondered whether I should dress first, but when Grantley turned over and hugged my pillow to him, my resolve to let him continue sleeping hardened.

I padded down the short hall, past the open door of Sue-Ann's room, and into the main suite. Barney was sitting on the sofa, dressed in jeans and a sweatshirt, drinking from a mug, while Sue-Ann stood in front of him, one hand on her hip, and pointing a finger at Barney.

"You need to tell him. You're his friend."

Barney raised an eyebrow above the mug which was paused at his mouth, evidently waiting for her to finish.

"He needs to be careful, he's a star."

Something inside, told me that Sue-Ann was talking about me. She wanted Barney to tell Grantley to be wary of me.

"Morning," I said, as brightly as I could.

Both heads swivelled towards me; Barney's with a smile and Sue-Ann's with a scowl.

"Hey there, Phoebe," Barney replied, putting down his mug. "You want coffee?"

I glanced at Grantley's mother and knew most definitely that she had been talking about me. There was pure hatred on her face as her eyes took in my bare legs and body covered with what was obviously her son's t-shirt.

"I can make it," I said, turning towards the kitchen area. "I know how to use the machine."

"I bet you do," Sue-Ann spat out. "Got those pretty little feet of yours firmly under the table, haven't you?"

I looked down at my feet with the bright pink toenails, which Sue-Ann was pointing at. I loved the colour and was a little bit put out she didn't feel the same way.

"Sue-Ann," Barney warned. "Leave her alone because you know what will happen if Grantley finds out how you've been speaking to her."

"Oh yeah, I know," she cried, turning back to Barney. "He'll take her side over his own mother because she's got her claws into him."

"It's not like that," I ventured. "Grantley and I-."

"Grantley and you what?" she snapped. "You're a money grabbing little whore who's getting into his pants because of how much money he's got."

"Now wait a minute." I strode forward and it was my turn to point. "Don't you dare call me that. You don't even know me, you've no idea what my feelings are about Grantley."

"Oh I think I do missy. You see the dollar signs while you're throwing yourself at him." She curled her lip and shook her head. "Like I said, a damn whore."

Her words were like a slap across the face, just like Declan's had been. She'd called me the same thing that he had. Was that really how people saw me, just because there was a mutual attraction between me and a film star? I'd be attracted to him if he was a refuse collector or a teacher – being a film star wasn't what defined him and she was underestimating him if that was what she thought.

"Don't judge me by your own shortfalls. I am *not* that person."

"What the fuck. Barney," she bellowed. "Are you going to let her speak to me like that?"

Barney sighed wearily and stood up.

"She called me a damn whore and you're just going to let her."

Sue-Ann's bloodshot eyes were wild, as she raged at Barney. Her twig-thin arms flailing around.

"You called me a whore first," I cried. "Something that is totally unfounded. You don't know me, you haven't taken any time to get to know me. You just decided to get drunk and be a total embarrassment to Grantley instead."

Sue-Ann flew at me, fists flying and screaming like a banshee.

"Sue-Ann," Barney roared and made a grab for her.

Sue-Ann was too quick and slippery and was on me in seconds, grabbing at my hair, scratching at my face. Unlucky for her, I'd been trained at wrestling by the best – Callum and Mack. I stooped down low, threw my shoulder into her chest and pushed. With a loud thud, she landed on her backside, looking up at me with astonishment and pain on her face.

"Why you little -."

Before she could finish, I was in her face pointing a finger at her.

"Don't speak to me like that ever again, and if you ever lay a finger on me, I'll punch you so hard you'll need to visit a plastic surgeon to fix what's left of your damn nose, if that's even possible."

As I stood up, I heard slow clapping behind me and my heart thudded to a stop – shit, Grantley was out of bed.

I whizzed around to the most gorgeous sight. Grantley in black boxer briefs, sleep filled eyes and sexily mussed hair.

"Hey, Phoebes." He flashed me a smile and moved to my side and looked down at Sue-Ann. "That's what you get for causing shit." he said. "So, in the future, keep your damn opinions to yourself and leave my girlfriend alone."

I gasped and wobbled on my feet. Grantley took hold of my chin, gave me a quick, soft kiss and then the most beautiful smile.

"Yeah," he said, "my girlfriend, so you'd better get used to it."

As he strolled over to the coffee table, he high-fived Barney, picked up the mug on it and drank it back.

"Okay," he said, turning to me. "What's our plan for today, pretty girl?"

Be still, my rapidly beating heart.

CHAPTER TWENTY-EIGHT

GRANTLEY

Phoebe Drinkwater kicked fucking ass and it was sexy as hell.

The only person I'd ever seen stand up to Sue-Ann like that was Marcia, and she was mean to most people all of the time. Phoebe wasn't, so to hear her give my darling mother shit, was a damn revelation.

"Okay, what's our plan for today, pretty girl?" I asked, drinking Barney's coffee.

"You're going to let her assault me and say nothing?" Sue-Ann cried, rolling onto her knees and staring up at me.

"I just said something," I replied, handing Barney his now empty mug. "I said you'd better keep your opinions to yourself, or did you not hear me?"

"I mean say something to her, for attacking me."

I looked over at Phoebe who still looked as though I'd just announced we were getting married in an hour, rather than the fact that she was my girlfriend. Her cute little mouth was gaping open and her eyes were as big and as round as plates. It was a shock to her, it might have been to me a few days ago, but after last night and then her kicking Sue-Ann's butt, and I knew she was the woman I wanted to be with. I'd thought about our conversation the previous day, on what we were to each other, and there was no way we were *just* friends. She wasn't my date either, she was more than that. So, it was decided she was my girlfriend. I just had to figure out how we did that once the shoot was over – but that could wait.

"Sounded to me like you deserved it."

I stretched, feeling as though I'd slept for a week. I hadn't slept that good for years and it felt amazing. I walked toward Phoebe and stopped in front of her, pushing her mouth closed with a finger under her chin.

"So, you thought about it – what you want to do today?"

"N-no, not really," she stammered. "I just assumed I'd go home and you'd be busy all day."

"Grantley," Sue-Ann screeched from somewhere on the floor. "She hit me. I cannot believe you're just going to let that go?"

Okay, now I'd had enough of her shit. I turned and held a hand out to her and as she took it, I roughly pulled her to her feet.

"Hey, that hurt," she complained.

"Good. Now listen to me carefully." I leaned into her space, almost recoiling at the stench of stale alcohol. "I don't want you here. I've been pretty clear on that, but if you insist on staying, you keep your damn vile opinions to yourself. I like Phoebe. She's my girlfriend and I will not have you disrespecting her. And before you shoot your mouth off about *you* being disrespected, don't. You need to be respected before someone can disrespect you and you do not have even an inch of it from anyone in this room." I looked at Barney. "Okay, maybe the big guy respects you a little, but that's only because his momma brought him up to respect his elders, no matter what a piece of shit they are. Is that clear?"

Sue-Ann looked at me warily and finally nodded.

"Good. Now, I don't know what your little plan is, or why you've even deigned me with a visit, but whatever it is, you can forget it. I offered you money and you weren't interested, so I'd say we're done and you may as well go back home."

"I don't want your money, I told you that."

"I know," I responded impatiently. "But whatever you do want, you're not getting it."

"You don't understand," she cried, taking hold of my bicep. "*I* don't want anything."

"But you do, Sue-Ann. You always want fucking something. You never visit me for any other reason than you need something, so just tell me what it is, so I can tell you no and you can go home and I'll carry on making a movie."

"Grantley." Phoebe's soft, gentle voice broke through the poison in the air.

I turned to face her.

"Maybe I should go. You obviously have things you need to discuss with Sue-Ann. I can get a train."

I shook my head. "No, I don't want you to go. We have a day off and we're going to enjoy it."

"Maybe she should go," Sue-Ann said, not without the tiniest bit of venom.

"Did you not hear me?" I bellowed at her. "I told you -."

"But this is a family matter," she interjected. "I know you like her, but you don't know her that well."

"What is?" I snapped.

"What is what?"

"You said it's a family matter, so I'm asking you what is."

Sue-Ann opened her mouth to speak, but before she had chance, I cut her off.

"No, don't even say it. If I'm happy to have Phoebe here then you should accept it."

"Grantley, maybe she's right," Phoebe offered.

I turned my gaze to her. "No, I want you to stay. Now tell me, what the fuck is a family matter?"

Sue-Ann looked over my shoulder to where Phoebe was standing and then over to Barney, who had now positioned himself next to me. Her hands started shaking as she chewed on her lip, seemingly deciding whether to give up her reason for the visit. Finally, she spoke. Her voice quiet but determined.

"Your dad needs a kidney transplant, so I'm here to ask for your kidney."

CHAPTER TWENTY-NINE

Grantley

"Your dad needs a kidney transplant, so I'm here to ask for your kidney," Sue-Ann said.

Phoebe gasped, Barney dropped his mug to the floor, and me... well I busted out laughing.

"You really are a piece of work," I snarled. "That has got to be the most -."

"It's true, he does. He has kidney failure. You probably don't remember, but he had one removed when you were a kid, you were maybe two or three."

I nodded slowly, remembering the long scar he had on his side and how he always told me it was from fighting a dragon. Of course, as I grew older his story never held up, but he'd always wave me away and say it was nothing, just an operation he'd had.

"And?"

Sue-Ann swallowed before continuing. "And now his remaining one is failing and he needs a transplant."

I dragged a hand down my face, before holding it over my mouth and exhaling deeply.

"And he wants me to donate one of mine?"

Sue-Ann nodded, looking at me warily, before moving her gaze past me when there was movement behind me. Phoebe was at my side and taking my big hand in her small, soft one.

"Go and sit down, I'll make something to drink," she whispered, before dropping a kiss to my bicep. "You're cold too, I'll grab you some clothes."

I stared at her vacantly, not knowing what to say, as she gave my hand a squeeze before disappearing out of the room.

"Come on Grant, let's sit down." Barney's deep voice broke through my haze.

I didn't move straight away, but stared at Sue-Ann, wondering whether this was some stupid joke and I was being punked in the worst possible way. A whole bunch of thoughts were swimming around in my head, trying to make sense of what I'd just been told. My dad was dying. He needed my kidney. He was dying – fuck.

"I just -."

"I know," Sue-Ann replied. "But you're the only one that can help him. If he waits for a donor, it could be too late."

I ran a hand through my hair, absolutely floored by the news.

"I haven't spoken to the man in twenty years, why the fuck would he think I would do this for him?"

Before Sue-Ann had chance to answer, Phoebe came back into the room. She was wearing the jeans I'd bought for her and one of my hoodies and fuck, despite the shit storm in my head, it struck me that she looked cute.

"Is it okay?" she asked, tugging at the sweatshirt. "It's a little chilly."

I nodded and took the jeans and sweater she was handing to me. "It's fine, pretty girl."

"I'll make some coffee."

"I'll come with you," Barney said, laying a hand on my shoulder. "You'll be okay for a few?"

I nodded. I was pretty sure he wasn't worried I'd kill Sue-Ann in the length of time it took to make coffee, so obviously he was worried how I was taking the news. As I slipped on my clothes, I thought about it– I had no fucking idea what to think. The man had left me when I was six-years-of-age, I owed him nothing, yet I'd be a cold hearted man if I didn't admit that I felt sick to my stomach about his situation; he was my dad.

"Grantley, baby boy," Sue-Ann whispered. "Tell me what you're thinking."

I flopped down onto the couch, resting my head back and looking up at the ceiling.

"I'm thinking why the hell hasn't he asked me himself?"

"Well, he's scared," she replied, in a tone that said she wondered how I could not know that.

I lifted my head to look at her and frowned. "I get he's scared at what's going to happen to him, but why should that stop him from asking me himself for one of my god damn kidneys?"

Sue-Ann lowered herself onto the opposite couch, perching on the edge.

"He's scared to ask you himself, because he hasn't seen you in so long."

"Twenty-fucking-years to be exact."

Sue-Ann started to chew at her thumbnail as wary eyes watched me.

"So why ask you?" I said, leaning forward. "You're the one who was a useless drunk, you were the reason he left us. So why the hell would he trust you to be the bearer of the shit news?"

"It was his wife," Sue-Ann replied. "She was the one who asked me. She said Trent was too scared or too proud or whatever, and so she thought I could ask for him."

"Does he actually know that you're asking, or is this just something you and his wife have agreed on?"

Sue-Ann colored and looked down at the floor.

"He has no fucking clue does he?" I bellowed. "You're fucking unbelievable."

"But baby boy, he's your dad and –"

"Yeah so you said, and quit calling me baby fucking boy."

"His wife, she said she told him to call you, but he's so riddled with guilt at leaving you like he did, he doesn't think you'd agree. He said he didn't want to put you in that position."

"No, but you and his god damn wife are happy to."

"I'm sorry," Sue-Ann said. "But you're his only hope and I loved him once, I kinda felt I owed it to him to ask."

I clutched at my hair with both hands and wondered where the hell Phoebe and Barney had gone to. The coffee machine took seconds, what the hell was taking them so long?

Blowing out a breath, I looked up at Sue-Ann. "If I say I'll do it, what happens?"

"You go to a private clinic and they'll remove it and put it into your dad," she said with a shrug.

"It can't be that simple. Won't I need tests?"

"Oh, yeah of course, but they'll do that at the clinic."

"And who is paying for this clinic?" I asked, knowing that it was most likely going to be me.

"Well he won't know you're the donor. His doctor is going to tell him a couple of days before and then he'll be in the clinic, ready and waiting. I thought you'd want something private, you know, no publicity. His wife is going to tell him their insurance paid."

"Do I get to see him or talk to him at all?"

I had no idea why, but the thought of seeing my dad again filled me with a nervous excitement. Yes, I was angry with him for leaving, but I wanted to see him and talk to him again. I wanted to know why he'd left me with her. I would have gone with him no question, if only he'd wanted me.

"Maybe afterwards." Sue-Ann cleared her throat as she played with the hem of her blouse. "Let's make sure it's all okay and then visit him. I know he'll be happy to see you, once it's over, but if you go before, his wife is pretty sure he'll refuse your help."

"Fuck."

I flopped back against the couch and pushed the heels of my hands into my eyes, not having a damn clue what to do. If I said no, I was being a cold-hearted bastard, sentencing a man to probable death. I could only imagine what the press would say if that got out. If I said yes, I was giving something to the man who'd abandoned me to a shit childhood, with the worst mom on the planet.

"I need to speak to Marcia about this," I stated, looking up at the ceiling.

"Why? This is your father we're talking about."

"Yeah, my father who fucked off out of my life." I lowered my gaze and glowered at her. "So, like I said, I need to speak to Marcia."

"I don't –."

I held up my hand. "I don't want to hear it."

As I watched Sue-Ann, daring her to speak, Phoebe and Barney came back into the room each carrying two mugs of what smelled like the shit, machine-made coffee.

Phoebe handed one to me and sat down, while Barney passed one to Sue-Ann.

"You got any hard stuff I can add to this?" she asked.

"Really?" I asked. "You think that's appropriate seeing as we're talking about one of my parents dying of kidney disease? You want to trump him with liver failure."

"Listen," she said. "If I'm going to get liver problems, I'd have gotten them by now."

"Whatever." I shook my head and turned to Phoebe.

Her eyes were full of sympathy, but her body was tense and I knew I should have let her go home when she suggested it. She didn't need to be involved in the Miller dramas.

"You want Barney to take you home?" I asked, gently running a finger down her cheek.

"No," she replied with a sigh. "Unless you want me to, of course."

"Nope. I need you here. I have no fucking clue what to do and could do with your input."

"I don't know, Grantley," Phoebe said, shifting in her seat. "I think maybe Sue-Ann is right, maybe it's a family matter and you should discuss your options with her."

"Phoebe, believe me, we haven't been a damn family in twenty years, and one of my parents needing one of my organs isn't going to change that."

"Grantley," Sue-Ann squeaked. "We're family. I'm your mom."

I turned to look at her, my lip curled in disdain. "Don't think we're going to get all warm and fuzzy just because you delivered the good news. This does not change the fact that you are a shit mother."

"Grantley." Phoebe's tone was chastising, but I'd bet she'd fucking agree with me if pushed.

"Maybe I could take Sue-Ann out for a while," Barney offered. "Get Marcia over here."

"I think you should speak to her," Phoebe said. "She is your agent after all."

"I don't get why you need to speak to her," Sue-Ann complained. "You need to do this for your dad. It doesn't matter what she says."

"Take her to a bar," I snapped, ignoring her. "That'll keep her occupied."

Barney nodded and stood up. "Come on Sue-Ann, go get your coat."

"The department store has a lovely cocktail lounge," Phoebe said. "It overlooks the city."

"Thanks sweetheart, we'll check it out."

"You got my credit card?" I asked.

Barney nodded. "Yep. There a limit?"

"Keep it to three figures if you can, but don't make that all booze."

"Will do and I'll call Marcia for you on the way out."

"Thanks buddy."

When the door finally shut behind them, I pulled Phoebe into my arms and kissed the top of her head. I sighed and wondered for the millionth time in the last five minutes, what the hell I was going to do?

CHAPTER THIRTY

Phoebe

As I threw my coat over the bannister, I felt like simply disappearing up the stairs and hiding under my duvet for the foreseeable future. What had promised to be a great day had turned out to be a hideous one.

Grantley and I hadn't ended up doing anything, which was fine, he had far more important things to think about, but Marcia's screaming and shouting hadn't helped. As soon as Grantley explained what he might have to do, she'd gone off on a rant telling him not to be ridiculous as he was putting his career at risk.

"As opposed to my father's damn life," he retorted and he slammed out of the suite.

He didn't return for half an hour; a half hour that I'd sat on one sofa and Marcia on the other in uncomfortable silence. Silence only occasionally broken by her sighing or raspy cough. When Grantley finally returned, we sat and they had a fairly civilised conversation. At one point Grantley asked me what I thought, and while I told him I sympathised with his situation and would be there for him, it wasn't for me to say. We were new and I hardly knew him to be able to give a measured answer. He accepted my response and my decision to get a train home, so that he and Marcia could talk. He kissed me goodbye and promised to call me later.

I'd hardly been on the train for five minutes when he sent me a text.

Grantley: So sorry about today. I'll make it up to you the next day off we get. See you tomorrow. - G x

Now I was home and I was missing him already. Now I was regretting taking things slow and wishing I'd not been so cautious and agreed to more than kissing. Just the thought of what might have been, was making me hot and bothered.

"Hey Phoebes," Beth shouted from the lounge.

"Hi."

I hung my bag with my coat and trudged in to join Beth and the boys. When I entered the lounge, Beth had her feet up on the sofa, with a magazine open next to her, while the boys were playing on the floor with some action figures – I think I spotted the Hulk in there somewhere.

"So," Beth said, bouncing in her seat. "How was your night? Did you...?" She nodded at me with her eyes really wide, silently asking me if I'd slept with Grantley.

"No, we didn't, but I did..." I made a sleeping sign, putting my hands together against my cheek. "In the bed with..." I drew a G in the air.

"But no..." Beth made a circle with her thumb and forefinger and then poked her other forefinger back and forth through it.

"No," I said a little sulkily.

"What, he didn't want to?"

"Yes, but I said no and am now regretting it."

"Why did you say no, you stupid idiot?"

"Because I didn't think I was ready."

"What the fuck?" she mouthed silently. "This is Grantley James we're talking about. What is there not to be ready for? You should have been on your back with your legs…" Beth then held her arms out in a wide V-shape. "As soon as he closed the bedroom door."

I shrugged and lifting her legs, flopped down onto the sofa. "Call me Stupid McStupid of Stupid Town."

"Queen McStupid you mean." Beth rolled her eyes and smacked me with her magazine. "Like I said, you're an idiot."

"Yeah, I know," I sighed.

"So did he send you home because you wouldn't put out?"

"No!" I snapped. "He's got a few things going on with his mother. They needed some time together."

"So it's still on?" Her eyes were bright with anticipation.

I nodded and Beth squealed, clapping her hands together.

"What are you clapping for, Mummy?" Callum asked.

"No reason, I'm just happy." Beth grinned at both the boys. "Auntie Peepee is going to get a really huuuge present from Dick."

"What are you getting Auntie Peepee?" Mack asked, getting up onto his knees.

I threw a glare at Beth. "Nothing special."

"What is it Mummy, what's Dick giving to Auntie Peepee?"

Beth winked at me and turned to the boys. "Dick's going to give her a really big sausage if she's a good girl."

The boys looked at each other and turned their noses up in disgust.

"A sausage?" Callum asked. "Is that all?"

"I hate sausage," Mack added. "They're yuck."

"Not this one," Beth said nudging me with her foot. "This one is really tasty."

Later, we spent some time watching a film, but after an hour I was feeling restless. Well, to be honest I was feeling frustrated. I'd flicked through Beth's magazine and seen a full page advert that Grantley had done for a cologne. He was stripped to the waist, wearing battered jeans with the top two buttons undone and showing off the sneakiest peak of his sculpted v-line. So, feeling a little desperate and with Beth's magazine safely tucked under my arm, I decided I needed to fly solo for a little while.

As soon as the door of my room was closed, I rid myself of the jeans that I'd got from Grantley and rushed to my chest of drawers. I opened my knicker drawer and reached to the back for my silver and pink 'special friend'. It was *the* best friend I had ever had. I loved it dearly and thanked it for being there for me when I was feeling alone. I hadn't given it a name like some women did; that would be stupid, but it did have a massive place in my heart.

Arranging my pillows, I sat back against them and wiggled around until I was feeling comfortable – call me precious, but I liked to be comfy while making my bald man cry – and once I was ready, I slipped my hand inside my black lace knickers and started the party.

After a couple of fairly satisfying orgasms, a quick shower, and a good wash and wipe over for my friend. I dressed in a pair of sweat pants and white vest top, pulled my hair into a messy bun, and finally felt relaxed.

I checked my phone but there was nothing from Grantley. It had only been a little over four hours since I'd left him and him and Marcia had some serious decisions to make, so I wasn't really expecting anything. Sitting on the edge of my bed, I thought about sending him a text, but decided against it. I didn't want to be that woman who pestered her boyfriend.

Shit, that felt weird – my boyfriend. My boyfriend who was Grantley James.

As a huge grin spread across my face, I heard Beth shouting for me. I jumped up and opened my door.

"Yeah."

"You should come down here," she shouted, sounding a little giddy. "Quick."

"If this is one of those stupid cat videos again, I won't be happy, Beth."

"Oh no," she replied, looking up at me from the hallway. "It's so much better."

I banged down the stairs and followed her into the kitchen, where I was faced with the biggest pink and cream bouquet that I had ever seen. It was huge with a whole host of different flowers. There were peonies and roses, tulips and freesias, chrysanthemums and gerberas – it was simply stunning.

"Oh my God," I gasped. "They're amazing. When did they come?"

"About five minutes ago. I was going to shout you, but I had to stop the boys from using my sofa as a diving board."

I rushed over to the table and gently touched the flowers, before dropping down to smell their gorgeous aroma.

"There's a card," Beth said, thrusting it into my hand.

"Mummy, can we play football in the hall." Callum and Mack came rushing into the kitchen, skidding to a stop in front of us.

"No, you can't. I've told you before."

"But it's raining." Mack grumbled.

I looked through the window to see that in the hour or so I'd been upstairs endeavouring to stem my Grantley induced frustration, it had indeed started to rain.

"There are loads of things you can do," Beth said, only half concentrating on the boys. "Go upstairs and play pirates."

Mack sighed. "Only if you promise I can be *Jack Sparrow* this time."

"Okay," Callum agreed. "But you're not allowed to make me walk the plank."

"Yeah, but I'm the pirate. Pirates always make you walk the plank."

"Boys," Beth snapped. "Just go upstairs and play."

When we heard their feet pounding up the stairs, Beth turned back to me.

"Go on, open it."

I tore at the small envelope and pulled out the card inside. On it was a bold, masculine scrawl.

"What does it say?" Beth's eyes were brimming with anticipation as she urged me to read the card.

I skimmed it quickly and grinned.

"Well? Is it dirty?" she asked. "Does it say what he's going to do to you?"

"No, it doesn't," I replied with a giggle. "It's really sweet."

"So what does it say?" she cried.

"Okay, okay. It says 'Dear Pretty girl, I'm so sorry our day was ruined, but I promise I'll make it up to you. I can't tell you how much I enjoyed our night together and I'm glad we're taking it slow, because all the best things are worth waiting for, and you are most definitely the best. Grantley xx'."

"Shit," Beth groaned. "He's made my nipples hard with that, so I've no idea how you must be feeling."

I felt my cheeks warm as, like a stupid, love-sick idiot, I held the card to my chest.

"So how *do* you feel?" My sister asked, grinning like a Cheshire cat.

"I feel-."

"Hey Mummy, look. Auntie Peepee bought us a sword to play with. It lights up and everything. It's amazing."

With horror, I looked at Mack to see him brandishing my 'Special Edition Glow in the Dark, Glitter Vibrator'. With a huge amount of effort, he was prodding and poking his 'sword' at his imaginary assailant, his little face red with the exertion of his fight. Mortified, I made a grab for it, but Mack was a better swordsman than I gave him credit for and moved out of my grasp.

"I'm Addison Yates and you're going to die. Take that!"

"Mack!" Beth cried. "What...where...what. Oh shit."

"Mummy," Callum bellowed, running into the kitchen. "Tell Mack he has to share the sword Auntie Peepee got for us."

"Give it to me," I snapped. "It's not a *sword*."

"What were you doing in Auntie Peepee's room?" Beth slammed a hand against her chest, as she looked on the boys in complete horror.

"Yes," I added. "What were you doing in my room?"

"Playing hide and seek," Mack replied, still lunging with the vibrator in his hand. "I was going to hide under your bed and I found it. It's really cool, thanks Auntie Peepee."

"It's my turn," Callum complained. "You've played with it for ages now. I want to be Dick."

"You were Dick yesterday." Mack thrust the pink, glitter, joystick under his brother's nose. "I'm being Dick for five more minutes."

"Please stop saying Dick," Beth whimpered.

"Beth do something. You're the parent, stop them."

"Hey, Cal," Mack said, nudging Callum in the stomach with the 'sword'. "Watch this."

He pressed a button and the bloody thing began to rotate as well as vibrate.

"Woah, cool," Callum gasped. "What else does it do? What are they for?" He pointed at the 'rabbit ears' and then starting flicking them with his finger. "They're bendy."

"I think it's a handle for close combat," Mack replied sagely giving it some serious tactical thought.

"No, it's not. Now, give it to me." I held my hand out, but Mack backed away.

"You can't give a present and then take it back. That's not fair, is it Mummy?"

We all turned to Beth who by now was a strange shade of greeny-grey.

"Beth," I hissed. "Get it off him."

Beth opened her mouth and her jaw moved but nothing came out.

"Hey," Mack said, turning back to Callum. "Let's go and see if Jack wants to play with us, and I'll let you be Dick."

Callum's eyes lit up with excitement. "Yeah. I bet he hasn't got a sword like this one. Can we Mummy?"

No, they couldn't take it to their friend two doors away. His parents collected the money in church. We'd be sent to hell and Beth might be made to run the Brownie's in order to atone for her sins – for my bloody sins.

"No!" I cried stamping my foot. "I've told you, it's not a *sword*. Give it back, now."

"It's not a sword?" Mack asked, curling his lip in disappointment.

"So what is it?" Callum asked.

"You may well ask." A deep, sexy voice, full of innuendo said from the back door.

We all shot around to see Grantley, rain beating down on his back, soaking into his black pea coat, as he stood at the open door.

"I did knock, but no one answered, so thought I'd come around the back."

"Dick!" The boys cried in unison.

"Oh shit," Beth groaned.

"Do you want to play with Auntie Peepee's sword?" Mack said, thrusting the pink, vibrating, rubber object at Grantley.

"I'm not sure that's what it is, buddy," Grantley said with a smirk.

"So what is it?" Callum asked. "No one will tell us. Where did you get it, Auntie Peepee?"

"It was a present," I said, holding out my hand. "Now give it to me."

"Hey," Mack cried, holding the vibrator aloft. "Dick, did you give it to her? Mummy said you were giving Auntie Peepee a present."

I looked at Grantley and saw the flash of fear in his eyes.

"Well, I-."

"I know, I know," Callum shouted, bouncing up and down. "It's the special, big sausage that Dick gave to Auntie Peepee."

"Woah," Mack said. "Dick, your sausage is huge."

I do believe that was the point where I wanted to die.

CHAPTER THIRTY-ONE

Grantley

"Okay, so tell me again why the dildo was out on your bed?"

Phoebe buried her face in her hands and groaned.

"Don't want to," she muttered.

"Don't care, now tell me."

We were on her bed, I was leaning back against the mass of cushions and pillows, with Phoebe snuggled into my side and it was fucking bliss. After the shit day I'd had, I'd needed to see her, so I'd driven myself over to Beth's house, leaving poor Barney babysitting Sue-Ann.

Yeah, I felt bad about it, but that's what he was paid to do. Admittedly, it was to babysit me, but by way of the fact that I shared that woman's DNA, I figured it was the same thing. Besides, Barney had a way with her. He always managed to keep her under control, whereas me, well I just lost it with her on a minute by minute basis.

"I don't have to tell you. You can't make me."

I cleared my throat and before she had chance to protest, I thrusted a hand up her tight white tank that had been enticing me for the last hour. I had no idea whether she hated being tickled or not, but most people did, so my fingers grabbed her waist and started their assault. Phoebe squirmed next to me and squealed. It didn't take long.

"Okay, okay. I'll tell you."

I withdrew my hand and straightened her top. "Why was your dildo out on the bed?"

"Because I'd used it," she replied in the quietest of voices.

"And?"

"And," she huffed. "I was thinking of you."

"Specifics please."

I gave her a shit-eating grin as her eyes widened.

"No. That's private."

"Not if it's about me, it's not. So, what exactly was I doing to you while you got yourself off with a piece of dick-shaped rubber?"

"Oh, now you've taken all the romance out of it." Phoebe looked up at me with a frown. "In my head it was your willy, but now it's just rubber."

"My *what*?"

"Your willy," she repeated. "Your penis."

"Ugh, now who's spoiling the romance? Penis is the worst word in the world. It's so clinical. It's what my doctor calls it when I go for my physical."

"Your doctor asks you about your penis? Ugh, now that's just weird."

"No it isn't. He gives me a full check, he has to, the studio insist on it."

"But your penis? No, I'm sorry," Phoebe said with a shake of her head. "That's just wrong."

"No, what's wrong is *you* calling it my penis. It makes it sound tiny. You know, peeny."

Phoebe burst out laughing and buried her face into my chest.

"What's so funny?"

"You and your peeny penis. I'm Auntie Peepee and you're Dick Peeny Weeny."

"It's not fucking peeny, I promise you."

"Oh I know that." She pushed herself up, laying back against the pillows with me.

"How do you know that?"

My eyes landed on her full, pink lips and with all the talk about him, and the thought of those lips wrapped around him, my not-so-peeny penis decided to wake up. When Phoebe let out a sigh, causing her tits to rise and fall, he was definitely ready to party. She turned and looked at me, her tongue darting out, the pink tip doing a quick sweep along her top lip. Her breath quickened, in pace with my own and her eyes darkened.

"Tell me, pretty girl," I said in a low tone. "How do you know?"

"I saw it in your sweat pants, and I felt it hard against me when we kissed in your suite."

"It was real hard that day. Just for you."

Phoebe swallowed and leaned into me, her tits pushing against my arm. Her top was tight against them and I could see her nipples were hard. They looked and felt amazing.

"As it's not peeny, I think I should call it something else," she whispered into my ear, her lips skimming against the shell. "Something much more appropriate."

My dick started to throb in my pants, pushing against the zipper of my jeans. My head was buzzing with thoughts of pushing her onto her back, ripping off those sweat pants, and pushing into her. I would take her fast and hard and she wouldn't know what the fuck had hit her.

"What would that be?" My voice was rough and edged with want and need. "What would be more appropriate?"

Phoebe moved and quickly straddled me, holding onto the headboard with both hands. Her rack was practically in my face, the curve of her tits poking out of the top of her tank, enticing me to pull out my dick and fuck them. She wriggled on top of me, adjusting her hips, the friction sending a tremor right through me to the end of my dick.

"I have a great name for it." She dropped her mouth to mine, giving me a long, slow kiss. "It's perfect in fact."

"Fuuuuck," I groaned quietly. "What pretty girl?" I breathed heavily. "What would you call it?"

"Little dick," she cried, bursting into laughter and rolling off me, onto her back. "You're Dick, so *it* must be little dick."

Phoebe howled with laughter, rolling around, clutching her knees to her chest and while 'little dick' was somewhat disappointed, I couldn't help but laugh along with her. The sound resounded around the room, pure and crystal clear and totally infectious.

"You little shit," I said, my hands pulling her to me, and wrapping my arms around her in a tight embrace.

We laughed together, our bodies aligning perfectly, and I felt lighter than I had in years. Phoebe Drinkwater was important to me and I knew I had to do whatever possible to make us last longer than the shoot.

Phoebe and I were sitting having dinner with Beth, while the boys were reading in the lounge. It had been a great meal of steak and salad, that Phoebe had cooked, while I'd told Beth all about my situation. Maybe it would have been wiser not to, I didn't know what it was with these two women, but I just wanted to be open with them both. It felt natural to let them in on all the shit in my life, and I didn't have fears of any consequences. No doubt Marcia would tear me a new asshole for giving away the family secrets, but I trusted both Phoebe and Beth.

"So, what've you decided to do?" Phoebe asked.

"I'm going to do it."

Phoebe gasped and grabbed for my hand. "Are you sure?"

"Yeah," I sighed. "I owe him nothing, but he's my dad and I couldn't live with myself if I let him die."

"You're a bigger person than I am." Beth looked through the glass double doors to where the boys were sitting, still reading quietly. "I'd never want those boys to help Steven. I'd actively encourage them not to in fact."

"I don't think you would."

"I would Phoebes. I'd keep it from them. He doesn't deserve

anything from them after abandoning us. You," Beth said, nodding at me, "I kind of get it. Your dad left because of your mum being a drunk, but he still left you with her."

"I know that," I said, reliving the pain. "But before that he was a great dad. Was Steven?"

"No." Beth huffed. "He left because he's a wanker and had been from the minute they were born."

I let out a laugh. "He does sound like a total piece of work, I've got to be honest."

"He was. He is," Phoebe said, turning up her nose. "I never wanted her to marry him in the first place."

"Why, didn't you like him?"

"Nope, I didn't. Plus, he self-tanned and plucked his eyebrows. What sort of a man does that?"

I kept my mouth well and truly closed, knowing that both were things I'd had to do in the past, usually on a director's say so, but I'd still done them.

"Oh and he had bad breath. I have no idea how you could even kiss him, Beth."

Beth simply shrugged and picked up her glass of wine.

"The thing is," Phoebe said. "If it's all got to be top secret and he isn't to find out you're the donor, how the hell is it going to work?"

"Sue-Ann says she and dad's wife have it all planned out. We'll be in the same clinic and he'll be told the donor is going to be taken off life support."

"Do you really think he deserves a kidney, if he's not willing to see or speak to you?" Beth asked.

"That's the point of why it has to be secret. His wife told Sue-Ann he won't accept it if he knows it's mine." I blew out a breath and rubbed my forehead.

"But?" Phoebe said.

"But what?"

"But you're not sure."

I looked at her and wondered how she'd known that I didn't feel right about keeping it a secret. I hadn't said anything, but she'd noticed.

"I want to go and see him," I announced.

"Really, after what he did?"

"Beth," Phoebe said softly. "This is Grantley's decision."

"I know, I know. I'm sorry, I'm just very anti men who abandon their kids, that's all."

I nodded, totally understanding Beth's feelings on the subject.

"I just feel that it should be his choice. It shouldn't be down to his wife and his ex-wife to decide. I want to help him, but I also don't want to do this behind his back."

"So what are you going to do?" Phoebe took my hand and gave it a squeeze.

"I've spoken to Alexi and he said I can have three days off. He'll shoot around me and do all the reverse shots that I'm not in. He's been pretty great to be honest."

Alexi couldn't have been more understanding. He'd listened and not once flown off the handle at my request. I'd only wanted a couple of days, but it was him who suggested I take three. Yeah, the jet lag would be a bitch, but I'd power through it somehow.

"When do you go?" Phoebe asked, her lips downturned and her shoulders slumped.

"When do *we* go, you mean?"

"You and Barney or you and Marcia?"

I shook my head and grinned. "No, you and me, pretty girl. You're coming with me."

"I-I can't go," she stammered, looking at Beth. "You need me here."

"I can get some help for Beth, if she needs it," I offered. "I mean I wouldn't send Marcia around, she'd scare the kids, but I could organize something."

"God no," Beth replied. "I can manage. I don't need her as much as she thinks. She's crap at the discipline thing anyway."

"I am not," Phoebe protested. "I can do discipline. Anyway, that's not what I'm talking about."

They stared at each other for a tense moment. I averted my gaze, to give them some privacy. Then Beth gave her a warm smile. "That's going to take two weeks, so go."

"Please," I begged. "I need you with me."

And who could refuse that? Luckily for me, not Phoebe.

CHAPTER THIRTY-TWO

Phoebe

The last couple of days had been a whirlwind. As well as shooting, or hanging around in the holding room in my case, Grantley and I were getting ready for three days in Ohio. Most of the organisation had been done by Marcia, who'd bitched that I was going, but Grantley had insisted. In those two days, I hadn't seen much of him, mainly because it was all being kept secret from Sue-Ann. Grantley didn't want to risk it getting out and Sue-Ann tipping off his dad's wife. I was pretty glad, because I was a rubbish liar and would have never pulled it off. Grantley on the other hand was an actor, it was a piece of cake for him. We were now on the plane, in First Class, on the last leg of the journey from O'Hare airport in Chicago.

Grantley seemed nervous, he'd barely spoken for the last hour and now, only thirty minutes from landing, he was bouncing his leg and rhythmically tapping his thick, silver rings against the arm of his seat.

"It'll be fine," I said, laying a hand on his knee to stop it from moving.

He looked at me from under the peak of his all black, DSquared2 cap and wiped away the thin sheen of sweat on his top lip.

"I haven't seen him for twenty years. What if he doesn't know who I am?"

I giggled and gave his knee a gentle squeeze. "You're the famous Grantley James, of course he'll recognise you."

Grantley exhaled and nodded. "I guess so."

"So the address you've got for him, are you sure it's still valid?"

"Yeah, I had an investigator find him a few years back and Marcia made sure he was still there."

We sat in silence for a couple of minutes, until Grantley's leg started to jig again.

"If he refuses my kidney, I may as well have killed him. Maybe we shouldn't go." Grantley looked at me for confirmation that he was right, but I didn't say anything and just smiled. "His wife will hate me if I tell him and then he refuses it."

"You have to decide what you want to do. We can get the hire car and just go to the hotel if you'd prefer. No one is forcing you to do anything, it's all entirely your choice. You're giving this man a piece of you to keep him alive, you need to do whatever it takes so that this sits right with you."

I wondered if Grantley was scared of seeing him, it can't be easy to turn up in someone's life, especially when they've made it clear that you don't matter to them. Grantley leaned his head back against the seat and closed his eyes for a few seconds. Finally blowing out his cheeks, he looked at me and nodded.

"I'm going to do it. He deserves to have a choice in this." He seemed more determined and settled. "And it's my condition for giving it to him. If he wants me to go through this, the least he can do is acknowledge where the fuck it's coming from."

"I'm not sure *deserves* is the correct word," I scoffed. "But I understand why you feel he should."

Holding hands, we then sat in silence until we landed. As everyone started to file off the plane, Grantley put on his sunglasses and pulled the peak of his hat lower down his face. I'd asked him whether Barney should accompany us, but he'd wanted him to stay and keep an eye on Sue-Ann, insisting shades and a cap would be sufficient to keep him incognito.

To get through security seemed to take years, but finally after picking up the keys to a rental car, we stepped out into the bright morning sunshine. I thought it was fairly warm, but Grantley, used to the LA sunshine, shivered and pulled a black track jacket from his carry-on case and put it on.

"At least it's not raining," he said, taking my hand and leading me to the car.

"I think it's lovely and warm."

"You think Manchester is warm, when it's actually fucking freezing." Pulling us to a stop next to a huge, black four-wheel drive vehicle, Grantley held out the key and beeped open the locks. "Get in and I'll put the bags in the trunk."

I handed Grantley my bag and jumped into the car, remembering at the last minute to get in on the right side – which was actually the wrong side, in my opinion. After getting inside and shutting the door, Grantley looked at me.

"I'm fucking shitting myself," he admitted as his shaky hand went to put the key in the ignition.

"It'll be fine and if it isn't and he's rude to you, well then he doesn't deserve your kidney."

Leaning in to kiss me, Grantley placed a clammy palm on my cheek. "Thank you."

"You have nothing to thank me for."

"Yeah, I do. You came with me instead of me having to bring Marcia. I knew you'd keep me calm, or as calm as I can be, so I really appreciate it."

"Entirely my pleasure," I said, giving him a quick kiss. "Why don't we go to the hotel, grab something to eat, maybe freshen up and then go and see him."

Grantley straightened up. "You don't think I should just get it over with?"

"No, I think you need to calm down and relax a little first."

He was all wound up, and I could see the tension in his neck and shoulders. Plus, I had an idea on how to relax him. He'd trusted me to do this with him – to be with him at an extremely important occasion, and it had made the last piece of ice drop away from my heart. I was ready to take that next step.

"Yeah, you're right. I think that's a much better plan."

I gave him a smile and pulled back, clicking my seatbelt into place. "Okay then, let's go."

CHAPTER THIRTY-THREE

Grantley

As we drove east on I-70 toward Yellow Springs, neither Phoebe nor I said a whole lot. I was still nervous as hell and she understood that, so she just held my hand and left me to my own thoughts.

After forty or so minutes, we drove up in front of the large, Colonial looking hotel and I had to admit it looked pretty nice. Marcia had, of course, made the reservation for us. She'd stayed here a couple of times, so it had to be good – Marcia only liked the best.

"Wow," Phoebe said, looking up through the side window. "It's so pretty."

"Yeah, it looks nice. Marcia says the rooms are pretty luxurious."

Phoebe turned to me and gave me a huge smile. "Thank you for inviting me. This looks as though it's probably the nicest hotel I've ever stayed in." I leaned in and kissed her softly. It was probably going to be the best I'd stayed in too, but because she was with me.

"Come on, let's get checked in."

"This bed is enormous," Phoebe said, bouncing up and down on it. "We could get four people in here."

"I think just you and me will be fine. Unless of course you want me to take the couch." I nodded to the pale blue couch, under the huge plate window with colonial shutters on it.

She looked up at me, her arms braced either side of her and grinned. "No, I'm quite happy to have you share with me."

"That's good." I bent and kissed her forehead and then moved over to the oak chest where we'd placed our bags, pulling my t-shirt over my head. "I'm going to take a shower, unless you want to go first."

As I bent to search through my stuff for some clean underwear, jeans, and tee, Phoebe's arms wrapped around me from behind.

"How about we shower together," she whispered, placing a soft kiss on my back.

Instantly my body came alive and my dick stirred. And as her delicate fingers popped the button on my pants, I let out an involuntary groan.

"Shit, Phoebes. Are you sure?"

"Never been surer."

Very slowly, she caught hold of my zipper and pulled it down, pushing her hand inside and taking hold of my rock-hard dick, her other hand squeezing my shoulder as she moved her kisses to my neck. "So this shower we're going to have."

"Phoebe."

"Hmm," she groaned, her lips on my neck.

"This shower, are you going to do extras, or am I just going to have to watch you, like those damn monkeys, and jack off to the sight of you wet and naked?"

"No, this is most definitely an interactive activity – not show and tell."

When she pumped my dick, I dropped my head forward on a groan, and reached around to twine my fingers into her hair with one hand. The other I placed over Phoebe's, urging her to take a firmer grip of me. She pumped me a couple of times more and, if possible, I went even harder.

"Take off your clothes," she said into my ear.

As she moved away from me, I felt the loss of her at my back. Her touch and the feel of her pushed against me, had felt so damn good. Without any hesitation, desperate to have my body against hers again, I rid myself of my clothes, leaving them in a heap on the floor.

I turned around to see the most magnificent sight I had ever seen. Phoebe was standing in front of me, in nothing but a tiny dove-grey scrap of lace covering her pussy. Her hair fell over one shoulder, covering one of her high, round breasts, leaving the other exposed. Her hips flared out from a narrow waist, to toned thighs. As my eyes grazed over her, Phoebe's hand went to her stomach, where she had an adorable, little potbelly.

"I don't go to the gym and I like chocolate and crisps," she giggled nervously.

I strode toward her, pulling her hands away and threading my fingers through hers. "You're fucking beautiful and perfect. Never think otherwise and don't ever hide yourself from me."

Leaning forward, I cupped her cheek and kissed her gently.

"So, how you going to relax me?" I asked, my dick straining and pulsating.

She grinned at me and turned.

"I'll show you," she said, over her shoulder as she moved toward the bathroom. "Just follow me."

I watched as her ass swayed seductively and I was pretty sure I would follow her anywhere.

"Shit Phoebes," I gasped, rolling onto my back. "I can't remember my name, never mind what the fuck we're here for."

"Good." Phoebe breathed heavily, her chest rising and falling rapidly. "I succeeded."

"Where the fuck did you learn that thing you did in the shower? Not from some damn glittery sword shaped like a dick, I'm sure. I think I saw stars."

"A girl never reveals her all secrets."

She giggled, her tinkling laughter filling the air and my soul. She was everything that a man could want, and she'd damn well side-swiped me into wanting that everything myself. I had not seen her coming and I was pretty glad I hadn't, because if I had, I may well have gone into hiding.

"What time is it?" Phoebe asked, turning onto her stomach.

I reached for my cell. "Just before two-thirty. You hungry?"

She shrugged and kicked her legs up behind her. "I ate quite a bit on the plane."

"Yeah you did." I laughed and slapped her ass. "You even finished off my dinner."

"Ow." Phoebe reached behind and rubbed her ass cheek. "It's the altitude, it gives me an appetite."

"Whatever. Hey let me do that." I moved her hand and started to gently rub where I'd slapped her. "Sorry, was it too hard?"

"No, I'm just being a baby."

"Even so," I said, pushing up. "I'm sorry. Maybe this helps."

I placed a kiss on the soft flesh.

"Hmm," she moaned, dropping her head to the bed. "That's nice."

"It is, hey?" I gave her another kiss, adding a little nip to it. "How about this?"

Slowly, I kissed down the curve of her ass and along the back of her thigh.

"Yes," Phoebe said breathily, her back arching. "That's really nice too."

"What about this?"

Another kiss while my hand caressed her backside.

"You're amazing," I whispered, kissing her other thigh. "Perfect."

Kiss and caress.

"You make me laugh like no one ever has before."

Kiss and caress.

"I smile all the time when I'm with you."

Kiss and caress.

"You make me feel normal."

Kiss and caress.

"Oh God, Grantley."

Phoebe's breaths were short and quick as I carried on kissing back up to her ass.

"I'm so close," she moaned.

I gave her one more kiss, touched her pulsing bud and watched in awe as my girl went off like a rocket.

CHAPTER THIRTY-FOUR

Phoebe

Grantley seemed to be a lot more relaxed since our shower and little bit of exercise on the bed. In fact, we both were, so much so, that we'd fallen asleep for almost four hours. I was a little disappointed as I would have liked to have had a look around Dayton, or maybe go to the RiverScape MetroPark and do a river walk. As it was, we had a couple of drinks in the bar and then dinner.

"I think we should go fairly early in the morning," Grantley said, popping a french-fry into his mouth. "Should only take forty minutes to get back into Dayton."

"You want to get it over and done with?"

He shrugged. "I guess so."

"Or is it that you want to spend some time with him, if it goes okay?"

Grantley averted his eyes to concentrate on his almost empty plate.

"It's okay to want that, Grantley. It's only natural, he's your dad."

"Yeah but he left me, Phoebes. Why the hell am I even giving him the time of day, never mind my damn kidney?"

"Because you can't help how you feel. You said he was a good dad before he left."

Grantley sat back in his chair and threw his napkin onto his plate. With a huge sigh, he ran a hand through his hair.

"What a fucking shit storm this is."

"Hey," I whispered, leaning forward to take his hand, "don't let all that work I did relaxing you go to waste."

He grinned at me. "You were phenomenal, I have to admit."

As I thought about our shower, I felt my cheeks heat up. Grantley gave me a cheeky grin and reached for the wine to pour me another glass. Just as he put the bottle back down, we heard his name being called.

"Shit," he muttered. "I thought we'd be safe in here."

We were eating in the hotel restaurant and as they had a strict privacy policy for their guests, Grantley had felt we'd be able to have an uninterrupted dinner.

"Grantley, is that you?"

Grantley's brow furrowed and he swung around in his seat. "Oh my God, Serena. How the hell are you?"

I looked up to see a tall, blonde woman approach us. She was wearing a tight, red dress and extremely high, black shoes. She looked sexy and sophisticated and made me feel extremely underdressed in my white linen trousers and vest top.

As she got closer to us, Grantley pushed up from his chair and held his arms out to her.

"What the hell are you doing here?" she asked, walking into his embrace and kissing his cheek. "Of all the places to see you."

"I'm just visiting family. What about you?" Grantley stepped back to look her up and down. "You look great by the way."

"Oh bless you, I've just got back from Barbados. My folks were celebrating their thirty year anniversary."

"Really, how are they?"

"They're good," she replied, looking Grantley up and down with a smile. "Really good."

"So why are you here?"

"I'm doing a restoration project here. A huge turn of the century house that the new owner wants to restore to its former glory. I'm staying here at the hotel, until I can arrange a rental."

I watched the two of them interact and felt like a spare part, an invisible one at that. After a couple of minutes, Grantley spun around.

"Shit, I'm sorry. Serena this is my friend, Phoebe. Phoebe, this is Serena, an old friend."

Serena leaned around Grantley and stuck out her hand. "Lovely to meet you, Phoebe."

"You too," I replied, trying not to feel put out that Grantley introduced me as his 'friend'.

"Why don't you join us," Grantley offered. "For a drink at least."

Serena gave him a beautiful smile. "If you're sure that's okay. I've just got back from dinner, but a nightcap would be wonderful."

Grantley looked to me and I nodded. What else was I going to say – no, she's too bloody beautiful to sit next to?

Grantley pulled back a chair and Serena sat down.

"So, I said to him, if you want that on your walls you need to employ a different contractor."

Grantley's deep laugh echoed alongside Serena's ladylike tinkling one and it took all my time not to stick my fingers down my throat and gag. It had been like that for the last half hour, a bloody mutual appreciation society. They'd barely said two words to me, and to say I was pissed off was an understatement. At one point, while looking at some photographs on Serena's phone, Grantley had actually turned his back on me.

I decided that I'd give it another ten minutes and then I was going to go to bed. Grantley could stay down here with Princess Serena. While they continued with their chatter, I wasted time, busying myself making a tower of sugar cubes. It was when I'd just managed to balance sugar cube number four that Grantley actually spoke to me.

"Sorry, what was that?" I asked, offering him the weakest of smiles.

"I was just telling Serena that you're from England."

"Hmm that's right."

She'd know by my accent if I'd actually been given an option to speak.

"Whereabouts?" she asked. "I went to London once, I loved it."

"No, I'm not from London," I answered and went back to my tower.

"Oh, okay." She gave Grantley a small smile – one that said 'wow, your friend is rude'.

"Phoebe's from near Manchester," Grantley answered. "Aren't you?"

I looked at him and nodded, not missing the hard stare I was getting.

"Yes, about forty miles away." I gave Serena a smile. "So, how do you two know each other?"

"Didn't Grantley tell you?" Serena said, rubbing his forearm, over his scar. "Gosh I'm wounded."

"Tell me what?" I replied, smiling sweetly, dreading what Grantley *hadn't* told me.

"We lived together," Serena announced. "In fact we almost got married."

My heart stuttered, did a fly up to my throat and then right back down to my stomach.

He'd lived with this woman. This woman was beautiful.

"Oh," I choked out.

Grantley closed his eyes momentarily and I saw his lips move in a silent curse. He looked at Serena.

"It was a drunken suggestion more than a proposal, if I remember correctly."

"Again Grantley, I'm wounded." Serena giggled and turned to me. "He's never been the romantic type. I think we thought about it for a day tops and then decided we'd just move in together – which lasted only a little longer than our 'engagement'."

I forced a smile and picked up my coffee, allowing Grantley and Serena to continue their reliving of old times. Once I finished the last drop, I decided I'd had enough.

"I think I'm going to go up to bed," I announced, pushing up from the table. "It's been lovely meeting you Serena, but I'm shattered after the travelling."

"You too, Phoebe. Hopefully we can meet up for dinner before you fly back home."

"That would be lovely." I held my hand out to Serena.

As she shook it, Grantley got up from his chair too and leaned in to give Serena a hug.

"Oh, you're going too?" she asked, surprised.

"Yeah, like Phoebes said, it's been a long day, we should get to bed. Was great to see you though."

Serena looked between us and gave a soft laugh. "God I'm such an idiot. I didn't realize you were together, when you said Phoebe was your friend, I just thought..."

"That's totally understandable," I replied. "He said I was his friend." My answer was pointed and I didn't really care. What did she think I was, his bloody body guard?

Grantley flicked me a worried look and took hold of my hand.

"Great to see you again, Serena."

"You too Grantley, and please let's do dinner."

Grantley didn't answer, but kissed her cheek and led me away from the dining room.

"Wow, crazy seeing her here," he said as we got inside the lift.

"Hmm, she seems lovely."

I pulled my hand from Grantley's and moved to lean against the rail at the back wall. I really didn't want to be a spikey bitch, but I just couldn't help but feel it. I could barely look at him. The disappointment I felt was overwhelming. How could he treat me like that? I dropped my head, angry that hot tears were threatening.

"You okay?" Grantley asked, stooping down to look at me. "Hey, what's wrong?"

He lifted my chin with his finger and looked at me. His shoulders sagged as he let out an exhale.

"What are you upset about?"

"I'm not upset," I snapped, as the lift shuddered to a halt.

As the doors opened, I pushed past Grantley and practically ran towards our room, wanting to get in the bathroom and hide from him for a while. Unfortunately, as I got to the door, I realised that he had the key card, having left the spare in the room, so I had to wait. When he reached me, I stood to one side, letting him open the door and usher me in.

"Okay," Grantley said, throwing the card on top of the chest of drawers. "What's wrong? Is this because I didn't tell you I'd lived with someone – lived with Serena?"

"If that's what you think, then you're more clueless than I thought," I replied, while rifling through my bag for my PJs.

"Well I must be, because if it's not that I have no fucking clue what's upset you."

Finding my pyjamas, I clutched them to my chest. "I told you, I'm not upset. I'm fucking angry and disappointed."

"What the hell for?" Grantley moved towards me and cupped a hand under my elbow. "I'm sorry I didn't tell you before, about living with her, but it just didn't seem important. Like she said, it lasted all of five minutes. As soon as we'd moved in together, we pretty much realized it was a mistake. We tried for a couple of months and then called it quits – on our relationship too."

"Grantley that was your life before we'd ever met. We've been together a short time, I have no rights to complain or worry about anything you've done in the past. If you chose not to tell me then that's your prerogative. I admit, it was a shock, but that's not what this is about."

"So what the hell are you angry and disappointed about?" he asked, throwing his hands into the air.

I shook my head. "You introduced me as your friend and then proceeded to ignore me. Do you know at one point you turned your damn back to me."

"No I did not." He shook his head. "I wouldn't do that."

"Yeah, well you did." I pushed past him to go to the bathroom.

"Phoebes," he pleaded. "I'm sorry, it's just I haven't seen her in a long time. It was kinda nice to catch up."

I swung around to face him, the anger pounding in my head. "And I understand that, I do, but you didn't have to ignore me. And as for me being your 'friend', well that's fine, but if that's all I am, I bloody well wish you'd told me before I had sex with you."

"For fuck's sake, it's one damn word. So fucking shoot me."

"It's a word that you insisted I was to your mother, or was that just to piss her off?" I cried. "If you just want to be friends now, then fine, but go and get your own fucking room because you're not sleeping in here with me."

Grantley stamped his foot. "God damn it. This is the exact reason why I don't do fucking relationships. You woman are all the same, damn bat shit crazy."

"Fine," I snapped. "There we have it, I'm bat shit crazy and you're a rude cock womble. All sorted, now fuck off."

With that I turned and stalked into the bathroom, just a few minutes later hearing the door to the room slam shut.

CHAPTER THIRTY-FIVE

Grantley

What the fuck just happened?

I slammed out of our room and down to the elevator, stabbing a finger at the button. What the hell was wrong with women? What the hell was wrong with Phoebe? She was normally so cool about everything, but she was spitting like a cornered snake in there. All I'd been doing had been catching up with an old friend.

"Fuck," I muttered, running a hand through my hair.

Was she right, had I concentrated on Serena and barely spoken to Phoebes? Yeah probably, knowing the dick that I was at times. If I had, I get why she would be mad, but to practically throw me out of the room, well that was a bit overboard.

Shit, did I really turn my back on her?

As the elevator stopped, I considered pushing the button for our floor and going back up, but figured it might be better to cool down a little. Plus, I was right, this was exactly the reason I didn't do relationships. We'd had a great day, with some amazing sex thrown in, and one little mistake and she'd flown right off the fucking handle.

I decided that I'd have one drink in the bar and then go back up and try and smooth things over. Shit, who was I kidding, I'd be going up there to plead her forgiveness.

"Draught beer, please."

The barman nodded and set about drawing me a large beer. As he pushed it toward me, I felt a hand on my back.

Phoebe. Thank fuck one of us was an adult, now I'd take her back upstairs and show her what she meant to me.

Grinning, I turned around.

"Serena," I said, shocked to see her there.

"Hey. I was having a smoke outside and noticed you come in."

"You still smoking? You do know it's bad for you, don't you?"

Serena pulled out a barstool, inching it a little closer to mine.

"I know, but I only have the occasional one these days. Must have been seeing you, made me feel the need."

She laughed softly, but the way she was looking at me, I could already sense where this was going.

"I just thought I'd have one last beer. Phoebe's taking a shower."

Serena nodded thoughtfully. "So how long have you been together?"

"A couple of months," I lied.

She didn't need to know our business, plus part of me hoped it might warn her off without me having to say the words. A budding two-week thing, well she'd be all over that like a rash, if I knew Serena.

"I thought maybe longer to be honest."

"Why so?" I asked, edging my stool back.

"New relationships don't usually see one of the couple drinking alone in the bar, last thing at night."

"Like I said, I fancied a beer and Phoebe is showering. No drama."

I took a huge long swig of my beer, and then pushed the still half-full glass toward the back of the bar.

"I think I'll get back up there. She's probably finished by now."

What the hell was I doing downstairs, sitting with Serena, when I should be with Phoebe? She was right, I had been rude and a fucking cock womble, whatever the fuck that was. I hated that I'd made her feel like that. She was here supporting me and I'd made her feel like shit while I chatted about old times to an ex.

"You could stay for another," Serena said, placing a hand on my arm. "Maybe take a bottle of your favorite Macallan back to my room."

I pushed off my stool, moving my arm away from Serena's touch.

"I don't think so, Serena. You know I'm here with Phoebes."

"It's just a drink, Grant," she replied, with a shake of her head.

"No, you and I both know you're thinking it would be much more than a drink. Which it could never be."

I went to move away, but Serena caught hold of my hand.

"For old time's sake?"

"No Serena. I'm going upstairs to my girlfriend, who I care a great deal about, because she'll be waiting for me, in *our* bed."

She dropped her head and sighed.

"You take care," I said and left her sitting at the bar.

When I let myself into the room, it was in darkness and I could just about make out Phoebe's body in the huge bed. She was deadly still, but I knew she wasn't sleeping because I could hear her sniffing.

Fuck, she was crying and I felt like a total shit.

Climbing onto the bed, I crawled up behind her, wrapped my arms around her body and kissed the back of her head.

"I'm so sorry," I whispered. "I *was* a fucking cock womble and I can't apologize enough."

"Where did you go?" she whispered, her voice breaking.

"The bar. Serena was there."

Phoebe's body stiffened in my arms and she tried to wriggle free, but I held on tight.

"She asked me to go back to her room, for a drink."

"What did you say?"

"I'm here, so you know what I said. But, if you want specifics, I told her no, because my girlfriend who I cared about a great deal, was waiting for me in our bed."

"You did?" Phoebe left out a sigh and her whole body relaxed.

"Yes, pretty girl, I did."

She twisted and turned over to face me, and in the dim light, with only the thin shafts of the moon shining through the shutters, I saw the sticky tears on her face. I leaned in and kissed them away, two kisses to each cheek and a final soft one on her lips.

"I didn't think," I whispered. "I got lost in catching up with her and acted like a rude prick."

"I felt invisible," Phoebe replied. "And I'm such a long way from home, it just got to me. I felt so alone, but I know I probably over-reacted."

"No, no you didn't. I was in the wrong. I should have introduced you properly, as my girlfriend and I should have afforded you the courtesy that you deserve – even as my friend."

"Are we friends again?" she asked, snuggling closer.

"You bet we are." I kissed her again. "Good friends, with special benefits."

"We are, eh?"

"Oh yeah," I nodded. "And I'm going to show my girl exactly how special those benefits are."

And I fucking did and my girlfriend damn well loved it.

CHAPTER THIRTY-SIX

GRANTLEY

"Do I look okay?" I asked, straightening my button down shirt.

Phoebe got up on her tiptoes and gave me a soft kiss. "You look extremely handsome. He's going to be very proud."

"I have no idea why I should care whether he is or not."

"Because he's your dad, and even though he left you, he was a great dad before he did."

I let out a long exhale, shoved my hands into my pockets, and leaned against the hood of the rental car. We'd parked a couple of blocks away from my dad's address because I figured a strange car pulling up outside his house would announce my arrival and I didn't want that. I didn't want to give him an opportunity to run again.

Phoebe had been great at keeping me calm. She'd worked her magic on me once again. I smiled as I thought about how she'd woken me a couple of hours earlier. Shit, that girl had skills. In fact, she was just amazing in every way. I'd been a total douche over the whole Serena meeting, but after I'd apologized, that had been the end of it. No sulking or pouting or bringing it up at every opportunity. She even apologized for overreacting, but she shouldn't have – I was in the wrong, not her.

Looking up from the sidewalk my eyes met Phoebe's, and all I could see was warmth and gentleness, and I was so damn glad I'd asked her to come with me. It had been a spur of the moment decision, made because of how damn adorable she looked in her embarrassment over the boys playing with her dildo. However, once the words were out of my mouth, I knew I'd made the right choice. The way she'd been with me since we'd got to Ohio only proved that.

"Okay, let's do this," I said, snagging her hand and moving away from the car.

A few minutes later, we stood a little ways down from his house.

"It's lovely," Phoebe said, looking up at the single-fronted two-story.

It was; it had a neat, well-tended lawn with a curved flowerbed cut into it with a few bushes planted. It was half brick and half clapboard, painted a brilliant white and on the driveway, at the side that blended into a path to the door, was parked a small sedan and his 1976 Harley Davidson Shovelhead.

"Shit," I muttered, squeezing Phoebe's hand.

"What's wrong?"

I nodded toward the driveway. "His bike. It's the same one he had when I was a kid." I swallowed the lump in my throat. "The same one he'd take me on around the neighborhood."

"Oh Grantley."

Phoebe kissed my bicep and moved closer to my side.

"We can go, if you want to," she said, her eyes firmly pinned on the bike.

"Nope. I came all this way for a reason, and I'm going to do it."

Taking a deep breath, I led Phoebe up the path and rang the bell. I heard it chime inside followed by a woman's voice.

"Hold on, I'm coming."

I looked at Phoebe and gave her a tight smile, as we waited for Deanna Miller, my dad's wife, to open the door. When it did swing open, I took a step back and drew in a breath.

"Oh hello. Can I help you?" Deanna, a pretty brunette, beamed at us.

When I opened my mouth, nothing came out. Deanna must have properly looked at me then, because she gasped and put a hand to her chest.

"Oh my God," she croaked out. "It's you."

I coughed and stepped forward again. "I guess that depends on who you think I am."

Anxiety gripped me, because if she said 'Grantley James, the movie star', if my dad had never acknowledged me, then I think it would have broken me.

"Trent's boy," she whispered.

I drew in a jagged breath, desperately trying to keep my emotions in place. Just those words: 'Trent's boy', made me want to drop to my knees and sob for the dad I'd missed. My dad.

"Is he home?" I asked, my voice unsteady.

Deanna nodded and stepped back from the door, silently inviting us in. As we walked into the spacious lounge, with a set of stairs off to the right, I felt my knees trembling.

"You okay?" Phoebe asked.

I nodded, my mouth too dry to speak. I knew I should say something to Deanna, about how I was going to spoil her and Sue-Ann's damn stupid plan, but no words would come. Deanna hovered next to us and looked between me and Phoebe.

"He's going to be shocked. I just can't believe you're here."

Thankfully, Phoebe spoke for me. "We know that this isn't what you want, but Grantley felt he had to speak to his dad about it."

Deanna slapped a hand across her mouth, stifling a sob, and shook her head. "No...you have no idea."

"I'm sorry." I managed to get out. "I had to."

She looked at me with tears in her eyes and I was sure I saw joy, but had no idea how could that be when I was about to tell my dad that it was my kidney he was getting. She must know that he was going to refuse it – or maybe Sue-Ann had got it all wrong.

"Please, take a seat," Deanna said, wiping her face. "I'll go get Trent."

"Thank you." Phoebe gave her a warm smile and led me to a brown leather couch.

We sat in silence, the only noise, the tick of a clock on the wall above the fireplace. I looked around and could see they lived a comfortable life. Their furniture was of good quality, their TV pretty big, and there was a bookcase, with books and framed pictures on every shelf. I was too far away to be able to see properly, but I was pretty sure I recognized one of the photographs. It was me and Dad, sitting on his Harley. I was in front, holding onto the handlebars, with Dad's hands over mine, and we were both grinning like we'd just won the damn lottery. If it was the picture I was thinking of, I had two front teeth missing and a huge scrape on my knee where I'd fallen over in the park. That was why I was smiling – Dad had taken me for ice cream and then for a ride on the bike to make me feel better.

"She seems lovely," Phoebe whispered, leaning in closer.

I nodded. "Yeah."

After a few minutes, I heard footsteps behind me on the hardwood floor and I thought my heart was going to explode, it was beating so fast. Adrenaline rapidly pumped through my veins, turning my blood to ice and electrifying the hairs on my arms. I could hardly breathe, in the corner of my eye, I saw the long, lean body of my dad.

I dropped my head and leaned forward, pulling my hand from Phoebe's to rest my forearms on my knees. He was here. My dad. My world for six years, before he left me.

"Grantley." Phoebe laid a hand on my back, her voice tender, yet full of urgency. "Are you okay?"

Breathing heavily, I nodded.

His boots came into view – biker boots like he'd always worn. The hems of worn denims draped over the tops of them. Then I smelled it, that familiar odor of my dad. Engine oil and juniper. He smelled exactly the same. Almost twenty years and he was still wearing the same cologne.

I couldn't look up, for fear of seeing hatred in his eyes. For fear that he'd disappear again. I wanted to scream at him, but I wanted to hug him. I wanted to punch him, but I wanted to cry because he was here. After twenty years, he was here. I started to shake, desperate to know what to do. Now wondering whether I was right to take his chance of life away from him. This was wrong. I shouldn't be here, he would refuse to take my kidney through guilt and he'd die. I would lose him again.

Then, I felt it. His big hand was on my head. Just like he used to do when I was a kid.

"It's okay, son," he said in his deep growl. "It's okay. I'm here."

CHAPTER THIRTY-SEVEN

Phoebe

I pulled in a breath as Mr. Miller placed his hand on Grantley's head. I looked up at him and saw his eyes brimming with tears. His worn but handsome face looked devastated as he looked at his wife. Deanna gave him a sad smile and swiped at the wetness on her cheeks.

"Grantley, son," he said, looking down at Grantley's head. "Look at me."

Grantley shook his head, still leaning forward.

"Please son."

"I'm sorry," Grantley said on long breath. "I couldn't do it without talking to you." He turned to Deanna, but keeping his eyes averted from his dad. "I'm so sorry."

Deanna blinked and looked at Trent, shrugging her thin shoulders.

"What are you sorry for?" Trent closed his eyes briefly. "You have nothing to be sorry for."

Grantley finally looked up at him and as soon as their eyes met, Trent flung his arms around his son, pulling him up to standing.

Grantley sobbed, and seeing him so distressed caused tears to flow freely down my own cheeks. I looked over to Deanna, who was also crying with her arms wrapped tightly around her waist.

The air in the room was thick with emotion as father and son clung to each other, both declaring how sorry they were. Twenty years of hurt and pain, washing around us and punching both men in their guts.

Finally, Trent pulled away and placed a hand on Grantley's cheek.

"I can't believe you're here," he said, his deep voice cracking with emotion. "All this time and you came. I don't deserve this, but I hoped. God, how I hoped."

Grantley silently stared at his dad for a few seconds and then pulled away, pacing over to the fireplace. Trent dropped his arms to his side and looked to Deanna, who flopped down onto a chair. My gaze turned to Grantley, watching to see what he was going to do or say. He did nothing at first, simply standing and staring at Trent, but when his dad took a step forward, Grantley held up a hand.

"No. Don't," he snapped, wiping his eyes with his forearm. "I need to say what I've got to say."

Trent stopped and nodded.

Grantley looked at Deanna. "I know you didn't want this, and I know you and Sue-Ann cooked up this damn stupid plan, but he has a right to choose."

"Sue-Ann?" Trent said, turning to his wife. "What's he talking about?"

Deanne shrugged. "I don't know honey."

"No point lying now I'm here," Grantley said. "I'm here now and I'm here because I thought you should know."

"Know what, Grantley? What are you talking about?"

"Your kidney. The kidney that you need, I'm going to give you mine. Your wife contacted Sue-Ann and asked her to ask me. It was supposed to be secret, because she said your guilt wouldn't let you accept it, but I couldn't do it without letting you know."

I looked up at Trent, waiting for him to blow like a volcano, but the explosion didn't come. He looked confused, looking between Deanna and Grantley.

"I have no idea what it is your mother has told you, but I have never spoken to her," Deanna said, moving to the edge of the chair.

Grantley took in a deep breath and shook his head. "Please stop lying, this is hard enough for me. I'm here because he needs to know."

"Just tell me what it is you're talking about son," Trent pleaded, holding a hand out to Grantley.

"The kidney you need, I told you."

Grantley's voice got louder and I could see he was getting agitated. I wanted to go to him and hold him, but wasn't sure it was the right thing to do. I sensed that he just needed to get it all off his chest and tell his dad why he was there.

"Grantley, son, I don't need a kidney. What would make you think that?"

I looked at Trent and had to admit, he looked fit and healthy, not at all like he was seriously ill.

"You don't need to pretend. I know you felt guilty about taking mine, which was why they came up with their plan, and I want you to have it, but I just couldn't do it without you knowing. You only have one and it's diseased."

"What?" Trent asked, shaking his head.

"Don't pretend that you don't need this," Grantley cried.

"I'm not pretending, I swear." Trent looked at Grantley as though he was crazy. "What on earth made you think I needed a kidney?"

Grantley looked around Trent to Deanna. "You spoke to Sue-Ann," he protested. "She said Dad needed a kidney but felt too guilty to ask me. You were going to tell him some guy had died."

Deanna shook her head furiously. "I didn't, I swear. Your dad is perfectly fine. Why would I do that?"

Grantley looked to me. "Didn't she say that, Phoebes? Didn't Sue-Ann say Dad needed my kidney?"

He looked anxiously at me, begging me with his eyes to prove he wasn't going mad.

I nodded and turned to Trent. "She did, Mr. Miller. Grantley's telling the truth. That's what Sue-Ann said."

Trent went deathly pale and I was certain he was going to scream at Deanna for telling his secret, but he didn't. His nostrils flared in time with his heavy breathing as he stood in front of Grantley.

"I will fucking kill her," he spat out. "She is one piece of shit."

"She only did what she thought was best," Grantley said. "I have no time for her, but this she did for good reasons."

Trent's eyes narrowed on his son as he moved forward and placed a hand on Grantley's shoulder. Grantley glanced down at it and I noticed how his breath hitched at his dad's touch.

"Grantley, I swear. I no more need a new kidney than you do. That piece of scum, who is your mother, lied to you. I have no fucking idea why, but she has. Deanna hasn't spoken to her. Have you babe?"

He looked over his shoulder at Deanna, who shook her head. "No, I swear."

Grantley looked at me, he was broken and desolate, and instantly I was out of my seat and going to his side to wrap my arms around his middle.

"Please don't lie to him, Mr. Miller," I whispered. "It took a lot for him to come here."

"I'm not lying honey. I don't need a kidney. I don't know what Sue-Ann has cooked up, but she's pulled a real doozy this time. And what the hell makes you think I only have one damn kidney."

Grantley tensed, his muscles going rigid beneath my touch and I held on tightly. He was going to detonate, I could just feel the anger building.

"I...she told me. The scar on your side. She told me you'd had a kidney removed."

"What the fuck bullshit has she been feeding you? I got that from a bike accident when I was nineteen."

"But she said..." Grantley trailed off and looked at me anxiously and then back to his father.

"I'm sorry Grantley. I don't know what to say." Trent went to touch Grantley, but at the last second pulled his hand away, looking at me with deep sorrow in his eyes.

"But she said you needed it. She said you wouldn't ask me because you felt guilty. She said you only had one kidney and you needed mine."

His voice was full of confusion and questions – questions that none of us could answer.

"You're not lying?" he asked Trent.

Trent shook his head and took a deep breath. "I swear." Trent glanced at Deanna and then turned back to his son, and swallowed hard. "Even if I did need one, I wouldn't ask you Grantley. I couldn't."

"Why?" Grantley snapped. "Why wouldn't you. I would do it, I'm here. I was willing to."

"I know, and I'm so grateful that you're here. I have missed you so damn much. There's been a huge space in my heart for twenty fu-."

"So why the hell did you leave then?" Grantley bellowed, pulling away from me and getting into Trent's space. "Why leave me with her? You were my damn world and you left me there."

Deanna let out a ragged sob as Trent stumbled backwards a step. He brushed her helping hand away and righted himself, standing up tall to face his son again.

"I am so sorry," he said. "Sorrier than you will ever know, but I couldn't stay, Grantley, I just couldn't."

"You could have taken me with you. I'm your son. You *should* have taken me."

Grantley had tears careening down his face, his chest heaving with the exertion of expending the emotions of abandonment and loneliness that he'd felt as a child. I moved to him and placed one hand on his back, and taking his hand with my other. I hated seeing him in so much pain and had to comfort him in any way I could.

"Grantley, please don't," I soothed.

"No Phoebe. He needs to know how shit my fucking life was without him."

Trent groaned and slapped a hand against his mouth. "I couldn't take you, Grantley. I just couldn't."

"Why not? *Just tell me, why the fucking hell not.*"

"Because I'm not your father, Grantley." Trent yelled. "I'm not your fucking dad."

CHAPTER THIRTY-EIGHT

Grantley

"No," I whispered, shaking my head. "No, it's not true. You can't say that. It's a damn lie."

My dad could barely catch his breath as he stood in front of me, repeating over and over how sorry he was.

"Did she tell you that?" I screamed. "Because she's a fucking lying bitch."

"Oh God, I'm so sorry," Phoebe whimpered, clutching tightly onto my arm. "I don't know what to say."

"Nothing Phoebe, nothing at all, because it's not true. Dad, please tell me it's not true."

I rushed to him and grabbed hold of his hand, tugging on it and pleading that he tell me he'd got it all wrong.

"I can't, I'm sorry. I really wish I could."

Dad's eyes were full of sorrow and remorse and worst of all, full of truth.

He wasn't my dad.

I'd grieved for his leaving for twenty years and he wasn't mine to grieve for.

I dropped his hand and took two steps back, finding myself in

Phoebe's arms. She wrapped them around me, laying a wet cheek against my back.

"How do you know?" I asked.

"Your mom confirmed it, after I figured it out."

I drew in a sharp breath. She might have been lying.

"No," Dad said. "I know what you're thinking, but it's true, son."

I gave an empty laugh. Son. How the hell could he call me that?

"I think we should leave you two alone," Deanna said, moving alongside my dad. "Phoebe, sweetheart, how about you come and sit in the yard with me for a while."

Phoebe looked up at me and then at Deanna.

"Will you be okay?" she asked, her voice breaking.

I nodded and as she let go of me and moved to walk away, I grabbed hold of her elbow and pulled her back to kiss her forehead.

"Are you sure?"

"Yep," I whispered against her skin. "Go with Deanna. We need to talk."

Once Deanna and Phoebe had closed the door behind them, my dad ushered me to sit down. As I did, I realized I couldn't think of him as that any longer. He wasn't my dad, but just Trent Miller, the man that raised me for six years.

"I still think of you as my son," Trent said, clutching a hand to the back of his neck. "I never stopped loving and missing you."

"So why the fuck did you leave me then?"

A vein pulsed in my temple, so fast I thought it was going to burst with the levels of anger running through it. I hated him for leaving, but I hated her more for making him. I hated them both.

Trent sighed. "If I could go back and make different decisions, I would."

"What, you'd have never had an affair with that biker whore you left with?" My words were venomous, my tone full of spite, and I knew distaste was etched all over my face.

"I mean, I would have taken you with me, no matter what Sue-Ann said."

Hearing his words should have comforted me, but the truth was they made my anger worse. He knew he'd done the wrong thing, yet in twenty years he'd never tried to make amends. I wanted to shake him and make him see how his decisions had fucked up my childhood. I would never be that happy kid that I should've been, because he didn't take me with him.

"If you'd really wanted me, you would have taken me."

"I wanted to, I swear, but she said if I did she'd have me arrested for snatching you. You weren't mine to take, Grantley. I'd have been charged with kidnapping and could have faced a long time in jail. I figured if I left you, I could come back one day, when she'd calmed down and persuade her you'd be better off with me."

My heart splintered as I remembered all the times I'd spent in the house, alone and scared. Times where she'd been drunk and unconscious, or high on drugs. Times when I had to put her to bed. Times I'd locked myself in my room while she partied with yet another stranger. Times and reasons that Dad could have used to bargain with her to give me a decent life.

"You know what the fucking sad thing is?" I cried. "She didn't even fucking want me. I was a thorn in her damn side. If you'd have come back and asked, she'd have gladly given me to you."

Trent let out a smothered sob. "Please don't, son. I can't-."

"Yeah, well tough shit. You need to hear how she left me alone for days on end, with just a few dollars to buy food. I wasn't even seven when she left me for the first time."

"No." Trent clutched at his chest, shaking his head vigorously.

His agony should have softened me, but I didn't have it in me to care. I was still hurting from years of neglect from both him and Sue-Ann. I needed him to see how shit life had been for me.

"Yes, *Dad*! She left me in that house to fend for myself. I had to go to school as normal, feed myself and put myself to bed. Every night I slept with a kitchen knife, petrified that someone would break in. I was so damn scared I pissed the bed every night that first time, and every fucking morning I washed those damn green sheets and my pyjamas, hoping that they'd be dry by bed time came because I couldn't get the fucking dryer to work."

Trent moaned softly along with his quiet crying. He sounded pained, as though he'd had his heart ripped from his chest – well hard fucking luck. I'd felt that pain the day he rode out of my life on his bike.

"I wish I'd come back. I should have made her see sense. Why the fuck didn't I come back for you?"

"You tell me," I scoffed. "In fact, tell me everything Trent. Tell me all about how you found out, tell me who the hell my real father is, because I can't wait to know."

"You don't need to know, Grantley. What good would it do?"

"I have no damn idea, but my whole life feels like a lie and I need to know the truth."

Trent wiped at his eyes as he rocked backward and forward, looking at me intently.

"Your biological father was an ex-boyfriend of hers," he finally said, his Adam's apple bobbing on a swallow. "I caught them, taking drugs and having sex one day. She'd promised me she'd stopped with the coke. I knew she still drank, but she at least stayed sober until you'd gone to bed."

"Yeah well nothing has changed," I griped.

"I came home early from work, and you were watching TV alone, so I went out back and caught them in the laundry room. There was a bag of coke on top of the counter and she was bent over the washer with him inside her and snorting that damn poison off her back."

He stopped and looked over at the bookcase and I knew he was staring at the photograph of us on his bike. The look on his face as he stared at happier times, told me that this was killing him, just as much as it was killing me, but I didn't care. His pain was the least I deserved.

"How did you find out he was my father? Did she tell you?"

He shook his head. "I lost it. It wasn't that I cared about her, we hadn't cared for each other for a long damn time. Maybe since you were a year old and she'd started using again."

"She'd used drugs before?"

"Before we were married."

"Why the hell did you marry her then?"

"Because she was different then. She was fun and pretty and I loved every bone in her body. From the minute we met, I couldn't wait to get her to County Hall and marry her."

"But the day you found her with him, you didn't love her anymore?"

"No, not for a long time." He blew out his cheeks. "But I loved you with all my damn heart, and I couldn't believe she'd let him into our house, taken drugs and fucked him, with you just a few rooms away, so I totally lost it. I beat the shit out of him."

Nausea rolled around my gut at the realization that Sue-Ann had never really cared about me. Trent had loved me like a father should have and I wanted to scream at the injustice of it all.

"And that's when she told you," I stated, giving my attention back to Trent, who looked pale and broken.

"She confirmed it," he said. "As I stood over him, about to punch him again, I saw your eyes looking up at me. There was no mistaking them. That pale green, with the flecks of brown. It could have been you. You even have his nose."

The pain he must have felt was back in his heart, I could see it. The way he held a palm against his chest, the way his face crumpled and the way his eyes looked at me with regret.

"Your mom knew what I'd guessed. She saw it in my face and she just nodded. That was all she needed to do."

"What happened to him? Did he leave, did she say anything to him?"

I didn't care about the man, I just needed to know my history. I needed to learn about my life, my *real* life for the first time. My life that was playing out like those shit scripts that I'd rejected time and again, because the family story sounded so unreal.

"He ran out the back door, as soon as he got a chance. She didn't care, she just said 'well now you know'."

"How come I never heard any of it? I don't remember any argument. I just remember the day you left."

Trent shook his head. "You had the TV so loud, you could have woken the dead with it." He gave a short laugh. "You always did. We even got you a hearing test once, because we thought you might be deaf, but you weren't."

An image of me as a young kid, pushed to the forefront of my mind and it gave me a hint of the happiness I'd felt, before life went to shit.

"I remember. The man gave me a lollipop when I passed with flying colors."

Trent smiled, creasing the corners of his eyes. "You were three years old and the spunkiest little kid I have ever known. Cute little fucker, too." Sadness shrouded his features as looked at me. "You just didn't take after me," he said wistfully.

"How long after you found them, was it that you left?"

"A couple of weeks. I got myself a job in Cleveland, rented us an apartment, and told your school that you were leaving. It was just a fling with Rebecca, the girl I left with. We'd hooked up a couple of times, but when she heard I was going she asked if she could come too. I didn't see why not. She was a good kid and I knew it wouldn't last, but she was nice. I'm not proud of hooking up with her, Grantley, but your mom and me, we'd been done a long time and I was lonely."

I heard everything, but the one thing that stuck in my mind was that he'd told my school I was leaving. My throat felt raw as tears pooled in my eyes at his words.

"You were taking me with you." I stated.

"Of course I was. I may not have put you in her belly, but you were my boy. I loved you."

I swallowed back a sob at his sentiment, and it took everything in me not to break down and collapse at his feet.

"So why didn't you take me?" I asked, my voice sounding small and fearful.

"Like I said, Sue-Ann threatened to get me arrested for kidnapping. She said..." He closed his eyes and sighed. "She said, she'd tell them I'd abused you too."

My blood went cold as I thought of the cold-hearted bitch who had ruined my life. The lies she had told from the minute I'd been conceived to now. This one, about Trent needing my kidney, the biggest and vilest of them all, was just another line on the never-ending list.

"She is fucking poison," I hissed, hating her with every single fiber of my being.

"Yeah she is," Trent said on a long exhale. "She was going to let you come with me, but when she found out about Rebecca, well that's when she said you had to stay. It damn near killed me riding away from you that day."

"Why didn't you stay? Why go to Ohio? Why not stay close?"

"I did for a few days. I put off my new job and hung around trying to persuade her. I went to the house after you left for school *every day* for a week, begging her to let me take you. In the end I thought I'd go and come back for you, let her calm down. It was going to be a week at most, but I broke my ankle at work and couldn't ride my bike for months."

"You could have called me, or written. Got Rebecca, or whatever her name was, to drive you. Anything, to let me know you were coming back."

I wanted to heave out a huge sob, for the boy I'd been. The lost and lonely boy who thought his daddy didn't love him anymore.

"I called seven times and every time she put the phone down on me. Wouldn't let me talk to you. I didn't see the point in writing, she'd have ripped them up and you were six, Grantley, were you really going to read my letters? As for Rebecca, she left as soon as I got laid up with my ankle. Said she didn't sign up to be a nurse maid. I could barely hobble around my apartment never mind come back to you.

My boss even put me on reduced pay because he had to give me a ride every day so I could work in the office until I healed. So, do you see how hard it was?"

I shrugged, realizing he was probably right, but it didn't make what happened to me any easier to stomach. No journey, pain, or suffering should be enough to stop you from getting to your kid.

"I finally made it back and you were in the front yard playing ball with her and I thought I'd die of happiness. I hadn't seen you for three whole months."

"I don't remember that," I said, furrowing my brow.

"You didn't see me. Before I got to you, he came out of the house, your real father. He picked you up and tickled you, making you laugh and then carried you on his shoulders inside the house while your mom held your hand."

I took in a shuddering breath. Knowing he had been so close made me want to scream. If only I'd looked up, or he'd called out to me.

"I don't remember him, or that day," I said, pushing the heels of my hands into my eyes, trying to stem the tears. "There were a lot of different men around after you left."

And there was a whole line of them, which started just days after Trent left. My 'real dad' must have been one in that line.

"I puked my guts up, seeing him with you," Trent said. "And I just knew I couldn't do it. I couldn't watch another man bring you up. You seemed happy with them both and I thought you'd forgotten about me. I called one more time after that and she told me the three of you were moving to Florida."

"We never moved to Florida," I protested. "We stayed in that house until I was thirteen and we only moved then because she couldn't afford it. And I certainly don't remember any particular guy hanging around for long at that time."

"I didn't know. I cut myself off and just transferred money for you into her bank account each month. I found out a few years back that he was already married and had died of a heart attack about a year after I left."

I looked at Trent and saw how he'd appeared to have aged in the last hour. He was still the tall, lean, and handsome guy I'd remembered, with bright blue eyes and sun-bleached hair, but he looked tired and pale, with a few more lines on his face than when we'd arrived at his house.

"I should have come to find you," I said quietly. "When I was old enough, I should have looked for you."

God, how I wished I had. It didn't matter that he wasn't my biological father, he'd been my dad. The man who'd loved and nurtured me. The man I'd looked up to. We had both wasted so much fucking time.

"No, son," he replied, shaking his head. "Do not blame yourself for this. There's only one person to blame and that's Sue-Ann. For not letting me see my boy all those years ago, and for lying about this now. And speaking of which, what the hell is she up to?"

I raked a hand through my hair and then scrubbed it down my face. I couldn't believe I was even thinking it, but I had a suspicion of what Sue-Ann was up to.

"I have an idea," I said.

I hoped to God I was wrong, but was fearful I wasn't.

"I don't know how she thought she'd get away with it," I continued. "But I think she was going to sell my kidney."

Trent's eyes went wide as he opened his mouth to speak but nothing came out. He was shocked, but what was so damn ugly about it all, was that I really wasn't. Sue-Ann was selfish and mean and only ever thought of herself. She was a take, take, take and fuck the consequences person – even if her own child got caught in the crossfire. That thought, even though it wasn't new to me, was like a dagger to the heart. I was that lonely, scared kid who just wanted his momma to care about him, all over again.

"I offered her money, but obviously it wasn't enough. Whereas if someone is desperate for a kidney, they'll pay a shit load more than I'd ever give her."

"You have to be joking," Dad gasped. "No way, she wouldn't."

"Yeah she would. She's still hooked on the booze and drugs and even coming to see me in the UK, she stopped over in Paris to pick up some drugs to mule over."

"What the fuck?"

"Oh yeah, she's a real treasure."

"So what are you going to do?"

"I'm not sure yet," I growled. "But whatever it is, she'll fucking wish I'd never been born.

CHAPTER THIRTY-NINE

Phoebe

Deanna and I sat in the garden, drinking lemonade and waiting for father and son to re-emerge. Could I say that, father and son? What exactly were they to each other now? My heart was breaking for Grantley, just thinking about it. He looked devastated by the fresh pain of finding out that Trent wasn't his dad. I doubted he had ever healed from Trent leaving twenty-years ago, so this on top must have crucified him.

How could that bloody awful woman do this to him? He was so worried about the visit and things had just magnified by a thousand. After what Steven did to Beth, I always thought some people should never be allowed to call themselves parents, but Sue-Ann, that bitch took the biscuit and the first prize in one fell swoop. She managed to damage two people who had done nothing but try and love her.

"Do you think they'll be okay?" I asked Deanna, glancing over at the house.

"Who knows, sweetheart. I hope so. Trent has lived in so much pain over it for all these years, but seeing Grantley today, there was a brightness in his eyes I've never seen before."

"I'm so worried about him."

"I know, but you have to let him work through this." Deanna took a sip of her lemonade before placing it down on the table and clearing her throat. "So, how much does Grantley hate Trent for leaving him?"

"I'm not sure that's for me to say," I replied. "It should be down to Grantley really."

I knew how Grantley felt about Trent, but it would feel like I was gossiping if I told Deanna. Aside from which, we'd been together such a short amount of time, it really wasn't my place.

Deanna nodded and smiled. "I understand."

We lapsed into another silence, both sipping our drink and looking everywhere but at each other. Finally, it became too quiet, and I felt an urge to speak.

"You have a lovely home," I said, spreading my gaze across the lawn and to the house.

"Oh thank you, sweetheart. We love it here. Trent's worked real hard on it. It wasn't much to look at when we first moved in about fifteen years ago, but he replaced a lot of the wood." She pointed to the wood cladding on the outside of the house. "And painted it too. He even knocked a wall down inside to open up the lounge area and decorated the place, the whole way through. We were hoping to have a couple of kids of our own, but it never happened. Trent and I, we've had a good life nonetheless."

She smiled proudly and I couldn't help but feel a twinge of hurt for Grantley. How much better his life would have been, living with Trent rather than the lonely existence he had with Sue-Ann. Growing up in this house with Trent and Deanna, he could have had the perfect childhood.

"I wasn't the one he left with, you know."

Deanna's admission surprised me. Did she think I blamed her – because I didn't, what happened was purely down to Sue-Ann and Trent.

"I-I didn't know that," I stammered. "But to be honest, I hadn't really thought about it."

"I just thought maybe you did – think it was me, I mean. Because if you did, you'd probably blame me for the crap those two have had to go through for twenty-years."

"The way I see it, Mr. Miller made his own choices."

Deanna smiled wistfully and looked up at the house. "Yes, he did. Choices he's regretted every day since. He wishes with every bone in his body that he hadn't left that boy behind."

"Well," I replied with an empty laugh. "From what I know of her, Sue-Ann wouldn't have made it easy for him."

"Yeah, I heard she was a real piece of work, and I guess this lie she's told Grantley just proves it." She frowned. "You have any idea why she would tell him Trent needed a kidney?"

I shook my head. "None whatsoever. I doubt that it was to help reconcile them though, she's really not that charitable and what I know of her only scratches the ugly surface."

Hearing the clatter of a screen door, we both turned towards the house to see Trent and Grantley coming down the deck steps. Grantley rubbed his temples, while Trent's head hung low. They were walking side by side and if it wasn't for the bombshell Trent had dropped, you'd have thought they were biological father and son. Both were tall, with wide shoulders and long legs, and while they didn't look alike, both were handsome. I was sure the comment 'you can see where Grantley gets his looks from', would have been a common phrase from people who didn't know the truth. It was also then that I noticed the thick rings and leather bracelets that Trent wore. They were almost identical to those that Grantley had on, and it made my heart ache just a little bit more.

"Trent says Grantley looks like his mother, except for the eyes," Deanna commented, as if reading my mind. "I guess they're his father's."

"He does a little," I replied, realising he did. "But it's what's inside that counts, and thankfully he's nothing like her in that way, so maybe Trent had more of an influence than he thinks."

Deanna gave me a beaming smile and took in a deep breath. "You two okay?" she asked as the men reached us.

Trent nodded and laid one of his big hands on the top of her head, just as he'd done with Grantley earlier. She closed her eyes and basked under her husband's touch.

"Hey, pretty girl." Grantley bent to kiss my cheek. "You okay?"

"I'm fine, how are you?" I took his hand in both of mine and lifted it to my lips.

"Okay." He glanced at Trent and then back to me. "We had a good talk."

"Why don't you both sit and have some lemonade," Deanna said, reaching for the jug.

"Sounds good to me, honey." Trent smiled at her, and sat down on one of the garden chairs.

"Please, Grantley," Deanna said. "Sit and have a drink."

"Thank you." Grantley pulled out the chair next to mine and lowered himself into it. "This is a nice back yard."

"Thanks so- err, thanks Grantley. It took a while to get it how we wanted it, but it was worth the hard work." Trent's face reddened at his mistake.

"Well you've done a great job, D-dad."

My heart doubled in size at the joy on Trent's face as Grantley said 'dad'. He might have stumbled over it, but the sentiment was evident. Trent was his dad, no matter what. I didn't doubt they had a long road to take, but Grantley was showing that he wanted to try.

"So," Deanna said, her voice breaking. "How long are you kids here for?"

"We have to go back tomorrow," Grantley sighed. "I only got three days grace from my director. He gave me enough time to get here, persuade you to take my kidney, and then get back."

"Shit," Trent said. "That's what I call a whirlwind visit. Although, I'm sorry you had to make it in the first place."

"I'm not," Grantley replied. "Otherwise I'd never have found out the truth."

"I take it you don't need a kidney, Mr. Miller?"

Trent shook his head. "Nope honey, I don't, and please call me Trent."

"It seems Sue-Ann was lying," Grantley added. "Dad doesn't need a kidney at all. In fact, he has two perfectly healthy ones."

"That's horrible," I cried. "Why would she say that? She told us you'd asked her for help Deanna."

"I've never spoken to the woman." Deanna took hold of Trent's hand. "Why on earth would she say that about you?"

Trent shrugged. "Grantley has his ideas on that."

We all looked to Grantley.

"As sick as it sounds, I think she was hoping to sell my kidney to someone."

Deanna and I both gasped. Ice flowed through my veins and nausea rolled around my stomach.

"The evil bitch," I said barely above a whisper. "Oh my God, Grantley."

Grantley took my hand and gave it a squeeze, before bringing it to his lips and kissing the top of it.

"She's not going to get away with it," he said, soothingly. "So quit worrying."

"But what if she had? What if you hadn't decided to tell your dad, and had believed Deanna was keeping it from him because he wouldn't accept it?"

The fear of what might have happened gripped me. Okay, so he was going to go into a proper hospital, but they must have been in on it for Sue-Ann's vile plan to work.

"The hospital, or clinic you were going into would have to be in on it," I said, voicing my thoughts. "She said you'd have tests there, so they have to know what she was up to."

"Maybe, but I'll find out more when we get back."

"What're you going to do?" Trent asked, concern written all over his face.

Grantley looked up at him, his own features set into a determined stare. "I'm going to report her and the clinic to the police."

"That's a big thing," Trent replied. "Giving your own mom up to the cops."

"I don't care. She's been a shit mother all my life and now it's time for her to pay for everything she's done. If that means her going to prison, well tough shit."

"Can I have five minutes with her first?" I asked.

Grantley laughed and leaned in to kiss my cheek. "It will be my pleasure, pretty girl."

"Shit," Grantley gasped, as he looked down at the box full of clippings and photographs. "You really did follow my career."

Trent dropped his head and rubbed the back of his neck. "Too much?" he asked.

"No, not at all." He placed a hand on Trent's back. "It's good to know that you cared."

Trent looked up at him and smiled. "I always cared, son. Never stopped. I just made some stupid decisions. I thought about coming to see you a while ago, but figured you had a relationship with him and I'd just be the memory of some guy who'd been in your life for a while when you were a little kid. But I had no claim on you, son." Trent's eyes shone as he looked reverently at Grantley. "Truth be told, I was scared to death that if by some chance you remembered me, you'd reject me anyway. Then you became a Hollywood movie star and I was the bum who walked out on you. So this lot," he said, waving a hand at the box, "was my way of staying close."

Grantley blew out his cheeks and swiped at his eyes, before reaching down and touching a photograph with his fingertip. "Can I have some copies of these?"

"Of course," Trent replied, clearing his throat.

"There's another box in the office," Deanna said with a laugh, trying to lighten the mood. "There's a lot more in there for you to choose from."

"You're kidding?" I asked, gazing at the mass of memorabilia, working with Deanna to help mend a rift that should never have been there.

"Nope." She sighed and kissed Trent's cheeks. "The box in the office is just this year's press and magazine clippings, so truth be told, it's only half full."

Grantley burst out laughing and picked up a newspaper clipping.

"'Addison Yates goes out for bagels'," he read, with a shake of his head. "I visit the bakery every damn week. Who the hell decides this shit is newsworthy?"

"I don't care. It meant I got to see you over the last few years."

"How did you know it was me?" Grantley asked. "Or even find out that I was acting?"

"I think it was fate. I bumped into our old neighbor, Mrs. Zominski, you remember her?"

Grantley nodded.

"She was helping to supervise her youngest daughter's class trip. They were visiting a couple of museums in Dayton and I happened to be delivering a bike back to a guy who worked at the Airforce Museum. I bumped into her while I was waiting for the guy and we recognized each other. She was the one who told me you'd just got that part, as the student in the drug movie. Apparently, she saw Sue-Ann regularly at the store and she'd been boasting about you."

"He went to see that movie six times," Deanna said, smiling lovingly at Trent.

"You recognized me okay?"

"Of course I did," Trent replied, his voice almost a whisper. "I'd know my son anywhere."

Trent held Grantley's gaze, his eyes pleading for forgiveness, yet again. He'd spent all afternoon saying that he was sorry, but while it would take time, I had the feeling Grantley blamed Sue-Ann far more than he did his father.

Sensing the atmosphere change a little, I picked up a photograph of Grantley as a young boy.

"Oh look how cute you were," I gushed, grabbing Grantley's attention. "How old were you?"

The picture was of Grantley holding in one hand a baseball bat, which was far too big for him, and in the other a helmet, which also looked huge.

"Damn, I don't know," he replied, looking over my shoulder. "Do you know, Dad?"

Trent looked at the picture. "You were four and that was Labor Day. We'd been to the park and you'd seen some bigger kids playing and wanted to join in, and threw a real tantrum when they said no. I had to give them twenty dollars for ice-cream to let you play. Then, on the way home you said you were going to play for the *New York Yankees* when you grew up. So, I got all my old stuff out from the garage."

"The Yankees, eh? Well it's not like Iowa has a major league team does it?" Grantley laughed and shook his head. "I really did have ideas above my station, didn't I?"

"Maybe," Trent replied. "But I always told you, aim high-."

"Because there's always someone out there who wants to be bigger" Grantley said, finishing off his dad's sentence.

Both men looked at each other and grinned.

"You remembered."

"Yeah Dad, I remembered. I also remember what a great dad you were before you left, so stop beating yourself up about it."

God, this man blew me away with his graciousness towards his dad, who now looked as though he was about to cry. Deanna obviously picked up on it too, because as in any difficult situation, she did what any woman worth her salt did – she offered us food.

"Who's hungry? I have left over pot roast and can steam some vegetables."

I groaned and rubbed my stomach where the sandwiches and cake from lunch still sat. "Not for me thanks, Deanna. I'm still full."

Grantley gave her a dazzling smile. "Me neither. In fact we

should think about going. I need to call Marcia, my agent, and we have an early start in the morning."

"So soon?" she moaned.

"Yeah, I'm sorry."

"Okay," she said, cupping Grantley's cheek. "But you make sure you come back and visit again soon."

I saw how Grantley slightly leaned in to Deanna's touch and for a brief second closed his eyes. He was getting the motherly comfort from her that he'd always needed and always wanted from Sue-Ann and it broke my heart. He missed out on this because of that woman, and I would never forgive her.

"You will keep in touch, won't you?" Trent asked, a few minutes later as he led us outside.

"Of course I will. As soon as I get back to the US, I'll call you."

Trent nodded and held out his hand, but before Grantley had time to shake it, Trent changed his mind and pulled him into a tight hug, clapping Grantley's back with his huge palm.

"Have a safe journey, son."

Grantley swallowed, and evidently too emotional to speak, merely nodded.

"You too, honey." Trent grabbed me into a bear hug and squeezed tight. "Both of you stay here next time, not some hotel that costs a damn fortune."

"Trent's right," Deanna said, grabbing both our hands. "This is your home too, so there'll always be a bed for you both."

Emotion scratched at my throat and hit the centre of my chest. I would probably never see them again, because once Grantley finished the film, he'd be back here and I'd be in the UK. The pain behind that thought was unbearable. Fearful to speak in case I cried, I simply smiled and nodded.

"I'll call you, I promise," Grantley said, and with one last hug for his father, we left the house and walked back to the rental car in silence. Both of us fearful of the future, but I suspected, for very different reasons.

CHAPTER FORTY

Grantley

We arrived back in the UK at just after one in the morning, with our body clocks thinking it was only 8 p.m. I knew I wouldn't sleep for hours, so I was relieved when Barney told us Alexi had given me a midday call time. At least I might get some sleep before I had to go be Addison Yates.

"Well, that's one fucked up story," Barney said after I'd explained what had happened in Ohio. "What you gonna do about her?"

"Call the police."

"Grantley," Phoebe said, placing a hand on my arm. "You need to think about it and talk to Marcia first."

"No, Phoebes, I don't."

We'd been having the very same discussion since we'd left my dad's house. I wanted to go to the police, but Phoebe thought I should hear what Marcia had to say first. She was worried that it all coming out might hurt my career.

"There will be a huge amount of publicity, Grantley," she said. "Is that something you need right now, especially as you're looking for some more serious projects."

Barney looked at us through the rear-view mirror. "Phoebe has a point. You don't need that shit."

"But, she can't get away with it," I protested.

"No one says she has to," Barney replied. "But there's more than one way to catch a 'gator, and I reckon Marcia knows every fucking one of them."

"Where does the old witch think we've been, anyway?" I asked.

"I told her you were on location. She's been sleeping or drunk most of the time, so hasn't questioned it."

"Won't she find it odd, us coming back at this time of night? And the fact that I'm with you?"

"You're not going home, Phoebes." I kissed her temple, inhaling her scent at the same time. "I want you with me."

"Don't worry, Phoebe." Barney let out a deep chuckle. "I gave her a sleeping tablet with her dinner. She'll be out for hours."

"Oh my God, isn't that dangerous, giving her pills with alcohol?" Phoebe asked, gripping my arm.

"So," I snorted at the same time as Barney said, 'No'.

"I swapped the vodka for water, she was asleep before she realized."

Our deep laughs mingled together while Phoebe gasped.

"You two are terrible."

"No pretty girl, she's the terrible one. In fact, she's the fucking evil one. I'm surprised her body didn't go into shock with the introduction of water anyway."

"I have to say, I'm shocked," Barney said, shaking his head slowly, his smile over my water joke fading quickly. "Never thought she'd go this far," he mumbled.

"It's no big shock. She's a lowlife drunk and junkie and nothing she does surprises me."

When we got to the hotel, we were shocked to see Marcia waiting for us in the suite. She was pacing up and down, screaming at someone on the phone. From the conversation it sounded as though one of her clients had failed to turn up for an audition and was getting the choicest of Marcia's language.

"I'm telling you, you little bastard, turn up for tomorrow's audition or I will drop you quicker than a hooker drops a puss ridden cock."

"Nice." I grimaced at the visual and flopped down onto the sofa, pulling Phoebe down with me.

"Oh you're back," Marcia growled, ending the call and throwing her cell onto the coffee table. "So, what the fuck happened? Did you and Daddy Dearest have a warm and loving reunion or did you punch the twat into next week?"

Barney rolled his eyes and nodded toward Phoebe. "You want a drink, honey?"

"A tea would be lovely," she replied.

"Anyone else?"

"Whiskey." Marcia snapped.

"Grantley?"

"Nothing for me, thanks buddy."

As Barney walked toward the kitchen, I turned to Phoebe. "Are you letting him make your tea? You didn't let me."

"Barney makes lovely tea and I don't think you would."

"Oh is that so?" I asked with a grin.

"Yep."

As I watched her cute little face break into a smile, I couldn't help but snatch a kiss. That's how I'd been all the way home, wanting to kiss and touch her – I'd even suggested joining the Mile High Club, but she hadn't been up for it. Good job really, because some poor bastard definitely had bad guts. It wouldn't have been the most romantic of liaisons, me fucking Phoebe with the smell of shit permeating the air.

"Will you two quit acting like high school kids and tell me what the fuck happened." Marcia sank down onto the opposite couch and scowled at us. "Is your dad taking the kidney?"

"Nope he isn't."

"The fucker feels too guilty?"

"Nope not at all," I replied. "But it's a long story."

"Well go on then," she cried, throwing her arms into the air. "Fucking tell me."

"No fucking way?" Marcia squawked. "What a fucking cunt."

I'd told Marcia the whole story and her reaction was pretty much what I'd expected. Her eyes were almost popping out of her head as she gripped the edges of the throw cushion on her lap. I was like a son to her, and this was momma bear about ready to rip Sue-Ann's head off.

"Get the bitch out of bed now and throw her out," Marcia demanded.

"That might be a problem," Barney replied. "I gave her a sleeping pill. Didn't want her upsetting Grant on his first night back."

"I don't care. Still throw her out." Marcia threw the cushion to one side, grabbed the bottle of whiskey from the coffee table and took a long slug.

"Marcia just calm down," I said, rubbing at my temple. "We need to decide what to do."

"What I've just said, throw the fucking cock-sucking whore out."

"Believe me, it's tempting to do that right now, but I don't think it's that simple."

"Grantley wants to call the police," Phoebe added. "But I think it might harm his career if he does that."

Marcia stopped mid-swig of her whiskey and eyed Phoebe.

"What?" I asked.

Marcia put the bottle down, folded her arms over her chest and grinned at me.

"I do believe your little missy there has some brains."

"I'm not stupid," Phoebe complained, copying Marcia's body language. "And I care about Grantley. I don't want to see all his hard work go to waste because of his bloody, putrid mother. The publicity from this could be damaging, especially as he's looking for more serious roles."

"Wow, I like your thinking girly." Marcia laughed. "She really does have balls, doesn't she?"

Pride filled me as I watched Marcia smile at Phoebe. The woman who had done more for me than any other person, who protected me like a mother, who fought my corner when no one else was interested, actually liked my girl. I'd never given a shit before what she'd thought of past dates or girlfriends, but now that she actually seemed to like Phoebe, I realized it mattered. It only hadn't mattered previously, because they hadn't mattered- the women I'd dated and even lived with, weren't important to me - not like Phoebe was.

"So, what do you suggest I do?" I asked, pulling Phoebe under my arm and hugging her to my side.

Marcia inclined her head and looked at me. "You really like this girl, don't cha?"

"Who, this girl?" I pointed at Phoebe. "Nah, not particularly."

"Hey you." Phoebe slapped a palm at my stomach. "That's not nice."

I grinned and kissed her hard, and when I heard her let out a satisfied little sigh, 'Little Dick' woke up.

"Alright, alright," Marcia groaned. "Cut it out."

"This is what I had to put up with all the way back from the airport," Barney offered.

Still kissing Phoebe, I gave him the middle finger.

"Grantley, stop with the damn kissing. We need to talk about your fucking mother."

Reluctantly, I pulled away and turned to Marcia. "Okay, I'm all ears. What do you think we should do? I'd be happy to call the police, but I understand what you're saying."

"It's gonna be a shit storm if you do," Marcia said. "Because once the press finds out about this, they'll dig into every other thing she's ever done. They'll get onto your prick of a father-."

"Hey, no." I held my hand up to stop her. "My dad is not to blame in any of this. I found a few things out over the last couple of days."

"What, how to abandon a six-year old kid and still have him worship you? Yeah, great fucking lesson kid."

"It was more than that, Marcia."

"Well go on, I'm all fucking ears."

"He's not my dad."

I rushed the words out, hoping that if I said them quickly enough the pain in my chest wouldn't start up, just like it had a million times since I'd walked into his house.

"You're fucking kidding me?"

"Seriously?" Barney asked.

I turned to him and nodded, slamming my lips together in a thin line. "Yeah Barney, seriously."

"So what he found out and left? Still a shit trick if you ask me."

"It wasn't quite like that," I replied. "He wanted to take me, but Sue-Ann said she'd get him arrested for kidnapping and threaten to tell the authorities that he abused me."

"Wowzer, that cunt of a mother of yours just keeps getting better and better."

"Yeah, she really does. The point is, Dad wanted to take me even though he knew I wasn't his. She then told him we were moving to Florida with my biological dad. Social media wasn't a big thing then, so he cut himself off from me and lost touch."

"How you feeling, buddy?" Barney asked. "You okay with it all?"

I shrugged. "As good as I can be. It's going to take time, but I'm positive about our relationship."

"That's good, real good."

Barney looked a little shell-shocked and I knew he must have been thinking about his relationship with his own father. Their argument the day his dad died haunted him, which is why he'd always pushed for me to keep faith with Sue-Ann. I guess even he had to now admit that she was a lost cause.

"Okay," Marcia said on a sigh. "This is what I think we should do.

We don't say anything until I try and find out about this clinic she said you'd be going in to. Then tomorrow night, when I have more information we decide what to do. If the clinic appears to be in on her fucked-up plan, well you have no choice but to call the cops. Either way, I'm getting her on a plane out of here tomorrow." She picked up her iPad and started tapping at the screen. "I'll sort a flight now. I take it she isn't going First Class?"

"No way," I replied, vehemently. "Not a chance. She can go in the hold with the animals for all I care. Or maybe put her next to the john, right where she can smell shit for the whole flight."

"Aren't you worried she'll go missing, if the police become involved?" Phoebe asked.

"She's got no money, no friends, and no fucking brains, so no," Marcia responded, while tapping away.

"She must have some brains, to come up with this plan."

"Either that or someone is helping her, Phoebes," I answered. "Which is my guess. She doesn't have the brains to pull something like this off."

"Grantley's right," Marcia said. "She's gotta be the fall guy, but I'll find that out. There, that's it. She's booked on a flight. Has to be day after tomorrow, but it's an eighteen-hour trip with two lay overs, leaving Manchester at six in the morning."

"Nice," I replied, giving Marcia a grin and a wink.

"And you ain't taking her Barnabus," she growled. "She gets a damn taxi."

Barney shook his head. "If you say so."

"I do," Marcia snapped. "And if I find out you did, I'll cut your fucking balls off and feed them to my neighbor's dog."

Barney and I winced as Phoebe giggled.

"And on that note," I said. "I'm off to bed."

"I'm not sure I'll sleep," Phoebe said, turning to me.

"Me either, but who mentioned sleeping?"

As Marcia and Barney groaned, Phoebe gave a sexy little moan and now 'Little Dick' was well and truly awake.

CHAPTER FORTY-ONE

PHOEBE

Waking up in Grantley's arms for the past few days had been wonderful, especially when he had an extra special way of doing it. I could thoroughly recommend an orgasm – or two – before breakfast, it gave you a much better glow than porridge ever could. However, having been woken with his fingers or 'Little Dick', as I now liked to call it, I was now dreading going home. I'd missed Beth and the boys like mad, but I had a feeling my yearning for Grantley at six each morning would be just as great. But, I guess I had to go home sometime. I just didn't want it to be yet.

Going home also got me thinking about what was going to happen when Grantley left. We only had a few weeks of filming left and then he'd be gone. Back to LA, his life, and numerous women desperate to get inside his undies. In all the time we'd spent together, we'd never discussed what would happen post filming, and if I was being honest, I didn't really want to. It was ridiculous of me to even contemplate him keeping in touch, never mind there being anything more, but the alternative was a horrible thought.

"So, how was your trip?" I heard Penny ask Grantley, as he prepared to shoot his last scene of the day, with Francesca.

"Good, just some business I had to deal with."

I was watching from behind the camera. I hadn't had any scenes to film, but Grantley had insisted I go with him to the studio, so that he and Barney could drive me home afterwards and maybe get some dinner with Beth and the boys. I loved the idea, although I was definitely starting to flag with jet lag, and wasn't sure I'd stay awake through dinner. But, I'd soldier through it, because I had a suspicion that Grantley wanted to do it because he was filming his sex scene the day following our rest day, and after the Serena incident, probably suspected that I would be feeling a little insecure.

"Phoebe enjoy it too?" Penny asked with a smirk and a glance over at me.

Grantley's eyes followed Penny's and I returned his stare with my mouth gaping open.

"Yes, she did," he replied, while staring at me with a beautiful smile. "We had a fantastic time."

Penny patted his arm, powdered his nose and turned to leave. As she did, there was a loud bang and shouting behind me. I quickly turned to see the studio door fling open and Sue-Ann stumble through, wearing boots which I was pretty sure were replicas of Julia Roberts' in Pretty Woman.

"Where the hell is my son?" she yelled, pushing a boom operator to one side. "Grantley, where the hell are you?"

Grantley fisted his hands at his sides and took a deep breath before storming in my direction.

"How the hell did she get in here?" he shouted to whoever was listening. "Someone get security and then fire their damn asses."

"Grantley," I said, trying to catch hold of his arm. "Calm down."

He swung around to face me, his pale green eyes burning with anger. "I'll calm down once she's out of here."

"Grantley," Sue-Ann called as she spotted him. "I need to talk to you now."

Grantley pulled away from me and stalked to Sue-Ann, with me following behind.

"What the hell are you doing here?" he hissed, taking her arm and turning her around.

"I need to talk to you. Do you know what that bitch has done?" Sue-Ann stopped dead, causing me to barrel into her. "Watch what you're doing," she snapped, looking over her shoulder at me.

"Don't you dare speak to Phoebe like that." Grantley poked a finger in his mother's face. "I told you before, you treat her with fucking respect. Now get the hell off this set."

With a hand against Sue-Ann's back, he pushed her to the double doors. Kicking them open, Grantley ushered her through them and marched her down a corridor towards his dressing room. I followed part of the way and then stopped.

"I'll tell Alexi," I called.

Grantley looked over his shoulder. "No, I need you in here with me."

"But Grantley-."

"Phoebe please, just get in here."

As they disappeared inside, I looked back to where we'd come from, expecting to see Alexi following us, but the corridor was silent. So with a deep breath, I jogged to the dressing room, went inside, and closed the door quietly behind me.

"What the hell are you doing, letting her put me on a flight out of here in the morning?" Sue-Ann screeched.

"Marcia told you then?"

Grantley placed himself in front of Sue-Ann, his hands on his hips. He was wearing a scowl that I'd never seen on his face before, and it was at that moment I saw the true likeness between him and his mother.

"Yes, she fucking told me. You've put me on a six am flight that takes forever to get home. And why the hell are you sending me home, anyway. We have things to sort out."

"Do we?" Grantley asked, shoving his hands into his trouser pockets. "And what would that be?"

"You know," Sue-Ann said, looking at me and then back to Grantley. "Things with your father."

"Oh my father." Grantley nodded slowly. "The same father who died of a heart attack years ago, probably brought on by his liking for blow, or the one you told me was my father?"

Sue-Ann's face blanched as she took a stumbling step backwards.

"I have no idea what you're talking about," she said, guilt written all over her face. "Who's told you that crap?"

I couldn't help my snort of derision, as she straightened herself up and jutted out her chin defiantly.

"What's your problem?" Sue-Ann snapped at me.

"I don't have a problem, but I'd say you do."

"You going to let her speak to me like that?"

Grantley sighed. "We've had this fucking conversation before, Sue-Ann. So, let me spell it out for you. Yes, I am, because you are a lying piece of work, who should have been sterilized at birth. You have no rights being a mother and I'm damn well ashamed to call you mine." Grantley took a step forward and leaned into Sue-Ann's personal space. "The person who told me that 'crap' was Trent Miller, the man who for twenty-six years I've believed to be my father."

Sue-Ann's breath faltered as Grantley moved in even closer.

"He told me everything," he hissed. "About your sordid hook-up while I was watching TV and how you wouldn't let him take me with him."

"You're my damn son," she cried. "You weren't his to take."

"But he wanted me. You didn't."

"I did want you. I loved you, I do love you, baby boy."

"You left me alone for days on end and thought I'd be okay because I had ten fucking dollars in my pocket."

A vein on the side of Grantley's head was bulging with the rage inside of him as he poked a finger at Sue-Ann. His other hand was fisted at his side, as his fury of the last twenty years spilled out. I was worried he was going to collapse, or have some sort of aneurism, as his face grew redder with each word he spat at Sue-Ann.

"Grantley," I whispered, moving alongside of him. "Please, just take a deep breath."

"She's right, Grantley," Sue-Ann simpered. "Calm down."

"*No, I won't calm the fuck down*," he bellowed, so loudly that both Sue-Ann and I jumped. "I am sick to death of having to deal with you. Either giving you money, or bailing you out of some other shit or other. Well this time, you've gone too damn far."

As he took a step forward, I moved with him. I didn't think he would, but he was so angry I wondered whether he was going to hit her. I held my hand up to stop him, but he didn't raise a finger, but moved his face to within an inch of his mother's.

"I know you're fucking game," he said, his voice dripping with venom.

"W-what game?" Sue-Ann flicked her hair over her shoulder, trying to appear nonchalant, but the tremor in her voice and the tremble in her chin gave it away.

"Who did you really need my kidney for, Sue-Ann?"

Grantley's voice was so quiet and measured that it scared me. Grantley being in control was more worrying than when he was losing it with her. Sue-Ann must have recognised it too because she gasped and tried to make a run for the door. Grantley was too quick for her though, and grabbed hold of her arm, pulling her back in front of him.

"Who the fuck were you going to sell my kidney to?"

"I-I. Grantley you don't -."

"I asked you a damn question. Was it some dealer you owe money to, or were you just going to sell it to the clinic. Tell me now."

Sue-Ann flinched and closed her eyes.

"It wasn't...I wasn't."

"Now, Sue-Ann, because I swear to God, I'll-."

"Stop," I said, pulling on his arm. "She won't talk if you keep badgering her."

Grantley turned his head. "Badgering her? This is nothing to what the damn cops will do."

"Sue-Ann, just tell him what he needs to know."

I didn't care about her, whether Grantley badgered her or not. She deserved every last bit of shit she was going to get, but I didn't want him doing something he might regret. Yes, she was an evil, vindictive woman, but she was still his mother and if he did hurt her in some way...I dreaded the thought.

"Phoebe, I wouldn't touch her if that's what you're worried about," Grantley whispered, cupping the side of my face. "I swear."

"You can't say that," I protested. "Because I'll tell you something, I'd gladly slap her face and she's not done this to me. She's not my mother who has betrayed me."

"Don't you dare touch me," Sue-Ann cried, pointing at me. "I'll scream."

"Just because I want to, doesn't mean I will," I replied. "Some of us were brought up with manners."

"How dare you?"

"I dare because you have to be the most odious woman I've ever had the displeasure to meet."

"I don't smell," Sue-Ann said, her eyes wide. "You can't say I'm odious. I take a shower every day."

Grantley rolled his eyes, and when I took a breath to start and explain he held up a hand.

"Leave it pretty girl, she has the brain cell of a dung beetle."

"What do you mean?" Sue-Ann asked, pushing her hands to her hips.

Grantley shook his head. "Nothing. Now tell me who you wanted my kidney for."

"I told you-."

"And I heard a crock of shit. Now, one more time, tell me who my *fucking kidney was for*."

"Okay, okay," she said, rubbing a hand up and down her arm. "It wasn't for anyone."

"What do you mean?" I asked. "It wasn't for anyone."

She looked at Grantley and swallowed. "I put it on Craigslist."

"*What*?" Grantley bellowed. "*Tell me you're fucking joking*."

"What's Craigslist?" I asked.

"I needed the money," Sue-Ann cried.

"You tried to sell your own son's kidney in a damn paper?" Grantley grabbed at his hair, almost pulling it from his head. "You're insane."

"It wasn't in the paper, it was on the website," she countered ridiculously, like that made it any fucking better.

"What the hell is Craigslist?" I asked again, a little louder this time.

Grantley swung around to me. "Fucking Ebay for those with more money."

My eyes went big as I looked at Sue-Ann. "No way, you didn't?" I gasped.

Sue-Ann started to wring her hands together, her eyes shining with tears. "Please Grantley, you don't understand."

"I know I don't," I yelled. "How can you do that, to your own son?"

"Because I'm fucking desperate," she cried back. "I need the money."

"I offered you fucking money." Grantley turned, picked up a mug, and threw it at the wall.

"It wasn't enough. I needed more."

"I offered you a blank check. You only had to name your price."

Sue-Ann started to cackle out a laugh. "Hah, and how much would you have gone to? A few grand, not a million that's for sure."

Grantley stopped pacing. "A million dollars. You need a fucking million dollars?"

Sue-Ann hung her head, and I damn hoped it was in shame because this was the most ridiculous and evil thing I'd ever heard.

"Please," Grantley said with a burst of laughter. "Please tell me this is a damn joke. That I'm being punked and a camera team is going to jump out of that fucking closet."

He pointed to the wardrobe where he kept his own clothes, his eyes still on Sue-Ann.

"*Well!*"

"No, it's not a joke," she whispered. "I figured I'd get a nice sum for a movie star's kidney."

"Please tell me you haven't listed it as mine," Grantley cried, looking as though his eyes were about to pop out of his head.

"No, of course I didn't." Sue-Ann snapped her head up. "I listed it as the kidney of a famous PI who likes to drive a Jenson Interceptor."

"*What the fuck?*"

"Oh my God," I groaned. "You didn't?"

From her description it was obvious it was Grantley. Addison Yates was a Private Investigator who drove a classic, pale blue, Interceptor.

"Fuck my life," Grantley muttered, pinching the bridge of his nose. "How much interest have you had?"

Sue-Ann bit her lip.

"Well?"

"None," she whispered.

Grantley let out a sigh of relief. "Thank God."

He moved over to a safe, unlocked it, and took out his phone and started tapping away.

"What are you doing?" I asked, glancing at Sue-Ann, wondering if she might bolt.

"Getting Marcia to take the fucking listing down."

"But I need-."

"Don't you bloody dare," I yelled. "How dare you expect him to go through with it. Are you actually crazy?"

"But you have no idea-."

"No, don't even speak." I pointed at Sue-Ann. "You're not having his fucking kidney and if you need money do what everyone else does and get off your bony arse and get a job, instead of drinking your damn life away. Just a suggestion, but your wardrobe already screams hooker, so you're half way there."

Sue-Ann watched me with her mouth open, while Grantley gave me a huge and gorgeous smile.

"Shit, you rock," he said, pulling me in for a quick kiss.

"But what about my money?" Sue-Ann complained.

"For fuck's sake." Grantley and I chimed in unison.

An hour later, after Alexi reluctantly agreed to call it a day, Sue-Ann had been taken back to the hotel to pack by Marcia and Barney, and Grantley and I were driving one of the studio's cars to take me home. Marcia had taken the listing down and Sue-Ann had finally confessed she had no plan. There was no clinic as she was hoping that Grantley would have arranged one once she had a buyer for his kidney. She also told us she needed money to pay off a dealer, but the other nine hundred and ninety four thousand dollars that she hoped to get was for her. She didn't see why she couldn't enjoy the good life, because in her words 'People can't believe my son is movie star, when they see how poor I am'. At that point, I feared for the drinking glasses that were stacked in the dressing room. Poor Grantley, he just couldn't get her to see that while he was successful and had a decent amount of money, he was only just starting on his career. Addison Yates may well be a prestige role, but he was still a relative newcomer and wasn't quite commanding the huge, multi-million-dollar fees just yet.

"You know, all this with Sue-Ann," Grantley said, bringing my hand to his lips. "It's pretty funny if you think about it."

"It is?" I raised by brows in surprise. "How do you work that one out?"

Grantley paused as he manoeuvred into the next lane.

"Because she had no idea what she was doing. She thought she could list it and that would be it. Never once did she think about how it got from me to its new owner. Was she just going to shove it between a six pack in a cooler and deliver it?"

"It's not the best plan, I'll admit, but I wouldn't say it was funny." I reached up and brushed the hair from his forehead. He may well be laughing, but the whole episode had given him another insight into what an awful mother Sue-Ann was to him.

"Farcical then," Grantley replied. "Farcical, idiotic, and so fucking Sue-Ann."

"Thank goodness you went to see Trent. Imagine if you'd gone ahead with it, believing your dad didn't want to know."

"Yeah," he sighed. "And then I would have still been gloriously in the dark about the fact he's not *actually* my dad."

I watched his profile and saw his nostrils flare and his jaw go tight.

"And you would still be alienated from each other." I leaned in and kissed his cheek. "So there's your silver lining. And the fact that when you get back tomorrow, she'll be gone."

"If she gets on that flight."

"She will," I said with confidence. "She'll be too scared that Marcia will give her another black eye."

Yes, Marcia kind of lost it when she arrived at the studios.

Grantley smiled and gave my hand a squeeze and I knew then that I was falling deeply for him. Despite everything I'd ever thought about men, this one had most definitely got through to my heart, but soon he would be gone from my life.

Thinking about our impending separation and wondering how I was going to cope, I was shaken from my thoughts by my phone ringing out 'Sisters Are Doin' it for Themselves'.

"Hey Beth," I chimed. "We're just on our way back. I've missed you."

"We've missed you too. So, how far away are you?" she asked.

I looked at the scenery outside. "About twenty minutes. Why, have you made something nice for dinner?"

"I-I...well, no not yet...I."

"Beth, what's wrong?"

She sighed deeply and then said. "My results are back. I have the letter in my hand."

As nausea threatened to overcome me, I turned to Grantley.

"Grantley, put your foot down. We need to get to Beth as soon as possible."

CHAPTER FORTY-TWO

Phoebe

"Beth!" I called as I burst through the front door. "Where are you?"

Beth appeared from the kitchen, putting a finger to her lips and pointing at the lounge.

"The boys are watching TV."

"Hey Beth," Grantley said, wrapping an arm around my chest from behind. "You okay?"

"Hi, Grantley. Did you have a good trip?"

"Yeah, it was great, thanks, but what's going on? All Phoebe would say is that we had to get back here."

Beth sucked in her bottom lip and placed a hand at her throat, her fears stemming the words she wanted to say.

I turned in Grantley arms. "I just need some time with her," I whispered.

Grantley nodded and kissed the top of my head. "How about I keep the boys occupied, while you two talk."

As he walked away, I caught hold of his hand.

"Thank you."

"My pleasure, pretty girl."

As Grantley let himself into the lounge, a snippet of noise burst through the open door, only to be silenced as soon as it closed again. I smiled as I heard, "Dick, you're here", shouted from the boys, and walked down the hall towards my sister.

"I thought they were going to take a couple of weeks."

"That's what the hospital said." Beth shrugged. "Maybe this means it's bad news."

"You won't know until you open them." I said, following her into the kitchen.

"I know."

Beth chewed on her lip as she looked down at the envelope that was shaking in her hand, so I held my hand over it, to stop the trembling. As Beth looked up at me, she took in a deep breath.

"I'm petrified."

"Open it," I said. "Whatever it says, we'll cope."

She nodded, glanced at me with tear filled eyes and ripped it open. Clearing her throat, Beth unfolded the letter and read it. I watched her eyes as they moved across the words typed on the paper, my heart beating rapidly, as Beth showed nothing on her face.

"Well?" I asked.

Beth looked up at me and held a hand to her mouth.

"No." I shook my head. "Please tell me it's not bad news."

"No, it's not," she whispered. "It's all clear. It says it's a cyst and I'm to contact my doctor to discuss my options."

"Really?"

Beth nodded vigorously. "Yes, really."

"Oh thank God," I breathed out.

"Shit, Phoebes, I have never been so scared." Beth flung her arms around me and hugged me tightly. "I am so relieved."

As we hugged it out, I heard Grantley clear his throat behind us.

"Hey ladies, sorry to interrupt but the guys wanted a drink. I said I'd get it, I kind of figured something was going on in here."

Beth let me go and wiped at the tears on her cheeks. "Of course, I'll sort it."

"Is everything okay?" Grantley asked.

"Everything's fine," I replied, gazing up at him. "Beth just had some test results back, and it's good news."

"Well that's fantastic, Beth."

"Thanks, Grantley. It's been a really worrying week or so, I'm just relieved it's all over."

Grantley leaned forward and gave Beth a kiss on the cheek. "You've had a rough time, eh?"

Beth nodded. "Just a bit, but it's all good now."

Grantley looked at us both and then smiled. "Hey, how about I treat the two of you to a spa day somewhere this weekend?"

"No, you don't have to do that," Beth protested.

"I want to."

I watched Beth and I could see the glint of excitement in her eyes. She desperately wanted to say yes, but was too proud. We both were, but if it meant my sister was pampered for a day then I'd let my pride go, for her.

"If Grantley wants to, you should accept his generous offer, Beth."

Beth glared at me. "Phoebe, we can't accept it. It's far too expensive."

"Beth," Grantley said, placing a hand on her shoulder. "Please, it'd be my pleasure."

Opening the cupboard door, she pulled down a couple of blue plastic beakers and carried them over to the fridge, where she took out a carton of fresh orange. Pouring some into the beakers, she then added some cold water. All the time, Grantley and I remained silent, watching and waiting for my sister to agree.

"What about the boys?" she asked, turning around holding the drinks in both hands.

"I'll look after the boys."

Beth and I both turned to stare at Grantley, who was grinning widely.

"You?" I asked.

"Yeah, why not? Shooting has a rest day on Sunday, so I'll book your spa for then. Barney and I can come around and keep them entertained.

Beth and I exchanged surprised looks.

"Are you sure?" I asked tentatively. "You don't have to. I'm sure Wendy would have them, Beth."

"She's still on holiday," Beth replied, staring at Grantley. "Really, you'd do that for me, for us?"

Grantley nodded.

Before I knew what was happening, Beth had handed me the drinks and thrown her arms around Grantley, hugging him tightly.

"Thank you, Grantley," she said against his broad chest. "You are a very special man."

Grantley looked at me over the top of Beth's head and smiled.

Oh shit, I'm most definitely falling for him.

Grantley

As I watched Phoebe sleep, I gently pushed her hair from her face. She'd just about made it through dinner before practically falling asleep at the table. As I carried her up the stairs to her room, Beth followed and insisted that I stay the night. She was right, it wasn't safe for me to drive feeling as bushed as I did. I'd ridden out the jet lag, but at almost eight pm, sleep was dragging me under.

"Goodnight, pretty girl," I whispered against Phoebe's cheek.

"Hmm, night, night," she muttered, snuggling against her pillow and throwing an arm around my torso. "That's nice."

I smiled as she dropped a sleepy kiss to my bare pec. If I hadn't been so tired, or in the room next to the boys, I would have kissed her back and initiated sex, because I had to be honest, sex with Phoebe was fucking amazing. My pretty girl could be wild between the sheets and I fucking loved it.

Sex was just one part of being with her that I loved. She could be funny as fuck and feisty as hell, and I adored spending time with her. I couldn't imagine *not* spending time with her, but filming would be drawing to an end in a few weeks, which meant so would my time with Phoebe. I really had some thinking to do, not least of all, what the hell was I going to do with two six-year olds for a whole day?

CHAPTER FORTY-THREE

Grantley

"Are you sure about this?" Phoebe asked, as she packed her cosmetics bag into a duffle. "They can be a bit of a handful."

"I'm sure. We'll have a blast and you'll be back for us all to eat dinner together."

She bent over to check her purse and I got a fantastic view of her peachy ass. It looked damn good bare and a little pink from me spanking her, but in tight, figure hugging jeans, it was totally awesome. I was beginning to question my idea of sending her for a day out on our day off. We could have spent the day in bed, eating junk food, watching movies, and making love.

Making love - woah, and where the fuck did that come from?

"I've got the troops coming to help, anyhow."

I swallowed hard, trying not to think about the words that had just flashed into my brain. That was a brain dump for another day, not today, when I had two six-year-olds to entertain. I needed my head in the game.

Phoebe rolled her eyes. "And what a great idea that is, letting Marcia loose on a couple of kids."

"She needs to talk to me about a couple of films that I've been short-listed for. She's going home in a couple of days, and I'll be busy filming, so it has to be today."

"Well on your head be it," she said, leaning in to kiss me. "Have a great time, and thank you again for today. Beth is really excited."

The quick peck wasn't enough, so I wrapped an arm around her and pulled her in for a longer, deeper kiss.

Phoebe sighed, her eyes closed and her face tilted up toward me.

"That was lovely," she whispered.

"I know, and there'll be plenty more when you get back."

And there fucking would be. I couldn't get enough of her.

"Dick, Dick," the boys yelled, "it's your turn."

I dragged a hand through my hair and looked to Barney who was laughing silently. "Fuck off," I mouthed, giving him my middle finger.

"Come on *Dick*, it's your turn," he said with a shit-eating grin.

"Okay, okay."

I heaved myself out of the armchair and stood in front of the fireplace, took a deep breath and started to tap dance. I knew how to step, ball change, shuffle and single buffalo, but that was the sum total I'd learned for an advertisement I'd done in my early days in LA. After only about a minute, I knew I'd lost my audience.

"That's rubbish," Mack groaned, looking decidedly bored.

"What's he doing?" Callum looked to his brother, who shrugged.

"It's not the same on carpet," I complained, stopping with my hands on my hips. "It'd be much better if I was doing it on a stage, or even a metal serving tray. Does your mom have a tray?"

Considering I'd been dreading my turn at 'America's Got Talent', I was now enthusiastic to show the boys my dancing skills. Barney had told jokes about poop that had the boys in stitches, so how the fuck was I supposed to compete with that? What six year old doesn't find shit hilarious? At least I wouldn't come last, I was pretty sure Marcia had that position sewn up. She could barely crack a smile, never mind entertain kids.

Where the hell was she anyway?

"I'm sorry, Dick," Callum sighed. "But it's a no from me."

"Yeah, sorry Dick, but you're rubbish." Mack then pushed on the air horn that was sitting on the couch between him and his brother. "Next."

"I think that's your cue to get off, brother."

Barney's deep chuckle reverberated around the room and only served to make me feel more like shit than I already did.

"But, I can do it so much better," I pouted, flopping down onto the armchair.

"Don't sweat it, Dick," Mack said, copying the phrase he'd heard from Barney. "You can't be good at everything."

"And you're really rubbish at dancing," Callum added. "Marcia, it's your turn."

He yelled it so loudly, I had to stick my fingers in my ears.

"Come on Marcia," Barney yelled, joining in with the boys.

The boys started clapping and chorusing, 'Marcia, Marcia', as they waited for my agent to appear. Finally, after a crescendo of noise, the lounge room door flung open and in strutted Marcia.

"What the fu-."

"Woah," Barney cried, cutting me off from dropping the f-bomb. "Where the hell did you get that outfit?"

"They're my football shorts," Callum cried.

"And my football socks," Mack added.

"It's soccer, get it damn right." Marcia curled her lip at them. "And I needed an outfit, so suck it up boys."

She waved a hand at them dismissively and stood in the spot where I'd just bombed at tap dancing. Marcia was wearing a tiny pair of shorts, no surprise seeing as they belonged to a six year old, and a pair of long white socks with a black band around the top, which came just above her shins. I'd always thought she was small, in height and stature, but the fact she was wearing the boys' clothes showed just how tiny she was. On her feet she had her own sky-high shoes and her shirt tied around the waist, to show a hint of stomach. Added to that, she'd slicked back her bush of hair and added extra red to her lips.

"And what are you performing for us, Marcia?" Mack asked, sitting up straight and grinning at her.

Marcia gave a raspy smoker's cough, slapped at her chest and said. "A little song by Rihanna."

My head shot around to look at Barney, who looked as alarmed as I probably did.

"What song?" I asked, fear and dread washing over me.

"You'll see," she rasped. "I need to use my cell."

Turning, she propped it on the fireplace, stabbed at the screen and turned back to her audience. The boys jumped excitedly in their seats, clapping their hands and swaying their little shoulders to the opening bars of none other than 'Birthday Cake'.

"Marcia," I growled. "No."

"Ah go fudge yourself, Grantley."

Yep, we'd already had the conversation about the f-word.

As the boys howled with laughter, she scowled at me and then as soon as Rihanna started to sing, she put her game face on, pouting and lip syncing to perfection.

She slut dropped to the first line, slowly lifting her ass with straight legs then turning her back to us and damn well twerking.

"Oh shit," I groaned, covering my eyes with my hand.

"Yay, Marcia," Callum cried.

I peeked through my fingers to see him high-five Mack and Marcia grab her crotch and do some sort of hip-hop moves with her shoulders.

"Barney, make her stop," I yelled above the loud music and screaming six year olds.

"I can't even move," Barney groaned. "I'm paralyzed. Why the hell couldn't it take my sight instead of my legs?"

As Rihanna sang about 'licking the icing off', my sixty-year-old agent, actually put her pointer finger in her mouth, sucked it hard and then slowly pulled it out and wagged it at the boys. Callum and Mack squealed and bounced even harder.

"This is amazing," Mack yelled.

"We should sing this at our party," Callum screeched. "Instead of Happy Birthday."

Then as Marcia did a little ass shimmy – a sight that would forever be in my nightmares, while turning in a circle, Chris Brown started singing. Barney and I realized at the same time what was coming.

"No!" I cried.

"Marcia." Barney's eyes went wide.

"Girl I wanna fu-."

Barney and I leapt forward at the same time, arms outstretched, hands grabbing desperately to get Marcia's cell. Barney's huge shoulders barged into mine, sending me airborne into Marcia who was doing her second slut drop of her routine. I tried to throw my body to one side, but Marcia decided at that moment to bend forward and shake her non-existent tits. I took her clean out, sending us both crashing into a heap on the floor.

"Grantley, you stupid twat, get the fuck off me."

"Stop cursing," I yelled, spreading my arms out, so as not to touch her. It was bad enough my groin was against her back. I'd have to shower, like a hundred times or something after this.

"Shit," Barney cried. "How the hell do you turn this thing off?"

"What does he mean?" Callum asked. "He wants to foot her."

"It means he wants to kick her," Mack answered, ever the sage. "She's licked the icing off his cake, so he's going to kick her."

"Ah that's bad. Mummy says you should never hit a girl. He's not a nice man, is he Dick?"

Shit, out of the mouths of babes.

Scrambling to my feet, I shot a pained look at Barney, who was still desperately stabbing at Marcia's cell.

"Barney, damn well hurry up."

"What's your security code?" he shouted down at Marcia, who was groaning on the floor. "Marcia, quick. Code. Now."

"Alright, alright. Two, nine, seven, four." She spat out the code and flipped over onto her hands and knees, her bony ass sticking in the air.

"I'mma make you my bitch." Chris Brown just needed to shut the fuck up.

"He's kicked her and now he's giving her itching powder," Callum explained to Mack. "He's really mad about her licking that icing."

"Barney, hurry the fuc-, fudge up."

I glanced back at the boys who were still gleaming and dancing in their seats – Callum copying Marcia's tit shake.

As Marcia got unsteadily to her feet, Barney finally cut off the music. I heaved a massive sigh of relief and blew out my cheeks, thankful the trauma was over.

"Marcia," Callum cried. "You're the winner."

"Yes. You were brilliant." Mack pumped his fist in the air, giving the air horn a couple of toots. "Teach us the dance, pleeeeaaaase."

"No!" I cried at the same time as Barney.

"Yes, go on Marcia, teach us."

Callum jumped to his feet and started jumping around licking his finger and wiggling his backside. Mack joined him and did the hip-hop move followed by a perfect slut drop.

"Oh shit," I groaned, as Marcia joined the boys dancing around the lounge as they sang '*It's not even my birthday, but he wants to lick the icing off*'.

"You know what man?" Barney asked, slapping a big hand against my back. "If you can't beat 'em."

Barney started rolling his hips and clapping his hand together, even doing a butt bump with Marcia.

"Oh, fudge it," I muttered and joined in the dancing and had the best time ever.

CHAPTER FORTY-FOUR

Phoebe

As harps and bells strummed and tinkled, I gave a huge sigh of contentment and breathed in the aroma of jasmine.

"Oh my God," Beth whispered. "I don't think I've ever been so relaxed."

"I know. I feel like I'm about to melt all over the bed, I'm so floppy."

"You know, if you don't nab Grantley pretty quickly, I may just do it myself."

I lifted my head to glare at my sister, who was sporting a huge grin.

"Don't worry, I'm not interested really. You can keep him. Although," she said wistfully, "if you ever want to loan him out, I'd be up for that. It must be lovely to have a man who cares about you and likes to do nice things for you."

My heart clenched as Beth's smile disappeared. Steven really had been a shit. Not just for leaving her, but for never taking care of her. It had always been Beth looking after his every need, never once had he ever bought her flowers – not even a shitty, half-dead bunch from the garage at the top of the road. I swear he'd only married her because he thought it would get him regular sex without having to put the effort in. Obviously that had changed once the boys arrived, and so Beth had been usurped by Miss Cock Sucker, who evidently gave herself freely to Steven, for the price of a new handbag and matching shoes. Seeing as her social media accounts pretty much boasted of such purchases at least twice a month, Steven was getting everything he'd ever wished for in a partner – someone as twatty and vacuous as he was.

"Stop thinking about Steven," Beth hissed. "I don't give a shit about him, so neither should you."

"Did I have that constipated look again?"

"Yep."

"It's just so unfair, Beth. He's living the life of a playboy, obnoxious dick, while you're the one struggling with the boys."

"I don't struggle," she replied. "My mortgage isn't much and I earn a good wage."

Thankfully, having worked in a bank since leaving school, my sister was incredibly good with money. She'd always saved and contributed to a pension. She knew how to budget and with great foresight had put the mortgage in her name because she got a great deal for working at the bank. She did admit to me after Steven had been gone for a couple of months that in the back of her head, she'd always worried whether he'd get flaky one day, which was why she'd done it.

"It's still not fair."

"Not everything in life is. But," she said, pulling herself up on her lounger. "What is fair is that you've found Grantley, and I want to be sure you're not going to let him go."

I closed my eyes and pictured Grantley. He wasn't wearing his sexy, smart Addison Yates' suit in my mind's eye, but his worn jeans, a t-shirt, and his sexy black glasses.

"Phoebe," Beth hissed. "Are you listening to me?"

I opened my eyes and turned to her. "What do you want me to say, Beth?" The film finishes shooting in a little over three weeks and then he goes back to LA."

Beth sat up and swivelled her legs around to place her feet on the floor.

"You could visit?"

"I could, if he'd even asked me."

"He hasn't said anything?" she asked a little nonplussed.

"Nope, but I don't expect him to." I sat up and hugged my knees to my chest. "I knew what this was going to be when we started it."

"And what was that, sweetie?"

"An on set fling."

As I said the words, the sadness I felt threatened a storm of tears. I hadn't had many relationships, but I certainly had never felt the way I did about Grantley. We were good together, in every sense, but more importantly he took me for who I was. He never made me feel less than him, because he was the big star. He didn't come into my sister's home and look down on it because it wasn't some fancy penthouse with its own infinity pool, and he certainly didn't treat my beloved nephews as a nuisance. Despite everything with his mum and dad, and all the crap he'd had to deal with, he'd wanted to do something special for my sister, because she'd had a bad week.

"You know it's so much more than that."

I hadn't noticed Beth join me on my lounger, I'd been so caught up thinking about Grantley.

"Do I?"

She nodded and laid a hand on my knee. "Yes, and now you just need to tell him what you want to happen, after the film wraps."

"I don't know what I want," I protested.

"Bullshit."

I rolled my eyes at Beth. "Okay, I know I want to be with him, but I'm not sure I can do the long distance thing, Beth."

"Okay, tell me why?"

I gave her a look that pretty much said 'are you stupid?'

"Well what about the fact that I'll be worried every day that he's found someone else, or is cheating on me."

"As if," she scoffed. "I know I hardly know him, but he doesn't seem the cheating type to me."

"They never do. Steven aside."

Beth's eyebrows shot up, almost hitting her hairline.

"I'm sorry," I cried. "But I always thought he looked like a cheating knob. I think it was the too shiny shoes. Besides, if you were honest with yourself, you did too."

Beth thought about it for a few minutes and then nodded. "Yeah, you're right," she replied with a matter of fact tone, "but I just don't see that in Grantley."

We sat in silence for a couple of minutes, Beth picking at a thread of my luxurious velveteen dressing gown and me watching her with great interest, contemplating what she'd said.

She was right, Grantley didn't appear to be a cheat. He'd left his home with Serena when he knew the relationship was over, he hated what Sue-Ann's affair had done to his life, and I couldn't imagine him putting anyone else through such pain.

"I think I'm going to tell him I want to do the long distance thing," I blurted out.

Beth's head shot up. "You are?"

"Only if he promises to tell me it's over, if he's even tempted to cheat."

Beth's eyes glistened as her smile widened. "I'm so happy for you."

"Well he may not want to. This is me telling him what I want. Grantley may have a totally different idea on what happens in three weeks."

"What, like he might want you to move their permanently?" she asked, excitedly.

"No you numpty," I cried, shaking my head. "Where do you get these ideas from?"

As Beth giggled, I couldn't help but wish, deep down in the hollows of my head, that it might just be a possibility.

"It's all very quiet," Beth said, as we closed the front door behind us.

"Maybe they're watching TV."

Beth opened the lounge door and stopped dead. "Aww, look," she whispered.

I moved up behind her, looked over her shoulder and felt my heart do an excited skip. Barney was asleep in a chair, his head lolled back and mouth open. Marcia, for some strange reason dressed in what looked like the boys' football kit, was lying on the floor, star-fishing over the rug with her head on a beanbag. But the sight that made my breath quicken, was Grantley. He was lying on the sofa with both boys lying on his chest, his arms protectively wrapped around them, while Mack had one hand in Grantley's hair and Callum had a finger up Grantley's nose.

"Phoebe," Beth whispered as she turned to me.

"Hey, what's wrong?" I asked, seeing tears welling in her eyes.

"That's the first male hug they've had, in all their lives."

My eyes widened as I looked over at the three men who held my heart. Beth was right. Steven's parents were both dead, so his dad hadn't been present in the twins' lives and as for our dad – well he wasn't exactly the cuddly grandpa type. The boys were lucky if they got a pat on the head, the three times a year that they saw him, despite living just a thirty minute car ride away.

"He's such a good man," Beth said, grabbing hold of my hand. "Don't you *dare* let him go."

As I watched them sleeping, Grantley's arms instinctively went tighter around the boys, and I knew Beth was right. Grantley James was a keeper.

"Beth," I whispered.

"Yes," she replied, turning to me. "What is it?"

I gazed over her shoulder and smiled. "I love him."

CHAPTER FORTY-FIVE

Grantley

I woke to a warm, soft hand stroking my forehead, and then a gentle kiss to my lips.

"Hey, wake up," Phoebe's voice whispered.

Slowly opening my eyes, I looked up to see her face gazing down at me. Fuck, she was beautiful. Her face was bare of makeup, her cheeks rosy and clean, and her gorgeous brown eyes had never looked so bright. I lifted a hand and cupped her face.

Then something hit me.

"Fuck," I cried, scrabbling around. "The boys, they were here, asleep. Where are they?"

"Ssh," Phoebe replied. "It's okay. Beth took them to bed after extracting Callum's finger from your nose. I'm surprised it didn't wake you, the little bugger was clinging on in there."

"Were they okay?" I asked, pushing up and rubbing at my eyes.

"Fine. Although, we're a little concerned what Callum meant when he asked if Marcia could do the birthday cake dance at their birthday party."

My eyes widened as my gaze shot across the room – no Marcia or Barney.

"They're drinking coffee in the kitchen, with Beth. You're the only one we couldn't wake."

"Oh, okay."

I yawned and stretched my arms, then hooked one around Phoebe's neck and pulled her closer for a kiss.

"Hmm you taste like cherries," I whispered against her mouth.

"That will be the lip balm gift we were given at the Spa. Beth got orange." Phoebe grinned.

"Well I like it. Did you have a lovely, relaxing day?"

Phoebe tapped a hand against my thigh, urging me to move up and pushed onto the couch beside me.

"It was perfect. Thank you."

As she rested her forehead against mine, and ran a hand through my hair, I felt more contentment than I had ever had in my whole adult life. Nothing could better this moment, not a damn film role, a prestigious award, or even millions of dollars. Being here with Phoebe, tasting like cherries and smelling like wild flowers, was my nirvana.

"I don't want to leave you," I blurted out.

"W-what?"

Phoebe looked startled as she pulled back, looking at me with huge wide eyes.

"I...I...what did you say?"

I took a breath and threaded my hands through her hair. "I said I don't want to leave you. I know I have to, but I don't want to."

Phoebe swallowed. "I can't stand the thought of you going," she whispered. "It's going to be awful."

I breathed a sigh of relief, glad that we were actually on the same page. I hadn't planned on telling her how I felt, not yet anyway. I wanted to be sure that was how Phoebe felt too, before I said anything, but as usual, my mouth had engaged before my brain. Having her here, looking radiant and so fucking adorable, it had just come rushing out.

"What do we do?" I asked.

Phoebe looked unsure, and lowered her gaze.

"Hey," I whispered. "Tell me what you want to do."

"I..." She took a deep breath. "I want to keep seeing you and if we have to do the long distance thing, then we do it."

I wanted to jump up and punch the air. I hadn't realized how damn much I needed her to say those words. I'd been through so much shit over the last few weeks and she'd been there with me, supporting me; having my back and every day she'd become more important to me.

"I will make it as easy as possible for you," I said, cupping her face with both hands. "I'll come to you as often as I can, and don't worry about the cost of flying in to me, I'll cover it, pretty girl. If it means I get to see you, I'll pay anything it costs."

Phoebe let out a little whimper and swiped away a tear.

"Hey," I soothed. "What's wrong?"

"I'm just so happy that you want the same thing."

"Well I do," I replied, confidently, because I damn well did. "And we will make it work."

"You think we can?" she asked tentatively.

"Without a doubt."

Phoebe squealed and the next thing I knew, I was on my back with Phoebe squirming on top of me, peppering kisses all over my face. My pretty girl was happy and that made me fucking delirious.

CHAPTER FORTY-SIX

PHOEBE

Grantley and I had had three weeks of bliss and every day I'd fallen a little more in love with him – not that he knew that. I might like to think I'm a feminist, but that was one rule I could never break. He had to say it first, and that was most unlikely. I knew Grantley cared about me, and enjoyed being with me and wanted to keep seeing me, but love? I was pretty sure he wasn't at that point.

Now, I had a feeling my sense of serenity was about to disappear. Grantley and Francesca's sex scene had been postponed because Francesca had a raging temperature, Alexi decided to make it the very last filming of the shoot.

It was supposed to be a closed set, as Francesca and Grantley weren't using body doubles, and while it was no *Fifty Shades* level of sex scene, there was some boobs and butt on display. The butt I was most interested in because it was Grantley's. Finding out that Grantley had insisted that I be on set, Francesca had thrown a real tantrum and complained to Alexi with a stamp of her foot. Grantley in turn had suggested I body double for Francesca, if she was that worried about it. So, while I'd been throwing him dirty looks and shaking my head, Francesca yielded to Grantley's demand and allowed me to stay.

I knew Grantley thought he was doing the right thing, showing me that nothing untoward would happen and everything was totally professional, but I still couldn't help but feel some trepidation. I'd seen lots of sex scenes while being an Extra, but none that involved my boyfriend whom I would be conducting a long distance relationship with. Life sucked donkey balls at times, and watching Grantley getting Francesca off was one of those times.

"You okay?" Penny asked as she sidled up beside me. "Or is this your worst nightmare?"

I grimaced and pretended to gag.

"As I thought." She flung an arm around me and gave me a tight squeeze. "You know how mechanical these scenes can be."

"I know, but it's different when it's the guy you're actually sleeping with," I whispered.

Penny laughed. "You do know everyone knows you're an item, right? I mean, if the hand holding and nose rubbing at lunch didn't give it away, the soppy ass grin on his face every time he looks at you did."

I looked over to Grantley, who was taking some last minute direction from Alexi. He was wearing nothing but a fluffy white robe, slippers, and a modesty pouch and it was making me anxious.

"Go if you want to. He'll never know."

"I can't, Penny. I said I'd stay and I wouldn't feel right about not being here and I don't want to lie to him and tell him I was and then have to fake being okay."

"Okay," Penny sighed, "but for what it's worth, I think he's wrong for asking this of you. Especially as it's no secret she's desperate to be in his pants."

"I know, and I think that's why he asked. I think he thinks I'll feel more comfortable seeing it."

"Well maybe close your eyes, at least then you're keeping your promise but not having to watch." She gave me a huge smile, and another squeeze with her arm. "I'd best go and touch up Francesca, if you know what I mean."

I giggled and nodded. "I do. Go, go do your thing."

Penny left and I was alone doubting my sanity.

Yep, I'd just about had it with Francesca Bloody Woodfield. The bitch had delighted in smiling over at me at every opportunity – okay, so I hadn't closed my eyes, I'd watched all the gory details. Then if that hadn't riled me enough, she kept putting her hand under the thin cotton sheet that was covering them, when hands were most definitely supposed to be above the covers.

"Go tell Francesca to stop acting this out like it's a porno," Alexi said to the First Assistant Director. "Those fucking moans are totally over the top and unnecessary."

I lifted my hand to high-five Alexi, but then thought better of it. Still, I was glad he'd noticed her antics too. A few minutes later, when Alexi shouted action once more, I turned back to the bed with Grantley and Francesca writhing around on it. With a sigh, I looked at my watch, wondering how long they'd been 'at it', when I heard a shit, from the action.

"What the hell was that?" Grantley asked. "That's not in the damn script."

I looked over to see him clutching at his neck and frowning down at Francesca.

"I thought it would look good. Realistic."

"Francesca!" Alexi shouted. "What the hell? You giving him a hickey could mess up continuity. Are you crazy?"

My eyes widened. Yes she *was* fucking crazy, marking my man. How dare she, knowing that it wasn't in the script and that I was standing right there, watching.

"Sorry," she simpered. "I just didn't think. I was so caught up in the moment."

"Go again," Alexi said. "And this time keep it PG and stick to what we agreed on."

The action started again and even though I took deep breaths, trying to quell the jealousy in the pit of my stomach, I couldn't help but let it take over me. I felt as though I wanted to vomit, and then following that, I wanted to march over there and pull her out of the bed by her hair.

As Grantley kissed up Francesca's neck, it took everything in me not to cry out and tell him to stop, but like a morbid fool I continued watching, hating every second and wishing I'd taken Penny's advice. The sad fact was, this would be my life from now onwards. I would forever be second guessing what women wanted from Grantley. Would every woman try to entice him and would he be enticed? Hideous images flashed through my mind, and I knew I was going to have to use every bit of strength I had to get through our times apart. Shit, I'd even need it through our times together – Francesca didn't give a damn that I was standing a few feet away, she was still trying to get Grantley to forget me.

God, I hate that I feel this pathetic and insecure. I knew I should have stayed away from him.

Looking down at my feet, I decided I needed to get out of there. Grantley had seen me watching, so he'd known I'd stay for some of the time and that would have to be enough. As I turned to leave, Alexi shouted.

"Cut! And that's a wrap everyone."

The few people onset cheered, and wardrobe rushed to Grantley and Francesca, offering them their robes as they jumped up from the bed. Immediately Grantley's eyes sought mine and I forced out a big smile and gave him a thumbs up. He didn't need to know how hideous the last hour or so had been for me. The returning smile from Grantley was beautiful and I could see there was a great amount of relief in it too. He hadn't just wanted me here to show me it was going to be okay, he'd wanted to know whether I'd be able to handle it. This had been as hard for him as it had me.

I held my smile as Grantley approached me, swigging from a bottle of water.

"Shit," he groaned, "that was hard work."

"Generally or because I was here?" I asked, with a giggle, trying to lighten the situation.

"No, because it was with Francesca. She fucking bit down on me." Grantley moved the collar of his robe. "Has she left a mark?"

I peered at his neck and sighed with relief. "No. There's nothing there, but I'd still recommend a trip to the hospital for a tetanus injection."

"Good," he smiled and then chuckled at my remark.

Laughing, I leaned forward to kiss him, but was shocked when Grantley pulled back.

"W-what's wrong?" I asked, glancing at Francesca who was taking her time to cover up.

Grantley grinned. "I ate tuna and onions before the scene and you know... she's been there. I should maybe shower first"

"You didn't," I gasped.

Grantley nodded. "Yeah, I did. Which is probably why she bit me, the stink must have been fucking awful. I don't want you to have to smell it."

"Just a quick peck then," I offered, pulling him to me by the belt of his robe.

"Patience pretty girl," he said, moving his mouth to my ear. "If you'd like to come to my dressing room, I could clean my teeth, maybe gargle a little, scrub myself clean and then I'd be more than willing to kiss you. In more places than just your mouth."

With a little quiver between my thighs, I nodded at Grantley, glanced over at Francesca who was now watching us, and then linked my fingers with Grantley's and followed him off the set to his dressing room, where he kissed me in places I didn't even know the name of.

I loved him, and wanted us to work, despite the distance and time apart. The following day when he left for LA would be awful, but we'd get through it because it would only be for a short time. We were going to work, I was sure of it.

But what if...

CHAPTER FORTY-SEVEN

Grantley

As Phoebe folded one of my sweaters, I took it from her hands and threw it into my case.

"Leave that," I said, pulling her into my arms. "I can do it later."

"You won't fold it properly. It'll be creased as hell by the time you get home."

She buried her face into my chest and wound her arms around my waist, holding on tightly- so tightly, it felt as if she was trying to get inside my skin. I got it, I really did, because I didn't want to let go of her, ever.

"I don't know why you can't just come home with me tonight," I whispered. "I don't start shooting for another week."

Phoebe didn't respond, but drew in a breath, snuggling closer to me. I inhaled her scent and kissed the top of her head, desperate to take her to bed, but I knew if I did I'd never leave and Marcia had fucking arranged for me to appear on the *Tonight Show*. I was already cutting it close and would no doubt be appearing with damn jet lag.

"When *do* you think you'll come over?" I asked.

Phoebe looked up at me, her eyes shining with tears and her bottom lip trembling. Dread and fear gripped me as I looked at her beautiful, sad face.

No, no way.

"No," I said shaking my head. "Don't do this Phoebes. Don't you dare tell me you're not coming, please."

Tears slid down her cheeks as she chewed on her bottom lip.

"I'm sorry." Her voice cracked. "I can't do it. I lay awake all night, after you fell asleep and it just kept going round and round in my head. And, I can't."

"*Why*?" I asked, swallowing hard. "What's changed since yesterday?"

We'd had an amazing time in my dressing room, enjoyed the wrap party, and then I'd made love to her here at the hotel, and I'd fallen asleep with her wrapped in my arms. A blissful end to a fucking amazing day, where I thought we were on the same page.

"I just realised that I wouldn't be able to stand it. You being there and me being here. The distance is too far. The time in between visits would be too long."

"But, I can organize a jet for you. It wouldn't take as long," I argued, cupping her face with my shaking hands. "We can do it, you know we can."

"But I have to work, Grantley," she sobbed. "I can't keep jetting over to you. I need money to live, to help Beth."

"I'll help you with money." I knew I was pleading, but I could give a fuck less. "I'll help Beth."

"No, Grantley, you can't. I wouldn't let you, and Beth certainly wouldn't."

Tears dropped from the end of her nose and chin as she gulped out a breath.

"Please, Phoebe."

She shook her head and swiped at her face. "I can't Grantley. You know it won't work and it will hurt so much more than if we end it now."

"But I don't want to end it."

"Neither do I, bu-."

"Well, don't do this then. Come to LA as we agreed. Do the long distance thing."

"I'm sorry, Grantley. I'm so sorry. I can't."

I looked down at her and I felt the same pain I had all those years ago, when my dad left. Only this time, it was so much worse. This was my adult heart being ripped apart after feeling fuller than it ever had before. But, as I watched her cry with pain in her eyes, I knew that if this was that hard for her, then she was doing what she thought was the right thing and I had to accept that, no matter how shitty it was.

But I couldn't, I wouldn't accept it.

"Please. Let's just try it out. See how things go and if it's not working, we call it a day." I placed my hands on her shoulders, stooping to look deep into her eyes. Begging her to listen to her heart.

"But that would be so much worse. At least this way, this time we've had will always be special."

Determination shone from her eyes and I knew that there was no changing her mind. Maybe she was right, having her for a few days a month would never be enough, but it was better than nothing.

"Please reconsider. Please, Phoebes."

"My mind is made up, I'm sorry," she whispered.

"What will it take? You want me to beg?" I asked.

"No. God no, I don't want you to beg." She cupped my face with both of her delicate hands. "You know I'm right about this."

Like fuck I did.

"No, you're not. I have never felt this way about anyone, not even Serena."

Immediately I wanted to take the words back, as Phoebe's face crumpled.

"I'm sorry, I didn't mean to mention her. I-."

"Grantley, don't be sorry. That is my stupid insecurities, but it's also another reason why I can't do this. I would forever be in fear."

"But I'm not a cheat," I protested. "I wouldn't do that to you. Was it seeing me acting with Francesca, yesterday? Because you know that's all it was – acting."

"I know," she replied, wiping at her face. "And I know you're not a cheat, but it wouldn't stop me worrying and I can't live like that. At least this way, it will always be my most perfect relationship."

I blew out a breath, trying hard not to think about her in a relationship with someone else. I also couldn't stand the thought of not seeing her again.

"Please Grantley, I've made my mind up. I can't be swayed."

As I looked down on her, she jutted out her chin, determined and unmoving. She was right, she wouldn't be swayed.

"Are you sure?"

Phoebe nodded and wiped away more tears. I dropped my head and let out a long exhale.

"I can't stand this. I'm going to miss you so fucking much." I choked out the last word, barely able to get it past the lump in my throat.

Phoebe gave a ragged sob and flung her arms around my neck. "Not as much as I'll miss you. I will think about you every day, and my heart will miss you every single minute of those days."

"Fuck, Phoebe. Please don't do this."

My words a muffled sob as hers slayed me and clinging on to her, I wrapped myself around her like ivy.

We held each other tightly, breathing each other in and basking in those last moments together. Eventually, I pulled back and dropped my forehead to Phoebe's, cupping the side of her face.

"I'll never forget us," I whispered.

"Me neither and I'll always remember this as the best time of my life."

"The *very* best," I breathed out.

Slowly she moved out of my embrace, and getting onto her tiptoes, she kissed me softly.

"Be happy, Grantley."

A huge sob wracked from her body as she pulled away, her hand lingering in mine and it took all my willpower not to tug her back into my arms and make her stay. I wanted to tell her goodbye, but my mouth was too dry and my breath too shallow to be able to utter even one word.

As the bedroom door quietly clicked shut, I realized that was it.

Phoebe was gone.

CHAPTER FORTY-EIGHT

Phoebe

After Barney had dropped me home, I ran to my room, covered myself with my duvet, and sobbed into my pillow until it was soaking wet. Beth had rushed up the stairs after me, but I was ashamed to admit that I'd slammed the door in her face.

I knew she'd looked in on me, because I felt her rub my back and my old teddy bear was pushed under the covers, but she hadn't forced me to talk, for which I was grateful. I guessed a couple of hours at least had passed because I heard the theme music to the boy's favourite tea-time TV program, drift up the stairs. Taking in a deep breath, I poked my head out and looked across the room to see Beth sitting on the floor, her back against the wall.

"How long have you been here?" I croaked.

"About an hour, maybe less."

"Beth," I groaned. "Your arse must be numb."

She shrugged and pulled her knees up, wrapping her arms around them.

"I know it must be really hard," she said. "But you'll see him again soon."

I inhaled sharply, remembering that the last Beth knew, I was going to help Grantley pack and arrange when I'd go out to LA to visit.

"I'm not going," I whispered.

"What?" She scrambled around and crawled over to me. "What do you mean, you're not going? What happened?"

"I can't do it Beth. Shit," I muttered, wiping my nose as the tears started again. "The distance, it's just too far."

"But you were so adamant it was going to work. *Grantley*, was so adamant it was going to work."

"I know, and he wanted it, but I can't stand the thought of him being there and seeing pictures and reading gossip about him. Like you said, I was an idiot over Serena and he was only talking to her, so imagine how I'll feel if I'm thousands of miles away and see a picture of him with someone."

I'd told Beth all about Serena and she'd call me an idiot, but she also understood. Steven had put her through that sort of crap their whole marriage – not that Grantley was anything at all like that dick.

"But this is just stupid," my sister cried, throwing her arms into the air. "You're heartbroken and you don't have to be."

"Yes I do, I have to be heartbroken now because it won't be as bad as when I'm deeper in love with him."

"Have you told him?" Beth asked.

"What?"

"That you're in love with him."

My mouth gaped. "Of course not."

"Well you should have. But that doesn't matter," Beth snapped, getting up on her knees and leaning against the bed. "The thing that does matter is that you're being stupid, ending things when you could have something amazing."

"No I can't. He might be shooting a film in Paraguay soon, and then where will he be after that?" I cried. "He could be anywhere in the world, and I just know there'll be times when I can't see him. Those times will get more and more until eventually I get the call that says 'this isn't working, Phoebe', or worse, 'I've met someone, Phoebe', and I won't be able to take it, Beth."

"You can't end things just in case *he* ends it in the future, or meets someone else. You're being stupid."

"No I'm not!" My voice cracked as I shouted at Beth. "He's a gorgeous film star, Beth. He's never going to be able to stay faithful."

"He's not fucking Steven, Phoebe. Not every man is like that piece of shit I married. Give him some credit."

"But even if he doesn't cheat, I can't go there all the time. I have to work and who would help you with the boys if I was jetting off to LA for a few days each month?"

"Oh no, no you don't." Beth pushed herself up to stand, and slammed her hands to her hips. "You are not, not doing this because of me and the boys. We will be perfectly fine. In fact, if you want my damn opinion, I think you should go out there for good. Go and live with the man if you're that worried about a long distance relationship."

"Beth," I gasped. "You don't mean that."

"Yes I bloody well do. You love him and I know without doubt that he loves you. I can see it in his eyes, the way he looks at you, and if you lose him because of some stupid idea that he may or may not cheat on you in the future, then you're a bigger prick than Steven."

"I am not," I cried in dismay, throwing back the duvet. "I'm being sensible and I can't just go and live there, he hasn't even asked me."

"So just tell him that's what you're doing. When have you ever been scared to say what you think?"

"When I fell in love with a film star."

"A film star who loves you back, you idiot. Just tell him that's what you want and I bet you a tenner he'll want it too."

"You're betting my future on a bloody tenner?"

Beth grinned. "Well once you're gone, I'll need money to pay a babysitter."

"You see, I can't possibly go." I rubbed my temples, wishing I hadn't appeared from under the duvet. Life was much simpler under there.

"Don't be so dramatic. I was joking."

Beth stood in front of me and taking my hands pulled me to standing. She brushed my hair away from my face and cupped my cheek.

"Phoebe, I love you so very much and I can't tell you how much help and support you've been, living with me and the boys, but it's your time sweetheart."

"But I don't want to leave you."

"Yes you do, especially if it means you're with the man you love," she said in a hushed tone.

"What if it's not what he wants?" I asked, feeling sick to my stomach at the thought. "What if he only wants the long distance thing?"

"Well then, you have to make a choice," she replied. "But if that's all he wants it will only be because he doesn't want to rush things, not because he doesn't love you."

"I don't know Beth."

"I do," she said with a grin. "Go and get your man and show mum and dad that Melania isn't the only one who can bag a rich and successful man."

We both burst out laughing at the thought of our parents' imaginary, perfect daughter.

"I suppose it would piss them off a little. Does a film star trump a doctor?" I asked.

"Hey," Beth said with a mock frown. "He's not just any old doctor, he's a brain surgeon."

Laughing I pulled her into a hug, swaying us from side to side.

"I love you," I said into her hair.

"I know, I'm the best." She pulled away and looked at her watch. "What time is his flight, because it's almost six now."

Dread thundered in my chest. "He's leaving the hotel around seven, his flight is at nine-thirty. I'll never get there in time."

"So call him, stop him from going."

I shook my head. "No I can't. If I call, he won't go, I know he won't and he can't miss this flight. He has to get home to be on a live show tomorrow night. Marcia will kill him if he misses it."

"Hah," Beth said waving a dismissive hand. "As if she's scary."

I looked at her wide eyed. "Would you really want to break the news to her?"

Beth thought about it for a second and shook her head. "No, you're right. Don't stop him getting on that plane, but at least try and get there to tell him."

"Really, you think I should?"

Beth huffed and turned to pick up my shoes, before thrusting them at me.

"Just go. Take my car and don't you dare come back here without telling him. Chase him to the airport if you think you've missed him at the hotel."

I lifted a leg and pushed on a shoe, stepping into the other as I rushed from my room.

"Are you sure I'm doing the right thing?" I called over my shoulder.

"You won't know until you ask him," Beth shouted as I ran down the stairs. "Just don't drive too fast."

"I won't," I replied as I picked up her keys from the hook on the wall and flung open the front door. "Wish me luck."

"What do you need luck for, pretty girl?"

My heart stopped to a shuddering halt, as I came face to face with Grantley.

"What are you doing here?" I gasped, touching his face with my fingertips, checking he was real. "You have a plane to catch. You're going to be late. Marcia will kill you."

"I don't care." As he breathed out the words, his eyes watched me with an intensity that heated my veins. "This is more important."

"W-what is?" I stammered.

Without warning, Grantley's mouth slammed against mine in the most amazing of kisses. It was hot and hard and it took command of my senses. My hair twined through his fingers as he held my head in place, pushing his hard body against mine as our tongues and lips collided. Finally, breathless and with my body buzzing, he pulled away.

"*That* was more important," he stated.

"You came all this way and missed your flight for a kiss?" I asked, still reeling.

"Nope. I also came to tell you I love you."

My heart didn't just stop this time, but it dropped like a stone and then, as if electrified, jumped right back up to my chest and thumped wildly. My hands started to shake and my chest heaved with the exertion of the adrenalin battling with the blood in my veins.

"You do?" I asked, my voice quiet and breathy.

"Yes, I fucking do. More than I can tell you and I don't want to spend even one minute without you in my life." His big hand cupped the back of my head, as he looked at me with heat and passion in his eyes. "I don't care what you say, this is not ending."

"Grantley -."

"No Phoebe, you're going to damn well listen to me. This is not ending, it's just starting because you're coming to LA with me and I don't just mean for a fucking visit."

"You don't?" I asked dreamily, hardly believing that he was here, holding me.

"Nope. I need you in my life, every day and you're right, long distance wouldn't work."

"It wouldn't?"

"Nope. So this is how it's going to be. You're coming to live in LA, I'm going to marry you and we're going to have lots of sex and have us some beautiful kids and an amazing life together. You on board with that?"

I nodded, wondering if maybe I'd been drugged, but when Grantley trailed his knuckles down my cheek, making me shiver, I knew it was real.

Grantley James loved me and wanted to marry me.

Wait, what?

"You want to marry me?" I asked, shocked.

"That's what I said." He grinned and kissed me. "Not the most romantic proposal, I know, but I'll do the mushy shit when I get you a ring."

Tears of joy had now replaced those of sorrow from earlier, as I leapt into Grantley's arms, wrapping my legs around him.

"I love you," I cried, planting a big, wet kiss on his lips. "So very much."

"You do?" he asked, giving me a gorgeous, shy smile.

"I do. I was on my way to tell you and to ask if you'd mind too much if I came to live with you."

"Really?"

I nodded and squeezed my thighs at his waist.

"Are you going to get into trouble with Marcia?"

Grantley shrugged and leaned in for another short, sweet, kiss. "Don't know and don't care."

"You really love me?" I asked incredulously.

"Yes pretty girl, more than anything. You make me smile, you make me laugh, and you fill my heart to bursting and I can't imagine a life without you."

"Well you don't have to," I sighed, nuzzling into his neck, "because I'm not leaving you ever again."

"Good," he breathed out, his voice full of relief, "because I wouldn't let you anyway."

As Grantley kissed me again, I thanked Genesius- the Patron Saint of actors- for giving me this beautiful man and was grateful for the day I was too busy on my phone to notice him.

"Hey," Grantley said, breaking the kiss. "Who do you love?"

I smiled and kissed his nose. "I love you. Always you."

EPILOGUE

Grantley

As I looked at Phoebe, I couldn't believe she was actually mine. She was so fucking beautiful and yet an absolute mess all at the same time. Her hair was all over the place, mascara was smudged under her eyes and she had one leg in a pair of yoga pants and one leg out.

"Hey, pretty girl," I whispered, gently shaking her awake as my eyes raked down her body.

Fuck, she was sexy and I could feel myself getting hard just looking at her.

"Oh hi," she yawned.

"What happened?" I asked, pointing to her disarray.

"I was bored so was dancing to Wham and got all hot and sweaty."

I grinned at her, that damn obsession she had with fucking eighties music was crazy. We could be anywhere, a red-carpet event, a dinner party, or even at the food market and if any eighties music was played she always squealed, clapped her hands like a damn seal, and then did a sexy shimmy of her hips and ass, always, without fail, in time to the music.

"You did, eh?" I sat myself down on the edge of the couch, and reached up to try and smooth down her hair. "I'm sorry I was late and you got bored. We had to reshoot a scene because the lighting wasn't right."

"That's okay, you have to work."

I smiled at her, thanking every damn star, planet, and god above that I had her. She got me. She knew who I was and what I needed, which namely, was her.

"So," I said. "What's with the one leg in the pants and one leg out?"

Phoebe looked down at her legs and slapped a hand against her mouth. "Oh God," she gasped. "That's awful."

"What?" I asked, grinning. "What's awful?"

She looked up at me with her huge brown eyes and crimson touched her cheeks. "I was having a rude dream about you and me. I think I was touching myself," she whispered as if there were other people in the room who could hear.

My cock certainly heard and woke up, wanting in on any action that was available.

"You were," I groaned, shifting to adjust myself.

Phoebe nodded and sucked on her lip. She looked so fuckable, even though that wasn't what she was trying to do. Phoebe had no idea about the art of seduction, she was just sexy without trying. Sexy, fuckable, and damn well adorable and she was mine.

"Yep, I must have needed better access."

"Shit, I love you," I said on a long breath. "So damn much."

Phoebe's face broke into a beautiful grin. "You do?"

"You know I do."

I bent to kiss her and snaked a hand up her bare leg, all the way, until I met the hem of her t-shirt. My fingers pushed under it, until I felt a hard, tight, little nipple. Phoebe moaned as I pinched it at the same time that I deepened the kiss.

"Grantley," she gasped. "I love you."

Her hips bucked and instantly my cock got even harder. Just knowing she wanted me as much as I wanted her, turned me on much more than any woman ever had before.

"Get your clothes off," she whispered. "I need you naked and inside me, now."

"Fuuuck," I groaned, pulling myself away from her hot, delicious lips.

I stood up and unzipped my pants and was just about to push them down my legs when a little voice instantly poured cold water on my hard-on.

"Daddy."

I turned to see my gorgeous baby girl careering toward me, wearing an orange all in one that had a prison number and 'I stole my daddy's heart' on the front.

"Hey baby." I dropped to my knees and held open my arms for my gorgeous four-year-old, Lowry, to run into – yep, who knew I could be sentimental and name my baby after the hotel where I first kissed her mother. "What are you doing out of bed?"

I pulled her against my chest and inhaled deeply. She smelled of baby soap and Phoebe and it filled my heart with joy.

"In fact, how did you get out of bed?" Phoebe asked, pulling herself to the edge of the couch and reaching from behind me to stroke Lowry's soft hair that was the exact same color as her own.

"I climb," came Lowry's muffled reply from against my chest.

"You climbed over the side?" Phoebe cried. "You need to be careful sweetie, what if you'd fallen?"

"I'd have hurted my ass."

Phoebe and I both snorted a laugh as the angelic cherub in my arms snuggled her nose against my neck. How the hell could I want anything more from life than this – oh yep, right on cue, my boy started to cry, reminding me of the other great joy in my life.

"I'll go."

Phoebe got up and stumbled across the lounge, trying to put her leg back into her pants.

"Momma is silly," Lowry giggled.

"She is," I agreed. "She's beautiful too."

Lowry nodded enthusiastically. "Yep, she's the beautifulest pwincess ever."

A few minutes later, Phoebe appeared carrying our one-year-old son, Chester. It was as close to Manchester as I could get, so yeah, you get the picture now on how sentimental I am. He was my mirror image and at a year old, already strong-willed and a little defiant at times, but he had his momma's smile and loving nature – thankfully both my kids did.

"Hey my man. You wanted to join in did you?" I asked, cradling his face as Phoebe sat next to me on the floor.

Chester's little hand came out and gently smacked my nose, and when I winced as if it hurt, the little demon giggled.

"God, I love my life," I whispered leaning to kiss Phoebe's temple. "You and the kids, you are my everything, you know that, right?"

Phoebe gave me a starry eyed smile and nodded. "I know. Same goes for us too. We three adore you."

I gave a long, contented sigh as Lowry snuggled down against me and Phoebe pulled Chester closer to her chest, gently rocking him.

"Can you imagine if I'd not got on that film?" Phoebe asked, as she often did when we were thanking our lucky stars. "Or I hadn't been looking at my phone, instead of watching where I was going."

I shook my head. "Don't even want to think about it."

"Me neither."

We had a damn good life, thanks to my success. I'd made my last Addison Yates' film a couple of years before, finally signing off with a desire to do some more serious movies. It worked, because now I was two days into filming a hard-hitting movie about a Vice cop and before that I'd recently finished shooting a political drama. Word on the street was, I was a shoe in for an Oscar nomination based on my performance as a crooked Senator. I wasn't counting on it, but it would be pretty cool if it happened. As for Phoebe, she didn't do Extra work any longer, but with the kids and helping to manage a charity I'd set up for disadvantaged kids, she had her hands full. Plus, after I'd petitioned for Beth's permanent visa, she and the boys had made the move to LA too. She worked at a bank close to our house, and the boys went to school nearby, so Phoebe picked them up for her on the days that Beth was working. As for Beth, well she was dating a fire-fighter, Joshua, who was, according to my wife, a real hottie – no pun intended. He'd helped rescue Beth and some other people from a broken-down elevator in a shopping mall and he told me, was pretty smitten at first sight. Beth was just as crazy about him and they'd been dating for almost eight months. Joshua got along great with the boys and they loved him right back – I'd even heard Mack call him dad once, by mistake. They were a great little family unit and Joshua had mentioned to me about asking Beth and the boys to move in with him. Of course, I'd had him checked out. I loved Beth with all my heart, she was an amazing woman for bringing up Mack and Callum alone all those years and I needed her to be happy and safe. Thankfully, Joshua passed all the checks and had even been given a bravery award a couple of years back that he'd never mentioned. He was a great guy and good enough for my sister-in-law and nephews.

Barney still drove me around and looked after me, but even he was thinking of settling down with a women he'd met in a hotel bar when we'd been staying on location. He was smitten and Marlena seemed good for him – my only worry was she lived in Washington and I wasn't sure she liked the idea of LA life, which meant I could lose Barney, but hey, I wanted him to be happy too, so what would be was what would be.

As for me, I was happier than I'd ever been and Phoebe gave me that; my pretty girl, my world. I admit, there were still times when I acted like a pre-menstrual bitch, but that was usually when my mom called. Yeah, things were no better with her, she still annoyed the fuck out of me. Phoebe said she couldn't stand to be in her parents' company for more than three hours, well my fucking limit with my mom was three minutes – ten tops. But hey, we were making progress, three was better than zero. I would never forgive her for what she'd planned to do, no matter how ridiculous her plan was. Unbelievably, my fucking kids adored her and I would never keep her from them. We kept things amiable for their sake, and after a stint in rehab, she appeared to have been clean and sober for the last year and a half. I asked her what was different this time and she said 'Lowry and Chester. I need to rectify my wrongs.', so maybe I should give her credit for that. As for Trent, my 'dad', he and I were getting there, much quicker than me and Sue-Ann, it had to be said. The guilt and heartache he'd felt over the years was visible in every line and crevice on his face. Every time he looked at me, I saw deep, dark regret in his eyes and yes I was still angry and disappointed that he hadn't fought harder for me, but I understood. The thought of finding out either Lowry or Chester weren't mine would gut me, but I'd still want to be in their life. That said, if I thought they were going to live with their real father, well I'm not sure I could stand that and maybe I'd run away too. Thank god, I didn't have that worry, my kids were most definitely *my kids*. As for the kids, they adored Dad and Deanna, and if I was on location and wanted Phoebe to come out for a few days, Granpy and Granma were more than happy to babysit them.

Phoebe and I sat in silence for a little while, until we heard the gentle snores of our babies.

"Hey," I whispered, turning to Phoebes. "What do you think about a sleepover tonight?"

She looked down at Chester and then Lowry, finally her eyes landing on mine.

"I can't think of anything better."

Leaning to her, I gave Phoebe the softest of kisses, delivering enough pressure that she would understand every word I wasn't saying.

"Who do you love?" I asked my pretty girl.

"I love you," she replied when I slowly pulled away. "Always you."

The End

Pelvic Flaws

I'm Katie Grainger, I'm 45 years old, a divorced mother of three, slightly annoying at times, but always loveable, kids and I can wet myself at the drop of hat. Actually, it's more like a sneeze or a cough than a drop of a hat, but whatever the reason, let's just say I am forever grateful for the invention of the ultra-thin panty pad.

I don't have a bad life, there's book club where I discuss the menopause with my friends, there's Clubbercise where I wet myself and dance like my mother with my friend Mandy and there's my work which is pretty boring, where I get to learn a lot about reality TV from my much younger co-workers. All of which makes me content – yes, I'd like more sex, but who wouldn't when their castle hadn't been breached for four years.

Do I have regrets in my life?

Yes, I do. I regret that my ex-husband, Carl, and I didn't realise we'd grown apart sooner. I regret having a perm in 1993 – I looked like Roly the dog from *Eastenders*. I regret not trying more online dating when I first got divorced and I regret that my youngest, Charlie, feels torn between pleasing me and his dad. What I don't regret is my bag breaking and spilling everything over the pizza place floor, the night Dex Michaels was in there ordering a 9inch meat feast.

What can I say about Dex?

Dex is the sort of man that dreamy sighs are made of. He's tattooed, has impeccable pecs and amazing abs and has the most gorgeous blue eyes I've ever seen. He's a true Southern Gentleman, with an accent that makes me want to wear a pair of Daisy Duke's and ride across the range on stallion called Champion. Dex Michaels is 46 years old, owns his own Tattoo Studio, has no baggage, likes my kids and seems to think I'm cute. A match made in heaven – right?

Pelvic Flaws is the story of one woman's struggle with hot sweats, mood swings and perilously poor pelvic floor muscles. It's the story of Dex, who thinks all those things about Katie are funny and adorable. It's the story of a romance that could turn into something big. It's the story of what might be the love affair of the century, as long as it's not ruined by the baggage that neither of them knew existed.

ACKNOWLEDGEMENTS

There are always many people I need to thank, once I've finished a book. Each time that list gets longer and longer, but that is why this book world is so bloody amazing. People want to help you, no matter whether they are readers, bloggers or fellow authors, there's always someone willing to lend a hand in some way. We stick together, we fight the cause as one and we always have each other's backs – what a cocky bunch we are!

Some special thanks goes to Suzie Cairney and Laura Nelson of SL PA Services. Thank you both, for everything you've done to help make the release of this book a success. I'm a total dunderhead when it comes to anything to do with social media or administration of any type, so I couldn't have done this without you. The members of PictPublishing, a big thank you to you too for all your help.

JC Clarke – yet again you've been a star. I love your work and you blow me away with your professionalism and hard work.

Brooke Bowen Herbert, it was a pleasure working with you especially as you got my stupid British sense of humour.

All of my Angels, who make stroke my ego daily by telling me how much they love my books. I love you ladies and please never stop posting and commenting in the group. You always manage to make me laugh and brighten my day. Kimberly Newman and Leanne Johnson, keep up the laughs you gorgeous pair of Sugar Tits.

My Beta readers – Sarah, Patsy, Cal, Laura, thank you for your honest opinions and for loving my words. I know you're probably biased, but it means a lot when you tell me I did a good job.

Lots of love to our newest member of the Angels; Savannah Williams. Ally, you and Sam have produced a beauty and I can't wait for cuddles when I finally get to meet you.

To my family and friends and most of all Mr A, who has to force me to take in some fresh air most of the time. I know I'm needy and at times I'm precious, but I just want you all to be proud of me, so thank you.

Finally, to those of you who read my books there aren't enough words to show gratitude to you for everything you've done for me. If you've read one book, or read them all, it doesn't matter because you took a chance on me and I'll be eternally grateful.

Thanks again everyone and much love always.
Nikki x

Printed in Great Britain
by Amazon